MW01264889

RISING

RISING

To anyone who needs to hear it—you are strong enough.

PLAYLIST

HOLD ON - CHORD OVERSTREET

WHAT'S LEFT OF YOU - CHORD OVERSTREET

TORTURED SOUL - CHORD OVERSTREET

ALL I WANT KODALINE

BROTHER - KODALINE

WAVES - DEAN LEWIS

ALWAYS - ISAK DANIELSON

BROKEN - ISAK DANIELSON

HOLD MY HAND - ISAK DANIELSON

BROKEN - LOVELYTHEBAND

FALLING APART - MICHAEL SCHULTE

I LOST MYSELF - MUNN

DANCING WITHOUT MUSIC - BRDGS

SUPERHERO - HAYD

HAPPIEST YEAR - JAYMES YOUNG

PROLOGUE

Rush—8 years ago

"We're so proud of you." My mom turned around from the front passenger seat to look at me in the backseat of the car, my long legs curled up to nearly my chin so I'd fit in the backseat of the tiny Toyota Prius. "A basketball scholarship ... it's incredible."

Pride radiated off of her and I felt my chest puff out. All I'd ever wanted was to make my parents proud of me.

"Thanks, Ma."

"Seriously, son, this is quite the accomplishment," my dad added, his eyes meeting mine in the rearview mirror. "This is one step closer to your dreams."

I'd wanted to be a professional basketball player since I was four-years-old and got a Fisher Price toy hoop and ball for Christmas. My friends, they had different dreams, to make it to the big times with our band. That'd be cool, but basketball was my first love, music second. This was my chance to attend a great school, further my education, and if the stars aligned join the NBA.

"I know." I glanced out the window at the dark cloudless sky. The stars were bright, one of the advantages of living in a small town. Maybe it was looking at the stars all these years that made me dream of bigger things.

"Where do you want to go to celebrate?" My mom asked me, once more turning to look at me. If she kept that up she was going to get a crick in her neck.

They'd picked me up from practice, despite having a car of my own, because the full-ride scholarship to Duke University had come in and they'd been desperate for me to open it. After the good news there was no way they were parting from me. I wouldn't complain. I loved my parents.

I was an only child—their miracle child they called me. After years and years of trying they'd finally conceived me. Growing up, we'd always had a close relationship, and I was man enough to admit I'd miss them when I left for college.

"Can we get pizza?" I asked. Over the years, any time something good happened we always celebrated over pizza. I didn't see why this should be any different.

"Sure." She glanced behind at me again, smiling. "We are so happy for you, Rush. This is more than we ever dreamed for you." Her eyes crinkled at the corners. To me those wrinkles didn't show her age, but her happiness instead. My mom was always the happiest person I knew.

I couldn't help feeling choked up by her words. My parents had spent years driving me to practices, attending every game, buying everything I needed to play the sport I loved and I knew at times it'd been a burden for them money-wise, but they never complained. Not once.

"This isn't my victory alone," I told her, meaning it. "It's all of ours."

Her smile spread. "We lov—"

"Dad!" I screamed, my eyes widening in horror at the incoming lights, but it was too late.

He jerked the wheel, but the car drifting from the other lane slammed head on into our tiny car.

My body lurched.

My mom screamed.

Glass rained everywhere.

Then, there was only darkness.

Until, there wasn't.

I blinked open my eyes, strapped to a gurney. An oxygen mask was pressed over my mouth and nose. Red and blue lights flashed everywhere, nearly blinding my sensitive eyes. My body hurt, and I tried to lift my arm but it was immobile.

"Mom!" I called out. "Dad!" My screams were muffled by the mask. I twisted and jerked my body and the paramedic tending to me came into my line of sight.

"Don't move," he warned, his voice stern but kind. "What's your name?" he asked, lowering my mask. I didn't notice the pity in his eyes, not yet anyway.

"R-Rush. Rush Daniels."

"We're going to take care of you, Rush."

He put the mask back over my mouth and nose before I could ask about my parents. The gurney I was on jerked and raised into the air. As I was wheeled away I saw it.

The blood, so much blood in the car, and on the ground...

Two shrouded bodies lying side by side.

Tears leaked out of my eyes as emptiness filled my heart, a pain like nothing I'd ever experienced cleaving the organ in two.

Seconds.

Seconds was all it took to change my life forever.

For me to lose my parents, my chance at playing basketball, for my entire future to go up in flames.

I vowed then, as the ambulance doors closed and I could no longer see the two bodies covered in white sheets, that I would never again allow myself to feel—to love—anything, ever again, because all it took was a single heartbeat to rip it all away.

ONE

Kira

"We shouldn't be doing this," I pant, my breath lost somewhere on the floor along with my panties and any sort of common sense I once possessed.

Rush grips my hips tighter, and I grind down on his cock. I try to contain my moan but it's impossible. The things he does to me sets my body on fire.

He grins up at me. "You didn't accidentally fall on my dick," he reminds me.

I roll my hips and grab my breasts, wishing he didn't make me feel so fucking good. Rush knows what he's doing when it comes to sex and it shows. I can't think of any man I've been with who's made my body come alive the way he does. Normally, it's always been about the release, with Rush it's about the journey.

"Yeah," I breathe, "but we've been doing this for..." I try to calculate how many months this no-strings-attached relationship of ours has been going, but with his cock buried inside my pussy and doing magical things to me, my brain can barely function. "Too long," I finish. It's close enough of an answer.

He flips me over and a surprised scream leaves my throat.

I expect him to pound into me, fuck me senseless, but instead he grabs my legs pushing my knees toward my chest and rolls his hips oh-so-slowly into me. My whole body shudders from the sensation and my eyes roll back into my head.

He lowers his head and nips my neck. "We've just started."

"That's not what I meant and you know it." My fingers shake as my body is overridden with pleasure. I'm not normally this chatty during sex, but for some reason today I'm feeling supremely guilty, because I've broken all my rules with Rush and I don't like blurred lines.

I've always vowed to never fuck someone I know. Strike one against Rush is he's the best friend of my best friend's boyfriend. But I couldn't seem to stop myself when it came to him. Strike two—we've slept together multiple times, hell probably hundreds of times at this point, and my rule was always once and done. Strike three—sometimes he stays the night, a lot of times actually, and I've *never* let a guy do that.

By all accounts, with three strikes against him, Rush should be out.

I can't get enough of him, though. I'm like an addict. Addicted to the rush he gives me. How funny, Rush is a *rush*. He gives me a high no one and nothing else can.

He kisses me, his tongue tangling with mine and silencing anything else I might say.

I let the conversation drop for now. While he's making me feel this good and giving orgasms galore I really shouldn't complain. The rules have already been broken many times over, so why am I bothering to get upset now? It's pointless.

"Get out of your head," he growls, nipping my ear. "Nothing's changed."

He's right. Nothing *has* changed. I don't want any more from him than just sex, and it's the same for him.

It's weird for me though considering I've never slept with the same guy. I want them for sex and nothing else, so beyond bringing me pleasure I don't need anything else from them.

Then, Rush came into the picture.

He rolled into town with all his pompous L.A. boy grins, thinking he could say whatever he wanted and panties would drop—most would have, but not mine.

It all changed when I ran into him at the gym with my best friend Mia and I saw what he was packing in those gym shorts. Oh yeah, I knew I had to get my mouth around that glorious cock and I hoped a guy as hot as him with *that* kind of tool could live up to it and give me plenty of orgasms. Boy, has he delivered. Something I've learned over the years is guys can talk the talk, but not walk the walk. Honestly, guys should be forced to take a class on what a clitoris is and how to rub it *just right.*

Rush, thankfully, could talk the talk and walk the walk.

My vagina sang a song of glory in his honor and continues to every chance it gets.

"It has changed, if you think *you're* in charge," I snap back, because it's easier to argue with him than to admit I agree.

I push him to roll over and—

A scream erupts out of me as we fall.

Rush slams onto the floor beside my bed and lets out a groan as my weight falls on top of him.

"I think you broke my dick," he huffs out, his face red.

"Don't be a baby. Man up." I smack his muscled chest, right over the tattoos on his pectoral muscles.

"Man up," he growls in a repeated mockery.

I scream again as he grabs me and stands up with me in his

arms. My breath leaves me in a whoosh as I find my back slammed into the wall, his fingers biting into my hips. His cock rams into me and I gasp, grabbing his shoulders. In one hand he grabs my hair, tilting my head to the side and exposing my neck. He bares his teeth.

"Don't tell me to man up, Kira. You might not like the consequences—also you're not in charge. Neither am I. We're fucking equals. That's why this works."

Before I can retort he bites my neck.

Bites. My. Neck.

Like some kind of fucking vampire or some shit.

I scratch his chest and he releases the spot with a wicked grin.

"Don't do that." I narrow my eyes at him, daring him to push me and try it again.

"Fuck, I love when you get mad."

"You're seriously messed up," I scoff.

He growls lowly. "Shut. Up. Kira."

Before I can argue with him yet again, he presses a bruising kiss to my lips. His tongue slides against mine and it feels like he's fucking my mouth with as much vigor as he is my pussy.

I grab at his hair, tugging roughly and he hisses. Pulling his mouth from mine, he growls, "You want it rough this time, babe? I have no problem with that."

His fingers squeeze my ass with bruising pressure and I gasp. He silences the noise with a raging kiss.

He sucks my bottom lip between his and lets it go. He caresses his nose against my cheek and I shudder as his mouth brushes my ear. "You can tell me you're in charge, and act like it all you want, but the way your body surrenders to me tells me *everything* I need to know."

My body shakes in his arms. I'm silently glad he's strong

enough to hold up my body, because I've lost complete control of it.

My head lolls back against the wall, my eyes drifting closed from pleasure as he fucks me.

I wish he was wrong, that I had the voice to tell him I don't surrender to him, but I *do*.

He's the only man I've ever done that with.

Growing up watching my mom be battered around by jerk after jerk set me up to make sure I took control of my life and who I slept with.

But while he might be a cocky prick half the time, I know he's not a *bad* guy, not like the ones my mom always gravitated to. With his band destined for great things, he can't be a *total* screw up. Plus, it helps that he's basically me in male form.

He loves sex.

I love sex.

He likes it rough.

I like it rough.

He doesn't want a relationship.

I don't either.

It's the perfect situation—we can fuck anytime we want, schedules permitting, and don't need to know anything else about each other. I don't even know his middle name or his birthday, and I don't care.

He sucks on the skin near my neck and I grab his hair roughly, pulling his head away.

He grins, his denim blue eyes shining with humor. His blond hair, sweaty from our marathon sex that started hours ago, hangs messily in those eyes that seem to mock me.

"Give me a hickey and you'll regret it," I warn him with venom in my voice.

He cups one of my breasts in his big hand and gives it a

squeeze. "You won't be saying that when you're screaming my name."

I scream as I find myself tossed back on my bed. In seconds, his big body is over me. He flips me over and slams into me. I bunch the sheets in my hands and let out a low moan despite myself, my body pushing back into his as I wiggle my ass.

He slaps his hand against my ass and gives it a squeeze, eliciting another long moan from me.

He lowers over me, and growls lowly, "I'm going to fuck you so hard, so thoroughly, you'll be begging me to put my mark on you."

Wetness pools out of me at his words and I hate my body for betraying me.

"I thought you said we were equals," I pant, struggling to find my voice as he pounds into me.

His voice lowers to a whisper as he says, "Did you think I wasn't going to let you put your mark on me? Fuck, Kira, I'd love to see what you'd do to me."

I moan again at the very idea of leaving behind a visible mark on Rush. It's this primal feeling of marking him as mine, and it scares me that I even think about wanting it.

Obviously, I've done gone and lost my damn mind all over this fucking blond Adonis and his monster cock.

Does that mean I'm going to stop our arrangement? Hell no. He's the best sex I've ever had and I'd be dumb to give it up easily.

Besides, it's laughable to think I've caught feelings as easily as the common cold. I'm above such frivolous things as *feelings*.

"You like the idea of that, huh, don't you?" His breath is a rasp in my ear and my body tingles. "You don't want to admit you *like* me, but you do."

Fuck, he sees me too well.

"I don't like *you*," I pant, struggling to catch my breath from his relentless pace. "I like your *cock*."

He chuckles huskily and my nipples tighten in response to the sound.

He bends and presses a tender kiss to the back of my shoulder, near my neck. "Keep telling yourself that, Kira."

Before I can retort his hands tighten even more around my hips and he fucks me relentlessly until I forget everything except the pleasure he brings me.

With a groan and a shudder, he reaches his climax at the same time an orgasm wracks my body. He holds me, my back cradled to his chest as I lose control of myself. He nips my neck where it meets my shoulder.

"You're fucking gorgeous when you cum. It's the only time you're ever completely free and not in control."

His words barely register. My mind is lost to pleasure.

I don't know how much time passes before I regain some power over my body and we collapse onto the bed.

I lay on my stomach and Rush reaches over, squeezing my ass with a grin.

"I love fucking you."

I snort, my nose twitching with amusement. "Um ... thanks, I think."

"It's a compliment, believe me." He rolls to his back, and stares up at the ceiling.

Both of us are still struggling to regain our breath, and I don't know about him but I feel exhausted with it growing more difficult by the second to keep my eyes open.

I force my body up and head to the bathroom to pee.

Returning to my room Rush is already asleep with his arm crooked over the top part of his face. I toss a blanket over him before slipping beneath the sheets.

The first time we fucked it happened by accident, him falling asleep in my bed, and then after that it didn't seem to matter. He's good about staying out of my way and since he doesn't ask personal questions and try to get to know me I don't mind it. Don't get me wrong, we do talk, but about basic shit. Like, what our day is like or what we want to eat. I think we might even be friends in some weird way, which probably makes this whole thing a lot more complicated than I try to make myself believe.

I stifle a yawn and roll away from his big body—seriously, the guy is huge *everywhere* and takes up almost my entire queen size bed.

When I fall asleep I dream of him, the dream world showing me impossibilities of our future—impossible, because I don't want a future with him, or anyone.

TWO

Rush

"Um..." I look at the menu board, scanning the items as if I haven't seen them a million times before. "I'll take six glazed donuts and six chocolate covered. I also want a large black coffee, and a small toasted almond latte," I tell the Dunkin' Donuts worker, pulling out my wallet from my back pocket.

It's early and the line behind me is long from the work crowd, needing their caffeine fix before they face the day.

She rings up my order and I hand her the cash for it while another worker starts gathering my order.

"Here's your change," she says with an appreciative smile, checking me out.

I grin. "Thanks, darlin'." I wink and she blushes as I move to the side to wait for my order. I can't help it that I ooze charm and girls can't help but be enamored.

Standing with my arms crossed over my chest, I wait for the donuts and coffee. When I left Kira's place she was still asleep. I don't know how it started, but shortly after we started having sex regularly I began going and getting breakfast and coffee. I bring it back to her place and sometimes I stay, other times I go depending on whether or not I overslept and have to be at the studio.

Our arrangement suits me well. She's hot, fucking amazing in bed, and she doesn't want to get to know me. I've never had a problem getting a girl if I need to get laid, but I have to admit it's a lot more convenient having one girl I'm sleeping with and I don't have to put any effort into it to get what I want. Maybe that makes me sound selfish, but Kira wants the same thing. As long as neither of us is getting hurt by the arrangement I don't see the issue.

"Your order, sir," the guy says, holding out a bag to me and a cardboard drink carrier with the two coffees.

"Thanks, man." I take everything from him and head out to my truck.

The bright red Chevy Silverado HD is a gift from our producer and mentor Hayes. When we signed our contract with him all four of us requested vehicles of our choice since we had to move all the way across the country from L.A. to a small town in northern Virginia close to D.C. There was no way we could tolerate being stuck here with no wheels.

I open the passenger door and place the bag of donuts on the seat and take the coffees from the carrier and put them in my cup holders. No way in hell am I risking the coffee sliding off the seat and staining my interior.

I close the door and climb in the driver's side. At six-foot-six it's no struggle for me to get into the massively tall truck, but I've had a chuckle at time or two while watching Kira get in and out of it. Lucky for her, I'm always willing to put a helping hand on her ass to get her inside. I'm a gentleman like that.

I drive back to her apartment and park on the street. I make sure to feed the meter—having learned the hard way how quickly the cops around here are willing to give me a ticket. Apparently they're all bored out of their minds since nothing interesting ever seems to happen around here.

I take the outdoor steps up to her second floor apartment, sliding my key in the door and opening it. The hinges creak eerily. I guess since she doesn't have security this loud ass door is the next best thing.

The shower is running, so at least Kira's up and getting ready for her classes. She's a beast when I have to wake her. She tossed her phone at my head once. That shit hurt.

I set the bag of donuts on the counter along with the coffee. Popping open the lid I grab a glazed donut and in one bite half of it is gone.

The shower shuts off with a squeak and I hear the suction of the door opening. A moment later Kira pads out into the kitchen with a towel wrapped around her body and one around her damp hair like some sort of turban or some shit.

"Mmm, coffee," she hums. "Gimme." She holds out grabby hands and I give her the black coffee.

She eyes my latte with a smirk. "I still can't believe you drink that girly shit. Honestly, is it even coffee?"

I pick up my coffee and take a large gulp. "Black coffee is for people who either hate themselves or have no soul."

She pats down her body with her free hand and I fight the urge to tear the towel off her body. Neither of us has time for morning sex today, even if it'd be fucking amazing. "Definitely no soul here." She shrugs her slender shoulders and reaches past me for a chocolate covered donut.

"Luckily mine is pure and holy enough for the two of us," I joke, licking glaze from my lips.

She snorts and fuck I find it kind of adorable.

"Thanks for the breakfast," she says with a dismissive tone.

Her code for *get the fuck out of my space.*

I make a noise of protest and press a hand to my chest as if I'm wounded. "Ready to get rid of me so soon?"

"I orgasmed. You ejaculated. We got a good night's rest, now coffee and donuts, frankly, what's left?" She raises a single dark brow in challenge. I love challenges.

"I could paint your nails while you tell me stories about your childhood," I jest.

She narrows her eyes and bites out a deadly, "No."

I have no problem with the fact that Kira doesn't want to talk about personal shit. I don't want to either, having to explain about my parents, and all that happened after the wreck ... the downward spiral it sent me into, is not something I like to talk about. But even I have to admit, after all the months we've been doing this *thing* it seems a little weird not to know more about each other.

"All right." I hold my hands up innocently. "I'm going as soon as I finish my donuts."

"Lock up when you leave." She gives me a warning look, but it's unnecessary. I learned a long time ago she loses her shit if the door isn't locked.

She takes her donut and coffee, disappearing into her bedroom. The door closes behind her—shutting me out.

It's funny how she continually shuts me out, yet I have a fucking key to her apartment.

I only wish I had a key into her mind, because despite myself I'm desperate to know more about Kira Marsh.

I pull open the door to Mist Records & Studio. I still don't understand the fucking name. All Hayes has told us is it's an inside joke—well guess what, I want in on the joke.

It's almost ten and I'm not surprised to see Cannon already in the studio with Hayes. He's a fucking overachiever.

"Hope I'm not interrupting anything—actually, I don't care," I quip as I join them.

Cannon shakes his head, pulling a beanie low over his ears and gives Hayes an apologetic smile. "I'm not responsible for the dumbness that leaves Rush's mouth."

Hayes gives a small chuckle. "Believe me, I learned with my band there is no controlling each other. I'm glad you're here on time for once," Hayes spins his chair toward me, "you're up first today."

"When am I ever late?" I ask, disgruntled.

Cannon begins to tick off on his fingers. "Last Wednesday, the Friday before that, you were late that Monday too I think, and—"

"Okay, okay." I hold up my hands, urging him to shut the fuck up. "I get your point."

I stand up and yank my sweatshirt off, dropping it on Cannon's head.

"Fucker," he grumbles, grabbing my sweatshirt and tossing it on the floor.

As I stroll into the recording booth, Fox enters, stifling a yawn. Like always he looks like he rolled right out of bed and forgot to brush his fucking hair. One of these days I'm shaving it all off while he sleeps.

I sit down behind the drum set and pull my drumsticks out of my back pocket. I never go anywhere without them, the same way I used to always seem to have a basketball glued to my hand.

It's not often I think about that lost dream. How basketball meant more to me than music, unlike my friends who always put the band first. I lost my dream of going pro when both my legs were broken in the accident. After that, it was never going to happen, and the next thing I was most passionate about was music. So, here I am today.

I hold my drumsticks in one hand and slide on the headphones.

Before Hayes can tell me to start Hollis arrives.

Hayes gives him a narrowed eye look before swiveling his chair back to face me behind the glass.

I'm thankful there's no outright hostility between Hayes and Hollis. When Hayes found out Hollis had been fucking his daughter, Mia, we'd been temporarily fired and shipped back to L.A. Thankfully they worked their shit out, we got our contract back, and we've been back in the studio since, working hard.

I watch Hollis drop onto the leather couch beside Fox. He sports a smirk and says something to Fox. It's strange looking at Hollis now, how much he's changed. He's not hollow-eyed anymore, not nearly as angry either, and he genuinely looks happy. Mia's been good for him. That path isn't for me, though. I'm not ready to settle down, not now, probably not ever.

Hayes waves his hand, bringing my attention back to him.

I wait for his signal and start drumming.

My eyes close and I feel the rhythm of the drums. I've come to crave this feeling, this unleashing of something. When I'm playing the drums I can drown out the world, the thoughts in my head, and for a moment nothing else exists.

Even I don't exist.

There's a freedom in it I can't get anywhere else.

An hour passes before Hayes has me switch with Cannon so he can set down some bass recordings.

My right leg jumps restlessly as I sit and wait with Hollis and Fox.

I hate being stuck, not being able to *do* something, which makes these in-between times incredibly difficult on me.

I don't know what I would've done if I hadn't found Kira to distract me. At least back in L.A. there were clubs, parties, and women. Here in this small town there are diners and bowling. Yeah, there's women here too, but none of them intrigue me like Kira does.

We don't talk about our pasts, not about anything personal, but from the moment I started hanging around her more, I sensed a kindred spirit. I don't know what she's gone through, perhaps witnessed, but I know it's something. I don't ask about it. If she wants to open up to me one day she will. We have this unspoken rule between us—I don't push her, and she doesn't push me.

What we have works for the both of us. Sex and companionship without the complication of feelings.

She's the first girl I've ever met that hasn't wanted more from me. It's refreshing to find a woman that's confident in the fact that she likes sex and doesn't need a man.

I pull out my phone from my pocket, bringing up my apps.

I haven't done it yet, despite the months Kira and I have been at this, but I delete every hook-up app off my phone.

I wonder if I'm doing the right thing, but I reason I can always add the apps back later if we decide to end this. We promised we'd be exclusive to each other for as long as we felt necessary, so there's no need for me to keep them.

I watch the icons disappear and I'm surprised when I find my shoulders feel lighter.

THREE

Kira

"I can't believe you invited me out for girl time. You spend all your free time with Hollis now," I joke to my best friend Mia.

She flips her red hair over her shoulder and holds out her hands to the nail tech.

"I don't spend *all* my time with Hollis. I have school and work too, you know."

"I do know," I quip, since we go to the same school and work together.

I don't begrudge her for falling in love and getting a boyfriend. While I might not be one for all the lovey-dovey shit, I do understand most people aren't me. But it's still fun to pick on her.

"The guys are in D.C. with my dad tonight," she explains on a sigh. "They're making some sort of appearance at a music club. I thought it would be nice for us to catch up on girl things."

"Oh," I say softly. Rush didn't tell me, and it's not like me to care that he didn't, so it surprises me to feel a sting of hurt. Schooling my features, I say, "Well, since you said you're paying I'm all about the girl things." I wiggle my fingers and the nail tech glares at me.

Things like getting my nails done, a haircut, and anything of the sort are a luxury I can't afford.

"I thought we could do this, grab a bite to eat, and watch a movie at my place," she explains with a shrug. "It's nice to do something relaxing, don't you think?"

"As opposed to going to a club?" I fight a smile.

My idea of a good time is going out in a sexy dress, taking some shots, and dancing until my feet bleed.

Mia's a homebody and would rather lounge in her pajamas eating ice cream out of a carton and watching Netflix.

Don't get me wrong, I like to chill too sometimes, but letting loose appeals to me more.

We only live once after all—might as well have some interesting stories to tell when I'm ninety.

"The last time we went to a club it was your idea for cheering me up—yet I ended up being the sober one who had to haul your drunk ass home."

"Point taken," I snicker, glancing down at my newly painted toes. The shiny black polish matches the one being put on my nails.

Mia, however, has a soft blue on her toes and now the lady paints a ballet slipper colored pink onto her nails.

As far as appearances go, Mia and I don't match up. She's pale, freckled, and red-haired, as well as always dressed in the finest clothes. I have dark, nearly black, hair, my skin is several shades darker than hers, I'm almost always in full-glam makeup whereas most days she's not bothered with more than mascara and some gloss, and my secondhand clothes definitely are not up to par with hers. But personality-wise we click. We're both tough as nails and take no shit. I'm quicker to fly off the handle than she is, but if Mia gets pushed too far, she'll do whatever it takes to make a stand.

When I moved here during high school, she didn't have any friends—not for lack of trying, but because everyone used her to get close to her dad and meet him and his band. I was the weird new girl everyone avoided. One day I sat across from her at lunch and the rest is history.

My phone vibrates on top of the faux marble table and I lean over to glance at the screen.

Rush: In DC with Hayes trying to be a good boy and work and all I can think about is that sweet pussy of yours and fucking you so hard you can't walk tomorrow. Every time you move I want you to feel me.

I can't help myself, I squirm in my seat and smile.

With my hand that's not being painted I pick up my phone and respond.

Me: Tell me more.

"Are you sexting?" Mia asks, interrupting my thoughts. She wears a knowing smile.

I press my lips together and then mutter, "Maybe."

"You so are!" She shrieks trying to snatch my phone from me.

The woman doing her nails yells something unintelligible and Mia frowns, but stops wiggling.

I look down watching as the three little dots appear telling me he's responding.

Rush: First, I'll have you lay down on your bed. Naked, of course. You'll spread your legs and touch yourself because you want me to see those pretty pink pussy lips of yours. I'll

watch, stroking my cock while I do. Then when you're wiggling and making those little noises I'll tell you to stop—and you will, because you know I can bring you more pleasure than your fingers. But I'm not going to fuck you just yet. Instead I'm going to kneel between those sexy as hell legs of yours and I'm going to tongue fuck that sweet pussy. When you're dripping wet and glistening from your orgasm, then I'm going to kiss you so you taste yourself on my lips. I'm going to kiss you until you're begging me to fuck you—then I'll finally, blessedly, fuck you until your legs are shaking, the neighbors know my name, and the only man you ever remember is me.

"Holy fucking shit," I whisper out loud, moisture seeping into my underwear.

Before I can respond he texts again.

Rush: Fuck, I have to go. Hayes threatened to take my phone. Can I come over when we get in? It might be late.

I type back a simple ***yes.***

I CURL MY LEGS UNDER ME, TAKING A BITE OF DOUBLE DUNKER ICE cream. The coffee flavored ice cream mixed with cookie dough and Oreo cookie is to die for. Mia picks up the remote and puts on one of our favorite movies—*How to Lose a Guy in Ten Days.*

The way I see it you can't go wrong with Matthew McConaughey—or as I like to call him, Matthew McNaughty.

Mia hands me a blanket and grabs one for herself before settling down beside me.

"Are you sure you and Rush aren't together-*together*?" she asks over the opening credits.

I sigh. "For the millionth time, Mia, *no*."

"But you text all the time—he has a *key* to your place."

My jaw snaps open. "I didn't tell you that. How do you know?"

"Hollis," she answers with a shrug.

I groan. "Those four guys gossip more than school girls."

"Why does he have a key?" she pesters.

I sigh and narrow my eyes on her. *"Because*, he comes over often for *sex*." Before she opens her mouth with a retort I don't want to hear, I add, "Nothing else, and it's easier if he can let himself in and lock up when he leaves."

She shakes her head. "All I'm saying is, for as long as I've known you you've never slept with the same guy. That has to mean something."

"It means nothing," I respond, and take a big bite of ice cream. "Fuck, that's cold."

"Don't take such a huge bite then," she reasons in the scolding tone a mother would use with a small child.

When I swallow the ice cream I reply with, "I can't help it that it takes a lot to fill up my mouth."

She smiles gloatingly. "Rush and you are seriously meant to be. Deny it all you want, but I know better."

"Now that you're serious with Hollis it doesn't make you an expert on relationships."

"No, it doesn't," she agrees. "But you can't deny chemistry. When it's there, it's there."

"You're making up stuff, because now that you're settling down you want the same for me—but it's not happening, Mia. Not now, not ever."

She purses her lips and doesn't say another word as we watch the movie.

HANDS TRAIL UP MY INNER THIGHS AND I WIGGLE IN MY SLEEP AT the dream.

Fingers curl into my panties, shimmying the fabric down my hips.

"Kira."

That voice. God, that voice is husky and raw with desire. It's the kind of voice that oozes sex. It's thick and syrupy, velvety in a way that makes my knees weak.

"Kira, wake up."

My loose sleep shirt is pushed up my body and large manly hands, calloused and rough, palm my breasts. My nipples pebble in response as a small sound escapes my throat.

"Kira, wakey-wakey. I'm not fucking you while you sleep."

My eyes crack open and I jump when a face materializes in the darkness.

Not just any face.

Rush.

His blond hair is messy, those blue eyes alight with desire. His chiseled jaw and angular cheeks are dotted with stubble. He doesn't look one bit tired. No, he's entirely alert.

I reach up with tired fingers and rub my thumb over the dimple in his chin. I have one too and it surprises me how much I love it on him.

He grins, his teeth blindingly white in the darkness of the room.

"There you are," his voice is a purr.

"Mmm," I hum sleepily. I try to push the recesses of sleep aside like a curtain, but it's not easily thwarted even with the promise of sex.

He lowers his head and kisses my bare stomach where he's pushed my shirt up. My back bows and another sound leaves my throat unbidden.

"God, you're fucking gorgeous," he growls, his voice vibrating against my skin. "You have no idea what you do to me."

I reach down, palming him through his jeans. "I have some idea." I stifle a yawn and he chuckles.

"Are you too sleepy?" he asks, still palming my breasts. "I can go."

I shake my head. "Stay."

His smile is back. God, I wish his smile didn't make my stomach flip like it does. It feels like a swarm of butterflies are trying to take flight every time he disarms me with one.

I trace my finger over the lines of one of the many tattoos snaking his arm and chest. I've always had a weakness for blue eyes and tattoos. Sue me.

"I want your shirt off," I demand, my voice raspy.

He chuckles huskily, his eyes twinkling. "Yes, ma'am." I watch in fascination as the muscles in his stomach ripple as they're exposed. There's something about the way he's built that reminds me of the smooth carved muscles of stone statues. He's almost too perfect, but he has his scars. We all do.

I reach for his belt, undoing it quickly.

We're both well-practiced at this dance by now.

Soon, sleep is long forgotten and I'm naked beneath him. His body wraps around mine, like he's shielding me from a storm. He's so large I disappear underneath him.

His fingers press against my clit, rubbing slow circles.

"Rush," I beg, my voice wobbling. My fingers fist in the sheets at my sides as I fight the desperate urge to bury them in his hair or claw his back.

He cracks a smile. "Tell me what you want."

"Your mouth," I plead brokenly, "on my pussy."

He tilts his head. "Is that so?"

I push against his muscular shoulder, his skin heated beneath the palm of my hand, and with a chuckle he moves down my body leaving dangerous kisses all along my body as he goes.

When his mouth finds my center my back arches off the bed.

I'd been sleeping well, a luxury I rarely get to indulge in, but this ... *this* is much better than sleep.

My fingers finally curl into his blond hair and I tug helplessly on the strands.

I beg him for more, then I beg him to stop, then I start all over again.

My orgasm shatters around me and I can barely keep a hold on reality.

He makes his way back up my body, and like he promised he kisses me so I taste myself on his lips. Those dirty, delectable, dangerous lips of his.

He cups my cheek, angling my head back so he can deepen the kiss. I feel as if he's kissing my soul out of me—like he wants to take my very essence and make it his to the point I won't even recognize myself.

His tongue tangles with mine and I gasp. His other hand finds my right breast, resting under the curve with his thumb rubbing ever so slowly against my skin. Each graze brings his thumb closer to my nipple.

"Tell me you want me, Kira," he growls, nipping my bottom lip.

"No," I gasp back as his lips move to my neck, sucking the skin there.

His teeth dig slightly into my skin. "Say it."

"No."

He chuckles. "Fuck, I love your spunk. I love how you fight me every fucking way. Challenge accepted, Kira."

He presses his hand to my throat, choking me slightly. His eyes meet mine, his lips closed but tilted in a smirk.

"You want me to fuck you. I want to fuck you. Why don't you

be a good girl and give us both what we want?" His fingers tighten ever so slightly.

"No," I rasp yet again.

He releases my throat and his lips sear mine like a brand as he kisses me. The kiss sparks with fire, our desire barely contained. I don't know why I love denying him so much, and I have no clue why he loves forcing me to beg. We're both crazy, I guess.

He moves slowly down my body, swirling his tongue around one nipple and then the other. He sucks one into his mouth and my back rises, eliciting that dangerous smirk of his that I love to hate to peek through for a moment.

A growl rumbles in his throat as he looks back at me, and in the blink of an eye he's kissing me again at the same time his hand moves to my pussy and rubs my clit.

Not fair.

The asshole knows I much prefer his cock to his fingers. He's playing dirty.

He smiles against my lips like he knows what I'm thinking.

I grab the short strands of hair on the back of his head and hold him closer. I don't do it because I crave his lips, which I do, but because if I don't kiss him he'll get me to spit out those treacherous words. I refuse to, not yet, because the longer I draw this out the sweeter the release.

My mouth opens beneath his and he kisses me harder. He bites my bottom lip, not lightly but not rough either. It leaves behind a small sting he's quick to soothe with small kisses that are far too sweet and tender for what we do.

We fuck. Hard. Fast. Any time, any place.

I won't stand for sweet. Sweet is for pathetic people who think love truly exists.

Spoiler alert, it doesn't.

So finally, I give in, like he knew I would.

"Fuck me," I beg on a breath. "Fuck me, now."

He rises up slightly, looking down at me. "Say it, Kira."

I roll my eyes.

"Say it."

"Please."

I gasp as he presses inside me roughly, my nails scraping against his strong back. His name leaves my lips with a soft exhale.

He grabs my left leg pushing it up toward my chest and I gasp as it presses him deeper into me.

"Yes," I pant. "God, *yes*."

This is what I've been waiting for.

This rough, desperate, aching meeting of flesh.

This is the only kind of connection I need, the only one I can rely on.

Everything else is fleeting.

FOUR

Rush

I pull my truck up outside of Kira's place.

Me: I'm here.

Kira: I'll be down in a sec.

Me: I'd rather be going up for some sex.

Our friends decided we were overdue for a group night out. I guess they're right since I've been spending all my free time in Kira's bed, and Hollis is so far up Mia's butt we might never see him again.

Fox came up with the brilliant idea for us all to go to a karaoke bar. "It'll be less competitive," he said, since our last few ventures out were riddled with teasing and taunts. The fact he thinks we can't turn karaoke into a competition is upsetting. Even *he's* competitive. I know there's no way tonight will end without an argument or two, and possibly a bet.

Kira: Do you only think about sex?

Me: Yes. It's all you think about too so don't judge.

Kira: Wouldn't dream of it. I'm coming.

Me: You will be later tonight, but I'd love to head up and watch the show.

Kira: I'M COMING DOWN TO THE TRUCK YOU FUCKING IDIOT.

Me: There's no need to yell.

A knock bangs against the passenger door and I glance over to find Kira bundled up like we're in fucking Antarctica. With her short stature all I can see is her dark brown eyes peeking up beneath a heavy gray-colored beanie and the puffiest black coat I've ever seen covers her torso. Around her neck she has a deep blue scarf wrapped around.

"Stop staring and let me in you idiot," she yells behind the glass.

I shake my head and unlock the doors.

She hops inside, struggling with her short legs and I suppress a chuckle.

"Stop laughing or I'll castrate you, and then you're no good to me or any girl," she grumbles with a slight shiver. "Remind me to give Fox a piece of my mind for dragging us out in this cold. It's supposed to snow six inches tonight!"

"You're going to get plowed with more than six inches tonight," I mutter, pulling away from the curb as she buckles in.

"Oh no I'm not," she declares. "I don't feel good."

"Are you sick?" I ask, true concern clouding my voice.

"I was nauseous all morning. I could barely eat and I'm sneezing my brains out. I finally managed to get some soup down. I told Mia I didn't think I could come out tonight, but she threatened me with bodily harm if I left her alone with all four of you, so here I am."

I pretend to feign hurt, as I turn right at the stoplight. "Does she think we're monsters?"

"You're something else," she mutters. "Cannon is the only normal one and I'm not sure how normal he is."

"I feel like I should be offended, but I'm not. Normal is overrated."

She gives a small laugh that turns into a cough. When she recovers, she groans out a ragged, "I'm dying."

"Sorry, doll, I don't think you're dying."

"I feel like it," she grumbles, leaning her head against the passenger side window.

"Remind me to kill Mia when we get there," she says, her eyes closing.

I glance at her for a moment, noting the dark shadows beneath her eyes and sallowness to her skin. It's only been three days since I've seen her—scratch that, two days, because I stopped by her job to get a sub—and whatever this is has come over her since then. But the early February weather has been icy and cold with snow showers, so we're all lucky we haven't fallen ill.

The restaurant and bar that hosts karaoke night isn't too far away. We arrive and the parking lot is packed with vehicles and a row of Harleys. I can't decide if that's a good or bad thing.

I hop out and jog around to help Kira out. She gives me a disgruntled look when I grope her ass as I help her down.

"I can only be so much of a gentleman," I tell her with a shrug, locking the truck behind us.

We walk in side by side, our arms grazing.

I hold the door open for her and we're immediately assaulted with an onslaught of voices and one shrieking a horrendous rendition of a Shania Twain song.

God help us all.

I shove my hands into my pockets, looking down at the grungy red and white tiled floor. It looks like at some point of time it might have shined with a polished finish, but now it's dull with gray scuffmarks.

"Are they here?" I ask Kira, my head swiveling.

She shakes her head. "I'm not sure. I asked Mia, but she hasn't answered."

"They must be here then," I reason. "You can't hear anything over this chaos. Come on." I grab her hand and she jolts as soon as my skin makes contact with hers. I glance at her, noting the way she looks at our joined hands like mine could bite hers at any second. "I'm only holding your hand. Not asking you to marry me."

Some of the tension leaves her and she smiles slightly. "Yet." She gives me a small smirk.

I chuckle as I drag her through the restaurant, looking for any sign of our friends. "Is that so? You think I'm going to get down on one knee and profess my undying love to you?"

She laughs, her hand small and warm in mine, but slightly clammy like she's still unsure of this hand holding thing. I only grabbed her hand so we wouldn't get lost in the crowd. The place is packed from wall to wall.

"I'm very lovable," she says casually.

"You keep telling yourself that."

She laughs again, but this time it turns into a cough. "Ugh," she groans, reaching up with her other hand to rub her throat. "I'm going home and drinking an entire bottle of Nyquil."

"You'll do no such thing," I scold seriously. "That stuff is bad for you."

"And what? You're going to take care of me?" She raises a brow as we enter the bar section of the restaurant.

"Yes, actually," I say, glancing at her and abandoning my search for the guys and Mia for the moment. I stop walking and Kira is forced to stop beside me. "I know all kinds of home remedies and shit. You'll be over this in no time." She looks at me speculatively. "I'm serious," I add in defense. "My..." I pause, choking on the word I know I need to say but seems to be lodged in my throat. "My mom was really into all the homeopathic stuff, the shit works too. I'd be sick as a dog and she'd brew one of her spells as she called them—really just herbal tea—and I'd be better the next day."

She shrugs. "Fine, I'm willing to try your ... spells." She smiles with the word. "But if I throw up on you, don't say I didn't warn you."

I chuckle. "It'll take more than that to send me running."

"That so?" Her tone implies she finds it to be a challenge and she can't hide her little smirk.

"Guys! Over here!"

The moment between us is broken by Mia waving like a deranged madwoman at us. I release Kira's hand.

"There they are," I announce unnecessarily.

"There they are," she echoes, looking down at her now empty hand.

I push my way through the crowded bar, Kira trailing behind me and we finally arrive at the table our friends have claimed.

I drape my coat over the back of a chair and sit down beside Fox, forcing Kira into the empty space beside me—though if she had a choice, we both know she'd still choose to sit there.

I'm awesome—who wouldn't want to bask in my presence?

Fox slides his menu over to me, and I peruse it for a moment before settling on my usual—a juicy ass cheeseburger and fries. Fucking delicious.

I go to slide the menu toward Kira but she shakes her hand in front of it. "No, thanks. I don't think I can eat."

"They have soup," I tell her.

She sighs. "I know, but..."

"Just get something and if you don't feel like eating it no

harm no foul. My treat," I add, because I know she hates spending money on things she deems unnecessary.

She sighs, picking at the edge of her fingers. A nervous habit I've noticed she has. The same way she bites her lip when she's either anxious or turned on—there's a difference in the way she bites it too, depending on which she's feeling.

"Fine," she agrees.

"So," I begin, speaking to no one in particular as I look around at the neon lights on the wall, red and white booths that match the floor, and the retro garb the wait-staff wears, "did we step back into the sixties or something?"

I half-expect Elvis Presley to jump out from somewhere.

Mia laughs lightly, tucking a piece of hair behind her ear. She leans unconsciously into Hollis beside her. He smiles, noticing her need to be closer to him. "Something like that. It's owned by this local guy. Cool, huh?"

"It's ... something," I say as a bunch of college girls shriek along to a *One Direction* song.

Mia bumps Hollis's shoulder. "You're going to have to get up there and give these poor people's ears a break."

He chuckles, ripping the paper apart that once held his straw. God, now I'm thirsty. How unfair they got here first and already have beverages. After all, I'm going to need a drink or two or even more to get through this night.

I don't fucking sing, ever, but I know the bastards will con me into getting up there. At least where I lack a voice I can make up for it in swagger.

"I'll get up there eventually ... with you," Hollis answers her.

"Oh, no," she protests swinging her arms wildly. "Not happening."

"Afraid?" Cannon asks, raising a brow.

"Of killing everyone in here with the sound of my voice ... um, yes," she replies.

Fox puts down his beer and I eye it enviously. Ever since the accident it's been pretty much impossible for me to go through a day without at least one drink. It doesn't erase the pain, the pain that even this many years later threatens to drown me, but it does dull it.

"Come on, Mia," he says to her, "you can't be any worse than these people in here. Besides, of all of us Hollis and Cannon are the only ones who can sing."

"You sing?" Mia's head swivels to Cannon at the head of the table. He looks like a fucking deer caught in headlights. I snort and turn it into a cough, but he glares at me anyway.

"I don't *sing*," he replies in a deadly calm voice.

"He does too," I pipe in and his death glare narrows. "He just prefers to ... use his *fingers*." I mime playing the bass.

Cannon shakes his head at me, muttering, "And you wouldn't know what I can do with my tongue so shut up."

"Dad's pissed," I hiss loudly enough for him to hear.

He tosses a rolled up napkin of utensils at me and I catch it easily—I've had enough practice tossing my drumsticks and a basketball, to become an excellent catch.

"Nice try," I say, slinging them back at him. They smack his chest and fall into his lap.

"Boys, be good," Mia scolds in an exasperated tone. "We're here to have fun, not fight."

"Fine," Cannon grumbles. "I can sing, but not at Hollis's level."

"I see the rest of your party has joined you," a waitress yells to be heard, and we cease talking to look at her. "What can I get you two to drink?"

"Bud Light for me," I answer—I'm a country boy, what can I say. "And a hot buttered rum for her."

"Actually a Coke for me."

"A coke and the hot buttered rum for her," I correct while

she glares at me. "Trust me," I whisper to her. "It'll help with the cold."

"Whatever," she mumbles. She still has her winter coat wrapped around her despite the fact it's two degrees away from hell in here, with all these people and the heat rolling out of the vents.

"Are you all ready to order too?" she asks.

After a nod of affirmation, we all take turns giving her our food order.

"I'll put this right in." She smiles, tapping her notepad against the wooden tabletop before walking away. She gives me a wink and I sit up straighter.

She's pretty in that homegrown small-town sort of way. Sandy blond hair, curvy body, light clear skin. She looks like she's college aged. She might even go to the University Mia and Kira attend. But ... as pretty as she is and how only a few months ago I would've been quick to tap that, I won't.

I made a promise to the dark-haired beauty beside me that for as long as we were fucking each other it would be exclusive. I don't make promises lightly, and I won't break them on a whim.

"She thought you were hot," Kira says. There isn't a trace of jealousy in her tone and for some reason it irks me.

I shrug. "Babe, I can't help it I'm this good-looking. I'm a stunner. The ladies like to look and I'm helpless to stop them."

"Yeah, you're as helpless as a baby tiger."

I snap my teeth together playfully. "I didn't pick my genetics."

"Just like you didn't pick that cocky personality either."

I lift my dark grey Henley and flash her my abs. "When you've got it, flaunt it. Rules to live by."

"I'll start walking through school naked then," she jokes, but it falls flat when she starts to cough.

I lean over and in a low voice I rumble in her ear, "Only if you want me to show up and haul you out of there. No one looks at what's mine."

She gives my chest a shove. "I'm not yours."

"Like hell you aren't. Maybe not forever, but right now, you are and I'm yours."

Her surprised brown eyes meet mine.

"You're crazy," she says, but her voice is higher sounding and she looks away, wrapping her arms around herself.

"Aren't you hot?" I ask, changing the subject.

She jerks back. "Excuse me?"

I groan and tap her puffy black jacket. "You're still in your coat."

"Oh ... I forgot." She slips it off and drapes it over the back of the chair, but leaves her scarf on. Without the coat she looks laughable in the scarf. It's so big and chunky and she's a tiny little thing drowning in it.

"What now?" she asks, tilting her chin up at me in defiance. "You keep staring at me."

I grin. "You're just so cute."

"Yes, my snotty nose is adorable. I'm glad to know that's your kink."

I snort. "You *know* that's not my kink."

Her cheeks redden. It's a rare thing to make Kira blush, but I can't help loving the way the scarlet color melts on her creamy skin.

"Here are your drinks," the waitress says, leaning heavily over the table so her arm brushes mine and she's practically all up in poor Kira's space.

"Thanks," I say tightly. "My girlfriend and I appreciate it."

She whips back so fast she nearly spills all three drinks she set down.

"Need anything else?" she asks in a clipped tone.

"Nope, we're good. Aren't we, sweetie?" I ask Kira, draping

my arm over the back of her chair. My tone is oversaturated with ooey-gooey gummy sweetness as I try to make my point.

"Just dandy."

After the waitress is gone, Kira and Mia say, "Girlfriend?" simultaneously.

I raise my arms innocently. "She kept checking me out. I just needed her to stop. Can't have Kira growing jealous and marking her territory like a mama bear. We've already been through that with Hollis."

Hollis groans, leaning his head back. "It was a fucking *baby* bear, and it barely scratched me. Besides, it was you three who freaked and thought I'd get rabies. I was cool as a fucking cucumber."

"Yeah, yeah, yeah," I chant, picking up my beer. With my other hand I slide the rum toward Kira. "Drink up."

She glowers, but picks up the drink and takes a sip. "Not bad," she admits. "Feels good on my throat."

"Told you. You know what else feels good on your throat?"

"Don't say it."

"My cum."

She kicks me under the table, how she does it with me beside her is beyond me, and I nearly choke on my beer. Some spews out of my mouth and onto my shirt.

"No sex talk during dinner," Mia warns, wagging a finger.

"Where's the fun in that?" I grumble.

"Rush," Cannon warns, his eyes narrowed and dangerous. He's the fun police.

"Yes, Dad? Are you going to ground me?"

"Possibly." Cannon crosses his massive arms over his chest. Honestly, it wouldn't surprise me if he did—not that I'd listen to him.

Mia nudges Hollis. "Go sign up."

"Everybody's doing it," he warns at her pestering. "Not just me."

She glares at him. "No."

"We're doing a duet."

She sighs. "Fine. Only if you go by yourself first."

"Don't sign me up," Kira begs. "My throat hurts."

Mia frowns. "You don't sound good. I thought you just didn't want to come."

"I'm coming down with something." Kira shrugs miserably. "I was bound to get sick at some point. I can never make it through the winter without getting a cold or the flu."

"Fine, are we all in agreement Kira doesn't have to go?" Mia asks and we all nod.

"I'll sit out for moral support," I volunteer.

Mia narrows her blue eyes. "Nice try."

"I'll be back," Hollis says, getting up to go add our names to the list, and undoubtedly pick our songs.

"Hang on, I'm coming with you," I say, suddenly knowing the perfect song to sing.

I meet up with him and we give the guy working the machine everyone's information.

"Do you have Under the Sea on there?" I ask. "Like from *The Little Mermaid*?"

Hollis flicks his head toward me. "Are you seriously going to sing that?"

"Fuck, no, it's for Cannon."

He chuckles. "I like the way you think."

"I occasionally have a brilliant idea or two." I pretend to brush dust off my shoulders. I then tell the guy what song I want. All the panties in the bar are about to land on the stage when I go on—even if I can't sing worth a shit.

"All right, is that all of you?" the dude asks.

"Yep," I say, reading over it one last time and seeing that everyone's down.

"You're going to embarrass the shit out of Kira," Hollis warns as we head back to the table. "Possibly, turn her on."

"Oh, I'll definitely turn her on." I smirk, walking with even more swagger than before.

He shakes his head. "The world broke the mold with you—that's how the saying goes, right?"

"Do I look like I know?"

"True," he agrees as we reach the table and sit down.

"Food," I groan in delight, finding my cheeseburger and fries waiting for me. "God, I'm starving."

Kira lifts a spoon of chicken noodle soup to her mouth. "Then shut up and eat."

I chuckle. "So, bossy. Me likey."

"You're incorrigible."

"You give me so many openings. I'm helpless here."

"I don't give you openings. You make them."

"I can't disagree," I admit, picking up my burger. I take a huge bite, suppressing a groan. I skipped lunch today and it was a mistake. It's rare for me to miss a meal—I'm always hungry—but I decided I better hit the gym today while we had a break at the studio. I've been neglecting going, but at least sex counts as exercise. I get plenty of that.

Hollis is halfway through eating his meal when it's his turn to go on stage.

"I'll be back," he says, hopping up.

He moves through the crowd and disappears for a moment before we see him hop up on the stage.

"This one's for Mia." He points her out and she covers her face. The music begins and she groans. "He didn't."

"He did," I confirm.

She shakes her head. "First the Halloween costume, now *this?* Why does he have to do a Willow Creek song? There are a million other songs out there."

He sings the words to her, to the crowd, playing it up.

They eat it up since he's the first person to grace the stage that can sing, at least since I've arrived.

When the song ends he crooks a finger at Mia. "Time to join me."

"Ugh," she groans, pushing away from the table. "If it's another Willow Creek song I'm stabbing him—y'all have been warned, that makes you accomplices." She waves two fingers from her eyes to each of us. "If I go down you're all going down with me."

"Is it a Willow Creek song?" Kira asks me once Mia's out of earshot. She struggles to suppress a laugh. I spy her bowl and I'm pleasantly surprised to see almost half the soup already gone.

"Wait and see."

"You suck." She pouts, jutting out her bottom lip in an effort to sway the words from my lips. "Just tell me."

"There's no fun in that, babe."

She looks toward the stage and we all wait for the music to start.

As the opening notes to *Dancing Queen* by ABBA start, she shakes her head. "You two aren't in charge of karaoke ever again."

"What's wrong with this? Would you prefer Justin Bieber?"

"Don't diss Justin. I like him."

"Should I get you a cardboard cutout then?"

"Yes—preferably shirtless."

"Well, babe, after you see my performance all you'll be asking for is a cardboard cutout of Rush—but lucky you, you get the real thing." I lean back in my chair, rubbing my abs through my shirt.

"Did you just refer to yourself in third person?"

"It seemed to work best to get my point across," I defend.

She reaches over and pats my chest mockingly. "Keep telling yourself that."

I capture her hand, holding it over my heart. "Keep pretending you don't actually like me all you want—but you do."

"I never said I didn't." She snatches her hand away like she's been burned.

"Mhmm," I hum. Lowering my voice, and my head to her ear, I say, "That's why you push me away at every turn."

"You like this arrangement just fine or have you forgotten the rules? Just sex, no talking about personal things, and when one of us wants out that's it."

"And do you want out?"

"No," she admits, crossing her arms and looking steadfastly away from me.

"My point exactly."

I pull away from her and straighten in my seat as Hollis and Mia return to the table. I was so engrossed in Kira I didn't pay one iota of attention to their performance. I'd planned on booing them. Everyone deserves at least one hater in life. Haters are motivators.

"Your turn Foxy boy." I smack Fox on the shoulder. With a roll of his eyes he stands. "I hate you all for this."

He pushes his chair back and heads for the stage. I swear one girl grabs his ass as he passes. Nope, not girl—cougar, definitely a cougar.

Fox hops up on stage, rolling up the sleeves of his maroon shirt. He grabs the microphone and looks at the digital screen that shows the lyrics. The music begins and he speaks into the mic, looking directly at me. "You didn't." He glowers, looking positively deadly—but Fox couldn't hurt a fly.

"Tell me, what *does* the fox say?" I shout above the crowd, earning more than a few looks of irritation.

He shakes his head and begins singing very loudly and very off-key to the gimmicky song. It was everywhere a few years ago, and considering his name is indeed Fox, and not a nickname, how can we not torment him with it? It's our duty as best friends to inflict endless torture.

I clap loudly and then cup my hands around my mouth to shout, "That's my Swiper-No-Swiping! Sing that song, Fox!"

He glares back, promising punishment later. I'd like to see him *try* to punch me. It's not happening. I might not be Cannon's size, but I'm definitely bigger than Fox. Not that he isn't muscular or anything, but he's kind of a string-bean. Super tall, super lean. I could probably push him over with one finger if I really wanted ... well, maybe not me but Cannon definitely could.

Honestly, Cannon is who I'm afraid of when he learns what song I chose. He'll know it's me, not Hollis, because Hollis isn't as much of a jerk as I am.

There was a summer when we were children when Cannon watched the fucking *The Little Mermaid* movie—yeah the Disney one with redhead Ariel—every single day and knew every song by heart.

In high school, he even joined musical theater.

The blasphemy.

I wonder what his drama teacher would think if she saw what the clean-cut Cannon looked like now—covered in tattoos and piercings, and no longer the baby-faced princeling he once was.

Fox's song ends and I turn to Cannon. "Your turn biker boy."

"Biker boy?" His pierced brow climbs up his forehead.

I sigh dramatically, like I'm suffering at having to explain myself.

"Because you look like a biker."

"There was an implied *duh* on the end of that," Kira adds and I smile at her.

She gets me.

Cannon shakes his head, pulling his beanie lower over his ears. "Whatever."

"Cannon Rhodes, ladies and gentlemen." I slow clap. "The man of few words and even less understanding of them."

He gives me the finger.

Kira laughs beside me. "You love tormenting people, don't you?"

"I didn't have siblings," I explain, shrugging it off. "I've got to make up for it somehow."

She's not amused.

The truth is the guys and I grew up like family. We went to school together practically from the start. As the oldest I was always a grade ahead of Cannon and Hollis, Fox being the youngest was two grades behind them. Despite the age differences we were inseparable from the start.

The defining moment that brought us together was in first grade for me. A bunch of older kids were picking on a scrawny preschooler and I came to his defense. Two more backed me up. Those two being Cannon and Hollis, with Fox being the poor kid being made fun of.

After that, we stuck together and nothing could separate us.

I lean back in my chair, the front two legs coming off the floor, and cross my arms behind my head as Cannon takes the mic.

He shakes his head as he sees the song.

"Fucker," he mouths at me.

I wink.

Much to my chagrin he sings *Under the Sea* in this low, gravely way that has all the girls swooning.

Swooning they may be, but *I'll* be the one having panties thrown at me.

But only Cannon could make a Disney princess song sound like something that should be on the radio today.

As he finishes I lean over to Kira and whisper, "My song is dedicated to you. Remember that when panties go flying."

She snorts, slapping a hand over her mouth so Coke doesn't go spewing across the table.

"That confident in yourself, huh?"

I feign nonchalance. "When you've got it, you've got it. Why would I deny it?"

I stand and slip through the crowd, hopping up on stage and taking the mic.

I might sound like a dying whale when I sing, but I can still make all the girls scream my name.

I nod at the guy working the machine that I'm ready and the opening music to Ginuwine's *Pony* starts.

I sing as best I can, but it's my dance moves I'm ready to impress with.

I roll my body and thrust my hips. I find Kira at the table in the back, covering her face with her shoulders shaking.

Oh hell no. She isn't going to laugh at me.

I play to the crowd for a moment longer before I hop off the stage and make my way through the crowd to her.

She lowers her hands and sees me coming. She immediately starts shaking her head no, and I nod my head yes.

This is happening. My eyes say. *Deal with it.*

I reach her and pull her chair out.

"Rush!" she shrieks, her face flushed. "Don't. Oh my God," she cries when I begin my lap dance.

"Oh my God," she says again, around the song as I roll my

hips into her like I'm fucking her. "You're way too good at this. Were you a stripper in a past life?"

I ignore her and continue moving to the music.

I grind against her and she tries to hide her face, but I grab her chin in my free hand. This show is for her, and I want her to watch. This is *almost* as good as fucking her in a public place.

Yeah, *that's* my kink, and my naughty girl gets off on it too. She won't admit it, which surprises me since she's so open about sex, but apparently it's one thing she won't fess up to.

But she fucking loved it when I fucked her in the empty ballroom of the hotel I'm staying at. She loved it even more when we nearly got caught.

I kiss her, not a safe for public viewing kiss either, and she melts into me.

She can protest, push against me all she wants, but she *likes* me despite what she tries to convince herself.

I mean, I can't help it if I'm an extremely likable and fuckable guy. It's in my DNA. That shit is engrained. Not learned.

As the song comes to a close I hurry back to the stage. Returning the mic, I bow, while all the ladies cheer and their boyfriends and husbands glower.

They're only jealous because they wouldn't know how to give a woman a squirting orgasm if their fucking lives depended on it.

Hopping down to an onslaught of applause, I toss a few winks here and there, and collapse back into my seat beside Kira.

I lift my beer to our waitress at another table and indicate I want another.

Kira shakes her head beside me.

"That was..."

"Panty-melting?" I supply. "I know." I toss in a smirk for good measure.

"It's a good thing there's only one of you. That's all I'm saying." She tries to hide a smile.

"Why is that?" I ask, taking the beer the waitress brings me.

"The world would erupt into chaos with more of you."

"I'll take that as a compliment."

She snorts and it's not an entirely unpleasant sound. "*You* would. I hope you never procreate."

"Aw." I feign hurt. "Are you afraid of the dominance my spawn would reign on the world?"

She shakes her head at me. "I'm afraid of the riots that would be bound to ensue."

"This has been fun," Mia says, loudly enough that my attention is stolen from Kira.

For the moment.

"I don't know why we don't hang out as a group more often," she says, genuinely meaning it, which is almost laughable. Every time it seems to turn into a disaster in some shape or form—like me turning a bar into a strip club. But at least all our shenanigans make for good memories.

"Because your idea of *fun* is more closely associated with *torture*," Cannon says lazily, sweeping his tattooed fingers.

Mia huffs. "Fine, then *you* can plan the next group outing," she challenges Cannon.

He shrugs, picking up his drink in salute. "I accept that."

"Fuck, we're all in trouble," I groan, shaking my head. "He's going to have us volunteering or some shit."

"Maybe you wouldn't be such an asshole if you contributed to society in a meaningful way."

"I spread joy through my cock."

Cannon sighs like he's so done with my shit. I mean, he's still friends with me so clearly I'm not that much of a burden.

"It *is* a thing of glory," Kira admits, holding her hands up innocently in an *I'm just saying* gesture, her head tipped to the side with a tight-lipped smile.

"See, I'm just doing my civic duty." I lean back in my chair with a smirk. "Spreading the love."

"And spreading STDs with it," Fox cackles with a disarming grin—I swear a woman at the next table sighs dreamily.

I smack him on the back of the head. "I'll have you know my junk is clean and perfectly groomed."

"Didn't ask." Fox raises his hands, wiggling his fingers. "But I'm sure the whole table is thrilled to hear about your man-scaping."

"I could give you some pointers." I shake his shoulder in jest. "Maybe then you'd get a lady."

Fox crosses his arms over his chest.

Beside me, Kira sneezes.

My eyes zero in on her, concern making me forget entirely about Fox.

"Do you want to go home?" I ask her, my tone now serious and my attention focused solely on her.

"Yes." She nods with the word, already grabbing her coat.

I stand, pushing the chair back with my legs. I pull my wallet out and drop a few twenties on the table that more than covers our share and a tip.

"Leaving so soon?" Hollis taunts with upturned lips.

"Kira's sick, I'm taking her home."

"Interesting," he muses, his eyes twinkling with amusement.

"What?" I narrow my eyes on him, willing that sparkle to leave.

"Nothing," he says in a tone that I know means something is *definitely* up.

I grab my coat from the back of my seat and shrug into it.

"See you losers later." I give them the finger as I leave.

I place a hand on Kira's back and we push our way out of the restaurant, the place still just as packed, if not more so, as when we arrived.

Outside I use the remote start to get my truck warm as we make our way through the slick parking lot to where the truck waits. I keep my hand near her, but not touching, in case she slips and I need to grab her.

When we reach it I open the passenger door for Kira and help her in. For once I don't grope her ass. I know she doesn't feel good and she's likely to punch me in the face if I get handsy, and my face is far too handsome to risk it—not that she'd be likely to actually get a hit in.

I have the reflexes of a ninja.

Closing her door, I slide around the front of the truck and—

My feet go out from under me as I slip on ice and hit the asphalt *hard*.

Maybe *reflexes of a ninja* was a *bit* of a stretch.

I pick myself up and glance in the tuck to find Kira laughing her ass off. Her laughter quickly turns into hacking coughs so I can't be irritated with her for long.

Dusting the cold as fuck snow off my ass I make it to driver's side and get in.

"I meant to do that," I tell her, sounding dead serious.

"Sure you did."

"So, we agree then? I meant to do it?"

She reaches over and pats my arm mockingly. "Whatever makes you feel better."

I pout playfully like a wounded puppy dog.

"Aw," she croons. "Don't be a baby about it. Do I need to kiss it and make it better."

I suppress a laugh. "As much as the thought of you *literally* kissing my ass amuses me to no end, you're sick and I promised to take care of you."

"Can we get milkshakes?" she asks with a little more energy

than she had before. "Ooh, a chocolate malt! There's a Sonic close to here."

I put the car in drive. "Sure, whatever you want."

"Thanks." She smiles and it's genuine.

"You're welcome."

There aren't many moments like this between us. Authentic moments where we aren't joking, arguing, mocking the other, or fucking.

Kira gives me directions and ten minutes later, less probably, I'm pulling in.

I start to go through the drive-thru but she points to one of the bays. "Park there. Let's both get one and sit here so we can enjoy it."

"Okay," I agree, because it actually sounds kind of nice to sit with her a bit longer.

I'm turning into a fucking sap.

Sick Kira is way mellower. It's nice, but kind of strange. I'm used to her barking orders at me, or whispering dirty things in my ear.

But if she wants milkshakes, and for us to sit together and drink them, then that's what I'll do.

I pull the truck into the nearest bay and keep the window up while I look at the ice cream menu, which is on the passenger side, so I basically end up in her lap. I *might* be leaning over more than necessary, but what she doesn't know won't hurt her.

"I want a chocolate malt," she demands again.

I swing my eyes to her. "You established that."

She laughs, and then coughs. Groaning she says, "Just wanted to make sure you were paying attention."

I look back at the menu again and when I know what I want, fall back into my seat, and roll down the window. I shudder from the chill pouring in through the open window.

I reach out and push the button.

A moment later static crackles and a female voice says, "Welcome to Sonic, what can I get you?"

"One small chocolate malt and a small strawberry cheesecake milkshake."

"I'm sorry, sir. This location doesn't serve malts."

Kira snarls. "The fuck—I want a malt."

"She wants a chocolate malt," I say to the speaker.

A heavy sigh and then, "*Sir*, we don't make them here. Therefore we don't have the malt powder. Would a chocolate shake suffice?"

Kira crosses her arms and huffs. "*Fine.* I will settle for a plain old chocolate milkshake."

"A small chocolate shake it is then," I say.

She gives me my total and I roll up the window while we wait. Sitting up I grab my wallet.

"I'll pay for it," Kira defends, fumbling for her bag on the floor.

"Don't worry about. I got it."

"How do you always *have* it?" She scoffs in disbelief. "Surely you're as broke as I am. It's not like you guys have released an album yet."

I shrug.

"Rush…?" she inquires.

I clear my throat. "Inheritance," I mumble.

It's the only answer she'll get out of me. There's no reason for me to go into all the dirty details about why I have an inheritance. I tried to refuse the money anyway. I didn't want it, but it was left to me, along with a house I haven't set foot in since the accident, and everything else inside of it.

They died and I got everything they left behind when I only wanted them well and whole.

"Inheritance?" she muses. "Why did—"

"No, Kira," I say roughly, raising my voice slightly. I'm

normally always easy going and never anger, but this is one thing I don't talk about with anyone. Not my friends who are practically family and definitely not *her*.

She slinks back in her seat and I drop my head.

"Fuck, I'm sorry. I didn't mean to ... yell or frighten you, it's just ... personal."

"Right," she says, looking out the passenger window and away from me. "And we don't talk about personal things."

"Kira—" I begin but she cuts me off.

"No, it's okay. You don't have to defend yourself. That's our deal. I don't tell you everything. We don't owe each other explanations."

Before I can respond there's a knock on my window and I roll it down, handing the girl cash and taking the shakes from her. I put them in the cup holder and Kira immediately grabs hers.

"Here's your change."

"Thanks," I say to the girl, handing her a tip before rolling the window back up.

Kira rolls hers down and tosses her cherry out. "I hate those things," she mutters.

"Me too," I say, picking mine out and throwing it out her window before it's sealed up.

She gapes at me. "How did you make that? The window was nearly closed."

I shrug and pick up my strawberry cheesecake milkshake—what happened to plain old strawberry? What the fuck did it ever do to anybody?

"I have magic hands," I explain.

She shakes her head. "Does anything serious ever leave your mouth?"

I pretend to think. "Nope, not really."

She gives a small laugh and wraps her mouth around the straw. She sucks, and sucks some more. I chuckle.

"Ugh," she groans, releasing the straw. "It's too hard."

"And *that's* what she said."

"Rush," she groans, knocking her head against the headrest.

"Give it here." I put my milkshake down and hold my hand out for hers.

"What are you going to do?" she asks, cradling her milkshake close to her chest like she needs to protect it from me.

"Do you trust me so little?" I pretend to be hurt.

She sighs, her eyes rolling slightly, and hands it over.

I take the lid off and stir it.

"Maybe I didn't want my whipped cream stirred in. Did you think of that?"

I eye her. "Too late now, isn't it?"

"You're insufferable."

"You're the one that keeps coming back for more."

"You're the one that sends dirty texts," she retorts.

"You're the one who screams my name. 'Oh, oh, Rush. Yes. More. Give it to me harder.'"

"Just give me my shake back," she snaps, snagging the Styrofoam cup and cradling it against her.

I chuckle, licking some chocolate ice cream off my finger that spilled over.

"Would you ... like your top back?" I hold out the lid to her.

Her mouth parts. "Jesus Christ, it's like some ridiculous, no good talent you have for making everything sexual."

"I mean, it's good for some things," I reason, picking up my shake once more.

"Like what?"

"It gets me laid." I shrug indifferently.

"The ridiculous part is, I know you're not lying."

"Didn't work with you."

"No, your monster cock did that for you."

I choke on my shake. "What?"

She smirks, pleased at herself with having surprised me for a change. "You know that first time I came up to you at the gym and then that night..." She trails off letting me fill in the blanks.

"Yeah, I remember."

"Well, as I'm sure you're aware those athletic shorts of yours leave little to the imagination. I had to see if you knew what to do with all of that."

"And do I?"

"Oh, yes."

"God, I want to fuck you right here."

"Here?" She looks around significantly at the parking lot.

"Like you pointed out earlier, I don't care who sees."

Her eyes turn dangerous. "Why don't you, then?" She challenges me to make a move.

I sigh good-naturedly. "Because you're sick, and you deserve to be taken care of, not have your body used. We're leaving here and going to Wal-Mart," I point across the way to the store sitting on the other side of the lot, "and I'm getting you everything you need to make you better."

"I'm still not sure I truly believe you're going to take care of me."

"Hey, I already got you milkshake. That's step one."

"Because I asked!" she protests.

I laugh. "Okay, you're right—but I *did* say I was going to make you tea, and tea is better for a cold than a milkshake. In fact," I add in a low conspiratorial voice, "I'm fairly positive there is no nutritional value in a milkshake at all."

"Don't mock my shake." She juts out her full bottom lip and dammit if it isn't adorable.

"Speaking of tea—do you even *own* a teapot?"

"Do I *look* like I own a teapot?" she counters.

I pause, considering. "I'm going to take that as a *no* then."

"What are you? Secretly British?"

I chuckle, and take another sip of my shake. "No, like I told you. My mom was into herbal remedies and shit."

"Was?" She raises a brown in inquiry.

I look away from her.

"Right," she whispers slowly. "We don't talk about personal stuff. Forget I asked."

I grit my teeth and turn to her. "It's not that I don't want to share stuff with you. I'd actually *like* to get to know you better. You're a cool chick, but ... there's some stuff I won't talk about with anyone."

"So, you definitely won't talk about it with me," she finishes.

"It's not about you." I look straight out through the windshield. "Some things are too painful. You know what I mean?" I glance at her.

She presses her lips together, her eyes sad and distant. "Yeah, I know." She whispers the words painfully with raw emotion.

We finish our shakes in silence, but not uncomfortable silence, before I back out and drive across to Wal-Mart.

"Stay in here where it's warm," I tell her when she reaches for her seatbelt. "I'll get the supplies."

"Are you going to battle?"

I give her a *duh* look. "Um ... *yeah.* I'm battling your nasty germs. I don't want to catch what you have."

I hop out of the truck before she can give me one of her sassy retorts and hurry into the store and out of the frigid air.

I grab a cart—I'm going to need it—and slowly begin my trek through the store since I have no clue where anything is and asking for directions is for pussies.

I stumble across some kind of weird looking animal thing that looks like a giraffe, or maybe a bear, but has lavender and can be warmed in the microwave so I toss it into the cart.

Near that are bath salts for soaking and I grab one with eucalyptus scent. I feel like I remember my mom saying eucalyptus was good for a cold, but I could be wrong.

Eventually I find the appliances and add a teapot to the cart.

When I reach the food aisle I grab Oreos because I know those are her favorite—they're always in her cabinet—and find the tea bags. I also grab some orange juice. My mom swore the acid in the orange juice could burn away any illness.

Heading back to the healthcare aisle I scour the vitamins for ones I know my mom said were good when you're sick. I dump a few in the cart and then head for the home stuff.

I finally spot a fluffy green blanket and get it as well. I know Kira has blankets, but who doesn't like to get new soft blankets? Blankets are the dopest shit ever.

Going over the items I've tossed in the cart I've decided there's only one more thing I need.

I head to the DVDs, and after fifteen minutes of looking I find what I want.

Pushing the cart to the checkout my phone buzzes in my coat pocket.

I pull it out and chuckle.

Kira: You've been in the fucking store for over an hour. Do I need to strip to get you to come back? If a nipple is free somewhere you're bound to appear.

Me: I mean ... if you're offering, a nip slip is fine by me.

Kira: Did you get lost in there?

Me: I'm a very thorough shopper.

Kira: Just hurry up. My sinuses hurt and I want to go home.

Me: I'm heading to the checkout now. Chill.

Kira: Tick. Tock. Motherfucker.

I shake my head and tuck my phone away.

Luckily there's an empty checkout lane so I begin unloading everything.

The woman scanning it though … pretty sure she could go down in history as the slowest person on the planet.

Somehow I manage to smile and grit my teeth as she takes a full minute to scan almost every item.

I swipe my card—no way in hell am I giving her cash to count—and my receipt prints out. I grab it from her, getting out of there as fast I can.

I wheel the cart to my truck and unload everything in the back behind my seat. Kira peers around to see all the bags, her jaw dropped.

"Did you buy everything in the store?"

I lift my shoulders slightly. "Close to it. But I did get you Oreos."

She presses the back of her hand to her forehead and pretends to swoon. "My hero."

I close the door and return the cart—I'm not about to be a jerk and leave it in the lot to hit someone's car. I jog carefully back to my truck, not wanting to risk taking another spill.

Thankfully, as I get inside the truck heat blasts out of the vents.

"I'm so glad I'm off tomorrow. There's no way I'd be up for working," she says, wiping her nose on a napkin I had stuffed in the glove compartment.

"Yeah," I pipe in, "I'm pretty sure no one would appreciate you getting your nose boogers all over their food."

"Rush," she groans like she's had enough of my shit.

"What?" I bat my eyes innocently at her before backing out. "You know it's true. You might be hot, but there's nothing remotely sexy about boogers and food mixed together."

She gags. "You're making the nausea come back. If I throw up in here, know it's your fault."

A laugh bubbles out of my throat. "You know, I threw up in Hayes's Range Rover our first night here. We flew into D.C. and had a hotel to stay there for the night so we wouldn't have to make the trip all the way out here with getting in late. We went out to a club and I ... well, I got us busted by Hayes since I posted where we were on Snapchat and things might've been a *tad* crazy."

"A tad?" she says doubtfully.

"Okay, more than a tad crazy," I relent. "I was totally wasted and threw up in his car. Got it all over Cannon's jeans too."

She snorts and wipes her nose again. "Bet he loved that."

"He might've threatened to kill me."

She stifles a yawn. "I hate feeling icky."

"Doesn't everyone?" I ask, turning onto the main road. "But don't worry, Dr. Daniels will fix you right up."

"Sounds kinky," she laughs.

"Hey, if you're into role-playing, I'm game. Can I be a dashing pirate and you be the damsel in distress?"

"Let me guess, you save me with your cock?"

"It's not a *cock* in this role-play. It's my mighty, gargantuan sword. Get it right, Kira."

"Oh, I'm terribly sorry I didn't think of that."

"Apology accepted." I grin at her.

We arrive at her place and she hurries inside where it's warm while I manage to gather up all the shit I bought. Two trips is for pussies. Anyone with brains knows you figure out a way to get all the bags inside in one trip, even if you have to carry one on your head and stuff something down your pants.

Not that I've ever done either before.

I bump my shoulder against Kira's door since I don't have hands to knock with and a moment later she swings the door open.

"Rush, this is nice and all, and I appreciate you getting this stuff, but it's after midnight. I'm exhausted and going to bed."

"Nope, not yet. First you're going to take a bath," I declare, setting the bags down and rifling through them. "With these."

I hold up the bag of salts proudly.

"And this is supposed to heal me?" She narrows her eyes.

"No, it'll help with your breathing. Along with this." I hold up a bottle of Vick's I grabbed while I was looking for vitamins.

"Rush, I really just want—"

I brush past her and into her bathroom. I start running her a warm bath as she stands in the doorway.

"You'll thank me later." My voice softening I say, "Please, just let me take care of you."

"Why?" she demands to know.

I swallow thickly. "Because I want to."

Her face loses its pinched and irritated look. "Okay, but I really am sleepy."

"You'll go to bed soon enough. Now get naked."

She laughs outright. "I think that's the first time you've said those words to me and it's not leading to sex."

"It was bound to happen eventually." I shrug and pass her to grab the salts.

I return and find her removing her clothes.

I pause, watching as her back is exposed. It has this delicious dip in it that I love running my tongue against. God, she's beautiful, and while she knows it to an extent, she's not truly aware of how captivating she is.

The way she gets under my skin isn't like anyone else.

She's in a league of her own.

She peers at me over her shoulder, smiling slightly.

"Like what you see?"

I let out a gruff laugh. "Don't ask stupid questions, Kira."

She removes the rest of her clothes and sinks down into the

water with a sigh. She grabs her bubble bath and dumps a generous dollop into the water.

I open the bag of bath salts and scoop two handfuls in.

She draws her knees to her chest and blinks up at me with her large, doll-like, eyes.

"Thank you ... for doing this. You don't have to."

"I want to."

She swallows thickly. "I know."

Clearing my throat I mutter, "I'll ... uh ... go start the tea."

I don't know why I suddenly feel so awkward. I guess, maybe, admitting that I want to help her, that I want to be around her, is difficult and strange. Beyond Cannon, Hollis, Fox, and their families I haven't allowed myself to get attached to anyone else.

The more people you love, the bigger of a chance you'll end up hurt.

Not that I love Kira, I don't, but ... I like her. She's become a constant the last few months and now it's strange to think of life without her. Even the short time we were back in L.A. in December it was odd not seeing her.

With a shake of my head I force those thoughts from my mind and make her tea.

When the water is hot enough I add the bag of ginger tea and a smidge of honey. I don't know if I'm supposed to do that, but I figure it can't hurt.

I carry it into the bathroom and sit down on the closed toilet lid beside the tub.

"Here you go."

"Thanks." She wraps her long fingers around the mug I found in her cabinet.

The mug, comically, says 'I don't spew profanities. I enunciate them clearly, like a fucking lady.'

It's the most Kira-ish mug that can possibly exist.

"You can go," she tells me with a shoo of her hand. "I'll be fine."

"Nope." I shake my head adamantly. "Dr. Daniels is not abandoning his post yet."

She gives a small laugh that turns into a cough. She groans loudly. "Fuck this cold. Also, can you *please* stop referring to yourself in third person? It's weird."

"No can do. Dr. Daniels likes third person. He also likes threesomes."

She rolls her eyes.

"Oh, come on, laugh. Tell me you've never thought about having a threesome before."

She bites her lip. "I'll admit ... I've wondered what it would be like to be with two guys at once."

"You want to be worshipped, huh, Kira? Lucky for you, you have me," I press a hand to my chest, "and I'm plenty enough for two guys."

She sips her tea. "Keep telling yourself that."

I frown.

"I'm kidding." She slaps my knee, leaving behind a wet mark on my jeans. "I definitely don't think I could handle *you* and another guy."

"I'm a handful," I agree.

"You're ... something."

She finishes her tea and hands me the mug.

She gives a slight shiver and I set the mug on the counter. "Come on, get out before you get chilled."

I grab a towel off the back of the bathroom door and hold it out for her to step into. She does and I wrap it around her.

"Oh, look. I made a Kira burrito." I kiss her and she makes a face.

"Don't kiss me. I'm germy."

"Kira, I've already been all over you for days, weeks, months. If I was going to catch this cold, I would've gotten sick already."

She sighs heavily. "I guess you're right. Now, let me through so I can put my pajamas on."

I step aside and she brushes by me and into her bedroom.

I let the water out of the bathtub and carry her mug to the sink, rinsing it out.

Taking everything else out of the plastic shopping bags I put it away and make sure everything is left in decent order. If I don't, she'll have my head and I like both of mine too much to let anything happen, thank you very much.

In her room I find her pulling back the covers and climbing beneath them.

"Thanks, Rush," she says, her tone implying I've been dismissed.

"Sure thing," I say with a forced smile. "I'll check on you later."

She nods and I ease her door closed behind me.

I go to the main door, open it and close it so she'll hear.

I click the lock in place from the inside.

No way am I leaving her here alone, sick, to tend to herself.

Nope, if she needs me, I'm going to be here.

I grab a pillow and blanket, creating a makeshift bed on her couch.

At my height I have no choice but for my legs to hang off the couch and it's hardly comfortable, but I don't care.

All that matters is that she's okay.

FIVE

Kira

My stomach rolls violently, and I burst upright from my sleep as I feel bile rise in my throat. Slapping a hand over my mouth, I topple out of bed running for the bathroom. It has to be early, because the sun is barely beginning to filter in my windows. I would've loved more sleep, but *no*, fate has other plans for me.

Dropping to my knees I manage to get the lid up on the toilet in time to empty the contents of my stomach. I don't ever remember having a cold where I actually threw up. When I'm done, I sit back on the cold tile, my body damp with perspiration.

My stomach rolls again and I lurch toward the toilet.

I jerk when I feel fingers pulling my hair back.

"I'm here. It's okay," Rush's warm voice speaks softly as he crouches down beside me.

After I'm done, I wrench away from him, wiping my mouth on the back of my hand.

"What are you doing here? Y-You ... I heard you *leave*. I don't want you seeing me like this."

"I pretended to leave," he admits, resting on his knees in front of me, still in his jeans. "I didn't feel right leaving you here alone and sick."

"Rush," I say softly, almost irritated, but also in a sort of awe. "You are the most confusing man I've ever met."

He cracks a grin. "What does that mean?"

"You don't want a relationship—to be anyone's boyfriend, but here you are doing boyfriend things. Can't you see how weird this is?" I flick a finger from me to him.

He shrugs like it's no big deal, which only grates on my nerves more. "I wouldn't do this for just anyone."

"Why *me*?" I ask, hating the way my voice cracks and spikes to a higher pitch.

His long fingers splay over his thighs. "I ... don't ... know." His answer is honest and I can tell even he's baffled by his behavior. "I guess when you care about someone you don't like to see them hurting, especially when you can help."

"Seriously, Rush. Go back to your hotel. You'll be more comfortable. I'm fine here. I've been taking care of myself practically since I was born. Why stop now?"

"Because you have me," he replies softly, sounding hurt.

I shake my head. I have a pounding headache and no brain power to deal with this confusing ass man.

I stand up, and Rush holds out his hand to help me but I refuse—not because I don't need his help but I wiped my throw up across my hand and that's just nasty.

I wash my hands thoroughly before brushing my teeth and swishing some mouthwash back and forth.

I spit it out, watching the blue liquid and white suds disappear down the drain. Rush hovers behind me, his presence large and looming like a fucking wall.

There's no point in telling him to leave again, because I know he won't. He's as stubborn as I am when he's convinced of something, and obviously he thinks here is where he belongs.

"Are you going back to bed?" he asks quietly, crossing his arms over his chest.

I ignore his probing gaze in the mirror. "No." I dampen a cloth with cool water and pat my face with it.

"Hungry?" he inquires with a tilt of his head. "I could make you some toast."

"You're going to make me toast?" I glance over my shoulder at him in disbelief and he chuckles, rolling his eyes.

"I might not be able to cook, but I think I can at least manage to make toast, not burn it, and smear some butter on it."

"Some toast might actually be okay," I admit. The sickness seems to be completely gone, and now that I've thrown up I feel pretty great—not well, but not as bad as I did. I'll take it as a small win.

I dry my face off as he leaves the small bathroom to undoubtedly make my toast.

"Should I make tea too?" He calls out from my kitchen.

"Sure, why not."

At least it'll give him something to do and stop fussing over me.

He and his friends might call Cannon the mother hen of their group, but right now Rush is giving him a surprising run for his money. To say I'm shocked is an understatement. It's weird and unnatural.

I turn the light off in the bathroom—Rush must've turned it on when he came in, because I know I didn't—and pad into the living space.

I can't help but smile at the pile of blankets and pillows on the couch.

Rush is a giant, I swear he's nearly seven feet tall, and the thought of him sleeping all night on my teeny-tiny couch is amusing. He must have had to perform some contortions to fit on it at all.

I sit down and wrap one of the blankets around me.

"Did you bring this?" I ask, looking at the fluffy green blanket.

"I got it for you when I was in Wal-Mart yesterday, but I got cold in the night and needed it. I should've gotten myself a Huggle."

"A *Huggle?*" I ask, not sure I've heard him right.

"Yeah, like a Snuggie, but better."

"*Okay*," I say, suppressing a laugh.

"I got a movie too—since you're sick and can't leave I'm forcing you to watch it with me."

"What is it?" I ask skeptically, watching him over the back of the couch as he moves around my tiny kitchen.

Everything about my place is small, but it's *mine* and that's all that matters to me.

"I'm not telling yet. You'll have to wait and see."

The toast pops out of the toaster and he puts it on a plate, slapping some butter across it.

He brings me the plate and says, "Tea will be ready soon."

"You need an apron."

"Huh?" he asks, raising a brow.

"A kitchen apron," I explain. "You're like my cute little personal chef."

"Baby," his voice lowers, "there's nothing *cute* or *little* about me."

There's a promise in his eyes saying if I wasn't sick he'd peel me out of my clothes and fuck me right here. I would let him too, but sadly I feel like a big ole pile of poo and that's not attractive at all.

A few minutes later he hands me the mug of tea and then crouches in front of my TV popping a movie in the DVD player. He fiddles with the controls, getting everything going, and the previews do nothing to give away what movie it is.

He places the remotes to the TV and DVD player on the coffee table before joining me on the couch and piling the rest of the blankets on him.

I stare at the side of his face. His straight nose, nice lips, and flawless cheekbones. Handsome seems too plain of a word to describe Rush. He's ... *godly*.

I would never dare to utter those words to him. His ego doesn't need any more inflation.

"Why are you staring at me?" he asks, still looking straight ahead.

"Because I can."

He finally looks at me with a crooked grin. He rubs the stubble on his jaw. "Like what you see?"

I roll my eyes. "If I didn't, I would've never slept with you."

He pretends to gasp. "Kira, are you saying you're so shallow you judge people based on looks?"

"The guys I sleep with? Yes," I answer honestly. "My vagina is a fickle bitch. Only the best for her."

He throws his head back and laughs. Dammit, if watching the way his throat moves with laughter isn't one of the sexiest things I've ever seen.

Just then I get distracted as the TV finally comes to the play screen for the movie.

I squint, not sure I'm seeing it right.

"*The Princess Bride*? Really?" I look at him like I don't know him, which I'm beginning to realize I don't. Not at all.

"It's a good fucking movie." He squirms beneath my scrutiny. "There are swords ... and killing ... and stuff."

"Mhmm, and it's also a romance." I cross my arms over my chest.

"Yeah, but it's *not* a rom-com, or Titanic," he mutters the last under his breath.

"What's wrong with Titanic?" I question curiously.

"Nothing." He shakes his head, his shaggy blond hair moving with the gesture.

"Sounds like there's a story there," I sing-song.

He pulls a face of disgust as he presses play. "A story you'll never ever hear."

"Oh, now you have to tell me," I say, perking up. The tea jostles in the mug as I wiggle on my beige couch.

"Nope." He mimes zipping his lips. "Be a good girl and watch the movie. I'll go get you some soup when it's over."

I shake my head. "One day you'll tell me."

He snorts. "Not likely."

I'll find out one way or the other, I know it.

I get settled on the couch beneath my blankets and sip at the tea while I watch the movie with Rush. I'm still beyond amused *this* is the movie he got. I file it away in the folder I keep in my mind with things I learn about him.

I have to admit, the tea isn't bad and I actually think it's helping with my cough and sore throat.

Beside me, Rush is zeroed in on the movie. I can't help but wonder what he thinks of my place. It's small, and dingy, definitely not in the best neighborhood and my furniture is all stuff I picked up at yard sales or flea markets. I've always thought it was cozy and cute, but coming from L.A., staying in fancy places ... it must seem gross to him, but he's never looked at it with disgust.

He's baffling to me, and despite myself and my rules, I do

find I'm curious to know more about him. But I don't dare step over that treacherous line.

Once I do, there would be no going back, and it's not a risk I'm willing to take.

Not now, not ever, not on any guy.

THE MOVIE ENDS AND RUSH STANDS, STRETCHING HIS ARMS ABOVE his head and exposing a sliver of tanned, muscled, stomach.

He grins when he catches me looking, so naturally I give him the finger.

He chuckles and stifles a yawn. I bet he didn't get much sleep, not on this small lumpy couch. He would've been better off sleeping on the floor.

"I'm going to go get you some soup. Want anything else?"

I bite my lip. "Another milkshake," I admit.

"From where?"

"Doesn't matter. Wherever is easiest."

He nods and starts shrugging into his coat. "I'll probably be back in about an hour. Try and get some rest. I ... uh ... I got you one of those lavender scented animal things yesterday. You can microwave them. I thought it might make you feel better."

I smile. "That was nice of you. Thanks."

It's hard for me to say thank you, so the fact I feel like I've done nothing but thank Rush in the past twenty-four hours says a lot.

Growing up, I had to fend for myself and take care of my mom. I've never had someone to look out for me before, and it's strange, but not entirely unpleasant. It gives me a new found respect for him.

He heads out, locking the door behind him.

I reluctantly get up, and start straightening things.

I hate a messy apartment, a messy anything. I like cleanliness and order when it comes to my personal space.

I didn't have it growing up and crave it now like someone with a sweet tooth craves chocolate.

Folding all the blankets I place them in the basket I keep in the corner beside the TV stand.

Heading back to my room I make my bed. I can't stand getting ready for bed and I haven't made my bed all day. It just seems gross to get in an unmade bed.

I finish fluffing the pillows when a wave of dizziness hits me.

"Oh." I press a hand to my forehead, swaying slightly.

I sit down on the bed quickly, worrying I might faint. It feels like my blood pressure has dropped suddenly. Closing my eyes, I breathe carefully in through my nose and out through my mouth.

It takes a few minutes, but the dizzy and lightheadedness passes.

Once it's gone, I go back to the couch and lay down, bundling the blankets around me once more—fat lot good it did me, folding them and tucking them in the basket. I put the TV on to a random channel. It's some mindless reality show, which is always the best thing to watch when you don't feel good.

It doesn't take long for my eyes to grow heavy and for me to doze off.

I startle awake when the door to my place opens.

Rush walks inside carrying bags from Chick-Fil-A and a milkshake.

I sit up, rubbing my eyes free of the lingering effects of sleep. He kicks the door closed behind him and sets everything down in front of me on the coffee table.

Before I can open my mouth to ask him to lock the door, he goes back to do it.

Safety is important to me and I can't stand an unlocked door.

You never know who might barge in. I don't need any sort of unnecessary stress in my life. I have enough stress as it is.

Rush sits down beside me as I pick up the chocolate milkshake, ripping off the paper from the straw. I smile to myself when I notice there's no cherry.

Rush's brain might be on a constant loop of thinking about sex, but he *notices* things. It's more than I can say for most people.

He pulls a black plastic bowl with a clear lid out of the bag and sets a wrapped spoon on top. "Chicken noodle soup," he says unnecessarily.

He then procures two chicken sandwiches and a large fry from another bag along with at least twelve packs of Polynesian sauce.

"Did you get enough sauce?" I inquire sarcastically.

"Hopefully so," he says seriously, taking the bun off one of the sandwiches.

He peels back the top of a packet of sauce and dumps the entire thing on the sandwich—then proceeds to do it *again*. He repeats the same process with the other sandwich and then opens another thing of sauce and dips a fry in it.

"What?" he asks around a mouthful of food.

"Nothing," I say, stifling a laugh. I wrap my lips around my straw and try to suppress a moan, because it tastes so fucking good.

I glance over and Rush is laughing at me.

His lips twitch. "You look like you're ... *really* enjoying that milkshake"

"Stop it," I whine, pushing his shoulder. "Let me enjoy it."

"All I'm saying is, nice suck job."

"Rush."

He laughs loudly and reaches for one of his sandwiches. "All right, all right. I'll be good."

"I should knock your sandwich on the floor," I grumble.

He takes a big bite. "Bvtynwt."

"Was that even a language?" I retort.

He chews and swallows, wiping his mouth with a napkin. "I said, 'but you won't'."

"Is that so?" I raise a brow and take a dramatic sip of my shake, daring him to make another comment.

He smiles, a big blinding smile that makes little crinkles appear at the corner of his eyes.

"Admit it, you like me."

"Nope." I shake my head.

His smile widens impossibly further. "You do. Maybe just a smidge." He holds his thumb and index finger the smallest bit apart. "But you do."

I sigh. "You're impossible."

"So are you."

"And incredibly stubborn."

"Again," he grins, "so are you."

"Let me enjoy my shake in peace." I turn away from him, curling my legs under me.

He stares at me for a moment, entirely amused. "Sure, whatever you want."

The problem is, I'm not sure what I want anymore.

Not from school.

Or work.

Or him.

Or life.

I used to have it all figured out, now I'm not so sure.

SIX

Rush

I hate leaving Kira Monday morning, but she has class and I have to get to the studio. She seems to be feeling better, but I know she's not well despite her protests. The woman is too stubborn for her own good.

I stroll into the hotel and up to our suite so I can shower and change my clothes.

Slipping the keycard into the door it swings open.

"You're alive," Cannon says gruffly from the kitchen area, making...

"Are those pancakes?"

"You're not getting any." His green eyes narrow on me. His normally groomed hair has yet to be tamed and he's only in his black boxer-briefs.

"Cover up, man. No one needs to see that."

He lets out a gruff laugh. "You're the one who walks around naked half the time."

"Gotta show you guys what you have to measure up to. I don't want your pancakes anyway. I already ate."

"With Kira?" He raises a pierced brow. When I nod, he says, "You've been spending an awful lot of time with her. You haven't caught those dreaded feels have you?"

I roll my eyes. "Of course not. I'm above such foolish nonsense. She was sick and I was taking care of her. That's all." I edge toward my room and further away from this conversation.

"You were taking care of her, huh?" He flips his damn pancake.

Cannon and his fucking pancakes. I swear he makes them every morning. Why not have a waffle every now and then? What did waffles ever do to him?

"It's not a big deal."

It's really not, not to me anyway. It was the right thing to do.

"Mhmm," he hums, "whatever you say."

"I'm over this conversation. I'm going to shower."

I hear him chuckle softly behind me and give him the finger over my shoulder. I don't know if he sees and I don't care.

I enter my room, closing the door behind me.

The hotel Hayes booked for our stay is pretty ritzy for this small town. It's a historic hotel, with most of the rooms harking back to the era of colonial America—I know because I looked online.

But not the top suites. There's one other on this floor on the opposite side.

Our room is decked out to the nines. It oozes money and splendor. It's far nicer than what any of us had back in L.A. where unless you have several million to spend, you're screwed.

My room is decorated in reds and purples—or I guess *plum* would be the more apt term for the dark shade of purple. The bathroom attached to the room is done in marble and it's all some of the fanciest shit I've ever seen.

I toss my coat onto my bed, drop my shirt on the floor, and I'm out of my jeans before I've even made it to the shower.

I turn it on and let it get steamy before stepping beneath the spray.

A sigh leaves my lips as the hot water pings against my chilled skin.

Even wrapped up, the walk from the garage to the hotel left me freezing.

I grab my soap, lathering it in my hands before smearing some into my hair and onto my body.

Rinsing it out, I deem myself clean enough. Turning the shower off I step out, grabbing a towel.

I dry and wrap it around my waist.

Padding into the carpeted bedroom area I open the top drawer on the dresser and yank out a plain gray long-sleeve tee. Another drawer—black jeans. Then I move to the closet and yank a sweatshirt off the hanger.

I can't handle the cold, not anymore. I've grown too used to L.A.'s always-sunny weather and this cold, icy, snowy shit is for the birds.

Finding some socks, I yank those on and then a pair of brown boots.

The last thing I do is grab my coat off the bed and shrug into that.

Heading out into the main living area, Cannon's now gone and there's no trace he was even there. The guy cooks and cleans. He's not normal.

Fox exits his room, drawing up the collar on his black coat. "You heading out?" he asks.

"Yeah," I answer.

"Should we wait for Cannon?" he asks.

I snort a breath in a disgruntled huff. "No."

Fox sighs, like I'm such a pain in the ass for not being nice or accommodating. "Yo, Cannon? You ready?" He hollers out to our bassist—and the biggest pain in *my* ass.

"Almost," he calls back.

"We're waiting," Fox tells me.

"Whatever." I give a small laugh.

I might give Cannon, hell—all of them—a hard time but at the end of the day we're friends ... no, family. They're the only family I have left.

Cannon leaves his room, bundled up as much as Fox and I are, with a beanie stuffed on his head. His heavy black boots clomp across the floor as he reaches us.

I bust out laughing and the other two glare at me, wondering what the fuck I find so amusing. When I finally recover, wiping an errant tear from my eye, I say, "Look at us. We're pathetic. We can't even handle a little cold."

Fox laughs first, then Cannon.

Sobering, Cannon says, "Who actually *enjoys* the cold?"

"It's all right some times," I admit reluctantly. "Snowboarding is fun." I give a lift of my shoulders. "But L.A. has turned us all into certified wimps."

Fox shakes his head. "You've got that right."

The three of us head for the elevator. It's still weird at times, Hollis not being around like he used to. Love, it turns us all into fools.

We step into the elevator and Fox pushes the button for the lobby.

Reaching the lobby, we walk across and out through the doors into the raging cold. The sky is a bleary dark gray and I worry more snow might be on the horizon. Even now there are piles and piles of it on every corner, long since turned a murky gray or brown color.

The studio is down the block from the hotel, meaning even with the cold it makes no sense for us to drive.

We hurry across the street and down to the studio, trying to be careful not to slip on ice. I don't need a spill like I had the other night. The last thing I need is my friends mocking me too.

Cannon reaches the door first and swings it open, Fox and I entering behind him.

The warmth of the studio hits me and I breathe a sigh of relief.

I shuck my coat off and toss it on the couch in the front area of the studio.

"Dude." Cannon glowers at me. "Don't throw your shit around, not cool."

"I haven't done that since I was like two, give me a break."

His eyes narrow to slits.

I groan. "Fine, *Dad*." I go and pick up my coat, then drape it over the back of one of the chairs. "Better?" I ask, waiting for his approval.

"It'll do," he says gruffly, and heads for the recording room.

I glance at Fox. "Why do we keep him around?"

Fox gives a small laugh. "Because we'd be up a creek without a paddle if we didn't have him."

I chuckle. "Is that one of your grandmom's sayings?"

"Yeah. That woman has the best sayings."

"She's pretty great," I agree.

We head back, joining Cannon, Hayes, and Hollis in the studio. I'm shocked Hollis is here first. That never happens anymore.

"Take a seat, guys," Hayes instructs and we do as we're told.

I end up on the couch with Cannon and Hollis. Fox takes the chair.

"What's up?" I ask, wondering if we're in trouble for something.

For once, I safely know it's not me.

Hayes swivels his chair to face the four of us.

"Your first single is premiering on the radio this Friday."

All of us blink at him in stunned silence.

"Are you serious?" Fox is the first one to speak.

Hayes grins. "As a heart attack. It's finally happening."

"Fuck, yeah!" I shout, fist bumping my guys. "We're fucking doing this shit."

I feel my heart stutter in my chest with fear but mostly excitement. We've been dreaming of this moment for so long, building it up in our minds to the point it seemed like it would never actually happen—that it was a dream way too far out of reach, some kind of make believe.

Even with the singles we've had reaching moderate success, playing clubs, and festivals ... it was exciting, but none of it compared to where we hoped to soar.

This shit is happening now.

I rub my hand over the stubble on my face. I seriously need to fucking shave. I've been at Kira's all weekend, so it wasn't like I could then, and when I stopped by the hotel this morning I didn't have time.

"This is a big deal for all of you and me too," Hayes says, steepling his hands beneath his chin and resting his elbows on his legs. "Your success is mine—it proves I wasn't crazy to take on this venture with all I have going on with my own band. It premieres at eight in the morning and most stations will be playing it throughout the day. I hope you guys are ready."

"For what?" Cannon asks, but I already know what Hayes is going to say before he does.

"For your lives to change. They'll never be the same after this."

SEVEN

Kira

Rush's hand is warm against mine as he pulls me onto the dance floor of the club.

Now that I'm better, we both wanted to get out for the night. Going to a club meant driving into D.C. but neither of us cared. I think we both needed drinks, dancing, and to let off a little steam.

It's Thursday evening, and normally I would never go out on a school night since I have classes tomorrow—but I needed to let loose. Being cooped up in my house, blowing my fucking brains out through my nose hasn't been my idea of fun.

"God, you look fucking sexy," he murmurs in my ear, head bent low as we bleed into the crowd. He twirls me around so my back is to his front. His hands settle dangerously low on my hips, his big hands closing around my narrow waist.

The song playing is loud, the lights blinking different colors with every change of the beat.

I grind my ass into Rush and I hear him hiss between his teeth.

This is the longest we've gone without sex since we started our arrangement. It almost feels like starting all over again. I know it doesn't make logical sense but that's how I feel.

His hands move up my body, stopping beneath the swell of my breasts contained in a tight-fitting black dress. My dark hair hangs in loose waves and I spent a good hour doing my makeup—a gray smoky eye and red lip. I wanted to feel girly tonight.

Hanging around in my pajamas hacking up a lung is not for me.

But *this*, going out, dancing, living it up ... this is what I live for.

Rush moves his hips against me to the beat of the song, and *fuck* can the man dance. He has this natural ability to feel the beat in his bones and move to it without a second thought. Maybe it comes from being a drummer, or maybe it's him. I don't know, but it doesn't matter, either way it's sexy as sin.

He flips me around so I'm facing him and I wind my arms around his neck. Normally it's hard to do, but in my stilettos the distance isn't nearly as far.

"You're fucking gorgeous, Kira. A goddamn temptress."

One of his hands makes a sensual stroll down my side, stopping when he reaches my bare thigh. Ever so slightly his fingers inch under my skirt.

He presses his forehead to mine. "I want you," he growls in a sexy rasp that sets my body aflame.

"Then have me."

He kisses me roughly at my words, stealing my breath.

His tongue finds its way into my mouth, tangling with my

own. Fuck, he's an expert kisser, possessing much more skill than most of the men I've kissed in the past.

There was one who I swore was going to drown me in his saliva.

It wasn't fun *at all*.

But Rush? Kissing, fucking, all of it is always fun with him.

Except when he takes care of me when I'm sick—that's just weird.

I still can't wrap my head around the way he stayed and tended to me while I was at my worst. He didn't have to do it, but he did, and as weird as I still find it, I can't deny it wasn't sweet.

Sweet seems like such a weird word to associate with Rush, but he was.

He bites my bottom lip, sucking it into his mouth and all my thoughts about the weekend flee my mind. It doesn't matter, and his motives don't either, this right now is all I need to focus on.

He kisses me until I'm aching and desperate for him to touch me, to make me cum. I need to tear at his clothes and have him fuck me raw.

I need to unleash this side of me in order to feel in control.

He drags me off the dance floor and we weave through the crowd. His eyes scan every available area for what he wants.

Finally he finds a darkened corner and turns to me.

"Can you be quiet while I fuck you?"

"Yes," I snap, slightly offended.

He grins. "Liar—but you moaning my name for everyone to hear is part of the appeal."

I squeal as he tugs me into the dark alcove. There's a small countertop, cabinets, and a mini-refrigerator. I don't know what it's meant for, and frankly I don't care, but it's incredibly open to the public.

We've fucked in his truck, my car, in his hotel room against the window, in the ballroom of the hotel, and God knows where else that I might be forgetting in my lust induced haze, but this is definitely the most open. The music still blares at a headache inducing level, and we haven't escaped the flickering multi-hued lights.

I swallow thickly, feeling nervous, but despite my nerves my nipples pebble beneath my dress and I feel wetness pooling between my legs from the idea of it all.

I have to admit, I've learned why Rush enjoys this—the threat of being caught, the idea of being seen, of someone watching you have sex ... it's very arousing in a way most things aren't.

It's dangerous, maybe that's why it appeals to him—to me too.

His big hands settle low on my waist and he pushes me against the wall, tucking us into the corner, so we're more hidden, but far more exposed than I'm used to. He's large enough that if anyone would stumble across us I'm mostly out of sight.

My breath stutters as he kisses my neck. I curl my fingers into his blond hair as his fingers slip under my dress, pushing it up my hips. He pushes my underwear to the side and rubs his fingers against me.

"So wet already," he growls lowly. "This excites you, doesn't it?"

"Yes," I pant, feeling his hardness press into my inner thigh.

"This is going to be quick and rough," he warns in a raspy tone that makes my knees weak.

"Shut up and fuck me."

He chuckles huskily, grabbing a condom from his pocket. Between us I undo his belt and free him from his jeans. I stroke his long hard cock and he hisses between his teeth.

"Fuck, Kira. I want you." He presses his forehead to mine, one hand against my cheek as he guides my head back.

He slips the condom into my hand and I rip open the packaging, rolling the condom on him.

I let out a small cry as he thrusts into me, not entirely prepared for the intrusion.

He holds me against the wall with his hands on my legs, his fingers digging in roughly, with my legs wrapped around his waist.

I do my best to quiet my noises of pleasure but it's difficult.

We're close enough to the dance floor I can only hope it helps drown out the sounds of our fucking—skin smacking against skin.

Rush covers my mouth with his, silencing a moan I desperately need to release.

"Quiet, Kira," he commands in a low voice against my ear. I can feel him smile, because he *knew* despite my protests I wouldn't be able to silence my pleasure.

I bite down on my bottom lip so no noises can escape.

My nails claw against his shirt, desperate to hold on to something, to anything, that might keep me from floating away.

"Let go, Kira," he whispers huskily. "I'm almost there and you are too, I can feel it."

I whimper, scared to reach that point.

He presses the back of his hand to my mouth. "Scream as loud as you want. Bite my hand if you need to. It's okay to let go, I have you."

A moment later there's no more fighting my impending orgasm and it rolls through me so powerfully I *do* bite his hand. The lure of getting caught makes my orgasm thunder through me, pulses of aftershock making my legs shake around him.

His cock twitches inside me and he groans through his own orgasm.

We stay locked in position, waiting for feeling to return to our limbs before he sets me down and we both work to right ourselves. He tosses the condom in a nearby trashcan and tucks himself back into his pants.

He stares at me for a moment, a bead of sweat above his lip, and before I can blink he grabs my face between his hands and crushes my mouth beneath his. Releasing me, he rasps, "You're making me fucking crazy."

"W-What do you mean?" I stutter, taken aback.

He shakes his head and steps away from me. He rubs his jaw like he's utterly confused and after a moment he murmurs, "I don't know."

It's an honest answer, I can see it in his deep blue eyes, and I'm terrified of what it truly means.

EIGHT

Rush

I shake Kira's shoulder in a desperate attempt to wake her.

"What?" she grumbles. "We fucked at the club and twice more when we got back here. My vagina needs a rest you fucking fiend."

I smack her bare ass where the sheet has dipped down.

"As delightful as another round sounds, that's not why I'm waking you up."

"Then *why*?" she groans, not opening her eyes. Her lips are pouted with sleep that still clings to her.

"We're going to get breakfast and then we're going to sit in my truck and listen to the radio."

"Why the fuck would we do that?" She cracks open one brown eye.

"Because," I draw out the word slowly and dramatically, "our song is premiering on the radio today."

She sits up so fast her head bumps my chin and I back out of her way.

"Are you serious?" she blurts, her eyes wide. "You guys are going to be on the radio today?"

"Well, our song." I shrug like it's not a big deal, but it is. Fucking huge, really. We've never had one of our songs make it onto the mainstream radio.

"That's ... wow, Rush. Um ... just give me a few minutes to throw something on."

"Sure," I reply.

She disappears into the bathroom and I quickly pull my clothes on from the night before.

Within ten minutes Kira is ready in a tight pair of jeans that hug her ass and a plain gray sweatshirt that somehow is sexy as fuck even with it hiding her shape. She has her hair tossed up in a messy ponytail and fuck I want to take it out and run my fingers through the strands.

She turns to the mirror above her dresser and swipes some kind of red lipstick on.

"I'm ready," she declares, turning back to me. I stare at her hungrily. She huffs out a breath and rolls her eyes. "Can you stop looking at me like I'm a snack?"

I suppress a laugh. "I can't help it you're sexy as fuck."

She shakes her head at me and grabs her bag. "Let's go. You've got me out of bed, now feed me."

"So demanding," I joke, and we go outside to my truck.

She hops inside, wiggling her ass as she struggles.

"Stop staring at me," she says, not even looking my way.

"How do you know I'm watching you?" I ask, laughter in my voice.

"Because you love looking at my ass."

She manages to right herself into the seat and pull the door closed. With a shake of my head I walk around the front of the truck and climb into the driver's seat.

There's a diner not far from here—we could actually walk, but since Kira's just getting over a cold I'm not about to let her get chilled.

Since it's early I manage to snag a spot right in front. I hop out and feed some quarters into the meter.

Kira opens her door and I hold out a hand to help her down and she stares at it for a moment like it's going to bite her.

"Kira," I say and her eyes lift up to meet mine, "why are you so afraid of my hand?"

She squirms a bit. "It's not your hand ... it's what it represents?"

I suppress a laugh. "What exactly does it represent?"

"Familiarity."

"Is ... that a bad thing?" I ask, raising a brow.

She swallows thickly. "I don't want to get too comfortable with you."

"Why?" I ask, slightly offended as she gets out, ignoring my hand. I let it drop to my side cold and lifeless without her touch.

"Because this isn't permanent, and we don't want it to be. You're going to go back to L.A. at some point and we'll both be nothing but a memory to each other."

"Is that you really think? That we'll never see each other again? Need I remind you my best friend is in love with your best friend—and he's in it for the long haul, which means weddings and babies and all that shit, so Kira, I'm sorry to inform you but chances are you're not getting rid of me that easily."

"I'm not trying to get rid of you," she says, as I open the door to the diner and usher her inside. It's a tiny hole in the wall place but the food is fucking amazing. It's one of those hidden gems you can only find in a small town like this.

"Really, because it sure seems that way," I say, as Kira pulls out a chair at the table by the window.

"Don't be so dramatic." She rolls her eyes as I take the seat across from her. "You're such a drama queen."

I sigh heavily as the waitress comes by to give us menus. "You act like I'm a fucking leech or something," I hiss under my breath as the waitress leaves to tend to another table. "I'm as opposed to relationships as you are, but I would think we could at least be friends."

She snorts, the sound laced with disbelief. "Rush, I highly doubt you've ever been *just friends* with anyone of the female gender."

I glower, unable to help my reaction. "Maybe not in the past, but it doesn't mean I can't change."

She levels me with a doubtful look.

"I like sex," I admit. "I like women. I like fucking. But that doesn't make me a bad guy. I'm open about what I want. It's not a secret. I don't feel like I deserve to be punished for *liking* you, Kira. I don't want you to be my girlfriend, and you don't want me to be your boyfriend, and that's fine. But there's no rule that says we have to hate each other otherwise."

"Maybe there should be," she says, looking down at her menu even though I know damn well she gets the same fucking thing every time.

"What's that supposed to mean?" I spit, anger lacing my words.

She breathes out heavily and lifts her eyes to mine.

"I just mean ... we've been doing this for a while. Maybe..."

"Maybe what?" I prompt with more bite to my words than I intend.

"Nothing." She shakes her head.

"If you want to fuck someone else I won't stop you." I mean

it, but the idea also pisses me off. I won't stop her if it's what she wants. I'm not that guy.

Her mouth works back and forth. "That's not what I want. I'm worried that this is becoming too easy—us, hanging out. It's more than sex now."

"Is there something wrong with that?"

Normally I'd be running at a full sprint in the other direction at the fear of attachment, but with Kira ... we're similar, and I guess I like spending time with someone who understands me without saying a word.

"Not as long as we both understand this will never be anything but what it is."

I smile at her. "Don't worry, Kira. I won't fall in love with you."

I mean the words, I truly do, but in the back of my mind a little voice tells me if I ever were to fall in love, she'd be the one.

We finish our meal in tense silence and get in my truck.

I don't want to be irritated with her, she's done nothing but speak the truth, but now I'm worried she might have a point.

What if this is becoming too easy? Too safe?

Neither of us likes commitment, maybe we would be better off to go our separate ways, but I don't want to, and I don't believe she does either.

I guess we do our best to remember this is sex, nothing more, but that doesn't feel right either, because she *is* different. This is different. It might not be a real relationship but we've grown close and I actually enjoy her company.

Fuck, I'm seriously overthinking this whole thing, letting her words eat their way under my skin.

I start the truck and glance at the time. It's five minutes until eight.

My stomach dips with anticipation.

I'm excited, nervous, and worried all in one.

This is a big fucking deal and I can only hope our first single goes over well. *Midnight Eyes* is closer to a ballad than anything else and there's no telling how it'll perform in the mainstream. It's nerve-wracking as fuck waiting to hear what people think. I might not care what people think of me, but I sure as fuck care what they think of my music and band.

I turn the volume up on the radio and Kira sits quietly beside me. I think she can sense my nerves.

This is huge.

Fucking monumental.

I watch the clock, my heart beating faster with every minute that ticks closer to eight.

"It's going to be great," Kira says, for a moment drawing my attention from the clock.

"I hope so." I scrub a hand over my jaw.

The announcer on the radio comes on and says, "We have a brand new single to share with you today coming from a band you might've heard of and if you haven't ... well, you'll definitely know them now. Here's The Wild with *Midnight Eyes*."

The song starts with a soft pattering of drums and my whole body seizes for a moment, because that's *me*. That's me playing the drums on a song that's playing on the fucking radio.

What the ever-loving fuck? How is this real life?

My throat closes up and I listen carefully to every lyric and every beat of my drums in the background. I've heard the final version of the song many times in the studio, but nothing compares to hearing it on the fucking radio where across the states thousands more are listening to it and will be hearing it all day long.

It's not often dreams come true, but when it does it shatters walls, walls you've built to protect your heart from the fact you might never reach them.

When the song ends, we sit there in silence. For once I have no cocky words or a smile to toss out. I need a moment to process this, the enormity of it all.

Finally, I look at Kira and I'm surprised to find her crying, not full on crying but a few tears and it's enough to stun me into further silence.

She looks at me in awe, her lips tilted in a small smile.

"Rush," she breathes my name, "this is going to change your life. Nothing will be the same for you guys."

"I know," I croak. "I know."

NINE

Kira

I still can't get over hearing The Wild's first single on the radio. Sharing it with Rush is something incredibly special. I don't even want to touch on my feelings when it comes to the matter. If I think too much into it I'll spiral down a deep dark hole I won't be able to climb out of.

God, I'm a fucking mess when it comes to him. I can barely understand my own thoughts half the time. I'm pathetic.

I can't believe I said all I did to him this morning and I'm even more surprised by his reaction. I thought a guy like him would be eager to cut ties and be free to fuck anyone he wants.

This *thing* between us is confusing to me. I know I don't have feelings for him *that* way, but I *do* like him and that's where the complication lies.

I've always avoided attachments. Mia is the only person I've talked to and seen on a regular basis the last few years.

I don't talk to my mother—*at all.* I have no desire to hear from her, talk to her, or even look at her. Not after the hell I had to go through growing up, because even after my father beat her to within an inch of her life, she still insisted on dating the worst of the worst, the slimiest guys she could find. The final straw for me was when her last boyfriend I know about, *Trevor,* tried to touch me. I was weeks away from graduating and stayed with Mia after that. Thank God her parents are as cool as they are and let me stay as long as I needed to. I'd been working since I was fifteen, and I stayed with them through that summer saving every penny so I could afford my own place before classes started at the local University where I received a full ride scholarship. Without that, I couldn't have gone to school. I've always wanted nothing more than to get my degree, get a good paying job, and *never* live a life like my mother.

It's why I've stuck so firmly by my rule of one-night stands only. I refuse to let a man degrade me and beat me like I'm nothing, like I'm beneath him because I'm a woman.

Then Rush came along and we agreed we didn't want a relationship, but we both liked sex and it would be convenient for the both of us if we fucked each other instead of having to seek someone new out anytime we wanted a roll in the sack.

Nothing's been wrong with our arrangement all this time, except for us both starting to *like* each other.

I don't do boyfriends, and I don't do friends—especially not guy friends.

So, this is weird for me.

I tried to get him to end the agreement, but we're at an impasse because frankly I don't want to end it either. I was only hoping he'd do it because it felt like the necessary thing to do.

I leave my class heading to the cafeteria to grab a snack. It's not even lunchtime and I had a hearty breakfast with Rush of biscuits and sausage gravy but I'm already ravenous.

I enter the cafeteria and grab a bottle of Coke and a cereal bar. I swipe my student ID card and find a table to sit at.

I open my bottle of Coke and take a greedy sip, twisting the cap between my fingers.

If Mia wasn't in class I'd ask her to meet me, but it seems like this semester we're on totally different schedules. She's studying music, wanting to get into producing and other things that are all gibberish to me. I chose nursing as my area of study. It wasn't an easy choice for me to make and one I question often, but in the end, I decided I wanted to help people. I didn't want my life to be completely useless. If I can be a part of saving someone's life then it'll all be worth it. But now that we're getting into the nitty gritty of everything I'm only on campus once a week and spend the rest of my time at the local hospital shadowing different doctors.

Who knows if I'll actually do anything good with it, but I at least have to try.

I open my cereal bar as some dude sits next to me with ... I smell the air, my stomach rolls.

No. Not here. Not now.

The smell of the chili he's about to eat hits me like an eighteen-wheeler plowing straight into my body—and my body is not at all pleased about it.

I abandon my cereal bar and Coke, running for the nearest bathroom.

I smash into the swinging door and into the closest empty stall. I drop to my knees as the entire contents of my stomach sprays into the toilet. I feel tears burn my eyes as my body tries to get every last bit out of my system.

When I'm sure I'm done throwing up I stand, not daring to sit on the unsanitary floor, and lean my back against the wall of the stall, tilting my head up.

I take a moment to think, to process, and then I text Mia.

I pace the length of my apartment, which isn't much so it's a miracle I haven't worn a hole straight through the floor.

I came home after the bathroom incident; my nerves were shot and I knew I couldn't stomach sitting through class the rest of the day.

Asking Mia to ditch her classes for me wasn't easy, but much needed, because I can't do this alone.

A light knock raps against the door and I rush to open it, yanking her inside.

"Did anyone we know see you?"

"No," she insists, holding the plastic drugstore bag out to me, "but why am I buying this, Kira?" She stares me down, daring me to deny it.

My bottom lip quivers and tears sting my eyes. Fear clings to me like a bucket of slime has been poured over my head. "Because I think I'm pregnant."

We stare at each other, neither of us saying a word. Tears form in her eyes, mirroring the ones in mine.

"Kira," she whispers my name.

"I know, I know," I cry, exasperated. "I have to be wrong. I mean, I'm on birth control. I *never* miss a dose. You know how anal retentive I am with it and Rush *always* wears a condom. I mean, surely between both those preventatives I *can't* be pregnant."

I know from my studies, I could be. Nothing is fool proof and with my track record of luck, I *would* be the person to end up knocked up using two preventive measures.

Mia inhales a shaky breath. Somehow it makes me feel better to know she's as nervous as I am.

"It's got to be negative," she says, but I can see the doubt in her eyes too.

I rip the plastic bag off the ridiculous pink cardboard box.

"Here goes nothing," I say, and head to the bathroom.

I leave the door open and Mia leans in the doorway. We're best friends. We've seen it all. What difference does it make if I'm peeing on a stick that might change the course of my life forever?

I mean, even if I am pregnant, I have options.

I don't have to keep the baby. I could get an abortion. Or put it up for adoption.

I don't have to become a mother if I don't want to, if I'm not ready, which I'm definitely not.

Somehow I manage to pee on the stupid stick. My hands shake the entire time and I'm not sure I've done it right, but it doesn't seem like it's that difficult to screw up.

Placing it on the counter I wash my hands and cross my arms over my chest.

"How long?" I ask Mia and she picks up the box.

"It says five minutes."

"Ugh," I groan, "this is going to be the longest five minutes of my life."

"Come on." She grabs my arm, tugging me out of the bathroom. "Standing in here is doing you no good."

"What else am I going to do?" I shriek, diving for the couch and landing on my stomach. I grab one of the throw pillows and cradle it under me.

She looks at me worriedly and perches on the coffee table in front of me.

"Kira," she says softly like she's afraid I'm a bomb she might detonate if she makes too much noise or moves the wrong way.

"What?" I reply bleakly.

I can see my entire future, everything I've worked for and strived for going up in flames. If I'm pregnant I don't see how I'll ever be able to salvage anything.

"It's going to be okay. No matter what it says, it'll be okay."

Tears sting my eyes. "You can't know that."

"No, I don't—but I have faith."

I roll my eyes. "I'm glad one of us does, but realistically I know there's no way this can work out well for me. It's just not possible," I mutter.

She reaches for my hand, pulling it away from the pillow. "I know you think you're alone, but you're not. If you're having a baby, I'll help you, and you know my parents will—God, my mom would spoil a baby silly—it'll be okay."

"Even if I am pregnant..." I pause, not sure I want to say my thoughts out loud, fearing her judgment. "I don't *have* to have it."

"Kira," she says my name slightly in shock, but surprisingly with no judgment. Shaking her head she says, "If it comes to that I'll support whatever you choose. But it could be negative."

I want to believe that, I really do, but I don't.

I've been feeling tired and draggy, I was so sick to my stomach with my cold and I've never thrown up from a common cold before, and if I go back and think I can't remember the last time my period decided to pay me a visit. I've been so busy with school and work I haven't had time to spare a thought for it. Now, I feel pathetic for not realizing sooner.

Mia looks at her phone screen, then me. "You can go look now if you want."

I don't want to. I want to avoid this reality for as long as I possibly can. I want to live in this blissful little bubble of not officially knowing where I can delude myself into believing it's not true.

As easy as it would be to ignore this, I can't. I have to be a big girl and face my reality.

I ease off the couch and stand. For a moment I don't move. I give myself one minute longer to live without knowing before I face my fate.

I walk back to the bathroom and Mia follows. She doesn't say a word but her presence is calming. I'm damn lucky to have a best friend like her. I step in front of the counter and let my eyes drop to the test.

Two pink lines stare treacherously back at me.

A sob bubbles out of my throat, and I turn, sinking to my butt with my back against the standard oak front bathroom cabinet.

Mia sits down beside me, wrapping her arms around me.

She holds me close and lets me cry into her shoulder, not saying a word, just being there.

TEN

Rush

The guys and I clink our bottles together, out to celebrate our first radio single together with Hayes and the rest of his band. It still feels like a fucking dream that Joshua Hayes, the guitarist for Willow Creek, is working with us. His band has reached international success few bands have ever seen. To have him on board with us, producing, mentoring ... fuck, it's an experience people would kill for.

"This is the first step on a journey you four will never forget," Hayes begins his speech. "Cherish every moment, each small step and each big one. It's not something many get to experience, but lots dream of."

I take a sip of my beer, feeling a bit choked up. There's something surreal about today, about this whole experience. I find myself questioning whether or not I need to pinch myself to see if this is real.

Two waiters appear, passing out our plates of food. My stomach rumbles. In my excitement I haven't been able to eat since breakfast and it's after six now. I'm so hyped up I'm not sure I'll be able to go to sleep tonight. There's a restless energy stirring inside me and normally the only thing that can settle it is booze and sex.

But I already sent Kira a text, asking if I could come over after dinner, and she said she wasn't feeling well again and had homework to do. A part of me wants to show up, but her place is her space and I don't want to make her feel uncomfortable like she's not allowed to be alone or something.

As per our deal, I can't sink myself into any other woman. Even if the hot bartender is eye-fucking me. Normally, I'd be all over her in a heartbeat, and even with the deal I've struck with Kira most guys would probably say screw it and break it. But I can't bring myself to do it. My word is my honor, and I swore to her as long as we're fucking, I won't sleep with anyone else and she agreed to those terms as well.

"Have you seen if they can play at Clarke County Fair?" Maddox asks Hayes.

I pick up a fry, dipping it in ketchup before popping it in my mouth.

Hayes nods. "I'm still working out the details."

"What's that?" Fox asks.

"Local fair not far from here, they always have live music. We've performed there many times," Hayes says, swishing his fingers through the air before they close around his bottle of beer. "It usually draws in a decent crowd. I know you all have performed at festivals, which are some pretty big venues at times, and this would be nothing of that magnitude but I think right now stuff like this projects the kind of image we want."

"You mean one of completely fucking boring?" I interject jokingly.

Hayes shakes his head, fighting a smile. "Not completely, but I don't need you dancing on bars with half-naked chicks either."

I tip my bottle in his direction. After all, there's not much I can say since I did do that.

When I'm wasted I do stupid shit. I can't help it.

"With you putting all this time into them, when are we going to record our new album?" Mathias asks in a low voice. His face is almost always pulled into a sneer.

The guy is scary and intimidating—nothing at all like his carefree, jokester of a twin Maddox.

Maddox pushes his brother's shoulder. "Shut up, man. We've got time. It's only been a year since our last album. We've gotta make the people wait or they'll get bored with us."

Mathias huffs out a breath.

Hayes shakes his head and Ezra mutters, "Ignore Mathias. He's just a salty bastard."

"Did you just use the word *salty* to describe me?" Mathias asks, and if I didn't know better, I would swear he's trying not to laugh.

Ezra shrugs. "Everly taught it to me. It means when you're upset over something stupid—which in your case is basically everything. Why Remy puts up with your shit is beyond me." Ezra cracks a joking smile.

Mathias hides his answering smile by lifting his glass of whiskey to his lips. "Remy loves me. It's more than I can say for you assholes."

I can't help but smile at the way they interact together, because it's the same as my friends and me. I can only hope that if we reach the same kind of success they have, that we manage to remain as close.

My friends are like family. They've been there for me through everything and vice versa. Losing my parents ... I barely endured it with their help, fuck I'm *still* coping with it, but if I hadn't had them ... it terrifies me to think of what kind of path I might have gone down.

Hayes clears his throat, looking at the four of us where we sit at the end of the table. "Depending on the reception Midnight Eyes gets I think we should shoot a music video in a couple of months. Today, all indicators are good, but it's only the first day and I want to gauge the lasting power of the song before we splurge on a video. It might be something better saved for down the road."

"Whatever you think is best," Cannon says.

"You're the boss," Hollis pipes in, and Hayes gives a small laugh.

Hollis only considers Hayes the boss when the rules and ideas are easy to follow—but Hayes saying his daughter was off limits? Of course, Hollis was never going to listen to that. You can't dangle a tasty morsel like her in front of Hollis and not expect him to act. I don't think he ever intended to fall in love with her, but somehow he did, and I think maybe even before something happened between them he realized his feelings were far more serious than he ever anticipated.

The rest of the dinner is spent chatting and eating. It's cool to get to hang out with Willow Creek—to hear their tales and get advice. Afterwards we part ways and I head back to the hotel with Fox and Cannon—Hollis, strolling in the opposite direction to Mia's apartment.

"Not seeing Kira tonight?" Cannon asks with a raised brow as we step into the elevator.

"Nope." I shake my head, which is a bad idea after too many drinks. Maybe one day I'll learn to *stop* instead of keep going. I always drank too much in high school at parties, as long as I didn't have any basketball games, and when my parents died I turned to alcohol even more. Since that first night when we arrived in D.C. I haven't gotten *that* wasted again, but it's only because I've been spending so much time with Kira engaging in my other vice.

"Why?" he asks. I'm sure he knows how much I'd rather be fucking than here.

We step off the elevator and Fox swipes us into the suite. My thoughts make me laugh, along with the alcohol in my system.

Swiper no swiping. A classic when it comes to Fox.

"She said she didn't feel good and has homework," I explain, following behind Fox.

Cannon lets the door swing closed behind us and latches the chain at the top of the door.

"You mean, you respected her wishes? I'm shocked."

"Hey, man, if you knew what we did last night you'd get it."

My thoughts drift back to fucking her in the club against the wall, where anyone could see us if they came along.

"I don't need to hear about your sexcapades," Cannon groans, turning away from me.

"Who said I was going to give you details?" I crack a grin. "I'm going to shower."

"Good, you smell like a brewery," he quips, opening the refrigerator and picking up a bottle of water.

"We can't all be one and done like you." I give him the finger and close the door behind me as I enter my room.

I head into the bathroom and shower. I stand beneath the hot spray of water longer than I normally do. My muscles are tight from sitting behind my drum kit for hours today. Don't get me wrong, I wouldn't have it any other way, but it does take a toll on my body.

Washing my hair and body I watch the white suds swirl down the drain and disappear. My blond hair falls forward, dripping wet and I shove it back with my fingers. I need a trim, but I haven't bothered, now it's becoming a nuisance.

I get out, drying my body with one of the hotel's fluffy white towels. I've become spoiled to having such luxury handed to me by staying here—even our clothes get washed for us. Back in L.A. my apartment was barely the size of the bedroom space I have in the suite, and I definitely had to do my own fucking laundry. Not that I mind taking care of shit like that, but does *anyone* actually enjoy doing laundry?

I pull on a pair of sweatpants and grab my phone from the floor where it fell out of the pocket of my jeans.

Me: How are you feeling? Do you need me to bring you anything? I'm a liiiiittle drunk ... okay, pretty drunk, but I'm sure I could get something delivered if you need it.

I settle on the bed, turning the TV on, and crossing my legs. A few minutes pass and I check my phone. It shows she's read my message, but no response and no little bubbles indicate she's typing back a response.

I grind my teeth together in worry, wondering if she's feeling so rough she can't respond.

If I was in better shape I would just go over there—but I can't drive like this, and while her place isn't far, it is far enough I need to drive so I don't have to walk in the freezing cold. Plus, as much as I had to drink, I'm not sure I could walk straight and the last thing I need is to get cited for public intoxication.

I try my best to focus on the show, but it barely holds my attention. I flip through the channels, not finding much on.

Finally, when thirty minutes have passed I can't take it any longer.

Me: I'm worried about you. Are you okay?

This time she responds immediately.

Kira: I'm fine.

Me: You're fine? That's all I get.

Kira: I finished my homework and I'm laying on the couch now. Does that suffice?

Even though it's a text message I can sense her sass in every word.

Me: I worry about you.

Kira: I'm not your concern.

Her tone is curt and I feel my throat closing up, remembering our conversation from this morning. Fuck, it feels like days ago, not hours.

I set my phone down, but my eyes keep straying to it every few seconds as I resist the urge to say more to her.

Finally, I turn it completely off so I can't be tempted, especially in my drunken state.

I can feel her slipping from my grasp, and for once I'm at a loss as to what I've done.

ELEVEN

Kira

I enter my apartment after a long day at the hospital shadowing Dr. Hawkins who works with cancer patients. I'm exhausted, my feet aching, but my mental state is in the worst shape of all.

I feel so lost and confused. A part of me is trying to pretend this isn't happening, that it's not real, but the fact of the matter is I'm pregnant and Rush is the father.

Locking the door behind me, I drop my keys on the counter and kick off my shoes. A shower is calling my name, and after that I'm piling into bed, pulling the covers over my head, and possibly having a good cry. I hate crying, it feels weak, but right now I'm afraid I might drown in my emotions if I don't.

I head down the hall into my bedroom and then the bathroom. I turn the shower on before stripping out of my clothes and piling them into the overflowing laundry basket. Glaring at the basket I know I have to make a trip down the street to the Laundromat tomorrow. There's no way I can put off not going any longer.

Taking a long shower, I let the hot water uncoil my stiff muscles. Stress has made my whole body curl into itself and now I'm paying for it with an aching back and shoulders.

With a loud squeak of the knob I turn the shower off and step out, drying my body with one of my cheap purple towels I got on clearance at Target, before wrapping it around me.

I brush my wet hair and sweep it up into a messy bun.

Padding into my room I let my towel drop and yank on a pair of sweater knit leggings and a soft t-shirt, piling a sweatshirt on over that. I add my towel to the precarious stack of dirty things and climb in bed, turning my TV on.

It's not even late, barely after five, but I feel like I could go to sleep and not wake up for a few years. Whenever I'm stressed, I tend to become ridiculously sleepy. It's my coping mechanism. If I'm asleep I'm blissfully unaware of how hellish my life is.

When I'm awake there's no escaping the reality.

I curl my arms around my pillow, cradling it against me.

I feel pathetic.

Pathetic and lost.

I've always been the take-charge person. I never doubted what to do in any situation and now here I am doubting *everything*.

I took strict precautions to prevent this kind of thing. Never missing a dose of birth control and making sure any man I slept with was wrapped up tight. I knew I didn't want a baby now, maybe not ever, so I thought I was being smart and safe—doing what needed to be done to prevent the risk, but leave it to me to be in the teeny-tiny category who covers all their bases and still ends up knocked up.

It isn't fair. I'm not ready to take care of a child, and I don't see how I could be a good mother, and the last thing I'd ever want to be is like *mine*. She gave me a clear outline of how not to treat your children. My father didn't help matters either. But at least he's in jail states away. The only decent thing my mother ever did for the both of us was move to this area after he was sentenced.

A knock on my door startles me out of my thoughts. Mia texted me earlier asking if I wanted her to come over or bring anything, I said no, but it's just like her to show up anyway. She's the kind of friend who always wants to make things better, even when she can't.

I force myself out of bed as another knock sounds against the door.

When I reach the door, I swing it open and my breath leaves me, because it isn't Mia standing on the other side.

"Rush," I breathe, rendered practically speechless. "What are you doing here?"

He shrugs nonchalantly, but I can tell from that one simple movement he's unsure of himself. "You were kind of ... short with me last night. Did I do something?"

Yeah, your fucking sperm fertilized my stupid, treacherous, no good egg.

"I just didn't feel good," I say by way of explanation. It's not a complete lie. I was so upset last night I *did* feel sick.

"Can I come in?" he asks, flicking his fingers toward the inside of my apartment. "I would've let myself in with my key, but that seemed rude."

I should ask for his key back right this second, but I know I can't raise his suspicions of something being wrong. Not until I figure out what I'm doing. This is my body, my future on the line. I know if I keep this baby I'm doing it on my own while he gallivants across the country with his band. It's what'll happen. I know it.

"I don't think that's a good idea," I hedge, blocking his way inside with my body and inching the door closer.

"Why not?" He raises one blond brow. The silver ring piercing in his right ear glimmers in the outdoor light beside the door.

"I'm tired," I explain, trying to sound light. "I just got in from class and I want to crash."

His shoulders drop ever so slightly. Someone else might not even notice it.

"Well, here," he holds out a bag to me, "I figured if you weren't feeling well, you'd forget to eat dinner. It's soup and a sandwich from Panera."

My throat closes up as I take the bag from him. "Thanks," I say softly.

He nods, tucking his hands into the pockets of his jeans, drawing his shoulders up close to his ears. "I'll go, then."

He starts down the stairs and I watch as he gets in his truck and pulls away before I close and lock the door. Setting the bag down on the counter I unpack the contents.

That's when I realize he got food for himself too, hoping we could eat together, and when I turned him away he said nothing more. Just gave me the food and left.

My heart seizes and I'm even more confused than I was before.

TWELVE

Rush

It's been days since I've seen Kira. Days since I dropped off that food for her, hoping she'd invite me in and I could join her. I was worried about her, still am, but despite all the texts I've sent her in the last five days she still hasn't answered a single one and I'm baffled as to what the fuck I did.

Did I get too close? Too attached? Is she scared I have feelings for her? I mean, I like her company, and I like her, but I don't love her. If that's what she's afraid of there's no need for it. But I'm the kind of guy who doesn't have many friends, because I'm picky, and when I do pick friends, I care about them and want to take care of them when they need someone and in Kira's case the only person she has is Mia. Is it wrong of me to want to help her? To be there for her?

I bang my drumsticks against my kit, trying to beat out my confusion and anger. I asked Mia for her keys so I could come back this evening to the studio. I thought an hour would suffice and I'd feel better, but I've been here for three hours and the alcohol I swiped from the hotel suite are almost gone and I'm nowhere near less confused than when I started.

I'm not even playing a song, instead banging out my own beat that sounds nice to my ears. Thank God these rooms are soundproof, or the surrounding buildings would be issuing a complaint at this late hour.

A bandana is rolled up, keeping my hair from flopping in my face, and it's wet with sweat now.

I stop drumming long enough to grab another mini bottle. I raided the hotel room's alcohol supply before leaving. I knew I'd need something to take the edge off, and the nearest liquor store was five miles away.

I know this is the wrong method of dealing with things, but it's the only thing I know how to do. Alcohol numbs my pain in a way nothing else can, and sex distracts me. But since Kira is the reason I'm confused out of my mind, that means sex is off the table. So liquor it is.

I giggle to myself and lift the tiny Jack Daniel's bottle in a toast, like someone else is there.

I drum out a beat with one hand while I tilt my head back, slurping down the liquid. It burns, but I don't care, it's part of the appeal after all. Maybe it can burn away my sins while it's at it.

The door to the booth opens and Cannon leans against the doorway.

"Caaannnnnooon," I drawl out his name. "Ahoy, my man. Come to hang out?"

"I've come to take your ass back to the hotel to sober up."

"Ach, I don't need to sober up. I'm dandy. Having a spanking good time."

He raises a brow.

"Ye can grab a drink. There's one left. Malibu, gross."

"Rush?" he asks hesitantly. "How drunk are you?"

I push air out through my lips. "Drunk? Not at all."

"Is that so?"

"Aye."

"Are you a fucking pirate?"

"Arrr, me hearty."

"Fuck."

"Yo ho, yo ho, a pirate's life for me," I sing, tossing my now empty plastic bottle on the floor. I start drumming again, bobbing my head to the beat. My stomach rolls, but I don't care. If I vomit all over my drum set it won't be the first time.

Cannon starts picking up the trash.

"Stop drumming, Rush. I'm taking you to the hotel."

"No, ye can't make me."

"Is that so, Captain Jack Sparrow?"

"Aye."

"Why do I always have to clean up everyone's mess," he grumbles to himself.

"No one asks you to."

When he has everything thrown away, he pulls out the trash bag and ties it off, swinging it over his shoulder so no evidence of my misadventure is left behind.

"We're going," he says sternly, grabbing my arm.

I drop my sticks and make like I'm going along with him, then I run for it, tossing the keys in my pocket behind so good, responsible Cannon will stop and lock up.

I push the door open into the cool night air. It stings the bare skin of my arms since I don't have a coat or anything.

"Rush!"

When I hear Cannon's voice, I run faster down the street away from the hotel.

His footsteps thump behind me and I laugh loudly at the

fact I'm running down the street away from my friend, who's carrying a bag of trash.

"Rush! Dammit!"

I trip over a bench and go sprawling on the ground.

"Aye, mate, when did that get put there?" I ask, rolling over and looking up at him.

"It's always been there. You're just a fucking idiot." He grabs my hand and hauls me up. He tosses my left arm around his shoulders so he can steady me.

"I don't feel so good."

"I'm not surprised."

"You don't understand—"

I throw up all over the bottom of his jeans and his shoes.

"I should throw you in the fucking sewer and let you rot. You have a fucking problem, Rush." He bites out the words in disgust and anger. Sober, I'd be bothered by his tone, but I'm too drunk to care.

"No, I don't," I say as he guides me down the street, back toward the hotel.

I don't have the energy to try to get away from him anymore.

He stops walking and glares at me.

"You're an alcoholic, Rush."

"No, I'm not," I defend, blatantly offended by his accusation.

I'm not. I can't be. Yeah, I like to drink. A lot. And often. But that doesn't mean I'm an alcoholic. I can handle my liquor.

"Clearly, you can't."

Did I say that part out loud?

"Yes, you did. Which further proves my point. You need help, man."

"No, what I need is people to stop pissing me off and fucking confusing me. It makes my brain hurt. Then I drink to feel better."

"Drinking is a weak ass, pathetic excuse and you know it."

I sniffle.

"I watched you go on a downward spiral when you lost your parents."

"Don't talk about them!" I shout with all the force I have in my body.

He barrels on anyway. "You drank yourself into oblivion, you partied hard, and for all I know you did drugs too."

I stop him. "No, I never ... I wouldn't. I didn't."

He stares at me for a moment and must see the sincerity in my eyes, because he nods.

"I don't know what's going on, but this has to stop. You can't turn to alcohol any time things get a little tough for you."

"God, can you shut up?" I groan, my head pounding. I'd been focused on playing the drums and didn't realize I was giving myself a migraine—not to mention the shit ton of booze cruising through my system.

"No," he thunders, his voice firm as he drags me into the hotel and over to wait for an elevator. He props me against the wall and stares me down. "You've got to get your life together, man. Your parents wouldn't want this for you."

I glower at him, pointing a finger in warning. *"Do not* bring my parents into this. No one knows what they'd want since they're *dead.*"

He pushes my shoulders roughly and my head knocks into the back of the wall.

"I won't watch my *best friend* throw his life away." If I wasn't so wasted I would swear there are tears in his eyes. He grabs my shirt between both his hands and holds me upright. "You're so fucking selfish you never stop to think about what it would do to *me,* to all of us, your *friends,* if you were gone, and that's exactly what'll happen if you continue down this path."

The elevator opens and he drags me inside.

"I have nothing worthwhile to give this world," I sigh, tilting my head up toward the mirrored ceiling—bad idea as my stomach rolls.

"Is that what you really think?" he asks, his mouth parted in horror.

A second passes, two, three.

"It's what I know."

THIRTEEN

Kira

"How are you feeling?" Mia asks me, as we take our break at The Sub Club and sit down to eat our dinner.

I pick at the sub I made to eat. I'm not hungry, but I know I *need* to eat. I haven't touched anything resembling food all day and I can't keep going if I don't give my body some sort of fuel.

"Fine," I answer. The word comes out as a breathy sigh.

She tilts her head. "How are you really feeling, Kira? How are you *doing*? You haven't said anything about the B.A.B.Y," she spells out the word, "since you took the test."

I shrug casually, flicking a piece of lettuce off the table and onto the floor. "There's nothing to talk about. I'm not having it," I say simply, like it's no big deal even though this is a huge deal.

I'm not even one-hundred percent decided yet, but I need to say the words out loud to see how they feel, to gauge how I react.

It doesn't feel good saying it. I feel dirty and like I'll never be clean.

"Are you sure that's what you want?" she asks. "I know it would be difficult, but … that's your baby, Kira."

"Mia," I say sharply. "I *can't* do this. I can't be a parent."

"Can't or won't?" she challenges.

I sigh in defeat. I don't have an answer for her.

Continuing on, undeterred by my silence she says, "I know for a fact you haven't told Rush, because Hollis would've said something if Rush knew."

"You told Hollis!" I shriek, getting a few head turns from nearby.

"Of course not," she scoffs, offended. "I'm not going to blab your secrets to my boyfriend, but Rush is his best friend, and if you had told him you're pregnant I'm sure he would've shared with the guys."

"No, I haven't told him," I admit reluctantly.

"Don't you think he deserves to know before you do something drastic? He should at least know, be allowed to be a part of the conversation. He might be loud, and obnoxious, and cocky as hell but he's still a decent guy … well …" She gives a sheepish look.

"What?" I prompt. "What'd he do?"

"He got shit-faced drunk the other night, because apparently you're ignoring him. Cannon had to drag him back to the hotel."

"Oh, God," I groan, burying my face in my hands. "See, this is another reason why I can't tell him. If he's so immature he goes and gets plastered because I'm not talking to him, what will he do when he finds out I'm growing his spawn?"

"Rush has a lot of growing up to do," she agrees. "But so do you."

I feel like she's slapped me. "What is that supposed to mean?"

She finishes her bite of sandwich and swallows. "I just mean it's clear you haven't dealt with things when it comes to your mom."

"You're bringing my mother into this?" I hiss, picking apart my sub. I need to eat, but thanks to this line of conversation there's not a chance in hell I will.

She tucks a piece of her pretty red hair behind her ear. I used to envy her for her gorgeous natural red locks. I've since learned to appreciate my dark hair and not nitpick every aspect of myself.

"I'm not saying you need to go speak to her if you don't want to, but maybe see a therapist or something."

"I *don't* need a shrink." I wave a piece of torn up bread at her.

"Don't take it so offensively," she snaps, straightening her shoulders. "It might help you."

My face screws up in irritation.

She reaches across the table and places her hand over mine, her eyes soft. "Kira, all I'm saying is *think* before you do something drastic. Make sure this is really what you want."

"To kill my baby you mean?" Saying it that way I feel like a monster to even be thinking it. It's a choice, a personal one each woman has to make depending on her situation, one I'm still not certain I'm ready to decide on.

"That's not what I was saying," she defends with a shake of her head. "I'll support you no matter what you decide. I would never judge you for *anything*, and you should know that by now. I only want you to understand, once you go down that route, go through with it, there is no changing your mind. It's done."

I press my lips together, my throat closing up. "I'm so confused," I voice aloud. "Lost ... nothing makes sense right now."

She squeezes my hand, having never let it go. "Then wait until it does make sense."

I've been avoiding Rush for two weeks straight. His texts finally stopped after the first week and he hasn't shown up at my place or come into The Sub Club.

I should feel good about this—this is what I wanted after all, to not have to see him. Having to face him, and *know* I need to tell him is too much. He doesn't need to know, not until I've made up my mind, because at the end of the day I'm the woman and this changes my life far more than his.

Pulling on my scrubs I get ready to head to the hospital. Queasiness hit me hard this morning so I'm not looking forward to my day at all, but I have to grit my teeth and get through it.

I grab my bag and swipe my keys off the counter, locking up as I head out.

My beat-up ancient Honda Civic sits by the curb. It's banged up, rusted, with peeling paint but it still gets me from point A to point B without sounding like it's going to die so in my book it counts as pretty reliable.

I climb in and toss my bag over onto the passenger seat.

Gripping the steering wheel in my hands I sit there for a moment, longer, unable to move. I feel frozen in time, suspended, and for just a second I allow myself to believe everything will work out, that it'll be okay.

But in my life only one thing has always remained true—it's never okay.

Swallowing past the lump in my throat I put the car in drive and pull away.

Glancing in my rearview mirror I spot a red truck. My heart skips a beat in my chest, thinking it's Rush, but a second later I realize the truck is too small to be his.

I feel stupid and ridiculous for my reaction, for the flood of emotions that hit me when I thought it was him. I'm the one avoiding him, but I can't help but miss him, and I wish I could hate him for that—hate him for making me like him and care about him.

I'm pathetic.

I force all thoughts of Rush from my mind—which is easier said than done.

Arriving at the hospital I park in the garage and walk through the new part of the hospital over to the older main part. It's a complicated labyrinth I once thought I would never master, but somehow I have.

I'm still shadowing Dr. Hawkins along with a few of my classmates, so I spend my morning with her as she makes her rounds.

Around noon we're dismissed for lunch and head to the cafeteria in the hospital to eat. I packed my lunch so I find a table and sit down. Sometimes I sit with my classmates. I'm not friends with any of them, but we do talk and chat. You kind of have to in order to make the time go by faster.

I finish my basic turkey sandwich and small bag of chips. Wadding up my trash I throw it away. I have time to kill before we have to join back up with Dr. Hawkins and since I don't feel like sitting by myself or joining my classmates, I start walking through the hospital.

There's no destination in mind, but I suppose I shouldn't be surprised when I end up on the maternity ward.

I find myself standing in front of the glass separating people from the newborns.

I watch the babies, some sleeping, others screaming, some just wiggling. All so tiny and innocent, helpless in this big bad world.

I press a hand to my stomach, to the small life growing there, already relying on me to take care of it. Tears come to my eyes. How can I possibly think of getting rid of my child? Some people have no choice, but I do, and I've always been able to do anything I've set my mind to—why can't that apply to being a mother?

A nurse walks up to me with a kind smile. "Student?" she asks.

I nod. "Yeah."

"Thinking about working in the maternity ward?" she questions. She's probably in her forties with dark hair pulled back in a ponytail and kind brown eyes.

"I don't know," I answer honestly.

She looks down then, noting my hand against my stomach. "Ah, I see. How far along are you?"

"I don't know yet?" I admit. "I'm not sure."

"Let me guess," she smiles, "you're terrified?"

"You have no idea," I breathe a sigh.

She pats my shoulder. "I think every woman, whether a pregnancy is planned or unplanned, is terrified."

"I don't want to be a shitty mom. Not like mine," I admit, my voice barely above a whisper.

"We all have a choice to be who we want to be—no one makes us into what we are, only we do. Some people make the wrong choices." She shrugs, gazing through the glass at the babies. "They have to live with the consequences of those mistakes—but not their children. You have the choice to rise above? So what will you do?"

"Be better," I answer. "For my child. For *me*."

She smiles. "Then you have your answer."

"What answer?"

"You already know," she replies and walks away.

She's right, I do know.

I have the power to be who I want to be in this world.

I've always chosen to be a fighter, to climb high above my

childhood and not let it shackle me to the ground, and now I choose to still do those things, but I'm adding another to the list.

I will fight.

I will climb.

I will be a mother to this child, the best one I know I can be.

FOURTEEN

Rush

"Pizza's here!" Fox announces and I look up from the couch as he carries in several large boxes. My stomach rumbles to life.

The last thing I want to do is be stuck here in the suite with Fox and Cannon, but Kira's still ignoring me, and there's nothing to do in this God forsaken town. I could go to D.C. and find plenty of entertainment, or hell I've heard West Virginia is full of strip clubs, but Cannon is watching me like a hawk. There's no way I'm making it out of here without him knowing, and I've given him plenty of reason to worry thanks to my drunken binge.

It was stupid to let myself get that wasted, I know, but I needed it. Sometimes the numbness is the only thing that comforts me and I wish he could understand. It doesn't mean I'm an alcoholic. I don't *have* to drink—but I want to.

Fox spreads the pizza boxes out on the coffee table.

"I'll grab drinks," I say, and hop up.

Cannon glowers at me where he lounges in one of the big oversized chairs.

"What?" I blink innocently. "I'm allowed to drink soda, right, Dad?"

He leans forward. "Is it so bad that I worry about you? Huh? Is it wrong I hate the idea of my friend continuing down a certain path? You've been toeing the line for years, and then when we got here, I thought you were doing better, only having a drink a couple times a week. I won't watch you spiral out of control again. I mean it."

"Don't worry, I'm not going to do anything that'll piss off Hayes and jeopardize our career."

He stands. "Dammit, Rush," he snaps, the veins in his neck straining. His hands flex at his sides like he's fighting not to punch me. "I'm worried about *you*, not our career, and it pisses me off you'd assume otherwise."

"I had a moment of weakness, is all," I explain, trying to sound rational. "It was foolish and it won't happen again."

He stares me down, those green eyes of his seeing far more than most people ever do.

"I wish I believed you," he says.

Between us Fox's head bobbles back and forth like he's watching a tennis match. His eyes settle on me, waiting to see if I'll say or do anything.

Looking away, my jaw clenched, I whisper, "I wish I believed me, too."

STOMACH STUFFED WITH PIZZA, I LAY ON MY BACK STRETCHED OUT on my bed, with my arms crossed behind my head. I stare up at the ceiling, confused and lost.

Everything used to make sense, then my parents died and nothing did anymore. I thought … I thought coming here I was doing better, I was happier and focused on music, and Kira was a welcome distraction … but now it all seems like it's just been a Band-Aid—an ill-placed one and it's falling off now.

The door to my room cracks open and I raise my head slightly.

"What do you want?" I ask, my tone sharper than I intend.

Cannon walks into my room and stands over me, his arms crossed over his chest.

"I feel like I should apologize for being a hard ass, but I'm not going to."

I snort, looking up at the ceiling and away from him.

"Then why are you here?"

He sighs and out of my peripheral vision I can see him run his fingers through his normally perfectly coifed hair before rubbing his stubble-free chin.

"I worry about you. I was there, all of us were, when you lost your parents. Watching you go through that … it fucking sucked, man. But it's been *eight years* and you still haven't dealt with it—don't you think it's about time you did?"

"There's nothing to deal with."

He shakes his head and I turn my head to him.

"If we were still back in L.A. you'd be at a club every night, drinking yourself into oblivion, and doing God knows what else. It's not *healthy*, Rush. You had to bury your parents, it sucked, I get it."

"No, you don't," I growl.

"I do!" He shouts. "Because there are so many times when I ask myself how long it'll be before we have to bury *you*."

"That's not fair," I snarl, my upper lip curling like I taste something unpleasant.

"Isn't it? The accident was just that, an accident—you're *choosing* this because you won't deal with your demons, blame Kira for not speaking to you all you want, but that's not the reason you're like this. It never was."

I sit up straight, my face contorted in anger. "It wasn't an *accident*. That asshole was texting instead of driving his fucking car like he was supposed to. My parents *died* and he lived, all over a fucking text message. How fucked up is that?" I throw my arms wide. "And here I am, left behind."

"Exactly." He pokes my chest. "You still have a chance to live."

"That's what I'm doing. *You* just don't approve of how I do it."

He shakes his head and starts to walk away. He pauses, looking back over his shoulder. "Do whatever you want, Rush. I'm done trying."

He leaves, slamming the door closed behind him.

Finality rings in the air, long after the echo of the door closing fades away.

FIFTEEN

Kira

"I'd rather be home in my pajamas right now," I grumble, walking with my arm looped through Mia's. She insisted on getting me out today.

She laughs, tossing her head back. "Look who's turning into me?"

I roll my eyes. "I'm pregnant and I'm pretty sure drinking and clubbing is frowned upon in this state." I stop walking and Mia halts with me. My eyes widen in horror. "I was having drinks and I had to be pregnant already. What if I've totally fucked up the baby by drinking?"

"Don't be dramatic, Kira. I'm sure plenty of women drink before they know they're pregnant. When do you see your doctor?"

"This Wednesday," I say, beginning to walk again. It's Sunday now, so only a few days to go. I'm dreading it, because while I *know* I'm pregnant I still wish there's a chance the doctor will tell me I'm not.

"Do you want me to go with you?" she asks lightly.

"It's at two, can you?" I reply in relief. It'll be nice to have her with me.

"Not a problem," she says easily. "I'll be there. I can drive you."

"I'll already be at the hospital," I tell her. "Just meet me there."

"Okay. Look," she points, "we should go in there."

I glance at where she's pointing and my mouth drops. "Not funny!"

"I'm serious," she pleads. "Come on." She pulls me into the —*gulp*—baby clothes store. "You told me you decided to keep the baby, you're going to have to get this stuff eventually."

"Yeah, but not now," I protest.

"It'll be fun."

She releases her arm from mine once we're safely inside the clothing store.

I move toward a table of tiny little pants and pick up one labeled newborn. I gape at the tiny size. "Is the baby really going to be this tiny when it comes home?" I ask her.

"You're the one studying nursing," she reminds me. "You should know the answer to that better than me. But yeah, they're that small."

"How am I not going to royally screw this up?" I voice the concern that's been eating away at me. "A baby is so small and helpless."

"You're going to do great. I believe in you. You're one of the greatest people I've ever had the privilege of knowing and you'll be an amazing mom. Not to mention, this kid is going to have the best auntie ever." She points to herself.

I laugh a little and put the pants down.

"I guess looking wouldn't be such a bad thing." My fingers graze over a tiny fluffy pink jacket.

Mia grins from ear to ear. "I knew you'd give in."

I shake my head. "You're impossible."

Lowering her voice, she says, "When are you going to tell Rush?"

I groan, swiveling away from her and over to a display of onesies.

"I don't know," I admit, picking up a plain white onesie.

"Kira," she says softly but in a warning tone, "you have to tell him."

"I know, I know." I swivel to her. "I'll do it soon."

She narrows her eyes. "I mean it, you have to tell him."

"I'll tell him after my doctor's appointment," I reason logically. "Once I know everything is okay."

She raises a brow. "Will you really?"

"Yes," I sigh, exasperated.

I'm terrified to tell Rush. It's scary as hell to think about telling him he's going to be a father. I don't imagine him having a good reaction. I sure didn't. I can't possibly begrudge him for it, either, when I was the same way. I have to make him understand I decided to keep the baby, and I in no way think he's obligated to be a part of our kid's life. I won't allow our child to ever be a burden, not when that's all I was to my parents.

Mia looks down at her phone. "Is it okay if Hollis meets us here?"

"Here, here?" I ask, pointing a finger to the mall store floor.

"Not *here*, but at the mall in general."

"That's fine," I reply. "Tell him to meet us at the food court. I'm starving. I think I could kill someone for one of those pretzels—oh my God I have to get Cinnabon." I grab her arm.

She laughs. "Is this your first craving?"

I frown. "Possibly. Don't deny a pregnant woman, Mia."

She shakes her head and types something back to Hollis. "Wouldn't dream of it."

We look through the store for a few more minutes before I can no longer resist the call of salty and sweet goodness.

Mia gets in the pretzel line to get our order and I hop in the one for Cinnabon.

Armed with food we take a seat at one of the tables against the row of windows overlooking the theater and parking lot.

I rip open a packet of sauce and dip a pretzel bite in it. "Oh my God," I moan, my eyes closing with pleasure. "That's the best thing I've ever tasted."

Mia laughs at me, breaking apart her full-sized twisty pretzel. "You're funny when you're hungry." She glances down at her phone. "Hollis is here." She looks around and spots him coming in the doors. She waves madly, like it's impossible for him to find her. I'm pretty sure Hollis could sniff her out anywhere like a bloodhound.

He grins when he sees her, his eyes lighting up with love. I selfishly hope one day someone looks at me like that. I'm sure as a single mom it'll be harder to find *the one*, but not impossible.

Jesus, what's happening to me? I never wanted to settle down before, what's with this newfound desire? I'm blaming the spawn.

He pulls out the chair beside her, placing a kiss on her cheek as he sits down.

Hollis Wilder, quintessential bad boy, is now wrapped firmly around my best friend's pinky finger.

He swipes one of her broken apart pieces of pretzel and she swats at him. "Get. Your. Own."

"You're so mean to me," he says around his mouthful. "Why can't we share?" He mock-pouts.

She glances at him in disbelief, her lips slightly parted. "You should know by now *I don't share.*"

Hollis steals another bite and pops it into his mouth with a grin. After he chews and swallows, he points somewhere behind my shoulder. “Mia, do you know that guy? He’s staring at you.”

Mia looks where he’s pointing and pales.

I glance over my shoulder and mutter, “Oh, shit.”

“Who is it?” Hollis asks, looking lost.

“Her ex,” I answer in a biting tone.

“Which one?”

“The worst one,” I mutter, rolling my eyes dramatically.

As I watch, Todd the Turd starts heading our way with his usual cocky swagger. He’s a good-looking guy, shaggy curly blond hair hanging down past his ears, tanned skin, and dimples—but he’s a complete asshole so it ruins the whole façade.

“Mia Hayes,” he says, stopping beside the table. “Long time no see.”

“Todd,” she says shortly.

“The Turd,” I add under my breath.

He glances at me and I give him a wide smile that’s anything but friendly.

I eat little boys like you alive, my look says.

“Kira,” he replies cuttingly, “always a pleasure.”

“It’s really not,” I say in a deadpan tone.

He clears his throat awkwardly. Tipping his head at Hollis, he says, “Does she make those little noises when you fuck her too?”

Rage overcomes Hollis’s face and he stands abruptly, his chair slamming into the one behind. “Did she scream my name when she was with you too, then?”

Todd’s face contorts in rage.

“Hollis, I’ve got this,” Mia says in a deadly calm tone, as she too stands. She presses a hand to his chest, urging him to stand down and let her handle this.

She moves in front of Hollis to face Todd.

"Todd," she says sweetly, and I stare at her in confusion because I know she hates his guts. "There's something I've wanted to say to you for a really long time." She smiles, the picture of innocence.

He tilts his head in confusion. "What?" he asks, unsure if he should dare to placate her.

Her whole face changes, contorting in rage. Before Todd can process the change, she says, "Fuck you," cocks her arm back and punches him square in the nose.

"Holy shit," Hollis chortles, clapping. "That's my girl."

"Never," Mia points a finger at Todd as he clutches his nose —he'll have a wicked black eye I'm sure, "speak to me ever again."

Todd mumbles, "Bitch," and stumbles to the bathrooms nearby.

"Fuck, that was hot," Hollis tells her, practically drooling.

I glare at him. "Don't eye fuck my best friend in front of my food. I'm eating."

He chuckles and Mia moves back into her seat. Hollis pulls his chair back up to the table, plopping onto it. You wouldn't know only a moment ago Mia pulled off one of the most badass things I've ever seen.

"Who was that guy exactly? There has to be more to the story than just an ex," Hollis inquires, stealing another bite of Mia's pretzel. She glares, but doesn't scold him this time.

"Todd," she answers.

He snorts. "I gathered that."

She sighs, glaring at her food. I know Mia's upset when she doesn't even want to eat. She *always* wants to eat.

"We went out a few times, had sex once, and he spread it all around campus that he bagged a rock star's daughter," she mumbles, looking at the table. "Not to mention, while I thought we were together he cheated."

Hollis's mouth widens in a surprised O-shape. "Is that guy who your dad had his car crushed?"

She snorts, her lips slowly but surely rising in a smile. "The very one."

"Savage." He drapes his arm along the back of her chair. "Do you feel better?"

She looks at her knuckles, there's not even a mark left behind—though I guess she *would* know how to punch someone and not hurt herself. "Much," she replies, and smiles fully at Hollis.

My heart pangs at the love shining in her eyes for him.

I've never wanted to look at someone like that, but as I think about the life growing inside me, I wish my child could grow up with two parents who love each other like that. Rush and I aren't those people. Maybe I shouldn't have given up on the idea of adoption so quickly, but I know in my heart I *do* want to keep this baby.

I might not be the best mom, but I know I'll at least be a good mom. I had trouble believing it in the beginning, but I know I can do right by my child.

Finishing my pretzel, I wipe my hands on a napkin and toss the wad at Mia.

"Stop looking at your boyfriend with googly eyes. You're my ride home."

She picks the napkin off her sweater and drops it on the table. "I should make you walk home for being mean to me."

I wave my hand dismissively. "You'd never make a pregnant woman walk home. Oh, shit." I slap my hands over my mouth.

Hollis's eyes widen in surprise, his mouth gaping in horror. "You're pregnant?"

I practically dive across the table and grab his wrist in my hand. "You cannot tell *anyone*," I hiss. "I know how to hide a body and get away with it."

"I take it by anyone, you mean ... Rush?" he finishes, looking awkwardly out of place. Nothing is ever awkward about Hollis Wilder, so clearly I've shocked him.

"I haven't told him yet," I whisper brokenly.

"This is why you've been ignoring him, for what? Three weeks now? The guy is going crazy, and it's because you're *pregnant?*"

I stretch my arm up and cover his mouth. "I mean it, Hollis, you can't say a word." He mumbles something behind my hand, I let it drop, and ask, "What was that?"

"Why *shouldn't* I say something? He's my best friend and ... wait," he turns to Mia, "you've known this whole time, haven't you?"

"I was sworn to secrecy." She shrugs, holding up her hands innocently. She looks completely apologetic, and I'm sure she was torn because of how close Rush and Hollis are, but at the end of the day she always has my back. "Girl code."

"Fuck," Hollis breathes out, low and slow, his eyes shifting from side to side. "You have to tell him." He raises his head, leveling me with a serious look that raises the hair on my arms.

"I know," I hiss, sitting back down in my seat. "I have a doctor's appointment Wednesday. I'll tell him after that." He lowers his head, giving me *the look*. You know, the one of complete disapproval and doubt. "I *will*," I defend. "Do I look so untrustworthy?"

"Oh, I don't know, maybe I don't believe you since you've known for weeks and haven't told him." He raises a brow, daring me to argue.

"I didn't know what I was going to do," I admit, biting my lower lip.

"You didn't know what you were going to do?" he repeats. "What does that mean? Oh." He glares at me and I didn't know easy-going Hollis could ever look so rage-filled. "You mean, you thought about getting an abortion without ever telling Rush you were pregnant with his child?"

"It's my baby too," I defend. "And my body, *and* my life because I'm the one ultimately responsible for caring for the baby."

Hollis snorts humorlessly. "You know, guys get the raw end of the deal—yeah, I get there are a lot of assholes out there who knock up girls and don't give a damn, and it's your body and choice as a woman, but the guy should still be considered in the decision. Rush deserves to know, he deserves a say."

"I'm keeping it," I bite out, "and stop looking at me with such judgment. You have no idea what it's like to be a woman, so just *don't*."

Hollis shakes his head and sighs. "I'm sorry. I'm not trying to judge you, but I've seen the downward spiral Rush has been going through for almost three weeks. He was doing so good after we got here. Now he's going back to that dark place, just when he was finally getting out of it."

"What do you mean?" I ask softly, hesitant and unsure if I actually want an answer.

He shakes his head and stands. "It's Rush's story to tell." Tapping the table, he says, "I know you guys had a sex only deal or whatever, and never talked about anything personal, but this," he glances down in the direction of my flat stomach, "changes things. Rush has been through a hell of a lot and it ... it makes him not the best person at times, and it's rare for anyone to know the *real* him, but I promise the real him is worth it."

"Worth what?" I ask.

He shrugs. "That's for you to decide."

He says goodbye to Mia, kissing her on the cheek before he goes.

Even as I follow her to the car, I can't stop wondering what

Hollis meant. I think I know, and it scares me even more than having a baby.

SIXTEEN

Rush

"Why the fuck are you looking at me like that?" I ask Hollis. "Why the fuck are you even here?" I spread my arms to encompass the hotel suite. "All your shit is at Mia's."

He stands there with his hands shoved into his jeans' pockets looking at me like he's never seen me before.

"Is something growing on my face or are you finally realizing you're in love with me? If I was going to go gay it wouldn't be for you. Possibly Fox."

"Hey, don't bring me into this." Fox raises his hands dismissively, sprawled in the chair beside the couch I'm currently laying on, a tumbler of scotch dangling from my hand. It's only my first drink but of course Father Cannon has already bestowed me with a scornful look. Judgmental asshole. He didn't spare a glance at Fox's drink.

Hollis shakes his head and mumbles, "Sorry."

"Seriously, man, what's wrong with you?" I ask, my brows furrowing in confusion because the guy looks seriously tortured by something.

"N-Nothing," he stutters awkwardly, not quite meeting my gaze. "What are you making in there?" he asks Cannon, who's making dinner in the small kitchen, wearing an apron and everything. He's fucking Martha Stewart.

"Nothing for you," Cannon retorts. "Why are you here?"

At least I'm not the one who has to ask again.

Hollis shrugs. "I can't hang out with my friends?"

I snort in disbelief. "You're too busy fawning all over Mia to have time for us anymore."

"That's not true," he defends a little too forcefully.

I raise my glass slowly to my lips, giving him a look that tells him exactly what I think of his bullshit.

He shakes his head. "I've only seen you guys in the studio these past few weeks and thought we could hang out."

"We might not have even been here," I retort in response, sweeping my arm wide. "I might've been balls deep in some much needed pussy, Martha Fucking Stewart might've been hitting up the local knitting ladies—I hear Maddox knits, maybe you two can be besties," I toss in Cannon's direction, "—and Fox here could be nerdgasming out at the nearest comic book store."

"You're impossible," Hollis says with a shake of his head.

"Thank you." I grin like it was a compliment. "It's the very essence of my personality."

Hollis drops onto the other end of the couch and I lean back.

"What's going on, man?" I ask him, serious this time. "You look like you've seen a ghost."

"No, no, I'm fine."

"You don't act fine," Fox adds, taking note of Hollis's troubled appearance.

Hollis runs his fingers through his shaggy brown hair.

"Mia's not pregnant is she?" I ask suddenly, connecting the dots of his behavior.

Hollis chokes on his own saliva. "Mia? P-Pregnant? Noooo."

I exchange a glance with Fox.

"Are you lying, bro?" Fox asks him.

"No, I swear."

"Always wrap it before you tap it." I tip my drink toward him and wink.

"Why don't we go do something?" Hollis prompts.

"Because I'm cooking fucking dinner, that's why," Cannon says from the kitchen, wearing fucking oven mitts now. I don't even know where he got them, because there's no way they came with the room. At least I don't think they did. It's not like I checked. Cooking is not my forte.

"You said I couldn't have any," Hollis defends.

Cannon huffs a breath. "Fine, you can have some if it gets you to stop acting weird."

"I'm not acting weird."

"I'm not drunk enough for this," I retort.

"You're *not* getting drunk," Cannon warns with a dark glare. "I shouldn't have to spend my life being your fucking babysitter."

"Didn't ask you to," I grumble under my breath.

"Are you okay?" Hollis asks me. "*Really*, okay?"

I inhale a breath and it's shakier than I intend. "Just peachy." Running my fingers through my hair, I add, "I'll be fine."

I don't even know why I'm still so bent out of shape over Kira. I used to have a different girl in my bed every night, there's no reason why I wouldn't have moved on by now. Except I'm completely fucking baffled by what I did to her. I'm used to ghosting girls, not being the one ghosted.

Did I get too attached?

I mean, I *like* Kira. She's a nice girl. She's pretty cool actually. But I don't know enough about her to be in love with her, if that's what she thinks was happening. I counted her as a friend, my first real friend outside of Cannon, Fox, and Hollis. I like to take care of my friends, but maybe I took care of her too much and it scared her away.

I'm sure Cannon would tell me *I'm* the one who needs to be taken care of anyway. He doesn't get it. The alcohol makes me forget who I am for a little while, and sometimes, okay, lots of times, I need the distraction. Any sort of pain I feel, emotional, physical, it doesn't matter—it takes me straight back to that dark place I was in after my parents died. I guess, I never really got out of it. Now, I'm only trying not to drown in it.

"Dinner's ready," Cannon announces. "I don't know why I cook for you sorry asses."

"Do you enjoy insulting us, *Dad?*" Hollis asks him.

Cannon cracks a small smile. "I'll admit I get some joy out of it."

"Dickwad," I mumble, and he whips off his oven mitt to give me the finger. I press a hand to my chest. "I've been blessed."

He shakes his head and grabs plates, setting them on the table.

"Dig in."

We all sit down and pile steaming lasagna onto our plates. I grab two pieces of garlic bread and add them to my plate.

Shoving a heaping forkful of lasagna into my mouth, with no concern for the temperature, I give Cannon a thumb's up of approval.

The man can cook. All those days spent in the kitchen with his mama paid off.

Honestly, Mama Rhodes is the fucking best. I miss her, but like hell am I going back home. I left that place behind when we moved to L.A. and swore to never go back.

You could say my coping mechanism is avoidance.

Maybe that's why I haven't searched out Kira.

If she doesn't want anything to do with me anymore, I'm not going to impose myself on her.

"See, this is nice," Hollis says. "All of us hanging out together."

I point my fork at him. "You're full of shit and I still don't believe you came over here to 'hang out.'" I add air quotes for good measure.

Hollis frowns. "I can't miss my friends?"

"You see us practically every day," Fox argues.

"In the studio," he defends.

"Which you can't leave fast enough so you and Mia can bone. Where is she anyway? If you're here I'm surprised she's not lurking about."

Cannon shakes his head. "Leave him alone."

"Nah, it's fine," Hollis says. "She's with Kira." He pauses, gauging my reaction to his words.

I blink, stone-faced, refusing to act like her name means anything to me.

I almost come back with, "Who's that?" But then he'd know how bothered I am by her radio silence. The best course of action for me is to act like it doesn't matter, because, honestly, it doesn't. I'll get over it. I'm a big boy.

"I hope they're having fun," is all I say, before turning my attention back to my food.

Hollis shakes his head, not believing my bravado, but I don't give a shit.

Kira's not my concern anymore. She doesn't want to be.

Conversation dissolves into talk of music, like it always invariably does. We seem to have a hard time forgetting not to work, since it's what we love. It's always on our minds in some way.

Fox and I clean up from the meal—I actually don't mind washing dishes, it was always my chore growing up—and Hollis eventually leaves.

Cannon and Fox head to their rooms to go to bed and I fill my glass to the brink of spilling over, and sink onto the couch, grabbing the remote. I settle on *Ghost Adventures*—I love paranormal shit.

My focus isn't on the show like it normally is, no matter how hard I try to make it so.

Finally, I give in to my desire and pick up my phone. I bring up all my text messages to Kira, the last few read but unanswered. Anger surges through me, and I click onto her contact, my finger hovering over the delete button.

I stare at it for a full minute, willing myself to push it.

But I don't.

I throw back the rest of my drink and go to bed angry.

SEVENTEEN

Kira

I stare at my phone, at the text message Rush sent this morning.

The waiting room of the doctor's office is packed, and I'm already nervous about this appointment, so his text doesn't help matters.

Rush: I don't know what the fuck I did to you, but I deserve more than this. Normally I'd be happy to go quietly away and fuck someone else, but not this time. You're going to give me an explanation to my face. Tonight. Either give me a time to come by or I'll just show up. I still have a key.

I haven't responded, I don't know what to say or do, not until this appointment is over.

I'm sure he's fuming at the fact I haven't responded yet, but he'll have to remain angry until this is over, and my vagina has been thoroughly probed—and not in the fun way.

The door to the office opens and I look up, breathing a sigh of relief when I see it's Mia.

"How are you doing?" she asks, sitting down and placing her purse in her lap.

"I'm freaking out," I admit. It's pretty obvious though, considering how jittery I am.

She takes my hand in hers, still slightly chilled from the cold outside.

"You're not alone in this," she reminds me. "I'm here for you, always."

My lower lip wobbles, and I dam back my tears. I hate crying, and I refuse to let this situation lower me to such barbaric needs.

"Thank you," I say, choked up. Mia truly is the best friend I could ever ask for. She puts up with all my shit and always remains calm, cool, and collected.

"You're going to be okay," she sooths. "I wouldn't tell you that if I didn't believe it."

I reach over and give her an awkward hug. I'm not the hugging type, but right now I need it, and I think she does too.

She squeezes me back.

"Kira Marsh?"

I look at her with wide panicked eyes and she squeezes my hand.

"Here goes nothing, I guess," I breathe out.

She stands with me and we follow the nurse back to a room.

"So, it says here you got a positive pregnancy test result?"

I nod. "I did."

"When was the date of your last period?"

"Um..." I bite my lower lip. "I'm not sure exactly."

She writes something down.

"Were you trying to conceive?"

"No."

"You were still taking your birth control then?"

"Yes—I stopped it after I got the positive result, I haven't been sexually active since, and we always used condoms. It has to be a fluke, right?"

She shrugs. "These things happen no matter how careful you are. A false negative is far more common than a false positive, but I'll send the doctor in to check things. You can take your pants off and drape this over you." She grabs a sheet from the cabinet and hands it to me. "You'll be fine," she adds, sensing my nerves.

I let out a breath as she closes the door behind her.

Hopping off the table I take off my scrub pants and underwear, not caring at all that Mia's in here with me. She's seen me naked, and now's not the time for decency.

I sit back down, draping the sheet over my bottom half.

I look at Mia, letting out a nervous breath as my heart roars in my chest. I don't think my heart has ever beat so fast. It's possible I'll faint, but hopefully I don't.

"Breathe," she says in a quiet and calm tone. "Freaking out doesn't solve anything. It only makes it worse."

She's right, I know she is, and yet I can't stop freaking out.

I want a miracle. I want the doctor to tell me I'm not pregnant.

But I am.

I know it as sure as I know my own name. I feel it in my soul.

There's a soft knock on the door and then Dr. Wren's kind face appears, framed by hair a deeper shade of red than Mia's.

"How are you, Kira?" she asks, closing the door behind her and pumping some Germ-X on her hands.

"Knocked up, apparently," I reply in a dry tone.

She gives a small laugh. She's younger, in her forties I'd assume, and I've always really liked her. Today, not so much—simply because of my reason for being here.

She sits down on the stool and rolls up to me. "Are you doing okay?" she asks, true concern in her eyes.

I nod. "I'll be fine."

I will be. One day at a time.

She claps her hands together. "Well, let's take a look."

Minutes later there's a small black and white graphic of a bean-sized baby on the screen.

My baby.

Rush's baby.

Our baby.

"It's ... so big," I murmur in awe.

She gives a laugh and Mia leans over me, getting a better look at the screen.

"It looks like you conceived in early December—"

"Early December?" I shriek. "It's the first week of March! How could I not know?"

She shakes her head. "It happens more than you'd think."

She clicks some buttons. "I'd say you're about nine weeks along and due around the end of August ... the twenty-seventh the way the baby is measuring."

By the end of the summer I'm going to have a baby in my arms. It's possibly the craziest shit I've ever heard.

She pushes another button and a booming sound fills the small room.

"What's that?" I ask stupidly. Something about this appointment has sent all my smarts soaring out the window. "Is that the heartbeat?"

"It is," she replies with a kind smile, like she understands how freaked out I am by all this, but at the same time in complete awe.

"Wow," Mia breathes, her lips parted in wonder. "That's amazing."

"It is," I say, choked up, looking at the tiny wriggling form.

The thing I was so afraid of doesn't seem so frightening now.

"I'll get some of these printed for you," my doctor says.

Thirty minutes later I'm walking out of the office with several ultrasound photos of my baby and my next appointment scheduled.

"I can't believe you're actually having a baby," Mia says, walking with me to the elevator. I get to head home now, which I'm thankful for. There's no way I could work the rest of the day, my focus is elsewhere. "I mean, I was there when you took the test, but it never really sank in."

"It's happening," I say as much for my benefit as hers. "I'm going to be a mom."

The doors slide open with a merry chime and we step inside.

Pushing the button for the main floor, Mia says, "I'm going to be the best auntie ever—rest assured, we might not be related by blood, but we're family and I'm this kid's aunt."

"Thank you for coming with me." I mean it too. I couldn't have done this without her. I probably would've fainted before they even called my name.

"No problem." She smiles at me, the kindness in her eyes nearly making me cry.

Fuck, look at me. This baby is already turning me into a pathetic weeping mess.

Not cool, little one. Not cool.

The doors open to the lobby of the hospital and I hug her tight before she heads out the main doors and I turn to my right to head for the garage.

A few minutes later I slide behind the wheel of my car. I turn it on, but I don't leave. Digging my phone out again I bring up my text messages from Rush.

Me: Come by around 5. Does that work for you?

Seconds later his reply appears.

Rush: I'll be there.

I bustle around my tiny kitchen like a crazy person.

I've lost my ever-loving mind. I rarely cook—unless pouring cereal into a bowl and adding milk counts, but here I am trying to make dinner for Rush, because I feel bad for ignoring him and also because...

Well, I have to tell him he's my baby daddy and that sounds about as fun as having nails driven into my eyes.

But by making dinner, at least it shows I've put in some effort for this, right?

God, what am I thinking?

Granted, grilled chicken, mashed potatoes, and vegetables is nothing extravagant, but considering I'm the one cooking it's a five-star meal.

I'm overthinking this way too much, and I've never been an over thinker. I couldn't be. I've had to put things behind me and move on, to live without a care.

Have you really been living without a care, or letting your past define every decision you make?

"God," I groan, shoving my fingers through my already messy hair and blowing out a disgruntled breath.

Rush is going to be here any minute and I look a mess.

I tie my hair back in a ponytail and rush to the bathroom, adding some color to my lips and swiping mascara on my lashes. It's not like I'm trying to impress him, but I know I'll feel a hell of a lot more confident with some makeup on. Something about dressing up and doing my makeup makes me feel like I can conquer the world.

Dashing back out to the kitchen I fix everything onto plates and set them on the coffee table. I turn the TV on, but keep the volume soft, because as much as I don't want to, Rush and I *do* have to talk.

I step back, looking everything over. It doesn't look horrible, in my opinion, definitely edible and not burnt. Wiping my sweaty palms on my jeans there's a soft knock on the door.

"Showtime," I mutter to myself, my heart racing.

I feel entirely silly for being this nervous, but then again this is huge, life changing, news. I've had several weeks to get used to it and accept it.

This will be the first Rush is hearing of it.

I open the door and my breath catches, because it's honestly unfair how good-looking he is.

His blond hair is still damp from a shower, the strands on top shorter than they were the last time I saw him, and the sides freshly buzzed—not to the scalp, but shorter than the hair on top. His earring catches the light and makes him look rakish.

The heavy stubble on his cheeks adds to his handsome features and his blue eyes are so dark I think I could drown in them.

"Are you going to stare at me all night or let me inside?" He says the words lightly, but there's no joking lift to his lips like usual or a twinkle in his eyes. After ignoring him I deserve much worse.

I shake my head. "Oh, yeah. Sorry." I step aside and let him in.

He shrugs off his navy coat and hangs it on my pathetic coat rack by the door. My eyes can't help but stray to his ass, looking way too delectable in the pair of jeans he wears.

Fuck, it's been way too long since I got laid. I'm certifiable.

He turns to face me and I have to suppress a moan, because his shirt is taut against his muscles and he's rolled the sleeves up, exposing the tattoos on his forearms.

God, how I've missed those tattoos, and him ... yeah, him too.

As much as I don't want to admit it, I have missed him. Maybe I haven't sheltered my heart as well as I believed.

"I ... uh ... made dinner," I say awkwardly.

I don't like this new side of me. I'm used to being confident, truly confident and not faking it, but getting pregnant has shaken me up and as the sand settles, it's shaped differently than it was before. Now, I have to puzzle out exactly what this means for who I am—because I'm not sure I'm who I've always believed. I think I've been wearing a mask, one I made to protect myself from the people who were supposed to love me no matter what, but did nothing but hurt me instead.

He shoves his hands in his pockets and looks me over. "I didn't come here for dinner."

"I know," I sigh heavily. "I'll explain, I swear, but this might take a while. Let's just sit down and eat."

"Fine," he agrees, and moves by me. His arm brushes mine and I inhale the scent of his cologne like a greedy high school girl.

I'm practically certifiable at this point. Where's the straight jacket?

I grab a beer for him and a Coke for me from the refrigerator. It's pathetic how empty it is otherwise. I guess I'll have to change that now that I'm growing a tiny human.

I sit down beside him and hold out the beer.

"Thanks," he mumbles, popping the cap off.

The can of Coke hisses as I crack it open and take a sip of the bubbly soda.

There's not a lot of space between us, simply because my couch is small and Rush is huge, but I can tell he's making an effort not to touch me and I'd be lying if I said it doesn't hurt. I'm being stupid, I know. *I'm* the one who ignored *him*. I'm not denying that I've done this, put this distance between us, but it still sucks. I could barely process the fact I'm pregnant, let alone tell him.

I set my drink on the coffee table and pick up my plate. I'm not hungry. Eating is the last thing on my mind actually.

"So, what the fuck happened?" Rush asks, cutting into the piece of chicken. He brings the fork to his mouth and pauses, assessing me. "Did I do something to piss you off? Is it because I consider you a friend? If that's the case, then you're not my fucking friend anymore. It's fine with me."

I shake my head. "It wasn't that."

"Then what?" he asks, exasperated, his tone short. "You completely ignored me. Normally I'd say whatever and go on my merry way, but this was different." He flicks his fingers between the two of us. "I know we set out for it to be sex, nothing else, and it was at first. But then," he pauses, gathering himself, "it became something more. If it scared you, fine, but you should've fucking said something. I would've backed off. Given you your space."

"Rush," I breathe, biting my lip as I feel the tears beginning to form.

Don't cry, Kira. Tears are for the weak and pathetic and you're neither.

"Maybe you met someone else," he muses softly. "Decided you actually wanted something serious, something I can't give you."

"Rush," I say his name firmer this time.

He looks at me fully, his eyes confused and hurt. "Just tell me what it is I did, Kira. I'm used to fucking everything up. I'm too loud. Too drunk. Too crazy. I'm too everything. I can handle whatever the fuck it is."

I shake my head back and forth, my throat closed up.

"Jesus Christ," he pleads, "tell me."

I force myself to look him in the eyes.

"I'm pregnant."

I barely hear the sound of his plate hitting the floor. It

doesn't even break from the short drop, but food goes everywhere, spraying across both our feet.

He looks at me, stunned and confused. "What did you say?"

"Please, don't make me say it again," I beg, my eyes closing.

"I need to hear it," he pleads, turning to face me. His knees brush mine and I force my eyes open.

"I'm pregnant," I say again. "You're going to be a dad."

He rubs his hands over his face, and stands, pacing the small length of the living room.

"Rush?" I ask hesitantly. "Are you okay?"

It feels like all the oxygen has been sucked out of the room and I'm struggling, gasping desperately for air.

He pauses and lets out a breath. "How'd this happen? We were careful."

I shrug, dipping my chin down. I can't quite meet his gaze right now. It makes me feel too much, hurt too much. "We won the lottery, but in reverse."

He shakes his head. I can tell he's stunned, confused, probably questioning everything the same way I did.

"I'm not ready to be a dad," he breathes. "How can I take care of and provide for someone when I'm a fucking mess myself?"

"I'm not expecting *anything* from you," I promise him. "Once I decided to keep the baby, I knew for certain I'd be okay doing this on my own. I don't expect you to be a parent. You didn't ask for this."

He stops his pacing and faces me, anger simmering beneath the surface of his whole body.

"Once you decided to keep the baby," he repeats in an icy tone. "And you didn't think to include me in these important decisions?"

"Rush ... I ..." I don't know how to explain myself to him. "I knew this responsibility was mine to bear. As the father you're free to walk away in a way I'm not."

He stares at me. "You think I'd walk away from my child? Just abandon it like it means nothing to me?"

"No, that's not what I'm saying—"

"It is!" he shouts, a vein threatening to pop out in his forehead. "It's exactly what you're saying. You're basically admitting you would've walked away from it too." He shakes his head. "It pisses me off beyond measure you've ignored me, pushed me away, and couldn't give me the common courtesy of being involved in this."

"I'm involving you now," I defend, my voice broken.

"Would you have? If I hadn't kept pressuring you?"

"Yes, I swear. I wasn't going to hide this from you forever."

"The fact you hid it from me at all is appalling, Kira. I thought I knew you—maybe not your inner most thoughts, or your past, but I still thought I knew *you*. Now, I'm not sure of anything."

I stand up, my hands held out in front of me pleadingly. "I didn't plan this, or want a baby, and I was scared. Can you really fault me for being scared?"

"I can fault you for lying to me, for keeping me away."

"Are you saying you want to be involved? I would never keep this baby from you, but I won't force it on you either."

"I don't know what I'm saying." He pinches the bridge of his nose. Lowering his hand he looks at me. "I'm ... this wasn't what I was expecting tonight, and I'm confused. I need time to process this."

I stare back at him. "I find it funny you need the same thing you're mad at me for needing."

His jaw clenches. "This is a fucking mess. *We're* a fucking mess. How can either one of us be a decent parent?"

I shrug like it's no big deal, even though this whole thing is *life changing*. "I'm not claiming I'll be the best mom ever, but I'll be the best one I can be and I'll try my damndest to be even better than I think I can be. The ball's in your court now, Rush, as to what kind of part you want in this child's life."

He stares back at me, breathing heavily. "I might have my concerns about what kind of father I can possibly be with as fucked up as I am, but I will be there for my child."

I swallow thickly, trying to keep my emotions at bay.

"Prove it."

EIGHTEEN

Rush

Leaving Kira's I head to the nearest bar.

I'm already scoring high on this whole dad thing. I'm a real fucking winner.

Sliding onto a stool I signal the bartender and order a shot of whiskey. Downing it, I ask for another, before switching to beer.

I wrap my hands around the bottom of the bottle.

Kira's pregnant.

When I came over to her place tonight that was the last news I ever expected to hear. I don't know quite how to process it, and maybe I was too harsh on her, or possibly not harsh enough.

I'm *hurt*, which isn't something I admit often. I'm hurt that after all the time we've spent together, she wouldn't tell me. I know she has to feel something more for me than she lets on. There's no way I'm alone in feeling like we've grown close.

But she's scared, and when she's scared she pushes people away.

Me? I drink.

But I also drink if I'm happy, or stressed, angry—pretty much any emotion is an excuse for me to drink.

Depending on the mood I'm in, the alcohol either hypes me up or sends me into numbness.

Lately, it's only been numbness.

I pull out my phone and ring the number of the one person I know will always be there for me no matter what.

"Hello?"

"I need you."

"A BAR, MAN, *REALLY?*"

"This is my first beer," I defend, lifting my beer in the air, not mentioning the two shots of whiskey I had prior. "Sit down." I pull out the empty stool beside me.

Cannon shakes his head at me, but takes the seat. I slide the glass of beer I ordered for him in his direction, it's his favorite, Guinness. I don't understand the appeal, but what do I know? Apparently I don't know shit about anything and I'm a worthless human being Kira doesn't think deserves to know he's going to be a father.

"What's going on? It must be serious if after all I've said and done you're willingly inviting me into a bar with you." He takes a sip of the Guinness.

I raise the beer to my lips and set it down, looking straight ahead.

"Kira's pregnant."

He chokes on the liquid and when I look at him some is dribbling out of the sides of his mouth. The normally calm and capable Cannon looks shocked and entirely frazzled. If I wasn't in such a bad mood I might smile.

"She's pregnant?" I nod in answer to his question. "Like ... with a baby?"

"No, a puppy, you idiot," I snap, exasperated. I feel strung out, at my wit's end. "Of course with a baby."

"Your baby?"

"My baby," I sigh, taking another sip of beer—well, more like a gulp this time.

"But ... how?" he asks.

"Well, the same way I assume most conceptions happen. I put my cock in her pussy and ejaculated."

He smacks the back of my head with his tattooed hand. "I could gather that part, but you always wear a condom, right?"

I nod. "And she was on birth control."

"You don't think..." he pauses and I shake my head vehemently.

"No, she wouldn't do that. Kira was as paranoid about protection as me, and..." I take a moment to gather myself. "She admitted she thought about having it taken care of before she told me."

"And by taken care of, you mean?" He raises a dark brow.

"You know what I mean," I sigh heavily like the weight of the world is on my shoulders. Honestly, it's exactly what it feels like. Ever since she told me I can't seem to shake this crushing pressure. "Is it wrong I'm beyond pissed she'd consider ... consider..." I close my eyes. I can't even say the word. "Ending it," I finally settle on, "without ever telling me? She could've done it, never told me, and I wouldn't have known the difference."

Cannon shakes his head. "That's rough."

A hefty sigh leaves me yet again. "I want to be in my kid's life, but she doesn't seem to think I'll show up. She told me to prove it."

He shrugs, wiping the condensation off his glass with the back of his index finger. Above, mounted behind the bar, the TV blares obnoxiously. "Then prove it to her."

"Maybe it'd be better if I stayed away," I muse quietly. "What kind of father could I possibly be? I mean, I want to be there for my kid, I do, but ... I'm hardly the best role model."

"We can always change," he reasons. "We're always evolving —maybe it's time you focused on being the best version of yourself you can be."

"What does that even mean?"

He raises his pierced brow. "Whatever you want it to mean, I guess."

I scrub my hands over my face. "I don't know if I can change," I mutter solemnly, resigning myself to my miserable no-good existence.

He looks at me sadly. "You *can*. Anybody can change. You only have to decide if you *want* to. As long as you don't want to better yourself, you'll continue down this path—and I guarantee you, if you do, you won't have anything to do with your kid. Kira probably wouldn't let you and I can't say I'd blame her. Clean up your act, Rush. You've already done a pretty damn good job of it since we got here, but there's one major thing you have to accept."

"What's that?" I ask, but I'm afraid I already know his answer.

"You have to admit you're an alcoholic and take the steps to stop."

"I'm *not* an alcoholic," I defend vehemently. "I like to drink, so what?"

He sighs wearily, his eyes narrowed. "You're my best friend, and it makes me sad you can't see what you are. I guess most addicts can't."

I bristle at his words.

"I don't say this to hurt you, or make you angry, I'm saying this because you're more than a friend, you're practically my brother, and it kills me watching you poison yourself. Kira's pregnant now, you're going to be a dad no matter what, but you have to decide what kind of dad you'll be."

He stands up, finishes the last of his beer, and slaps some bills on the table to cover the tab.

"Come back to the hotel with me. Don't sit here alone and drown in misery."

I shake my head. "It's what I do best."

He exhales an angry breath. "I don't know what more I can say to you."

"Then stop talking."

"*You* asked me to come here, remember? Don't snap at me for trying to be your friend. It's been *eight* years since your parents died. Don't you think it's past time you dealt with it?"

He doesn't wait for me to answer and a second later the door closes behind him.

I close my eyes and groan. I don't know why it is I constantly push the people closest to me away, the only people I have left in this world are ones I love. I believe Cannon is only trying to look out for me, I do, but I don't have a problem and that's where he's wrong and can't get it through his thick head.

Maybe I haven't dealt with my parents' death, but I'm *not* an alcoholic.

I don't have to drink. I can stop any time.

I finish the beer I ordered and head out.

It's the first week of March and the air is still way too fucking cold for my liking. I miss the warmth and clear blue skies. Ever since November this ugly ass gray sky has descended on Virginia and it's fucking depressing.

I walk with my hands buried in the pockets of my warm coat.

Mom, tell me what to do? I plead. *Give me some kind of advice. A sign. Anything.*

But like always, there's nothing—nothing but the twinge of disappointment I know she must feel if she can see me now.

My parents would've been the best fucking grandparents ever. Now, my child will never know them. What's worse is, will my child even *want* to know *me?* All the videos that exist on the internet of my past escapades are damning. What kind of child would want *me* as their father?

Sadly, I understand why Kira wanted to assure me she can do this on her own.

Heading down the street on the old walking mall I enter the bookstore.

"Can I help you find anything?" The kind lady behind the counter says, peering at me over the top of her glasses.

"Yeah," I breathe, as some of the warmth from the store seeps into me, warming my bones. "I need any kind of books you have on babies."

"WHAT'S THAT?" CANNON ASKS SUSPICIOUSLY AS I ENTER THE suite with two bags in hand.

"Here, take a look." I carry one over to him where he sits on the couch.

He takes it and peers inside reluctantly like he's afraid something is going to jump out from it and bite him.

"Baby books?" He looks mystified, and perhaps a smidge proud.

"If I'm going to be a dad, I have to know how to take care of the kid, right?"

"Whoa, whoa, whoa," Fox chants, sitting up from where he was reclined in the chair reading a Captain America comic book. "Did you just say you're going to be a dad? Where the fuck have I been? What year is it?"

Cannon laughs, and it's genuine, not forced. Even the dimples he has make a rare appearance. "He just found out today."

Fox turns accusing eyes onto Cannon. "You knew? Nobody tells me shit."

"Sorry, man," I say, truly meaning it. "I just found out a couple of hours ago. If it makes you feel better Hollis doesn't know yet."

He smiles, picking his comic book back up. "I do feel better."

I take the bag back from Cannon and give both a shake. "I'm going to go read."

As I turn toward my room I hear Fox mutter, "I didn't know he could read."

"I heard that," I say back.

"I meant for you to," he cackles.

Friends, the people who are there for you through thick and thin, but also know how to roast you unlike any others.

NINETEEN

Kira

"I told him," I confess to Mia, shoveling a forkful of salad into my mouth.

I hate salad—*loathe* it, actually. Does anyone actually enjoy feasting on pieces of *lettuce?*

But, I'm trying to be healthy for the baby—and I guess me too, but mostly the baby.

Mia's eyes widen at me across the lunch table in the university's cafeteria. I begged her to meet me, because this wasn't a conversation I wanted to have through text message, or over the phone, and definitely not at The Sub Club when we work this afternoon.

"You actually told him like you said you were going to? Wow, I'm impressed. If I was betting on it, I would've said you'd chicken out."

I throw a piece of lettuce at her. "Have some faith in me."

She flicks the piece of lettuce back toward me from where it landed beside her tray of delicious looking pizza.

God, I'd kill for some pizza. Why'd I get a salad? Oh, right—healthy. What a load of garbage.

"How'd he take it?" she asks.

I lift my shoulder indifferently. "Better than I thought, I guess. He seemed to be more upset with me for not telling him sooner."

"Understandable," she interjects.

"He said he needs time to process. Maybe he'll see where I was coming from."

I hope.

It's a scary thing learning your life is going to completely change. I'm only twenty-one—I'll be twenty-two in June—and a baby ... I'll never be able to go back to how I lived my life before.

"Do you think he'll be a part of things?" she asks, and I might drool a bit as she chews a bite of pizza.

"He said he wants to be, but we'll see."

"You're doubtful," she states.

I spear another piece of nasty looking lettuce—it's not that salad has ever done anything to personally offend me ... except exist.

"I mean—we agreed to a sex only relationship, and yeah we started growing closer, but at the end of the day he's a player, a partier, and a drinker. Not exactly the dad type."

She snorts. "You're all those things too—maybe not to his extent," she defends when she notices I'm about to protest, "but you can't deny you like to go out and have a good time."

"I don't see Rush growing up and rising to the occasion," I admit. "It's okay if he doesn't. When I decided to keep the baby it was with the assumption I'd be raising it on my own. I refuse to constantly rely on a man like my mother. I'm strong enough to take care of myself and my child."

She smiles at me. "Yes, you are." Reaching across the table she grabs my hand. "I really am proud of you."

"For what?" I blink stupidly at her.

Around us conversation stirs in the air, but it feels as if nothing else exists outside of our conversation. I'm tuned in to her every word.

"For realizing you're not your mom."

My throat feels tight, but I nod. I'm not her. I'm me—a person of my own making whom I choose to be. Just because she birthed me doesn't mean I'll be as miserable and shitty as she was, jumping from man to man, never caring how they treated her. I begged her many times to let them go, to stand on her own two feet—to let *me* be enough for her as her child, but I wasn't what she wanted. They were—and it's time I realized those actions define *her* not me.

"I'm not," I echo.

She releases my hand and wiggles around in her seat. "I still think you should go see her, get some closure or something."

Panic threatens to wash me away. "I can't."

There were good times with my mom, sure, but for the most part all she did was hurl hurtful things my way. Any time something went wrong in her life—like one of her boyfriend's hit her, or my dad showed up unexpectedly, or even if she didn't have clean underwear—it was always my fault.

"Kira Elizabeth Marsh! Can you not do anything right? You're pathetic. Sometimes I wonder why I ever I wanted a child. I'd be better off without your baggage.

The one thing I never told her was how I knew I would've been better off without *hers*.

Being loved by a monster isn't truly being loved at all.

It's only a curse, one that seems impossible to break when the monster is your own flesh and blood.

I won't be that to my child, and I won't let Rush either.

I believe in my heart Rush is a good person. The way he took care of me when I was sick is proof of that, but I can tell there are demons of his he's never taken care of, ghosts that haunt him the way mine have haunted me. This baby is already teaching me to love myself, to let shit go, but I don't know if it can do the same for him.

"Is it time to go home yet?" I ask Mia in a whiny tone. "My feet are killing me."

We've been making sandwiches and tending to customers for hours. All I want to do is go home and fall asleep in my bed—I'm not sure there will even be time to change out of my clothes.

"One more hour until close," she tells me reluctantly.

"I need to find another job," I mutter.

The thing I've always loved about working at The Sub Club is the flexibility with my schedule. But with school, my time at the hospital spent on my feet, and working here? It's going to be too much when I start to get huge—but who is going to want to hire a pregnant lady?

"Like what?" she asks, seeming to echo my thoughts.

I blow out a breath. "Good question."

She gives me a smile. "I'm sure if you really want to work somewhere else, we can find you something."

The chime above the door dings and customers stroll in, putting us back to work and out of conversation.

I'm not even far along in this pregnancy and I already feel more tired every night than I ever have. It's only going to get worse. Who knew growing a human took so much out of you?

When the time comes for us to close up shop, I'm ridiculously relieved.

Mia and I walk out to the parking lot and I halt when I notice a familiar figure leaning against my beat-up car.

"You okay?" Mia hesitates beside me.

I nod, a short jerk of my chin in affirmation. "I need to talk to him."

She nods and waves at him before heading over to her car.

Walking up, I stop in front of Rush. He leans against my driver's side door, barring my means of escape.

"We need to talk," he announces.

"I guess we do," I agree.

"Can I buy you dinner?"

I want to say no, not because I want to avoid him, but I want to get home and crash. My treacherous stomach comes to life and he chuckles. The salad I had at lunch was a pathetic excuse for food.

"Yeah, I guess so," I agree.

"Mind if I ride with you?" he asks.

The idea of being so close to him in my tiny car wants to send me running in the opposite direction, but I hold my ground.

"Where's your truck?" It seems like an important question to pose before I answer him.

"At the hotel," he answers. "I walked over."

"Guess you're riding with me then," I sigh, pinching the bridge of my nose. I can feel a headache coming on.

He cracks a grin, and for a moment it feels like it did weeks ago—easy, without this troubling complication of the fact we made a baby together.

"I knew if I brought my truck you'd insist on driving separately and then ditch me."

"I wouldn't do that."

I so would and he knows it.

He laughs, not believing me at all.

He steps away, allowing me into the driver's seat and he climbs in the passenger. He squeezes in and then pushes the bar beneath the seat so he can roll it all the way back.

He's never been in my car before, any time we've gone somewhere together we've either met up or ridden in his truck, and now I know why.

He has to duck, because his head would be curved against the low ceiling otherwise, and even with the seat all the way back his knees are still up to his chin. He leans it back and says, "Better."

"Really?" I question, because he still looks like a squished marshmallow—not that he's squishy or anything. He's delectably hard in all the right places.

"Are you staring at my dick?" His voice is full of barely contained laughter.

I whip my head away from him and shove the key in the ignition. The rumbling engine roars to life—sounding far mightier and angrier than a small car like mine should.

"I'm horny," I say in defense.

He laughs outright. "How do you think I feel?"

My head whips toward him so fast I feel slightly dizzy. "What do you mean?"

He looks at me like I'm dumb. "It means I haven't had sex. We never did call off our deal."

I gape at him. "You mean..."

"I haven't had sex with anyone since you."

I stare at him and the air between us grows heated.

No words will come to me.

In a low voice he says, "If you keep staring at me like that I'm going to fuck you in this car."

My breath catches and my thighs clench together. A low moan flies unbidden between my lips. He groans and reaches over, cupping my cheek in his hand.

"You're killing me, Kira. You have no idea what you do to me."

"I thought you were mad at me," I whisper in the darkness between us.

"I am." His deep blue eyes meet mine and I see the hurt there—hurt of my making. "But it's the people we care about the most, who can cause pain unlike any other."

His thumb brushes over my bottom lip.

"You care about me?"

"I wouldn't be here now if I didn't," he admits, and his perfect white teeth bite lightly into his full bottom lip. "I'm not asking anything from you, I'm sure you don't expect much from me, but we're going to be in each other's lives from now on. There's no changing it. We could at least try to get along and like each other."

"I already like you," I admit.

His grin is nearly blinding. Rush smiling truly is a thing of beauty. It transforms his whole face and brings a brightness to his eyes that's normally absent.

"Well, now that we've established that I guess we should get to know each other better."

I make a face.

He chuckles. "I know there are things you don't want to talk about, not yet, and I'm the same—but we can at least learn the basics, right?"

"I guess," I agree.

"Good." He rubs his hands together. "Now, let's go eat. I'm starving."

Ten minutes later we're seated at the diner for dinner—the same diner we had breakfast at the day I learned I was pregnant. I guess this place is sort of ... *our* place. It feels weird to be back here now, post baby news.

I play with the napkin wrapped around the utensils and Rush watches me.

"You really hate the idea of talking about yourself, don't you?"

I stop messing with the napkin. "What's there to talk about? I'm not very interesting."

"I beg to differ," he reasons. "Want me to go first?"

"Sure," I say softly. "Tell me something about you I don't know."

"I played basketball from the time I was just a little guy. If we have a son, I hope he likes basketball. I'd never force it on him, but it would be nice to share that passion with him. Teach him the drums. Shit, a girl can do both too—a daughter would be cool."

I choke on my own saliva at how easily he talks about a son and daughter.

Maybe it's strange, me being the woman and all, the one actually *carrying* the baby, but I haven't once thought about it being a boy or girl, or what it would even look like—*who* it would look like.

"God, our child is going to have a massive butt-chin," I blurt.

Rush laughs loudly, the sound genuine and carefree. "Where'd that come from?" He strokes the dip in his own chin. "You're right, though. There's no way our kid isn't coming out without it."

I feel the dent in my chin. "Poor thing."

"Poor thing? It's awesome."

I frown, sinking down in my chair a bit. "I've never liked having it."

"I think it's cute." He reaches across the table with his long arm and grazes his fingers over my chin.

I feel my cheeks heat at his touch.

"Sorry I'm only getting to you guys now," our frazzled waitress says, pen poised against the pad of her notebook. "What can I get you to drink?"

He removes his hand and sits back. I feel achingly cold from the lack of his touch.

"A Coke, please."

"Water for me," Rush replies. One of the benefits of coming to the diner—no alcohol. I don't think Rush even knows how one drink invariably leads to ten with him. He doesn't know when to stop.

She turns and leaves and I feel forced to fill the silence, the imprint of his fingers still fresh against my skin.

"Basketball, huh?"

"Could've gone pro after college, I'm sure. Didn't get that far," he sighs, looking away.

"What happened?"

His head swings back to me, his normally carefree blue eyes dark and shuttered. "It's one of those things I don't want to talk about. You have your secrets, Kira. Let me have mine."

I swallow and nod. I would never force him to tell me anything he didn't want to. I don't want to talk about my mom, or dad, or anything from my horrid past. There are too many difficult things to explain.

The waitress drops off our drinks and takes our order. I request a juicy cheeseburger and Rush copies my order. My mouth waters and I feel my stomach come to life.

"You know, those are terrible for you." Rush points to my Coke.

I rip the paper off my straw and stick it into the bubbling soda. I take a dramatic sip and say, "I *like* it. Also, with the amount of alcohol you consume you're one to talk."

His face narrows into something like irritation. "Not you, too."

"What?"

He scrubs his hands over the stubble on his cheeks. "Cannon has been up my ass about my drinking."

"Seems like he should be," I remark.

"I'm not an alcoholic," he growls defensively.

"Whoa," I force a laugh, "I didn't say you were."

"Sorry," he exhales heavily. "Touchy subject. Tell me something I don't know about you."

I tap my chin. "I can't think of anything."

"Kira."

"Fine," I groan in irritation. "Let me think." I have no idea what I can possibly tell him. There's nothing much interesting about me. I go to school, work, and before now—before *him*—I went to parties and usually brought a guy back to my place. "When I was in middle school I did plays—only two, but still."

He grins and it's incredible the way it softens his entire face.

"I have a hard time picturing you up on a stage."

"Believe it." I take another sip of my Coke. I've been craving them more and more—maybe it's my first pregnancy craving. "How are we going to do this?" I ask him on a sigh.

"What do you mean?"

I flick my fingers between the two of us. "You're going to go back to L.A. eventually. My life is here. I have work, school ... the baby will be with me. You say you want to be involved. How is that going to work?"

"Do we have to go over this now?"

"It's something we have to discuss. Putting it off doesn't change that."

He runs his fingers through his hair. "I don't know. I don't know how I'm going to be here. I don't know how I can be the father our kid deserves. All I know is I want to be there as much as I can."

I press my lips together. I don't think he gets it at all—how big of a deal this is, what kind of commitment a child is.

"We must be crazy," I whisper.

"Crazy? Why?" His brow furrows in confusion.

"You're going to *leave*. You're going to go on tour, and play stadiums, girls will throw themselves at you," he smirks at that, "and I'll be here with *our* baby. You'll forget about it ... and me."

"What do you want from me, Kira? Do you want us to try to date? You know that isn't my vibe, and you've always said it isn't yours. Also, you're getting way ahead of things. Our album isn't even out yet."

"That's not what I want. My point is you'll be *gone*, and I'll have to explain that to our kid, and then they'll see everything you do posted all over social media and the internet. Maybe..."

"Maybe, *what?*" he growls dangerously, eyes narrowed.

"Maybe it would be better if you weren't involved," I say as our food is set down on the table.

His hands close into fists on the table. "That's fucking *cruel* of you to say, Kira. How fucking dare you? What if it was reversed? What if I said that to you? That our baby would be better off not knowing you?"

I close my eyes and open them slowly. "I get your point."

"I'm going to be there," he vows. "I promise you. I can do this."

"But can *we* do this?"

He sighs, glaring down at his food. He raises his gaze to mine. "I don't think it'll be easy, but I know we can. It'll take time, and learning to trust each other in ways we haven't yet. I won't make you false promises and declarations that mean nothing. This is a big deal, a baby is a huge unpredictable thing." His lips twitching, he adds, "We'll take baby steps."

I want to believe him. I want to trust that everything will be okay, but in my life, I've learned that's rarely the case. I've come to accept the fact my life will never be simple or easy, but now I have a child to think about too—and I'll do everything it takes to protect him or her, can Rush say the same?

TWENTY

Rush

Sweat drips from my body as my drumsticks fly against my drums. My hair is kept back with a bandana to keep it from getting in my eyes. I feel good behind my drum kit, at peace. Peace is hard to find these days.

I worry about Kira, about our baby, about what kind of father I can be.

It's not a lie when I say I want to be in my child's life. I *will* be. But I've been selfish for so long, I wonder if I'll truly be able to set aside my wants and desires to put my kid first.

There are shitty parents out there who walk away from their kid every day—I don't want to be one of them. I have to be better, the man my parents believed I was. The man I thought died in the wreck.

I walked away from the accident changed forever. There's

probably no going back to who I was—there's a naivety I can never get back, but there has to be a middle ground.

"That's great. Take a break," Hayes says through the mic, breaking my train of thought.

Holding my drumsticks in one hand I stand from the stool and join the others.

Hayes pushes some buttons and it begins to replay everything I recorded.

My head bobs along to the beat and I high five Hollis. "Damn, I'm good."

I still haven't told him about the baby. I don't know why. I think I'm afraid since he's gone and fallen in love, he'll tell me I need to marry Kira. I *like* Kira, but I don't want to marry her. Our relationship has never been anything strong enough for me to be like, yeah, I'm going to put a ring on that. Though, if there was any woman in the world I could picture myself with long term, it would be her.

She's made it clear she doesn't want that, and I'm cool with it. I'm not the relationship kind of guy, not any more, at least we're civil with each other and I *know* we can find a way to co-parent our child.

Focusing on the drumbeat playback, I grin. When we were kids and started this band, I didn't believe we'd make it big. It's probably shocking to everyone now, since I'm the one who ran the most wild with the moderate success we found. The other guys always seemed to know we'd get here. I always had one foot out the door, focusing on another dream. Basketball was my love, my passion. Drumming was fun, exciting, a whole different kind of outlet.

After the accident it was my *only* outlet, but one I needed desperately. I came to love it even more, to realize drumming could become the spark I was missing. I still took it as a joke for a while ... a long while actually, this whole being a band thing, but when Hayes signed us ... I knew this was the real deal. We could do this, make something of ourselves that lasted long term.

"I have to say, this album is going to be fucking amazing," Hayes says, pushing another button so playback stops. "It's going to be crunch time soon to finish up recording so we can get the album ready and out into the world."

"I never thought four guys from Tennessee could make it big," I admit my thoughts out loud.

Hayes grins. "I never thought four guys from Virginia could make it big. Look what Willow Creek has done. Are you all ready for that?"

We exchange glances. "We're ready," we echo.

"I'M KNOCKED UP, I SHOULD BE EXCLUDED FROM ALL FUTURE going out plans. I know I used to *love* to go out, but now I fall asleep by eight o' clock." Kira glares at me with her hands on her slender hips, dressed in a pair of black leggings, a sweatshirt, and fuzzy slippers on her feet.

"Kira," I plead, clasping my hands in front of my face and mock pouting. "We're going to get tacos. You love tacos. Put on some real shoes and come on."

She frowns down at her fuzzy white slippers. "What's wrong with these?"

"Kira," I say slowly.

She grins. "I was kidding. I'll go—but only if you promise to buy me extra tacos so I can have them later—your spawn makes me hungry all the time now. I eat, and eat, then I eat more. I'm going to get huge."

"Extra tacos I can make happen. Scout's honor." I cross my fingers like I'm making a promise.

"I know there's no way you were ever a scout—that's not even what they do anyway." She points to my fingers.

"Stop arguing with me and put your shoes on."

"Fine." She disappears into her apartment, leaving me on the wooden stairs outside. I wonder if she'll ever let me back inside. She still hasn't asked for her keys back, and I don't know whether it's because she's forgotten I have them or ... I don't want to think about the alternative. Getting my hopes up sounds painful.

It's pathetic how I miss spending time with her—and frankly I'm desperate to get laid, but any time I think about fucking someone else I feel physically sick. I keep telling myself it's because we haven't broken off our deal, but I know deep down that's not the reason at all.

Kira appears again, this time with boots on, and closes the door behind her before locking it.

"I'm ready," she declares, looking up at me.

My heart seizes when I look at her. It's a feeling I haven't felt for a long time.

Clearing my throat, I say, "Let's go."

"After you," she says, motioning to the narrow stairs. "I'm not letting you look at my ass."

I laugh. "I so would—does that mean you want to look at *mine?*"

"Ugh, you're impossible." She brushes past me and goes down first.

I look at her ass just for the hell of it.

She hops in my truck, purposely scurrying in before I can help her.

I shake my head, slightly disappointed, but I try not to show it. What's the point?

Getting in the driver's side I pull out into traffic once it's clear, driving toward the opposite side of town to the Mexican restaurant we agreed to meet at—and by we I mean, me, the guys, and Mia.

Clearing my throat, I ask, "How was your day?"

What a fucking weird ass question to ask Rush? Can't you do better?

Kira looks at me, fighting an amused smile. "It was good. I spent the day at the hospital working in the ER. That was ... interesting."

"Interesting, how?"

"This old dude came in and couldn't get his erection to go down—he took three Viagra's, because that makes total sense, right?" She shakes her head. "I spent a full five minutes hiding in an empty room laughing my ass off."

I shake my head. "The poor guy only wanted a boner, Kira. Don't laugh at a man when he's down ... or up."

She cackles. "He still had a condom on—like please sir, safe sex is great and all, but we don't need to deal with that too."

I laugh. "Sounds like an interesting day."

"It was."

"Nursing ... do you like it? Does it make you happy?"

She bites her lip, pondering my question. "I like it."

"You didn't reply enthusiastically."

"I like it." She pumps a fist in the air.

I chuckle. "Still sounds fake."

She shrugs her slender shoulders practically up to her ears. "I had other dreams once, but the reality is a steady job is better than anything else. The world will always need nurses."

"You know what else the world always needs?" I glance at her as I slow at a red light.

"I'm scared to answer," she hedges.

I grin. "Morticians." I wink. "People always die."

She gags. "Nope, I can't do that one. Gross." She shudders.

"Oh, come on. I'm sure it's a very ... quiet profession."

"Rush." She smacks my arm. "Stop."

I laugh as the light turns green. I can see the restaurant up ahead on my right.

"What would you have done if you hadn't been a nurse? What was your dream?"

She still hasn't answered as I pull into the lot and park my truck.

I unbuckle my seatbelt and turn to her. "Tell me," I plead. I'm achingly desperate to learn more about her. It's pathetic. At this point I'm ready to lap up any crumbs she dares to sprinkle on the floor.

"It's so dumb." She gives a small laugh.

"Nothing you do would ever be dumb."

Her brown eyes meet mine, looking at me through impossibly thick lashes. She's been wearing less makeup lately. I like it, she seems more vulnerable this way—like I can see *her*. Don't get me wrong, she looks great in makeup too, but it's a different side of her, one I'm not used to.

"I loved baking. I used to dream of opening my own shop. Selling cupcakes and other sweets. Like macarons—God, I love those."

I grin, pleased she's shared this tiny bit of information with me. "Baking, I'm shocked."

"It's dumb, I know. Such a little girl's dream."

I shake my head. "I think it's awesome. But why did you say *loved*."

She shrugs with a small sigh. "I don't have the money to buy the ingredients *or* the things I need to do the actual baking. Being poor sucks."

I reach over and gently clasp her chin in my hand. We look at each other, the air taut between us. I want to kiss her, desperately, but I don't think she'd want that. I don't know what made me reach out to her, what I planned to do, and it feels silly now.

Opening my mouth to say something, I don't know what, I'm interrupted by pounding on the car window at my back.

Kira jumps and I let her go.

The moment is ruined, gone as quickly as it began.

I whip around toward the window and glare.

Rolling down the window I yell, "What the fuck are you doing, Foxtail?"

"I was sent to fetch you," he explains. "Can you stop with the nicknames?"

"Never." I roll the window up.

Fox rolls his eyes and steps out of the way as I cut the engine and open the door. On the other side Kira gets out as well.

Fox leads us into the restaurant and to a booth in the corner large enough to seat all of us.

He slides in first, then Kira, with me on the end. With all six of us Kira is plastered close to my side. I'm a selfish bastard for liking it.

I pick up the menu, looking over the items. We haven't come here to eat yet, and Mexican isn't usually my favorite. Unlike Kira, who I learned early on is a taco fiend.

"Get the tacos," she hisses under her breath. "They're delicious."

"What if I don't want tacos?" I counter, flipping to another page.

"What kind of monster are you? Tacos are delicious. They are life. They are the moon, the sun, and all things right in this world. Without them, Earth could not spin on its axis."

I roll my eyes, flipping back a few pages to the front of the menu. "I doubt that."

She pushes her menu aside. "All I'm saying is, if you don't get tacos don't even *think* about taking mine."

I press a hand to my chest. "I'm wounded."

The waiter comes by and we place our drink order. Mia orders a margarita and Kira grumbles beside me.

"I want a margarita too, but I'm not allowed. You just had to knock me up, didn't you?"

"I…" My eyes find Hollis across the table, but he doesn't look surprised.

"He knows," Kira adds. "I didn't tell him on purpose it just kind of slipped out." She gives a sheepish shrug.

"You knew?" I blurt at Hollis. "Since when? How long have you known?"

Kira sighs beside me. "Before you."

"Before me?" I blurt in disbelief. "Was I the last person you told?"

She gets a sheepish look.

I sigh, slightly irritated and hurt. I want to say more to her, but this isn't the time or the place.

Instead, I pick up one of the nacho chips in a basket and dunk it into salsa. I shove it into my mouth, quieting anything I might say and regret later.

Our waiter comes back with a tray full of drinks and I'm incredibly thankful for my Corona. Kira eyes me with pursed lips, but doesn't say anything. I guess we're both holding our tongues tonight.

We place our food order and much to Kira's chagrin I ordered steak fajitas.

"Don't touch my tacos," she warns.

"Can I touch your ass instead?"

"Depends on how nice you are to me." She gives me a coy smile.

I lean over, ghosting my finger along her collarbone. "I promise to be *very* nice. The absolute *best.*" Her breath catches and I smile in satisfaction.

I sit back and she squirms in her seat.

Job well done.

"How do you two feel about being parents?" Fox asks and our gazes swing to him. "It's not like you planned this." He crunches on a chip as I glare at him. "What?" He blinks innocently. "You didn't."

Kira shrugs, tucking a piece of hair behind her ear. "It's ... scary," she admits. "But I'll do what I have to do."

"*We'll* do what *we* have to do," I growl in a low reminder.

She gives me a doubtful look. It pains me how she doesn't believe me.

"Rush has been reading baby books like crazy," Fox tells her.

I glare at him. "Don't be a fucking tattle-tale, Foxglove."

Kira looks up at me with wide, surprised eyes. "You bought baby books?" I swear she looks like she's about to cry, which makes no fucking sense.

"Um ... yeah," I answer hesitantly. "You can borrow them if you want."

"That's so sweet, Rush." She hastily brushes away a tear.

"You made her cry," I admonish Fox.

"I'm not sad," she assures me. "It's ... unexpected and cute."

I roll my eyes. "There's nothing cute about me or what I do."

Mia chokes on a laugh. "She's pregnant and hormonal. Watch." She holds up her phone. "Aren't these baby penguins cute?"

Kira takes the phone and looks at it. "Aw, they're adorable. You know what's even cuter?" We all wait for her to finish. "Baby velociraptors."

Mia takes her phone back. "I have to agree."

Hollis chuckles and drapes his arm behind Mia. "You and your dinosaurs."

"All I'm saying is, if dinosaurs ever come back you can rely on me to protect you."

"Is that so?" Cannon voices. "How?"

She rolls her eyes dramatically. "I'm going to speak dinosaur to them, obviously. I'm Owen Grady's prodigy."

"You know he's not real, right?" Fox hesitates.

She glares at him. "He's real in my heart. That's all that matters."

"You really like this chick?" I ask Hollis in mock-disbelief. "She's weird," I whisper under my breath.

He places a loud kiss on her cheek and she pretends to wipe it away.

"I like weird," he replies. "I think I'll keep her."

Our plates are slid in front of us and in seconds Kira has the foil from around her tacos unwrapped and she's digging in.

"Hungry?" I jokingly ask.

"You have no idea," she mumbles around a mouthful.

I make a mental note to pick up some groceries for her—stuff that's already made she can pop in the microwave. I don't like the idea of her being hungry, especially pregnant.

"You know," Fox begins, "it's pretty crazy that we've only been here like six months, seven, whatever, and you got a girlfriend," he points his fork at Hollis, "and you got a baby on the way." He then points at me. "What's in the water here? Should I be afraid to drink it?"

Cannon snorts. "Rush lives off alcohol and he's still going to be a dad. I think your theory is moot."

"Moot?" He repeats. "I thought it was mute? Like a mute point?"

"It's moot. *Moot point.* Google that shit," Cannon tells him, typing something on his phone.

"Who are you texting all the time lately?" I ask him.

He looks up.

"You got a girl now, too?" Fox asks in a disgruntled tone. "Am I going to be the only one left single?"

Cannon shakes his head and sighs. "You know how my sister was sending me dick pictures?"

"Yeah," we all reply.

"Well," he starts, clearing his throat. "Every time she sends one I send a picture of a pussy back."

I laugh. "That's amazing."

"Dude," Fox scolds, looking unusually angry. "That's gross. Don't send that shit to your sister in retaliation."

Cannon sighs heavily. "Cats. I send her a picture of a cat."

He turns his phone around and sure enough below a picture of a pathetic looking dick and balls is a picture of a cat. It comically looks like the cat is jumping up trying to grab the dude's balls. Too bad those claws can't perform some manscaping.

"Why do guys send these kinds of pictures to girls?" Cannon asks, shaking his head. "Is romance dead?"

"Are you Mister Romantic now?" I ask him. "These are pretty good," I add to Kira. "I won't be needing your tacos."

"The tacos are still better," she says back.

"All I'm saying is, it's gross—and if I was home, I would make sure these fuckers stopped harassing my sister."

"Such a dad," I mock him.

"Make fun of me all you want," he tells me. "I'm your favorite friend."

"I can't argue with you there," I agree, pointing at him. "Even if I want to bash your head in most of the time."

"Jeez, if he's your favorite and that's how you feel I don't want to know what you want to do to me and Hollis," Fox jokes, tearing into his quesadilla. The guy always eats like it's going to get off his plate and run away from him.

When dinner's almost over I order more tacos for Kira to-go, as promised.

The others head out, leaving the two of us alone. She starts to scoot away from me now that there's more room, but I wrap my arm around her and pull her back against me.

"Rush," she exhales, trying to get away from me again.

"Am I really so horrible you don't want to touch me?"

Her eyes won't meet mine. "That's not the reason."

"Then what is?" I question, desperate for answers. She has me twisted in knots and she doesn't seem to care.

She swallows thickly, looking away from me.

I grab her chin in my hand, rubbing my thumb against the indentation she said she hated, but I love.

"You make me want things I've never wanted before." Her voice is soft, so quiet I'm not sure I've even heard her correctly.

"Like what?" I hesitate to ask.

Her brown eyes meet mine, soft and warm like the perfect shade of hot chocolate.

"Comfort in someone's arms, safety, instead of only pleasure."

Her words hit me hard, because day by day I feel it too. The draw to her, to *only* her. How I wake up and she's my first thought, instead of work, or the gym, or going out. Everything I've done lately has revolved around her. It's not because of the baby either, I only just learned of that. But I have this need to see her happy, to make her smile. She's closed off and cold at times, but those moments of warmth she gives me, a true insight into who she *is* and not who she projects ... lately I live for those moments, and it was painful when she ignored me, because what I'd been desperate for was yanked away from me suddenly. Perhaps Cannon's right, maybe I am an addict, addicted to booze and women, but now I have a new vice, an even scarier one—one with the power to crush me. I don't want to even think of it, to give it power, but it's staring me there in the face. Her. How I feel. But I choose to ignore it. The only thing I have left anymore is the power to protect my heart.

A throat clears and I let her chin go, my fingers feeling chilled to the bone, like I've stuck my hand in the freezer and left it there.

"Here you go, sir, and your ticket." The waiter leaves me with a check for our food and the to-go bag of Kira's beloved tacos.

I add a tip and sign the check, before sliding out of the booth. I loop my finger through the bag and Kira stands. She looks at me carefully, studying me, and it's unnerving.

I'm afraid I admitted too much after her confession—not in words, but in my expression.

I loved my parents completely, with my whole heart, and it crushed me when they died. But they didn't leave me by choice. It's terrifying to think if Kira and I were more than ... whatever it is we are ... if she *chose* to walk away, she'd take with her the last of my shredded heart.

Then there's the child growing inside her. My son or daughter, whom I already feel a connection to—one that will only grow more prominent once they're here in the world.

Two opportunities to lose myself completely stand in front of me.

I should walk away and never look back—to protect myself, what's left of me anyway.

But I can't. Maybe I'm weaker, or possibly stronger than I believe, but regardless, I can't help thinking a world of hurt stands ahead of me.

TWENTY-ONE

Kira

Rush has grown unusually quiet and introspective as we walk out of the restaurant.

"Are you okay?" I ask, grabbing onto his arm to keep him from walking ahead. My to-go bag of yummy tacos dangles from his finger.

He forces a smile. "I'm great."

"Liar," I scold in a joking tone.

His lips twitch. "Don't worry about me. It's my mind, as usual, dwelling on things it shouldn't."

"I know how that is," I exhale loudly. I spend way too much time thinking of things I believed I had put to rest. "Give me your keys."

"My keys?" His brows crinkle together and I itch to reach up and smooth them out.

"Your keys," I repeat, opening and closing my hand in silent demand. "You had a drink. I'm driving."

"Hell no." He shakes his head adamantly. "You're not driving my truck. You won't even be able to reach the pedals. Besides, it was only two beers. I'm fine."

I stick out my tongue. "I'm not that short, and if you think for a second it would be okay for you to drive our child because *it was only two drinks*," I mimic, "you're sorely mistaken, buddy."

He swallows thickly, looking slightly chagrined. "Fine." He shoves his empty hand into his pocket and pulls out his keys, depositing them in my waiting hand. "Don't hurt my baby."

I roll my eyes at his dramatics. "I'm carrying your *actual* baby. Relax."

I push the button to unlock his truck and he mopes as he gets in the passenger side. I clamor into the driver's seat. Since he's practically seven-foot there's no way my short legs are reaching the pedals, so I have to adjust the seat.

He grins, suppressing a laugh as the seat slowly moves toward the wheel.

"Stop laughing at me," I admonish. "I can't help it, I'm short."

"I think it's cute," he remarks.

"Still mad at me for confiscating your keys?"

"A little," he admits, "but it's worth it to see you drive my truck. It's kind of sexy."

"Kind of?" I raise a brow as my foot finally connects with the gas pedal.

"It's incredibly fucking sexy," he relents. Lowering his voice, he leans over the center console, brushing my hair away from my shoulder. He skims his nose against my cheek. "You make me so confused," he growls. "One minute I want to run the other way from you, the next I want to fuck you senseless. You make me uncertain about *everything*. I don't like it."

My breath leaves me in a shaky gasp and I swallow thickly. I feel my pulse in my throat as my heart works overtime.

Every time I convince myself I don't feel anything for Rush, my body proves me wrong. Time and time again, my reaction to him is undeniable. It's chemical, something that exists on a level I'm not sure I'll ever understand.

The two of us are wrong for so many reasons.

But it takes finding only one right reason to change everything—I think both of us are scared to look, to give in.

"Rush—"

"Don't say anything," he begs, his eyes pleading with me. "Don't."

Before I can blink, he kisses me.

It's a slow gentle kiss, one that strokes the flames in my belly —the ones that seem to burn only for him.

He's never kissed me like this before.

Deliberately.

This isn't a moment of passion, the heat of the moment getting to us.

No, this is more, so much more.

His tongue seeks mine and my mouth opens beneath his, giving him permission.

A small sound leaves me, pleading for more.

Not only has Rush never kissed me like this, *no one* has. I feel treasured, worshipped, a gift.

My fingers wind into the collar on his coat, pulling him closer.

I wish things weren't confusing between us, but we're both complicated people and I don't think it'll go away until we both open up and let things go.

It's easier to keep things bottled up than to trust someone with your deepest secrets and fears. Once you let someone in to the darkest parts of your soul, there's the chance they'll never look at you the same. Our demons hurt us every day, but once you unleash them there's the chance they'll smother you.

His lips fall from mine, but we stay huddled close, forehead to forehead, breath to breath. In this moment, in this tiny little space of time, I allow myself for a second to believe things could be real. It's not something I've ever dreamed of—having a boyfriend, a partner, someone to love. Possibly, it's being pregnant that has me feeling so sentimental, but I know in my heart it's Rush.

Once he pulls away, the moment is gone, and I have to go back to telling myself there's not an us and can never be one.

"What are you thinking?"

I look at him and blurt, "I want ice cream." I have no idea where the words come from, but now that I've said them, I *do* want ice cream.

He cracks a small grin. "You're the driver—go get ice cream."

"I will," I say, straightening in the seat.

I buckle my seatbelt, adjust the mirrors, and put the truck in reverse.

I feign confidence, but the truth is I'm terrified of wrecking this mammoth truck. It's a fucking tank—vehicles shouldn't be allowed to be this large.

I back out slowly and when I turn to my right, Rush is fighting a grin.

"Stop laughing at me," I chide. "I'm doing my best."

"I wasn't laughing." He raises his hands innocently. "I wasn't going to comment either."

"Sure you weren't," I grumble, somehow managing to get the truck backed out without crashing into any cars or pedestrians.

I adjust the wheel and curve around the lot, braking to wait for traffic to clear enough for me to pull out.

"Getting a milkshake?" he asks, pointing across the street to Chick-Fil-A.

"Nope." I shake my head.

"What then?" he questions.

"Dairy Queen," I answer, licking my lips.

"I could go for a blizzard," he admits.

"Even after two beers, fajitas, and rice?"

He rolls his eyes as I pull out onto the main roadway.

"There is *always* room for dessert. I'd prefer licking that sweet pussy of yours, but I'm assuming it's not on the menu for tonight."

I tap the brakes in shock and someone behind me honks their horn.

"Rush," I scold. "Don't say things like that to me while I'm driving."

I place my foot back on the gas, shaking slightly from weakness in my knees. Damn him.

He chuckles. "It's not my fault you can't drive a truck." I frown at his words. "What?" he asks innocently. "I was only kidding."

"No, it's not that. I was ... my car is a piece of shit. I need to get a new car before the baby comes, and a new place—my place is way too small and dirty for a newborn. What about diapers? I'll need those too, and clothes, formula." I start to hyperventilate.

"Pull over," Rush commands.

For once, I listen to him, turning into an empty lot of an abandoned building. I put the truck in park and he grabs my face between his hands, forcing me to look at him.

"Breathe," he commands, taking a slow breath in and letting it out. "Deep breaths like that. Can you do it?"

I mimic him.

"Good girl. Keep breathing."

He breathes with me, slowly getting me to calm down and my heart to slow to a normal rate.

"We have a lot of things to consider with the baby, but we're in this together, Kira. You're not alone. You have me."

I place one of my hands over his. My fingers shake with aftershocks from my anxiety attack. It came out of nowhere, with only a few thoughts. I guess that's how most manifest. It takes one simple thing to have to your brain spiraling out of control like a rock rolling downhill.

"You're okay," he says, his blue eyes staring into mine with concern. "You're here, with me."

I nod as I feel the edges of my attack seep away. The fear is still there, in the back of my mind, but for the moment it's quiet once more.

"I'm going to take care of you and the baby," he promises. "Don't worry."

I close my eyes. "Rush," I breathe out, reluctantly opening my eyes once more. "Don't make promises you can't keep."

His face hardens. "Taking care of you and our baby is an easy promise to make."

"Be quiet for a minute," I plead, feeling the panic creep back in.

He nods and releases me.

I lean against the headrest, my face tilted toward the ceiling. I breathe deeply, the way Rush had me do, and try to drown out my thoughts and the sounds of life continuing on around us.

A few minutes later I open my eyes and look at him.

"I'm better now. Thank you."

He nods. "I'll always be there for you, Kira. No matter what."

Words. They're just words. Like so many my mother's revolving door of men said.

They'd change for her. They loved her. They'd never cheat on her.

It was all lies—I want to believe Rush, I do, but my heart refuses to give in.

Abandonment is all I know. I won't allow myself to think he'll stay.

In my experience, no one does.

But for now, I'll enjoy his company and nothing more. I can at least indulge in that.

I put the truck into drive and pull out of the empty lot.

"I don't really want ice cream anymore," I mumble.

"Get the ice cream," he commands. "Otherwise, you'll go back to your place and freak out some more. Get your mind off of it."

I crack a small smile. "How do you know me so well?"

I come to a red light, the glare of the color shining into the car and cascading over his face as I look at him.

"Because," he answers slowly, his eyes serious in the darkened cab of the truck, "I pay attention."

"You do?"

He does.

"I do." He nods. "I always have. You learn so much when you study the things around you. Have you noticed anything about me?"

"You hate pickles," I blurt. "You always pick them off your cheeseburgers."

He grins like my answer pleases him. "We get to know each other even when we're not trying."

The light changes to green and I'm forced to turn away from him.

I turn left and when I reach the next major intersection, Dairy Queen is lit up down to the left.

Pulling into the lot I tell Rush, "There's no way I'm navigating this beast through the drive-thru. We're going in."

"Whatever you say." I park the truck in the front and he

adds, "Let me help you out, please? I really need to get a step-rail on this thing. It's too high for you and you're pregnant."

"I'm not *that* pregnant."

"Yet," he adds. "It's okay to let people help you, you know. It doesn't make you any less strong."

"All this serious talk is giving me constipation," I warn him.

He throws his head back and laughs. "You're something else, Kira."

He hops out and I decide that I will let him help me out. The last thing I need to do is injure myself trying to prove a point only to prove his instead.

He swings my door open and offers his hand to me.

The lights from the Dairy Queen sign reflect off his skin, making him glow and look like some otherworldly creature.

"It's only a hand, Kira."

I smile and take his hand—but for once, I wasn't hesitating because I didn't want to hold his hand, because of what it signifies. Instead, I wanted to look at him. I don't know what I was searching for, or maybe I do and I can't admit it.

He closes the door once I'm out and my feet are planted firmly on the ground.

I lock the truck and he releases my hand, only so he can hold the door open for me.

We're not a couple. I remind myself.

The lines are blurring—they have been for a long time, and even my weeks of ignoring him did nothing to reestablish them.

We get in line behind a couple of high school students and Rush looks at the menu.

"You're going to make me get fat," he warns, rubbing his flat stomach.

I roll my eyes. "Your nose grew ten inches, Pinocchio."

"You know what grows more than ten inches?" Before I can

retort he lowers his head to my ear and whispers in a dramatic tone, "*My cock.*"

I roll my eyes. "You *would* say that."

He shrugs, straightening. "You gave me the perfect opening. It would be a tragedy for me to resist."

"Mhmm," I hum, as the kids in front of us get their ice cream and move to a table.

We step up and I immediately say, "I want a small chocolate chip cookie dough blizzard."

"And for you?" The bored looking teenage girl behind the register asks Rush, not even looking at him, but as she raises her gaze her cheeks blossom with color.

I try not to laugh, because I understand the effect he can have on people. Forget about how hot he is, his height alone has people staring.

Once, when the two of us were out I heard a woman whisper that she'd climb him like a tree. I grinned and mouthed, "I did," at her, adding on a wink.

"I'll have the New York cheesecake blizzard," he says, looking at the menu, totally unaware of the girl staring at him with her mouth wide open. She can't be more than sixteen—seventeen at the most. "A small too," he adds.

"Only you would get the one with strawberries in it," I joke.

He looks down at me, his blond hair sweeping over his forehead. "I can't help it that I like strawberries in my dessert. You wouldn't know what a fruit is if it bit you in the ass."

"Point taken. I'm buying." He opens his mouth to protest. "No, Rush," I say firmly. "You always buy, and I want to treat you for a change."

He smiles at that, and I know he's pleased by the gesture. "Okay, I can't argue with that." He sweeps his hand forward. I pull my debit card out of my phone case and hand it to the girl, who manages to swipe it and hand it back to me with the receipt, all without taking her eyes off Rush.

Finally, she finds her voice. "A-Are you R-Rush Daniels?"

"Yeah, that's me," he replies.

"Holy shit," she cries. "Can I get a selfie? An autograph? Oh my God, my friends are never going to believe this. We saw you play at Griffin's and we're obsessed with The Wild now. Your band is amazing and my God can you drum."

Rush gives a chuckle. "Sure, whatever you want."

"Thank you so much," she shrieks with much more enthusiasm than she had two minutes ago. She yanks her phone out of her pocket and holds it out. He leans over the counter into the picture with her. After she's gotten her fill of photos, he signs the slip of paper she hands him.

Another worker hands me the two Blizzards, watching in confusion as the young girl continues to fawn all over Rush.

"I'll say goodbye before I leave," he assures her with a wink. "My ice cream is melting."

It's totally not.

He joins me, placing his hand at my waist and guiding me around the corner where the girl won't be able to watch us.

He picks a table beside the large glass window that overlooks the busy street and the strip mall on the other side.

I take a seat and slide his monstrosity he calls ice cream across the table to him.

Digging my spoon into my Blizzard, I make sure to get several chunks of cookie dough.

"Mmm," I hum. "I love cookie dough."

He grins, pausing with his spoon halfway to his mouth. "I think you just like ice cream in general."

"This is true," I agree. There's no sense in arguing. "Once, when the power went out in my apartment I used it as an excuse to eat all my ice cream—you know, so it wouldn't go to waste," I explain dramatically, gesturing wildly with the spoon in my hand. "Suffice to say, the power was only out for thirty minutes. I still ate all the ice cream anyway."

He laughs, tossing his head back. He seems free right now, untroubled. Too often there are shadows in his eyes, as if there's an ever-lingering worry he can't shake off.

"You would," he says, grinning as he digs into the ice cream for another bite.

"I have a sweet tooth. It's not a crime."

He chuckles. "I never eat this much ice cream, ever—but every time I'm with you somehow I get roped into getting some."

"It's a talent," I joke. "It's my goal in life to have everyone stoop to my level. The ideal life would include ice cream for breakfast, lunch, and dinner."

"You might go into a sugar coma."

I glance to the side as a chair squeaks and a couple sits down, side by side. They're laughing and being all lovey-dovey, hand holding, kissing—it's all so much. I'm ridiculously unromantic.

Looking back at Rush I say, "At least I'd be happy while I'm eating it."

"When is your next doctor's appointment?" he asks, and I'm jolted back to reality. Laughing, joking with him, for a minute it felt like how things were before. But now there's the reality of us having a baby together.

I stare across the table at him—at his messy blond hair, deep blue eyes, slightly crooked nose and full lips, to his chiseled cheekbones and heavy brow. There's more stubble on his cheeks than usual, and... He's the father of my child. No matter what, he's always going to be in my life in some way now. Even if he walked away and never looked back, he'll always be in the child we made.

"Why are you looking at me like that?" he questions,

confused. "Is there something on my face?" He wipes the back of his hand over his mouth.

"No, sorry. I zoned out," I lie. "Um, my next appointment is at twelve weeks, so in three weeks I go again."

"I want to go with you."

"You ... why?" My brows knit together in confusion. "It's just a doctor's appointment."

He looks at me like I'm crazy. "Because, I want to see my baby. Is that so crazy to believe?"

I let out a breath, and stare down at the chunks of cookie dough and chocolate chips in my ice cream. Slowly, I raise my tired eyes to his and give him a truth, a small one, but a truth nonetheless.

"I grew up with my dad being uninvolved, and anyone my mom dated was either an asshole or a pervert. It's ... this is different for me. I didn't expect you to be involved—it's not a reflection on *you* but me. I guess ... I've learned to expect nothing, because then it doesn't hurt."

He rubs a hand over his jaw, taking in my explanation. After a moment, he says, "We can pretend all we want not to feel, that nothing can hurt us, but it's a dirty fucking lie. It hurts anyway." He looks out the window, at the traffic beyond, but I know he's not seeing it—not really.

I guess we've both admitted small truths tonight.

We finish our ice cream and he tosses both the cups in the trash. I wait by the door, watching with a small smile as he says goodbye to the cashier.

As we walk out into the cold air I pause and look up at him. "You just made her whole year."

He gets a cocky grin. "Have you seen me? I made her whole fucking life. She's always going to tell the story of the time she served Rush Daniels ice cream."

I shake my head. "I'm glad to see your ego is firmly intact."

"Always." He winks. "I can drive now."

I shake my head. "Not a chance."

He sighs in exasperation. "I had two beers like an hour ago. I'm fine."

I narrow my eyes. "Is that the kind of philosophy you'll have when our child is involved—which it already is, considering I carry this thing wherever I go?"

"I see your point," he admits defeat.

The drive back to my apartment is a short one. I park on the street a block down, since everything was full that I could pull into and I was not going to attempt to parallel park this beast.

Shutting the engine off I hold the keys out to him. He opens his palm and I drop the keys into them.

"I'll walk you back," he says as he unclicks his seatbelt.

"It's barely a block. I'll be fine," I assure him.

"Kira," he says sternly, and my lips part in surprise. "I'm walking you back."

"O-Okay," I stutter in surprise.

I wait for traffic to clear before getting out of the truck. I meet him on the sidewalk and he shortens his stride so we walk beside each other. His hands are shoved into his pockets and the collar of his dark blue peacoat is pulled up to protect against the raging wind.

We reach the stairs to my place and he follows me up.

I slide the key into the door and turn to him. I'm not sure if he expects to be invited in, or if I even want to. I'm confused when it comes to him and it's bothersome.

He looks down at me, the slightest tilt to his full lips like he knows what I'm thinking.

"Goodnight, Kira." He bends and presses a kiss to my cheek but purposely kisses nearly half of my mouth while he's at it. With a wicked grin he steps down one step. "See you."

"Bye," I breathe softly, but he's already jogging down the stairs and the sound of the wind carries my voice away.

Stepping inside, I close the door and lock it before I lean my back against it.

I don't know what to do when it comes to Rush Daniels. He leaves me baffled and twisted in knots—but I can't help thinking that's the way he wants me.

TWENTY-TWO

Rush

After fifteen minutes of driving around the hospital parking lot, a spot finally opens up. I'm running late and I'm sure Kira assumes I chickened out of her twelve-week appointment. No way in hell was I missing this, despite what she thinks of me.

I shut my truck off and jog to the entrance. I bring up her text, telling me which floor to go to and what side her doctor's office is on.

Stepping into the elevator I push the button for level four and wait impatiently as it goes up. Thankfully, it's a short ride. Stepping off the elevator I head to my right and as I round the hall, I find her doctor's office on the left.

I open the door and—

"Holy shit," I mutter.

Pregnant women are everywhere, in every stage of pregnancy.

I scan the room and find Kira in the farthest possible corner sitting in a chair against the wall, like she's desperate to melt away and escape.

Heading over to her, she still hasn't noticed me.

"Mind if I sit here," I ask jokingly, indicating the seat occupied by her bag.

"Oh, yeah, sure—sorry," she blurts quickly, grabbing her bag. Finally she looks up, her hand shooting to her heart. "Rush, it's you."

"In the flesh," I reply, dropping down into the seat beside her. The fake leather lets out a gust of air. "Well, that's unpleasant sounding."

Kira gives a small nervous laugh. "I didn't think you'd come."

"I wouldn't have missed this for anything—though it was fucking awkward as hell telling Hayes where I was going. He's pissed at you by the way for not telling him. Apparently, he thinks he's your dad too, not only Mia's."

"He's a very protective kind of man," she agrees, looking a little green as she eyes the coffee table splattered with magazines of pregnant women smiling like they're having the time of their life with drooling babies cradled in their arms.

"But yeah, I'm here." I raise my hands awkwardly, looking around the dreary office. The walls are a grayish blue that makes my head hurt and there's dark wood trim. It makes no sense. Doctor's offices should be cheery, especially one for pregnant ladies. I feel like I'm sitting in the lobby of a funeral home. "They need more parking. I couldn't find a place to park to save myself. I drove around forever."

"It gets full quickly," she agrees, rubbing her palms nervously on her ripped jeans.

"Friday is Hollis's birthday," I tell her. "We're all going out."

"We?"

"You, me, the guys, Mia," I clarify.

"Where?" she asks. "I can't handle all these birthdays. I get them all mixed up."

Cannon's birthday was the fifth of January, but we didn't do shit to celebrate. All Cannon asked was to be left alone for the day—we have no clue where he went or anything. Fucking weirdo.

"The only birthday you need to remember is August first—that's my birthday," I add, like she didn't already figure that out. "I'm going to be twenty-seven," I sigh heavily, thinking about my impending birthday. "I'm getting fucking old."

"Jeez, I can't believe I had sex with such an old man," she jokes, looking a little more at ease. "What are we doing for his birthday?"

"Can you ditch class Friday?" I ask her.

"I think so. I don't have any tests or anything."

"And your weekend is clear?"

"My schedule is clear indefinitely now," she sighs heavily, touching her hand to her stomach. I swallow thickly as I notice the tiny bump her long-sleeve shirt doesn't hide. "You still haven't answered me on what we're doing or where we're going."

"And I'm not planning on it. All I can tell you is to pack your bags." I swallow past the lump that's formed in my throat. "Can I?" I hold my hand out.

"It's too soon to feel anything, but sure."

I place my hand over her small bump. It might be too soon to feel the baby move, but I feel something—the thrum of life.

Things are changing, faster than I'm prepared for.

With my palm resting against her stomach I look into her eyes and it's like a kick to the chest.

Everything I've avoided and run from for the last eight years is slamming into me like an eighteen-wheeler.

Before panic can crash into me, her name is called and we're heading back to a room. I sit on a chair as she gets fixed on the exam table.

I want to be here, to see the baby, but that doesn't mean I don't feel slight trepidation.

The door opens and her doctor, a kind woman who looks to be in her forties, enters the room.

"Kira, how have you been?" she asks, pumping disinfectant onto her hands and rubbing it together before she sits on the stool, wheeling it closer to Kira.

"A little nauseous, but I'm not clinging to the toilet so I won't complain."

"Good, that's good. Anything else?"

"I'm hungry all the time. I crave ice cream and cheeseburgers —literally the two worst things to crave ever," she groans. "I'm going to get so fat."

Her doctor chuckles. "I'll never allow that. Gaining excessive weight won't be good for you or the baby. Make sure you're getting variety in your diet and eating as healthy as you can. I'm not saying you can't give in to your cravings from time to time, but the majority of the time choose to eat healthy. What about exercise?"

"I haven't been to the gym lately," she admits with a wince. "Between school and work I've been too tired."

"But you're still active?"

"Except when I'm at home. Then I'm a couch potato."

"That's not too bad. Your energy level should pick up soon with your second trimester. So, hang on." The doctor turns to me with a kind smile. "And you are?"

"Uh ... I'm Rush ... I'm—"

"He's the dad," Kira finishes for me with a reassuring smile sent my way.

"Oh, well it's nice to meet you, Dad." She holds her hand out for me to shake.

"Nice to meet you too, Doctor." I clear my throat awkwardly.

I normally always have my shit together, but today I feel completely unhinged. This is not a place I ever thought I'd find myself. I swore off the idea of ever being with a woman long term, of getting married and having children, now here I am with one of those things definitely happening.

"Let's get started," the doctor says. She pulls out some sort of machine and presses it to Kira's stomach.

She moves it around and then a loud steady *bump, bump, bump* fills the room.

"Is that...?"

"The heartbeat?" The doctor asks with a smile. "Yes, it is."

Kira turns her head toward me and I'm sure she can see the look of awe and wonder on my face.

"I've never heard any sound more amazing," I admit on a breath. "It's like a drum beat, but better."

Kira holds her hand out for mine. I stare at it for a moment, the offer it holds, and with a smile I wrap my hand around hers. Hers nearly disappears in my grasp and I raise it, placing a kiss on the top of her hand.

No matter what the future holds, one thing is certain, this kid is ours and we have to be strong for it—be better people.

Looking into her eyes I see the promise of the future I threw away—it's mine for the taking, if I can step up to the plate.

The problem is, I've fucked everything up for so long I don't know how I can possibly not make a mess of things.

But not trying is a failure in and of itself.

I kiss her hand again.

"That's our baby, Kira," my voice cracks.

She smiles back, tears in her eyes. "Our baby."

Friday morning I pull up outside Kira's apartment. Hayes was nice enough to give us today off from working in the studio, so we have three whole days to do whatever the fuck we want for Hollis's birthday.

Me: I'm here. I'm already hopping out of my truck when the message delivers.

I jog up the steps and knock on her door. I still don't feel right using my key, since things aren't defined between us anymore. It feels like an invasion into her space. I had free reign before, but not now.

She swings the door open and I stare at her, stunned into silence. It's not like she looks much different than she normally does, but *damn*. A pair of jeans hugs her curves and she wears a red sweater that's falling off one pale shoulder. Her dark hair hangs down and she's curled it. She's done her makeup with a matching red lip, and I itch to take her face between my hands and kiss her until that color is smeared and all over the both of us. But more than that, I understand the glow they always talk about pregnant women having. She's positively radiant and more than anything, I want to soak in her warmth.

"Are you going to stand there and stare at me?" She props her hip against the door and crosses her arms beneath her chest.

I shake my head. "Zoned out," I lie.

"You were not. You were checking me out. I'm hot stuff over here, knocked up with this pudgy belly and my boobs hurting like crazy."

"You're beautiful." I mean it, too. She's the most gorgeous girl I've ever laid eyes on.

"Stop trying to butter me up." She dismisses my words with a wave of her hand. "I'm not sleeping with you."

I grin. "I didn't ask you to—but you still might change your mind." I wink and finally step inside.

She's recently cleaned the place and everything is put away in neat and tidy order. There's not even a blanket on the couch all scrunched up from use like there normally is.

"Where are you bags?" I ask her. "I'll get them."

"My room. I assume you haven't forgotten where it is." She smiles, messing with me.

"You wish I had."

I stride down the short hall and grab the two packed bags from the bed—one too small to hold clothes, so I assume it has her makeup and shit in it.

Returning to her living area with the bags in hand I find her tugging on her coat and fluffing her hair out from under it where it got stuck.

I can't make sense of the feelings coursing through me. It's confusion and madness all rolled into one. I'm no longer lusting after her like I once did—no, I desire her on a level I never knew existed.

"I'm ready," she announces, and I nod. I head out first, carrying her bags down to the truck while she locks up.

She meets me by the truck as I'm closing the back passenger door.

"Do I get any clue what's planned for Hollis's birthday this weekend? Obviously we're going out of town."

"There's a train involved."

"That's all I get?"

"Yep." I open the door for her and sweep my arm, bowing slightly. "Hop in."

"You're so dramatic and that was a pathetic answer, you know it too."

I grin, because she's right.

Frankly, I don't even really know what the plan is for this weekend.

Climbing in the driver's seat I enter the address Hollis gave me for the train station into my navigation system.

"Oh, here, I forgot to give some of these to you." Kira pulls something out of her purse and hands it to me.

I unfold it and I can't help but smile to myself. "Thank you," I tell her, and mean it. I fold the ultrasound photos back up and place them in the compartment on the side of my door for safekeeping.

"Have you eaten breakfast?"

She shakes her head. "No, I didn't have time."

"You have to eat," I remind her. "For you and the baby."

"I know," she sighs. "I'll get better."

Once traffic is clear I pull out and instead of listening to the navigation I head to the nearest McDonald's to get her breakfast. No way in hell are we making this trip without her eating first. I at least packed snacks for the train ride, but those will be useless if she's starving to death.

"Rush, where are you going?" she asks when the navigation system starts squawking at me to make a u-turn straight into a building.

"To feed you, woman," I declare. "You have to eat, and I'm going to feed you."

"You're so dramatic. I'm fine. I'm not going to wither away from missing one meal."

If I wasn't driving I would glare her into silence.

"You're eating, it's non-negotiable."

"God, you can be so bossy."

I laugh but there's no humor in it. "And you're not?" I counter.

Kira is the bossiest woman I've ever encountered. At times it's hot as fuck, at others it's infuriating as all get out.

I pull into the McDonald's lot and get in line. "What do you want?"

She thinks it over for a moment. "A sausage biscuit. Don't judge me," she warns before I have a chance to even open my mouth. "I know sausage is horrible, but I never eat it, so I'm allowed to be bad today."

I shake my head, fighting a smile. "I was only going to say I was going to get that too."

"Oh," she says in a surprised tone. "Well, then."

I sit up, reaching to grab my wallet from my back pocket.

The line creeps forward an inch at a time, but I don't complain. I picked her up early, so we have plenty of time to get to the train station before it leaves. I'm not worried.

Finally, I'm able to place our order and I can't help but smirk when I hear her stomach rumble.

"Glad I insisted on breakfast *now?*" I ask, pulling away from the speaker.

She looks out the window.

"Your stomach is betraying you, you know?"

She still doesn't answer.

"I'm only picking on you," I say, sliding my debit card out of my wallet.

I look at her reflection in the window and I blanch.

"Are you *crying?* What did I say? What did I do? Shit, I'm sorry, Kira. I was only kidding. I didn't mean to make you cry. Fuck, I'm a horrible person."

She turns to me, wiping away her tears. "I'm sorry, my emotions become too much lately. I'm not crying because I'm sad, I swear. It's just ... you're not what I expected at all. Things between us were only supposed to be on the surface. I was never supposed to get to know you or *like* you, but I do, and Rush? I've never had anyone take care of me the way you do. I don't think you even consider it anything special, but it *is* Rush. It so is."

"Kira," her name is barely a breath on my lips. I don't know what to say, or how to react, because I'm not used to this.

"I don't talk about my life much with anyone, and I don't plan on starting now, but I want you to know things weren't good, and I didn't have a lot, and I've always had to fend for myself. You make me realize there are people out there who want to take care of others. Thank you for showing me not everyone doesn't care."

I blink at her, still at a loss for words.

A horn honks behind me and I look in the rearview mirror and then ahead, realizing the whole line ahead of me has cleared.

I roll up to the window and hand over my card. As soon as it's back in my hand I speed forward to the next window and get the bag of food, handing it to Kira.

I'm still processing what she said in my mind, figuring out how to respond to it.

She hands me my sandwich and as I make a U-turn to head toward the interstate, I finally find my words.

"Kira, when you love someone you take care of them." It isn't until the words have left my mouth that I realize what I've said. Panic rises in my chest, threatening to choke me. I haven't told anyone I love them since my parents died. It's not like I technically came out and said I love you, but I kind of did at the same time.

She doesn't say anything. I know there's no possible way she didn't hear me. I think she's trying to give me an out.

I care about Kira, I do. I cared about her before the whole she's-my-baby-mama thing. But love? I don't know about that.

I don't know much about anything.

"My life's always been lacking in that," she admits. "Love," she adds unnecessarily and I glance at her long enough to see her looking down at her tiny barely-there bump and placing her hand over it. "It makes me wonder how I can possibly love a child the way it deserves to be loved, but ... I already love this baby. So much."

I force my eyes back on the road.

My parents might be gone, but I knew love. There was never a day that I didn't know they loved me. To think that Kira didn't have that, never has, suddenly makes my panic disappear and heart fucking hurt.

She's a beautiful, brilliant, kind, funny woman who knows what she wants and isn't ashamed of it. Anyone should've been proud to call her their daughter and loved her wholly.

I wallow in what I've lost, and she wallows in what could've been.

Finishing off my biscuit I get in the lane to turn onto the interstate and stop at the light. I toss the wrapper in the bag on the floor by her feet and wipe my hands off on a napkin, dropping it in as well.

Then, I rest my arm on the console, my hand up and angled toward her.

An invitation.

I watch from the corner of my eye as she contemplates it and after a moment puts her hand in mine.

Closing my fingers around hers I squeeze tight.

If I could hold on to her forever, I think I would.

TWENTY-THREE

Kira

When Rush invited me to whatever this shindig is for Hollis's birthday weekend, I didn't think I'd be sprawled on my knees practically hugging the porcelain throne in a moving train while he holds my hair back and whispers how it's going to be okay.

"It'll be okay *after* I punch you in the nuts," I groan, my stomach rolling again.

I've never experienced motion sickness in my life—but apparently pregnancy has made me super sensitive, because the moment the train started moving it was game over.

"You don't mean that," he says and there's laughter in his voice.

I whimper and throw up some more.

He bends down beside me, rubbing my back. I want to swat

him away, but his comfort actually feels nice, and if he's going to be a part of things, he should see the nasty side as well.

"I can't believe I'm kneeling on this dirty floor," I groan, shuddering at how disgusting it is.

The funny thing is, a few months ago I wouldn't have hesitated to drop to my knees in a public restroom and give him a blowjob.

Yet, here we are now.

Oh how the mighty have fallen.

There's a knock on the door and I yell, "Go away, it's occupied."

"Two people are not allowed in the restroom," a shrill voice says outside the door.

Rush rolls his eyes and sighs, unlocking the door and sliding it open to reveal a short tiny man in a uniform.

"My girlfriend is pregnant and sick," Rush explains with slight irritation. "Nothing illicit is going on here. Take your freak-out elsewhere."

The man looks at me on the floor hugging the toilet and snaps, "Just keep it in the toilet, please."

Rush slides the door back closed and locks it. He squats down again in front of me, gently running his fingers through my hair. It's so tender, and he looks at me with such softness.

"Girlfriend, huh?"

I have the skills to ruin any sweet moment.

He chuckles softly. "What was I supposed to say? The girl I fucked regularly until I knocked her up? My baby mama? That all sounds so ... wrong, like I don't respect you."

I snort. "Rush, there's nothing *respectful* about the things we've done."

He grins widely. "That's true, but I still respected *you*. We just have the same taste in debauchery."

"And look where it has led us," I sigh, feeling the nausea hit me again. "Oh." I press a hand to my head as I feel a wave of dizziness hit me at the same time.

Rush stands and grabs some paper towels from the dispenser, dampening them in the sink.

There's another knock on the door and Rush curses under his breath. "This fucking idiot again. *What?*" he yells the last part as he slides the door open.

"Whoa." Mia holds up her hands innocently. "I found some peppermints in my purse. I thought they might help." Leaning around Rush to see me, she adds, "Do you need me?"

I shake my head. "Rush has it covered."

Surprisingly, he does. Even if having him here with me as I puke up my guts was awkward at first, it's not completely awful. Despite his partying, drinking, and sex marathon ways, Rush is the kind of person who wants to *help*. He has a good heart.

"Okay. If you need me let me know." Mia walks away and he closes the door once more.

"Here," he says, pressing the damp wad of paper towels to my forehead. "This should help."

He holds it there and I place my hand over his. It's strong and warm beneath mine.

Meeting his denim blue eyes, I ask, "Why are you helping me?"

He lets out a gruff laugh. "I thought we'd established this already, Kira. It's because I care."

"But *why* do you care?" I probe. I'm desperate to know. I need some reason, some logical explanation for this.

He shrugs like it's no big deal. "I like you. We're alike in a lot of ways. I *get* you and you get me. I was content to let us run our course, but now..."

"Now we're in this forever," I breathe out the words on a slow exhale.

I know a baby doesn't mean we have to get married or even

be a couple, but it does bond us together for the rest of our lives. There's no changing the parentage of our child. I'm the mother, and he's the father.

He cracks a grin. "If I was going to knock up anyone, I'm glad it was you."

I give a small laugh. "You're so weird."

"I wish I felt like I was good enough for you," he confesses on a whisper. He looks surprised, almost like he didn't mean to say the words out loud.

"I wish I felt like I was good enough for anyone," I admit back to him.

"We're quite the mess, aren't we?" He sits down on the floor, awkwardly since he's still holding the towel to my forehead. I haven't moved my hand off of his. I should, but I don't want to.

"I'd rather be a mess, than neat and orderly. That's nothing but an illusion, everyone is a mess when it comes right down to it." I pull his hand away from my forehead, letting the towel drop onto the floor, and I squeeze his hand tight in mine.

"What are you thinking?"

"I don't know," I answer honestly.

My thoughts are jumbled and chaotic. There's no possible way I can sort through them.

I've always known what I wanted and didn't want. Life was simple. It was predictable.

Nothing about Rush has ever been predictable, now here we are.

"Are you feeling better?"

I nod. "A little. Give me one of those peppermints."

He hands one over and I pop it in my mouth, letting the taste of it seep onto my tongue. At first I'm afraid it's going to make me sick, but as the flavor melts across my tongue I finally feel my stomach settle.

"Think you're ready to head back out?" he questions, leaning his back against the door.

I shake my head. "Give me a few more minutes to make sure it has passed."

The last thing I want to do is leave the bathroom only to projectile vomit all over the train and passengers. I would never get over the trauma of it.

Rush stands up and flushes the toilet free of my sickness and then washes his hands.

"Do you ever think we'll be brave enough to be honest with each other? About our pasts?" I blurt.

The words tumble free of me, unstoppable. As soon as they're out I wish I could bottle them back up like marbles escaping a glass. They sound too pushy, too desperate. But the fact is, I realize now with the baby there is no getting rid of Rush. He's determined to be in our child's life, I didn't believe him, but he's still here ... and if he continues to stick around it seems necessary we be honest with each other.

But I think we both have trouble with that pesky word; honesty.

Lies are easier.

If you ignore the truth for long enough, you can make yourself believe a lie.

I think we've both been doing that for a long time, lying to ourselves and believing those lies.

You know the ones.

I'm okay.

Nothing's wrong.

I'm going to make it through this.

One more day.

Everything's fine.

On and on the list goes. One lie after another, until your entire foundation is built on them.

"I don't know, Kira," he answers on a breath, shoving his fingers through his hair, pushing the blond strands away from his eyes.

"Me either. Help me up," I plead, holding out my hand.

He grabs it and helps me up. My feet bump into his boots and I fall into his chest.

His arms wrap around me and he holds me close. I'm not sure he even knows he's holding me like this.

My fingers splay against his shirt and I tilt my head back, looking up at him.

Time seems to stretch thin.

"Hi," I breathe.

He cracks a small smile. "Hi."

Still, he doesn't let me go.

Being held like this by him feels good, almost too good. I wish I wasn't this comfortable with him. It would be easier to push him away, to keep him at arm's length, if I didn't feel so safe with him.

"Let me go, Rush." My words are a barely-there whisper.

"I don't want to." His voice is as hushed as mine.

"Why?"

He lowers his head to mine, until we're nose to nose. "Because I'm pretending."

"Pretending what?" My throat locks up. With fear? Anticipation? I'm not sure.

"That I'm just a guy, a normal guy. One who's nice, the boy-next-door type. That I don't drink too much or do shit I shouldn't. I'm pretending I'm someone worthy of the good in the world. Love and a family. For a minute, just let me feel like I'm not a complete and utter screw up."

"You're not a screw up."

He smiles slightly. "That's nice of you to say, but I am. I started down a path I don't seem to know how to come back from. Drumming is the only thing that's kept me sane for so long until..."

"Until?" I prompt.

"Until you," he professes.

"Me?"

"You."

I don't know what to make of his declaration. It both scares me and exhilarates me. I should pull away from him, put distance between us, but I'm caught in his stare and I'm helpless to move.

Idly, I wonder if he can feel my heart threatening to beat out of my chest. I haven't figured out yet if the strenuous beat is caused by his proximity or his words, or even whether it's in lust or fear.

Lately, I'm nothing but a wound bundle of nerves and emotions I can't untangle.

He presses a tender kiss to my forehead and my eyes close. It's at odds to how we were. Any time we were together we couldn't keep our hands off each other. We were a tangle of limbs, barely knowing where one began and the other ended.

Now, here we are, standing calmly in one another's arms. There's no tearing at clothes, or smashing of lips. It's just us, and the tender feel of his lips lingering against my forehead.

I've run from this feeling my whole life—of safety, of comfort, because the people who were supposed to give me that only left me living in fear.

All these years, I've done well in my practice of staying away from any chance of catching *feelings*. I've been smart about it.

Now, this one man might be my complete undoing.

"We should join the others now," I say, desperation leeching into my tone, because I need space from him before I do something stupid.

Like kiss him and *mean* it.

He nods slowly, looking slightly disappointed. "Yeah, we should."

I step away from him and he opens the door. I follow him down the narrow aisle and to our seats. Our seats are together, so there's no chance of escaping him entirely, but this time he takes the window seat and I give him a grateful smile.

Watching the scenery pass by us outside the window is not going to help my sickness.

Mia sits in front of me with Hollis and she turns around in her seat to look at me.

"How are you feeling now?" she asks, her blue eyes full of worry.

"Much better. Thanks for the peppermints."

"You're welcome. I'm so sorry you got sick. It shouldn't be much longer until we're there."

"Where is *there* exactly?" I blurt.

Her brows furrow. "Rush didn't tell you?" She shoots him a look.

He makes a noise of protest and covers her mouth with his hand. "Don't say a thing, Red. I want it to be a surprise."

She rolls her eyes as his hand falls away. "You're so weird, but whatever." Looking back at me she gives an apologetic shrug. "Sorry, Kira. Guess, I'm not allowed to spill the beans."

In two seats across the aisle from us Cannon and Fox sit. Fox leans over and says, "I'll tell you."

Rush presses a hand to my chest, holding me against the seat so he can speak directly to Fox.

"I'll drop kick you so hard everyone will know what the fox says."

"An insult and a joke rolled into one. I'm impressed." Fox smirks, fighting a laugh.

"Leave him alone," Cannon warns in his tone that brooks no

room for argument. "If he wants it to be a surprise for her, let it be a fucking surprise."

"I feel like I'm being scolded by my father," Fox grumbles, crossing his arms over his chest. "He's a scary dude when he's mad."

Sometimes, hearing the guys talk about their family and lives is super weird to me. I've gotten used to the fact it's always the four of them that it seems like, well, it's only the four of them. The fact they have lives, family, and friends that exist outside of here is weird.

I glance over at Rush as he watches the trees passing by outside. With us heading north only a few are beginning to sprout buds for spring.

There's so much I don't know about him, a whole *life*, and now here we are making one with each other. I idly stroke my stomach. Yet, we don't talk about things.

I refuse to open up to him, because the minute I do it makes things real.

And real ... real feelings, real thoughts, a real acknowledgement for more ... it'll change things in a way we can't come back from.

TWENTY-FOUR

Rush

Watching the look of awe on Kira's face as she spins around, taking in all the details of Grand Central Station makes keeping our destination a secret well worth it. She takes in every tiny detail, from the floors, to the ceilings, to even the light streaming in through the windows high above.

"I've never been to New York before," she says to no one in particular, still spinning around and around. I silently worry her nausea might return if she keeps it up. "This is incredible."

"And it's only the train station," I add in amusement.

It's cute the way she's taking in everything, as if every small detail matters to her.

She cherishes everything, even if she doesn't know she's doing it. She's not superficial like so many of the girls I've been with in the past. Yeah, she knows she's gorgeous, and she likes girly things, but she's not so obsessed with herself that it's obnoxious. When we first started fucking, I knew immediately she wasn't with me because she wanted to hang on a potential rock star's arm. We shared a mutual attraction and that's all she cared about. I wasn't an accessory to her, or merely my name and the potential it holds. I was a normal guy.

I wonder if she still sees me that way. I hope so.

I want to be more than what I can give someone.

Our friends have nearly reached the doors and look back.

Hollis raises his hand, waving for us to join them.

I shake my head no. I'm not rushing Kira. If she wants to stay here all fucking day and night, I will, as long as she gets her fill of everything she wants to see. I'll even buy a tent and set it up right here amidst all the people if I have to.

Hollis cracks a small smile, and I'm afraid I know what he's thinking, but it's not whatever he has in mind.

Kira and I aren't a couple, she's made it clear she doesn't want that, and I wouldn't know the first thing about being a boyfriend.

I watch them leave and then all my attention is on Kira once more.

Looking at her is like a punch to the gut, because she's *right* there, but it feels like I can't reach out and grab her. Months ago, I wouldn't have hesitated. Everything is different now that she's pregnant. Not because I'm freaked out about it or anything, but because she's made sure to put distance between us. I won't push her for anything, I don't expect it, and I don't want her to feel obligated. For now, I'm content to stay by her side and watch from afar. I don't know how long it'll last, I haven't gone this much time without fucking someone in ... years. But right now it makes me feel sick at the thought of being with anyone else. She's all I think about, all I see, and I won't degrade her or my feelings for her by fucking someone to fill a void that only Kira can soothe.

She lowers her head and looks over at me. Her brown eyes are warm, lit with a light I rarely get to see. Normally shadows haunt those eyes of hers, but not right now. I don't think she realizes what a gift she's given me by allowing me to see her happiness.

Her dark hair hangs down past her shoulders, curled on the ends, and with her coat on to ward against the early spring chill in the city I can't see her bump, but it's there.

"Look at how beautiful this place is," she murmurs, smiling at me. "Where did everyone go?" She frowns suddenly as she looks around and realizes our friends are gone.

"They went on to the hotel."

"Oh." Her frown deepens and I want to make it go away. I want her smile back. When she aims her smile my way it's like seeing the sun for the first time, basking in the awe inspiring light and feeling the heat warm you all over. "I guess I'm being silly. I just thought this was so pretty." Her shoulders slump, like she feels pathetic for being enamored with the architecture.

I reach out and with my index finger I tip her chin up, forcing her to meet my eyes.

"You're not being silly. Not at all. Thousands of tourists flock here every year to see this place." I motion to the design around us. "I wish more people stopped to appreciate things the way you do."

A little bit of that light returns to her brown depths, but not all of it.

"How far is the hotel from here?"

"Only a block, I think."

"Lead the way then. I have no idea where we're going."

I start toward the exit, shrinking my stride so she can easily keep up.

She keeps her hands in the pockets of her long coat, and I wonder if she does it on purpose so I can't hold her hand.

I've never cared about a girl's past before, but I often find myself wondering what happened to her that makes her fearful and desperate to keep her heart closed off.

I was never supposed to love again, not after the loss I suffered, but here I am now, already in love with the child growing in her belly, and I think I'm falling for her too. Maybe I have been all along and I was too fucking stupid to notice.

Stepping outside, wind hits us and she draws her shoulders up closer to her ears. It's sprinkling lightly, but not enough to get us damp. My backpack of overnight things is strapped to my back, one of her bags on my shoulder, and the other dangling from my left hand. No fucking way was I letting her carry anything.

"It's too cold out," she complains in exasperation.

I have to agree. It's fifty degrees, but with the wind and rain it feels much colder.

"It's supposed to be in the sixties tomorrow," I tell her. "No rain or wind, just pure sunshine."

"I hope so."

The sidewalk is full of people hustling to their destination and some douchebag bumps roughly into Kira, sending her slamming into my body.

"Watch where you're fucking going, asshole!" I shout after the businessman yelling into his cellphone.

Kira giggles. It's such a carefree sound from her that I'm actually startled.

I glance down at her as we continue walking. "What?" I ask, defensively. "He should pay more attention and not run into people. You're pregnant."

"Would you like to put me in a bubble for the next five months?"

"Um ... is that an option? Because, yes." I nod enthusiastically. "Let's make this happen."

"You're ridiculous," she says in a light tone, smiling at me.

"Ridiculously worried about your safety."

She laughs, avoiding a crack in the sidewalk and stumbling into me. She quickly rights herself, making sure to put as much distance between us as she can.

"This is it," I say, pointing to the hotel across the street and we stop at the crosswalk.

"There are so many people here," she remarks. "It's worse than D.C."

"It's a whole other league," I reply. "You should come to L.A. sometime, it takes over an hour to drive eight miles. I wish I was kidding."

She gasps, the barest inhale of breath but I hear it anyway.

"Are you inviting me to L.A.?" she asks in a joking tone, but when she tilts her head back her eyes are serious.

I shrug casually, like it's no big deal to talk about a future where I'm in L.A. and she'd be visiting me. "Sure, why not?"

"Do you have a place there?"

The crosswalk changes and we start across the street.

"An apartment," I reply. "It's nothing exciting, don't go getting grand ideas. It might be even smaller than your place."

Her eyes widen. "That *is* small."

We reach the next sidewalk and there isn't far to walk to the hotel entrance. We head for the revolving doors and once we're inside the brightly lit lobby, heated with warmth, I say, "My lease is up soon. I'll have to figure out what I'm going to do." I rub my jaw, heading for the line at the front desk.

"What is there to figure out?"

I look at her significantly. "You're here, and the baby will be here. I don't know if I want to live permanently in L.A. anymore."

"Rush—"

"Don't argue with me," I beg her. "We still have time before the baby comes to talk about it and figure things out. But I don't think I can go back to L.A. and live so far away from my child."

She exhales a shaky breath. "Okay," she agrees.

"By the way," I can't stop my grin from spreading, "we're sharing a room."

"What?" she blurts loudly, causing more than a few heads to turn our way.

I shrug nonchalantly. "Rooms weren't cheap. Don't worry, I made sure to get a king size bed." I wink at her and her jaw drops open.

"You ... you ... *you*—"

"Yes?" I prompt.

"Ugh," she groans, crossing her arms over her chest. "You're impossible and I see what you're up to."

"I'm not up to anything." *But my dick can certainly get up if you want it to.*

"I'm not sleeping with you."

"You don't have much a choice unless you want to sleep on the couch."

She scoffs as we move up in line. "That's not what I meant and you know it," she mutters under her breath.

"Kira," I say in a serious tone. "I'm not expecting anything from you. I'm joking. When we booked the hotel there weren't many rooms left. Hollis and Mia are sharing, of course, us, and Fox and Cannon have to crash together."

"Oh."

"I would've gotten you your own room if I could have," I promise, and I mean it.

Do I prefer having her in the same room with me? Fuck yes. But I'm not lying. I would've made sure she had her own room if we'd planned this farther out.

"This trip was last minute, and this was the most decent hotel we could get with three rooms. I think sharing a bed with me will be better than us each having our own rooms in a rundown dump with cockroaches."

She bites her lip and nods. "It is."

The couple in front of us leaves with their room key.

"Daniels," I tell the receptionist.

She types into her computer. "Rush?"

"Yes, ma'am."

She types something else and then hands me a piece of paper with two plastic keycards.

"Thank you." I smile at her and then Kira and I head for the elevators. I itch to reach out and touch her, to at least put my hand on her waist, but I know after our drive this morning and then what I said on the train, it's been too much for her.

In a lot of ways it's too much for me too.

I never expected to feel for her what I do, but I can't make it go away. I can barely understand it.

We ride the elevator up and get off on our floor. Our room is down a hall at the very end. I slide the key into the door and push it open, letting her go in first.

I set her bags outside the bathroom door to the left, along with my backpack.

On the other side of the bathroom wall is the bedroom. The king size bed is against the wall and in one corner there's a chair, and in the other a table with a different chair.

"It's cute," Kira remarks, undoing her coat. Once it's off she drapes it over the back of the chair by the table.

The room is mostly plain, with white walls and white bedding. But the pillows are bright yellow and the wall art uses bright colors.

"It's not bad," I agree, my head swiveling. "Are you hungry? I think the others want to get dinner."

She frowns. "Is it bad I'd rather stay here and get room service? Being pregnant is making me lazy. I used to love going out, but now I just want to chill in the bed."

I chuckle. "I feel the same. I'll let them know we're staying in for the evening."

"Thank you," she says gratefully.

I dig my phone out of my pocket and shoot Hollis a text that we won't be joining them tonight.

Hollis: But it's my birthday.

Me: We've been with you almost all fucking day. Kira's tired. She's pregnant. If she wants to stay in that's what we're doing. Deal with it.

Hollis. :D

Me: Asshole.

Hollis: You like her.

Me: What does that matter?

Hollis: It doesn't. ;)

I sigh and close out of my text messages, not in the mood to deal with him.

Tossing the phone on the bed I face Kira.

"I want out of these clothes," she groans, tugging on her sweater.

"I'd be happy to help you out of them." I grin, unable to help myself.

"Rush."

"You shouldn't give me the opportunity to say these things," I warn her. "It's your own fault."

"Or maybe you're just a pig."

"Could be that too," I agree with a shrug.

I have to admit, standing in this hotel room with her is awkward as hell. Normally, any time a bed is near we're fucking. Hell, we don't even need a bed to fuck.

Things are different now, and I have to get used to it.

Quiet falls between us and she stares at me. I can't tell what she's thinking and it bothers me. I wish I could read her mind, to understand if she's as conflicted as I am.

She shakes her head, as if she's trying to free herself of her thoughts and turns to her bags. She bends down, unzipping the larger one, and a moment later pulls out a pair of cotton shorts and an old ratty t-shirt I think might have her high school's logo on it.

"I ... um ... I'm going to take a shower."

I nod. "Okay. I'll order some food."

"Thanks. I could go for a burger."

I laugh loudly. "Of course you could."

Color stains her cheeks.

"I think it's cute," I add. "Burgers are giving tacos a run for their money right now."

She gives me a small smile and passes me by. A second later the bathroom door clicks closed behind her.

I heave a sigh and push my fingers roughly through my hair. I let out a noise that could be called a growl, but I think it's more a sound of despair because she's got me wound so tight I can't see straight.

It's difficult feeling like you had something, only to have it taken from you but still be within your grasp.

Talk about conflicting emotions.

I busy myself by searching the room for the room service menu. I finally locate it and call, ordering far more food than we need, but I'm starving and I'm sure she is too. I make sure she definitely has her burger and fries. I don't have a death wish.

While she's in the bathroom I change out of my clothes and tug on a pair of sweatpants. I don't bother with a shirt. When I'm hanging around like we are tonight I don't like to wear a shirt, sue me, and if she gets a look at my six pack and decides she can't resist me, well...

The door to the bathroom squeaks open, steam billowing out.

"Hi," she says awkwardly, facing me. Seeing her not know what to do or say is kind of cute.

"Hi," I say back, taking in her scrubbed clean face. Her hair is dry, pulled up in a messy bun. She looks back at me with round wide eyes, her full lips slightly parted.

For the longest time I only ever saw her covered in makeup and dressed in skimpy dresses. She's fucking gorgeous either way, but there's something about seeing her this bare and exposed that does something to me. She didn't trust me for a long time to see her like this. It's almost like the clothes, the sultry makeup, was a mask, a façade she put on to become someone else.

Now, I'm looking at *her*. The part of herself she hides away from everyone else.

"You're beautiful," I blurt the words in a soft confession.

She ducks her head. She doesn't contradict me, and I find that fucking sexy. She knows she's drop dead gorgeous and she owns it.

She takes careful steps toward me, looking at my chest, particularly the tattoos on my chest before she lifts her chin. Her lips quirk into a playful smile. I itch to touch my fingers to her jaw, for her to stand on her tiptoes, and me to lower my head to kiss her. But I know none of that will happen and it's wrong of me to wish for it, to hope for more than she can give me.

"Are you allergic to shirts?" she asks in a joking tone, poking my chest.

I shrug casually. "I put it on and it flew right off." I crack a smile. "It seems like the answer to your question is yes."

"Lucky me." Her eyes sparkle with playfulness.

Lucky me.

My breath catches.

I'm a pathetic bastard.

I never thought a girl could bring me to my knees, to want to be around her at all times, and not only for sex. But I never could've predicted meeting Kira. She's like a hurricane, plowing into me unexpectedly and destroying my foundation. Now, I'm rebuilding but the pieces are different and I barely recognize myself.

There's a knock on the door and a call of, "Room service," which has us stepping apart like we've been caught doing something we shouldn't have.

She sits down on the bed and I go to get the food.

I return with the cart and she laughs, covering her mouth to try to hold in her giggles.

"Did you order everything on the menu?"

"Pretty much," I reply nonchalantly. *And I'd do it all over to hear you laugh like that.*

"I'm starving and I think you're tempting fate. If I overeat, you might end up holding my hair back again."

I lift up some of the covers, looking at the food. It doesn't look half bad. I've had some questionable hotel food in the past.

"I wouldn't mind," I reply to her.

I mean it, too. Taking care of her isn't a burden. It's what you do when you ... *care* about someone.

"Hand me that," she demands when I lift the lid off the burger. She looks like she might attack me like a lion attacks a gazelle if I don't get the food to her stat.

I quickly hand her the plate and then grab some packets of mayonnaise and ketchup off the cart, giving her those as well.

"This smells so good," she moans. "This baby is either going to come out loving cheeseburgers or hating them." She opens the packet of mayonnaise and squirts some on the bun. She then empties a few of the ketchup packs on her plate and dips a fry. "So yummy." Her eyes close, savoring her food.

I'm hungry too, starving actually, but suddenly watching her savor her food is far more important than eating.

She opens her eyes and takes me in, staring at her like a fool. "I thought you were hungry."

"I am," I answer.

But now I'm hungry for so much more.

I've turned into a pathetic asshole.

Shaking my head I try to clear my thoughts and stop thinking about her naked and writhing beneath me. I look at the other things I ordered and settle on a steak and cheese sandwich.

"Let's get comfy," Kira declares, sliding to the other side of the bed and up near the pillows. "Maybe we can find something to watch."

I set my plate on the bedside table and grab the water and Coke from the cart, handing her the Coke.

I flop onto the bed beside her, stretching my legs out. Grabbing the remote off the side table I give it to her. "You pick something."

She swallows her bite of food, having already dug in, and takes it, turning on the TV.

Leaning over I grab my plate off the side table and settle back down.

"Fuck no," I growl, seeing what Kira's chosen to watch. "Turn it off."

She giggles, and again that sound hits me like a kick to the gut but in a *good* way. It's at odds to the always in-control Kira who never let her emotions show who I first got to know.

"Mia told you about this, didn't she?" I seethe playfully, shaking my head as the opening credits to *Titanic* begin.

"Maybe," she draws out the word. "Did you really cry when Jack died?"

"It was *one* tear," I defend. "He shouldn't have died. She

could've scooted over and made room or he could've found something else to lay on, but oh no he had to stay with poor precious Rose in the ice cold fucking water."

She clutches her stomach, completely losing it at my mini-rant.

"It's not funny," I defend in a light tone. "Jack was the best fucking character in the whole movie. That dude knew how to *live* and then he has to go and die. You know who should've died? Rose's mother. What a bitch."

She's laid her food to the side and now rolls around in the bed, laughing hysterically.

"Am I really that amusing?"

"Yes," she chokes out through her laughter. "You're so serious about all of this."

"I'm passionate about things I care about," I defend. "Passion is an excellent quality."

She keeps laughing.

"Fine, we'll watch it," I agree. "But when I bitch through the whole movie, don't say I didn't warn you." I pop a fry in my mouth.

She slowly recovers, wiping tears from her eyes.

"This is the most I've laughed in a long time," she admits. "Thank you."

"I'd say you're welcome, but it's at my expense. So, no."

She cackles some more.

She rights herself and tries to catch her breath. She picks up her plate and starts eating like she hasn't just been rolling all over the place laughing at my expense for the past five minutes.

Whatever. I can't even be offended because it feels so fucking good to see her let loose so freely, instead of projecting her normal icy cold attitude.

Bit by bit she's letting me in, she just hasn't realized it yet.

As the movie plays, we eat mostly in silence except for me interjecting random comments here and there.

"Oh, yes, let's just arrest the best character in the movie while its evil henchman walks free. He needs to be tossed off the boat and her douchebag fiancé with him. Feed them to the sharks I say. Walk the plank. You know what would've made this better? If pirates attacked the boat. Granted, that's not historically accurate, but who cares. Give me pirates. I like pirates."

I look over, in disbelief she hasn't told me to shut up yet and I find her curled on her side, her hands tucked under her chin fast asleep. Her dark lashes touch her smooth cheeks and her lips are slightly parted. She looks peaceful, at ease. She rarely looks like that when she's awake. Her past haunts her. I wish she would share those burdens with me, but I still haven't told her mine so I can't expect her to spill her guts.

I pause the movie and grab our plates. I pile the trash on the cart and roll it outside.

I don't have a blanket to put over her, but I don't want her to get cold either so I drape my coat over top of her. I know it's not exactly comfy, but I figure it'll keep her warm until she wakes up.

I stand over her, feeling like a creeper, but I just need to look at her.

I need to *see* her while she's not looking.

Once I have my fill I lean down and press a kiss to her cheek beside her ear.

"If I could love anyone it would be you," I whisper.

I close my eyes and sigh.

As soon as the words are out, I know I've lied.

It's not that I can't love her, it's that I already do, and I'm too fucking scared to admit it to myself or her.

TWENTY-FIVE

Kira

Sitting up suddenly, I blink around the now dark room. The TV is off, no lights are on, and Rush sleeps soundly beside me beneath the covers.

I look down and find his coat spread over me like a blanket. Gingerly, I touch my fingers to the soft fabric and a small smile graces my lips.

My bun has flopped over, turning my hair into a complete rat's nest. I pull the hair tie out and run my fingers through my knotted hair.

With a sigh I lean over and look at the digital clock on Rush's side of the bed. It's barely after five. I flop back down and let out a hefty breath.

I feel bad I bowed out of whatever was planned last night, and therefore Rush stayed behind with me. Normally I'd be all about going out and living it up, but now that I'm pregnant I'd rather relax, watch movies, and stuff my face with food like we did last night.

I'm turning into such a bore.

Beside me, Rush stirs slightly and his sleepy eyes blink open slowly.

"Hey," he says around a yawn. His voice is so much deeper and raspier when he's half asleep. I'd be lying if I didn't say it turns me on. "You okay?"

"Yeah, I feel like I got all the sleep I need though," I admit. "What time did I crash?"

"Early," he answers. His nose wrinkles as he thinks. "A little after seven I think."

I snort in disbelief. "I bet you wish you had gone out with everyone. I'm not much of a party animal these days."

His face softens, his eyes widening a bit more. "I want to be with you, Kira. Wherever that is."

I sit up, drawing my legs up to my chest. I wrap my arms around them as his coat falls to a heap on the bed. "Rush..." I begin, unsure where I'm going with this.

He shakes his head. "Don't say anything to ruin it, please?" He begs brokenly. "There's nothing wrong with us spending time together. There are no expectations. Not on my part at least."

I nod, but I'm not sure I believe him. Some of the things he's been saying, the looks he's been giving me ... it says things I'm scared to believe.

Growing up, the love I witnessed was toxic.

My father was a drunk asshole who beat my mom and spent most of his time yelling. I'm not sure I have a single memory of him speaking at a normal volume. Then, my mom was attracted to nothing but assholes. Men who bruised and abused her and she was willing to let them do that. She spent her time getting high and bedding whoever she could. I was an afterthought.

Something tossed aside as carelessly as the bills she continuously let pile up.

"What are we doing today?" I ask, desperate to change the subject. It doesn't solve anything for me to dwell on things I can't change.

"I think Hollis wants to go to Liberty Island—see the Statue of Liberty."

"Really?" I'm shocked. I was expecting something different, I don't really know what, but sightseeing was not on my list of things Hollis would want to do for his birthday. I guess I have to remember my best friend has changed him. He's not the playboy he once was. "That sounds fun," I add as an afterthought because of my surprise.

Rush stifles a yawn and rolls over onto his stomach, clutching the pillow to his chest. The muscles in his back flex with the motion and I have to suppress a moan.

I'm fucking horny, okay.

I already love sex, and now my hormones are all over the place, so with Rush flashing his gorgeous body all over the place I can't be held responsible for my fantasies ... or what I might do about them.

I shake my head rapidly at my thoughts.

I can't sleep with Rush again. I need to keep distance between us. We're having a baby together and we need to be responsible adults.

"Go back to sleep," I tell him. "I'm going to run down to the lobby and see if I can get some juice and a bite to eat or something."

Before I can blink he's rolled back over and hops out of the bed. "I'll get it for you."

"Rush," I begin, saying his name slowly. "I can get it myself."

He grabs his sweatpants from the floor, tugging them back on, and over his boxer-briefs. "I'm aware you can take care of yourself and get your own shit. I don't think you're helpless, Kira, not at all. But I do think you need to learn to sit back and let others be there for you."

"But I don't need any more sleep," I defend. "I'm sure you're still sleepy."

He crosses the room to his bag and digs out a t-shirt, tugging it on. I'm kind of sad when his perfect chest disappears but at least the tattoos on his arms are still visible. He pushes his hair out of his eyes and the slim silver ring in his right ear sways.

"I'm up now," he explains. "I'll be back in a few."

He disappears around the corner and the door shuts softly behind him, and I know he purposely eased it closed instead of letting it slam shut behind him. He's incredibly considerate of others. I don't think he notices he does it.

I look around the room, not quite sure what to do with myself with him gone. I showered last night so it's not like I need to do that, and it's way too early to get dressed or bother doing my hair and makeup.

Suddenly, my bladder decides for me.

Definitely time to pee.

I pad into the bathroom and empty my bladder. Like the room it's mostly white, but the tile in the shower is bright orange. This place has a strange vibe, but I like it. It's unique and the world always needs more of that.

Rifling through my makeup bag on the counter I go ahead and put my moisturizer on my face.

Back in the room I open the curtains on the large window that overlooks the street below. Traffic is busy, shocker, and it's incredibly lit up. It's beautiful in a strange way.

The door opens and I look to my right to see Rush entering the room.

"Jesus, what is it with you getting so much food?"

He shrugs and closes the door behind him, carefully

balancing the tray in one hand. "Figured we should have options."

I shake my head. "You're crazy."

"Sanity is for pussies," he responds and I roll my eyes.

He sets the tray on the bed and drops his room key on the table.

I grab the plastic bottle of orange juice and twist the cap off before taking a sip.

"They didn't have any with pulp," he says apologetically.

I raise a brow and wipe my mouth with the back of my hand. "How could you possibly know I like pulp in my orange juice?"

"Again, I notice shit, Kira. You always have it in your fridge."

My breath catches slightly. He truly does notice everything. I think he's the first man I've ever encountered that's observant. Every guy in the past has wanted the same thing I wanted from them—a quick fuck and that's it. Besides, I think most guys are pretty clueless when it comes to this kind of thing. Not Rush.

"You really do," I mutter, staring at the bottle of orange juice like it holds all the world's answers.

I pick up an everything bagel he got and spread some cream cheese onto it.

He grabs a banana and bites into it. "I think I'm going to run down to the gym after we eat. Are you okay here or do you want to join me?"

I frown. "Honestly, the gym sounds like the last place I want to be, but I haven't been going, so I should. You heard my doctor, I need to stay active."

He nods, chewing a mouthful. "It's not like you have to go full out. Do what you can."

We sit together side by side on the bed, eating our breakfast, and I can't help but laugh to myself.

"What?" he questions. "What's so funny?"

I finish munching my bite of bagel and swallow. "I was thinking about how…" I pause, gathering my thoughts. Looking at him face to face I finish, "I've never spent so much time with a guy before. Ever."

He cracks a grin. "I've never spent this much time with a woman before. I guess we're even."

I bump my shoulder against his. "We're kind of friends, I guess."

He looks slightly hurt by my words, but I don't take them back. Friendship wasn't something I ever planned to offer him, he should be thankful I've come this far.

Finishing our breakfast in silence we get ready to head to the gym. He switches out his sweatpants for basketball shorts and I decide to go as I am since I wasn't anticipating working out. I'm lucky I packed my tennis shoes—I wanted to be prepared since Rush wouldn't tell me where we were going. I'm glad now for the surprise. Coming to New York City is something I've always wanted to do, but never had the cash for. Mia asked me to come along once when her family came during the holidays, but I couldn't get away from work.

It's a little after six when we leave the room and head to the hotel's gym.

"Well, this is anticlimactic," Rush blurts, opening the door to the gym.

I snort in disbelief. "You're right."

There are two treadmills, an elliptical, a stationary bike and a puny selection of weights.

"It'll have to do." He waits for me to go in first. I head for the bike, because I figure that takes the least amount of effort for my lazy ass.

Rush heads over to the treadmill, muttering something about warming up.

I settle on the bike and bring up my reading app on my

phone. Exercise and time to read my steamy romance novels? Yes, please.

Rush takes a moment to stretch before getting on the treadmill and you bet your ass I watch him. Just because I've told myself I can't touch, doesn't mean I can't look.

He leans over and grabs his toes and I mirror him, getting a great shot of his ass. I nearly fall off the bike in the process and a choked scream leaves my throat as I catch myself.

He straightens and I quickly look away. He chuckles and I know I've been caught. I smile confidently back at him, owning it.

He merely shakes his head and hops on the treadmill.

"Warm up, I call bullshit," I mutter when he begins to jog and then speeds up further.

I'd be flat on my face at that speed.

Forcing myself to look away from him, I focus on pedaling and turn my attention to my book. It's almost time for the hero to ravish the heroine—my favorite part. I love reading the quick historical romances where there's lots of dirty forbidden sex.

I'm so into the story I don't notice when Rush gets off the treadmill.

"He guides his velvet covered sword into her warm sex ... what the hell are you reading?"

I let out a scream and nearly break my neck when I flip toward the sound of his voice.

"Don't sneak up on me. That's rude." I swat at his shoulder as he peers over me, squinting his eyes at my lit phone screen.

"I take it sword means cock? Can I poke you with my sword, Kira?" He grins at me, his blue eyes playful and teasing.

My cheeks heat. "Don't mock me."

"You're the one reading about velvet swords."

"Well, I can't help it. Now that I'm abstaining from sex, this is all I have."

He raises his brows as he moves over to the bench with weights. He sits down so he's facing me.

"I'd be happy to help you un-abstain."

I roll my eyes. Sweat dots my skin and I don't think it's from the bike.

"I'm sure you would," I reply in a higher than normal voice. "That's the problem."

"Why?" he asks, picking up one of the weights.

I exhale heavily. "I think things are complicated enough without adding sex into the equation again."

His arm flexes as he lifts the weight and I nearly whimper. Why am I saying this to him? We need to find the nearest closet, stat. Actually, he could just fuck me here and I'd be okay with it. I'm desperate. Why did I ever think us not having sex was a good idea?

I shouldn't listen to me. I'm done. I make stupid rules for myself and then I have to suffer. I shouldn't be allowed to control my own life.

"Kira?" he prompts.

"What?"

He nods toward my chest and I gape in horror at my nipples pebbled against my tee. I grab my boobs, hiding the signs of my arousal.

"I think your body is disagreeing with you."

"Yeah, well ... it's wrong."

Why is it wrong again? I forgot.

He laughs at me, entirely amused. I know I make no sense. I'm not sure I even understand what I'm saying, but it seems like not having sex with him is the only thing I can do to protect myself.

"Keep telling yourself that." His blue eyes sparkle with laughter he does his best to keep contained.

"I will," I snap. "Now, if you'll excuse me, Lord Barnell is about to take Miss Georgina against his desk."

Laughter bursts out of him. "You should let me read that when you're done. Maybe it'll help me with my blue balls, but your mouth would be better." He winks.

How dare he wink at me like that? I'm already vulnerable enough as it is. Don't guys know a cute grin and a wink sends panties flying? Or maybe it's just me.

"Fat chance," I mutter, forcing my eyes to the screen.

I can't see the words anymore. Instead, as I pedal, my mind plays fantasies of him taking me up to the hotel room and fucking me in the shower, then against the window, after that he'll—

Get a grip, Kira Elizabeth! This is ridiculous. He's just a guy. Pleasure yourself why don't you and get over it. You have fingers for a reason.

Rush laughs to himself like he knows what I'm thinking. I'm tempted to toss my phone at him, but he'd probably keep it and start reading the book.

An hour later, and after starting another romance novel, we head back to the room.

Rush hooks his thumbs into the back of his sweaty shirt and yanks it over his head as soon as we're through the door. He turns around and faces me with a cocky grin.

"Should we..." he nods his head toward the bathroom. "... conserve water, together?"

"Nice try." I roll my eyes, but dammit if I wasn't fantasizing about the same thing earlier.

He grins rakishly. "Your loss. You can go first." He gestures to the bathroom.

"Nah, you go ahead."

"You sure?" He raises a brow.

I nod. "I need to catch my breath," I lie.

"Okay." He tosses his shirt over his shoulder where it lands in a heap on the floor. "But remember, I offered." He warns, pointing a finger at me.

I smile. "Noted."

He steps into the bathroom and closes the door behind him.

A moment later the shower starts up.

I count to sixty and when I'm sure he's not coming out any time soon, I hurry to the bed. Between the book, his sultry gazes, and his comments I'm in desperate need of release.

I kick my shorts and underwear off, lying on my back across the bed with my legs slightly bent, my fingers skim down my body finding my center. I let out a small moan, finding myself already wet and pulsing with the need for release.

Coating my fingers in my wetness I find my clit and rub it in slow circles. A small moan threatens to escape my throat and I bite down on my lip. It feels good, not as good as what I know Rush could do to me, but getting off is all that matters to me right now.

I move my fingers down to my center, slipping them inside. I bite down on my lip again as I ride my fingers.

My body is a taut live wire, waiting for a spark to ignite it.

Close.

Riding my fingers harder, I grab my breast over my shirt with my other hand.

My heart beats faster and faster.

Almost there.

I can see my orgasm shimmering on the edges of my vision. I have to get this taken care of before Rush finishes his shower. He can't catch me like this. I'll never hear the end of it.

My pussy throbs and I know I'm almost there.

I toss my head back, my eyes shutting as I cry out. My orgasm shudders through me, my whole body pulsing with the shocks.

"Fuck."

My eyes shoot open, my legs twitching with the remnants of my orgasm, and I find Rush standing beside the bed. His towel lies forgotten on the floor and I'm helpless as the small whimper leaves me at the sight of him stroking his cock.

My heart jolts, beating even more rapid than before. I'm not sure the poor organ can withstand the sight of him. He's fucking magnificent. A work of art. A feast for my eyes. A—

"Fuck, you're so hot, Kira. You have no fucking idea." His voice is a low guttural rasp as he continues to pump his hand, his eyes on the wetness between my legs.

"Rush." My voice shakes and my brain empties of all common sense. I should close my legs, tell him to stop, hide in embarrassment. *Something.*

But I can only stare back at him.

I want to sit up, to move his hand out of the way and replace it with mine. I want to drop to my knees and wrap my mouth around him. But I'm frozen, my eyes locked on him, his movements, his expression, the pleasure evident on his face.

More wetness floods my pussy and I let out a helpless cry.

I start stroking my center again as he watches and he growls low in his throat. His blue eyes are the deep stormy blue-gray color of the ocean as he watches me.

Me.

I'm doing this to him.

He's getting off on *me*.

On my body.

On what *I* do to him.

My fingers slip easily inside my body and I bring them back out, rubbing my clit with their slickness.

"Please," he begs brokenly. "Please, let me touch you. Please, let me get you off. That's all I want. To pleasure you. I won't fuck you, not yet. I promise."

"Rush."

"Please, Kira. All I want is for you to feel fucking good."

I nod once and he lets go of his cock, dropping to his knees in front of me. He spreads my legs further and I cry out when his tongue licks in one swipe from the bottom of my pussy all the way to my clit, which he sucks into his mouth, swirling his tongue.

My fingers delve into his hair, tugging harshly on the blond strands as my hips writhe against him. If I'm hurting him, he doesn't ask me to stop. He tongue fucks my pussy, worshipping my body in a way I didn't know was possible.

His name becomes a prayer, a fucking plea from my lips.

"Rush. Oh my God, Rush. Please. Yes."

He pushes down on my hips to keep me from moving. I bring my closed fist to my mouth and bite my knuckles, quieting my desperate noises. Whoever is next door is probably getting an earful anyway. I'm not fucking sorry for it.

I didn't expect this to happen, didn't think I wanted it to, but now I'm glad he caught me.

He slides two fingers into my pussy, hooking them slightly—that, combined with his delectable mouth, sends me over the edge.

My vision blurs, stars exploding across my closed lids. I don't know where I end and he begins.

We've become one.

We are one.

"Thank you," I whisper brokenly, slowly blinking open my eyes, but he's already gone and I can't help wondering if he was nothing but a figment of my imagination.

TWENTY-SIX

Rush

Holy fucking hell, I can't get the image of Kira lying on the bed pleasuring herself out of my head. It's the hottest fucking thing I've ever seen. When I walked out of the bathroom after my shower to grab my clothes the last thing I ever expected to find was Kira rubbing her sweet pussy.

I was instantly hard, and I had to have a taste. The fact she let me is a fucking miracle. But after I made her orgasm I knew I had to get away from her and finish myself in the bathroom before I did something stupid. I wanted to fuck her senseless and the last thing I wanted was for her to say yes during the high of her orgasm and then regret it later.

So I jacked off in the bathroom after leaving her, cumming harder than I ever have from my hand alone.

Now, trapped in this fucking Uber with six other people,

seven if you include the driver, I'm trying to stop thinking about it. Even now I can feel myself getting hard again, and I can't exactly take matters into my own hands at the moment. Normally, I wouldn't give a shit, but I'm trying to have this thing called dignity.

Besides, once again I'm stuffed in the third row with my knees practically up to my ears. Why I get subjected to this tiny ass seat is beyond me. I'm the tallest, I should have priority seating. The only thing that keeps me from griping is the fact Kira is beside me.

She hasn't said a word about what happened in the hotel room.

It has me feeling lost. Does she want to forget it ever happened? I'm not sure I can. I don't want to.

Beside me, her legs point toward me, so at least she's not trying to get as far from me as possible. But she does look steadfastly out the window. I watch her reflection, and maybe it's my imagination but I think her eyes look sad.

I don't know who I am anymore, who I've become, because it makes me feel fucking awful if she's sad because of me.

"You're quiet."

"Huh?" I glance at Hollis, who's turned around in the seat in front of me.

"I said you're quiet. Normally you're running your mouth non-stop."

"Just tired." It seems like a plausible explanation, but he looks at me doubtfully. There's no way I'm opening my mouth and telling the entire car what's on my mind. Kira would beat the shit out of me.

"You sure?" he asks, and he turns slightly looking at Kira before back at me.

"Everything is fine," I assure him.

"Okay," he replies, but the one word is full of doubt.

He turns back around and faces the front of the car.

I feel like we've already been in the SUV for thirty minutes, we probably have, and who knows how much longer it'll be. I'm not sure I can survive being shut up in here beside Kira with no fucking idea what she's thinking or feeling.

I need a drink.

I scrub a hand over my face.

Maybe Cannon's right—maybe I do have issues with alcohol. When things get tough or confusing, my first thought is usually of getting a drink because I know it'll make me feel better, mellow me out.

Ten more minutes of driving through stop and go traffic has me ready to pull my hair out.

"How much longer?" I whine. "My legs are asleep."

"Don't be a baby." Fox turns around and grins at me.

I lean over and smack the back of his head. My knee touches Kira's in the process and she jumps slightly.

"Easy for you to say, Swiper, you have more leg room."

"Not much," he responds.

It's true they don't have much more, but they *do* have more.

"My dick needs to breathe. Crush is being suffocated."

"Crush?" Kira's head whips toward me, her lips twitch as she fights a smile. "Who or *what* is Crush?"

"My cock, of course."

"Rush," Cannon scolds from up front beside the driver.

"Yes, Dad?" I call back.

He sighs heavily—the world-weary sigh of a true parent whose patience is being tested.

"Stop talking about your dick," he begs.

"But it's such a magnificent thing of beauty," I defend. "Epic poems have been written in his honor." Kira cackles beside me. "What?" I turn toward her. "Do you disagree?"

She wipes a tear of laughter from the corner of her eye. "I just think it's hilarious you think your *penis* is so beautiful it's worthy of poetry. I don't understand why guys think their penis is a gift to the world. It looks like a dead naked mole rat. You know, like that little critter from *Kim Possible.*"

My mouth falls open. "Did you just say my dick looks like a dead *rat?*"

Mia begins laughing from beside Hollis, leaning her head against his shoulder as she absolutely loses it.

"That's exactly what I said."

I pause, not sure what to say next. Finally, I blurt, "Well, is it at least a *large* dead rat?"

"Sure," she pats my knee, "it's a *large* dead rat."

"I feel like you're being condescending."

Her lips quirk. "Am I?"

"Most definitely." I nod.

Up front the Uber driver turns up the volume on the radio, I guess he's irritated by our conversation. Lucky for him, we all grow quiet because it's our song playing on the radio.

Even though we've all heard it many times, every time it comes on we pause, soaking it in.

That's us, our hard work, our blood, sweat, and tears poured into endless hours to get this final product.

The driver hums along, tapping his fingers against the steering wheel.

He doesn't even know it's our song.

"Good song, yes?" he asks Cannon, who sits beside him in the passenger seat.

"Yes," Cannon replies, "it's a good song."

He doesn't tell the man it's our song, that we're a band.

I used to think making it big was about bragging rights, but really it's about having your voice heard, having your music and passion impact someone else.

Bragging about it diminishes the effect it has on people.

When our song ends, we don't start talking again. I think we all need a moment to appreciate what this life has brought us so far, and all that is yet to come.

"God, it's fucking windy," I complain, pulling my beanie out of my coat pocket and yanking it down to cover my ears.

Kira draws the hood of her jacket up over her head.

It's a nice day—bright, sunny, but on Liberty Island it's windy enough that a small kid walking in front of us with his parents falls to the ground because of it.

The kid begins to cry and the father stops, picking up his son to console him.

Looking down at Kira, I think of the child growing inside her.

A father, I'm going to be a father.

I'm going to have a son or daughter to pick up when they fall down.

The problem is, I can barely pick myself up.

I want to be a good dad, I want my kid to look up to me and love me, but...

"You know," Kira begins, interrupting my thoughts as she looks up at the Statue of Liberty, her head tilted to the side as she inspects it, "I thought it would be bigger."

I join her in looking and have to agree. "It's plenty big, but I thought it would be bigger too. I guess in our minds it was larger than life."

"It's amazing being here. I never thought a girl like me would get the chance to see something like this." She wraps her arms around herself, warding against the chill of the wind.

"What do you mean, a girl like you?"

She shrugs, not looking at me. "A small-town girl from the wrong family and the wrong side of the tracks."

"But I still don't understand why you'd think that?" My brows knit in confusion.

She sighs heavily, the sound carried away by the wind. "Because, I'm the type of girl who usually gets knocked up by some equally small town boy who invariably leaves and I'm left stuck on welfare raising a child by myself." She presses a hand to her stomach. "Things might not have happened exactly like that, but ... they still happened."

I don't know what to say. I'm torn between confusion, sadness, and anger.

"I hate you think that about yourself," I whisper, my words laced with pain and a twinge of irritation.

She looks up at me with a sad expression. "What I grew up with taught me to expect such things. I didn't grow up believing in love. It wasn't until I met Mia, and saw her parents, that I finally saw proof it exists. But I still think it's a rare thing for people to love like that."

"My parents did," I whisper, shoving my hands in my pockets to protect from the cold. Talking about them feels like small knives digging into my throat. Thinking about them sucks, speaking about it is even worse. I gaze straight ahead, my jaw tight.

Bringing them up hurts like a physical punch to the gut.

"Did?" she voices.

I feel my whole body seize up as my emotions threaten to choke me—emotions I've dammed back for eight long years.

"Rush?" she voices.

I walk away from her. Getting away becomes the only thought in my mind. I keep walking until I find an area mostly free of people. Spotting a bench, I sit down, stretching my legs out in front of me. I stare at my brown boots like they hold all the answers to the world, and have the ability to wipe my feelings from me.

I lean my head back. Above me the sky is a clear blue, completely cloudless. It looks like a canvas, smeared with the perfect hue of blue.

Resting my elbows on my knees I bury my head in my hands.

Why do I continue to do this to myself? To painfully shutter my emotions back?

I'm smothering myself, slowly but effectively, cutting off all oxygen to my blood stream. It's a coping mechanism, I know. My way of pretending they're not really gone. If I don't talk about them, don't think about them, I can delude myself into believing they're still alive.

But they're not.

They're dead—and I'm left behind with my life I've done nothing but make a mess of. I can't help feeling like they'd be ashamed. They didn't raise me to be like this. To use women the way I have. To drink endlessly and party like there's no end to the day.

Every day I tarnish their legacy a little more.

Growing up, I was a good kid. Basketball was my focus, with drumming in my free time. All my other time was spent on schoolwork, time with my friends, and my parents. I had a few girlfriends, all whom I treated with respect. I even went to prom with one. Back then, I was a lot like Cannon. We were really fucking close, not that we still aren't, but it changed when my parents died.

Suddenly, I wanted to become the opposite of everything I'd always been. The opposite of *him*.

Things are changing again, more and more of my old self is appearing every day and I don't know how to handle it. I'm scared to look in the mirror and see that version of myself again —the one I was sure died in that car with them.

My eyes fill with tears.

"I can't do this," I whisper to myself, my voice choked.

"Can't do what, hot stuff?"

I whip my head around in surprise and find the tiniest old woman I've ever seen on the bench beside me. I swore it was empty when I sat down, but I know no one has come since I've been here.

"Nothing," I reply.

She clucks her tongue. Her wispy gray hair is held back with a scarf around her head. Her wrinkled face is kind, her brown eyes warm and intelligent.

"Don't lie to me, sonny. Mona knows there's much more to this than nothing." She waves a thin hand at me, her skin pale and covered in age spots.

"I can't do *this*. Life," I add. "I can't accept my parents are gone. I can't be the man I was before when they were alive, because it hurts too much. It hurts to know *I'm* alive, and they're not. I can't be happy, because if I'm happy then I might forget them. I'm the only one left to remember. If I forget ... they won't exist anymore."

She stares at me for a moment and then reaches over and pats my hand. Her skin is soft and smooth over mine.

"They'll always exist, boy. Right there." She lifts her shaky hand and presses it to my heart, over top of my coat. "Your misery is your anchor. It weighs you down and it's suffocating you. Take a breath, my dear. It's not so bad up here." She smiles kindly at me. "It's an insult to the dead for the ones they love to stay stagnant. The greatest gift to the ones who are gone is for life to go on. Live it, boy. Live it for them. Live it for you. Love and be loved. Experience joy and bring joy to the world. And when sorrow enters your life again, in whatever form, remember nothing is good forever. If we were always happy we'd never learn anything. It is through our suffering that we earn the strength to seek happiness in even the smallest of things."

I stare straight ahead, out at the water and city skyline beyond it.

"Thank you, Mona. This has been ... insightful."

When I look back, she's gone.

TWENTY-SEVEN

Kira

I hook my arm through Mia's, and we laugh, spinning in circles, as we take in Time's Square lit up at night.

We come to a stop, swaying slightly.

"This is more incredible than pictures," I yell in awe, over the sound of traffic and hundreds of people strolling the streets. "Look at all the colors."

Mia giggles. "If you weren't pregnant, I'd swear you were drunk."

Up ahead, all four guys stand looking up at the colorful TV screens plastering every inch it seems. Rush hasn't spoken to me since he walked away during our trip to Liberty Island. He hasn't been cold, exactly, but he's withdrawn into himself. His eyes are the cloudy blue color of a murky pond and the normal playful smile he wears as a mask is long gone.

I guess he revealed too much to me, and now he doesn't know what to do—how to get that tether of information back.

From what he said, how he reacted, it's easy for me to deduce his parents passed away. I might not know when, or how, but I do know he's haunted by it.

I've always known we both had our demons, but I'm finally getting a glimpse at his.

"I'm so glad you came this weekend," Mia says, giving my arm a small squeeze. "It wouldn't have been the same without you."

I roll my eyes. "Please, you would've been fine. I'm a bore now. I didn't even want to go out last night."

She gives a small laugh and raises her shoulders in a shrug. "If I'd spent practically the entire train ride throwing up, I wouldn't have felt like going out either."

"I guess that's true," I exhale, watching as the lights—reds, blues, purples—an entire rainbow of hues, ignites across her face. "It's weird how so much has changed."

"You're having a baby," she states simply. "That's bound to change anyone's life."

As much as I'm aware this baby is coming, I don't think I've begun to truly comprehend how different my life will be from now on. I'll no longer be living for only myself. I'll have this child, *my* child, whom I put first. Their needs will be more important than mine.

"Come on guys," Hollis calls out to the both of us. "We need a group picture."

Mia tugs me over to the guys, and Fox—

"Is that a selfie stick?" I blurt, absolutely appalled.

"Don't diss it. It's great," he defends.

He holds it out and the six of us scoot around until we're all in the picture.

"Smile," Fox tells us, holding his fingers up in a peace sign near his chest.

I smile, but at the last second I turn and look at Rush standing behind me. His head drops and our eyes connect.

One second, that's all our gazes hold for, but in that small blip of time I see more, feel more, than I ever knew existed in the world.

I've spent my entire life running from my feelings, from my fears, and now they're crashing into me all at once and I don't know what to do—how to handle it.

Knowing me, it won't end well.

IT'S LATE WHEN WE GET BACK TO THE HOTEL ROOM. RUSH HASN'T spoken one word to me yet. His silence hurts me more than I care to admit. I feel like I've done something wrong, but I know it's nothing personal.

His silence is for himself, not me.

I change into my pajamas and climb into bed. A few minutes later he joins me, his breath smelling like peppermint from his toothpaste.

I'm surprised when he rolls to face me, instead of away.

With my heart pounding a vicious beat I reach out with shaky fingers to touch his stubbled jaw. He places his hand over mine, his eyes still sad, in a place far away from me. A place I'm worried he might lose himself to.

"We're a mess, aren't we?" I whisper into the dark hotel room, horns blaring outside from cabs and other vehicles.

He moves my hand to his mouth, placing a kiss on my palm before curling our fingers together and holding our joined hands close to his chest.

"I'm so confused, Kira." The confession scratches at his

throat, his voice raw and desperate. "I can't make sense of anything anymore."

I swallow thickly, the sound of it audible in the space between us. "Does it have to make sense?"

"Yes," he whispers. "I want it to at least. I'm tired of this purgatory. Of being afraid of my own feelings."

"Why are you afraid?"

"Because," he swallows, and I swear his eyes begin to fill with tears. "Because I think I love you. No," he closes his eyes, "I *know* I love you, Kira. I swore I would never fall in love, have a family, but I never could've predicted you."

"You ... you *love* me? But *why?*" Panic threatens to choke me and I try to pull my hand from his but he won't let go.

"Because I do," he sighs, the sound weighted and heavy in the room. "It's ... I've been struggling to accept it, but I do. I love you."

He stares at me, waiting for a response, I'm sure hoping for a declaration of love to come from my lips for him.

But I have nothing.

"You can't love me," I tell him, fighting tears.

"Why?" He sits up in the bed, looking down at me. Anger and hurt cloud his handsome features.

"Because I can never love you."

TWENTY-EIGHT

Rush

Because I can never love you.

Her words are an endless echo inside my skull. They rattle around like the little silver ball inside a pinball machine.

Because.

Ping!

I.

Ping!

Can.

Ping!

Never.

Ping!

Love.

Ping!

You.

Not that she could never love *anyone*, but that she couldn't love *me*. Am I that horrible of a person?

After her admission last night, I packed up my shit, beat down the door to Cannon and Fox's room, and crashed on their floor.

Now, on the train ride home I made Fox switch seats with me so I didn't have to be beside her.

I never wanted to fall in love, to have a family I could lose like I did my parents, but my mind couldn't control my heart, and now I've fallen in love with the one person who can't, or won't love me back. *Doesn't* love me back.

She feels nothing for me, which is a sad fact I have to keep reminding myself.

She does feel something for you, my treacherous mind whispers to me.

I can't believe it, though. Hope will only cause me more pain in the future, and I'm going to do everything I can to avoid it.

I'll numb myself from it.

I'm done with her, I have to be for my own sanity. I don't know what that means for our kid, I still want to be involved, but I can't fucking deal with her. If that means I'll have to take her to court for rights to my child, I will. I don't want to fight her, but if it comes to it I will. She won't walk all over me anymore.

When the train finally rolls into our stop, I grab my shit, and haul ass off of it.

"Rush!" Kira calls after me, her feet pounding against the concrete behind me. "Slow down!"

"No!" I yell back.

Done with her shit. So done.

Her feet stop. "Are you just going to leave me here?"

I don't turn around. I can't. If I do, I'll give in, and I refuse to let her have power over me any longer.

My heart was beginning to open up, the more time we spent

together the fuller it became. Now, it's closed off again, even more tightly sealed than the last time.

"Get a ride with Hollis and Mia," I tell her in a gruff tone. "You're not my problem anymore."

"Rush," she pleads brokenly.

But I start walking again. She made her bed, now she has to deal with the consequences.

RAGE CLOUDS MY VISION. I HAVEN'T FELT THIS ANGRY SINCE THE day I had to lay both my parents to rest.

With a sound that's more animal than human I shove all the baby books off the nightstand beside my hotel bed where they go crashing to the floor.

It's not enough.

I'm not sure anything will *ever* be enough.

I'm sure as hell not enough for anyone.

Grabbing the lamp off the nightstand, the cord yanks from the wall and I throw it against the opposite wall where it shatters.

"What the fuck is going on?" Cannon roars standing in the doorway, he ducks as I throw my computer next. It hits the floor near his feet, cracking.

"Jesus Christ," Fox blurts, joining Cannon in watching my meltdown.

My hands shake as my emotions threaten to overwhelm me like a massive wave crashing to shore. I have no control. I've become something I don't recognize.

I tear the covers off the bed, rolling them into a ball, which I throw too.

The whole room already looks like a hurricane has blown through.

I want to destroy it, to rattle it until it somehow closely resembles how I feel on the inside.

"Rush, man, what the fuck is going on?"

I can't answer them. I'm beyond words. I exist entirely in another form now.

When there's nothing left for me to throw, I drop to my knees and I scream. It's the painful noise of years of pent up anger leaching out of me. Everything I've bottled up comes roaring from the depths of my soul. I feel the veins in my neck pop out and tears leak from my eyes.

A hand touches my shoulder and I flinch.

Cannon moves in front of me and crouches down until we're eye to eye. I feel Fox's presence steady at my back.

Cannon stares at me for a moment, waiting for my breathing to slow. His eerie light green eyes seem to anchor me somehow —to remind me I'm *Rush*, and I'm in Virginia, and I'm still human.

"I'm sorry," he says simply, and hugs me. The tight, powerful hug of one brother to another.

Slowly, I hug him back. My tears fall and I can't stop them. My whole face is damp with them. I haven't broken down like this, not once, since they died.

The rage, I let myself feel that.

At least the anger was something familiar I knew how to channel.

But grief? I'd never experienced it before, so I buried it deep inside myself along with the man I was before. I thought if I buried everything far down enough it could never surface. I was fucking wrong. It's been biding its time, waiting for me to crack.

All it took was falling in love with a girl who will never love me for it all to come crashing to the surface, ready to drown me.

"I'm sorry," Cannon says again. "I'm so fucking sorry, man."

"I told her I loved her," I choke on the confession. "I love her, and she doesn't love me."

He squeezes my shoulder and pulls back slightly in order to look at me.

"I'm not supposed to be loved, am I?" I ask brokenly.

Lost, I'm fucking lost.

He shakes my shoulders slightly. "We love you, man. We're your best fucking friends. We grew up together. We're practically brothers. No matter what, you have the three of us."

"It hurts," I tell him, touching my heart. "I feel like my heart is bleeding."

Cannon gets a sad look, and Fox moves in front of me too.

"I'm so fucking angry," I continue. "I'm angry my parents are gone when they shouldn't be. I'm angry at Kira. I'm angry at myself. All I have is this anger left inside me. It's all I feel right now."

"Don't let it consume you," Fox begs, looking at me sadly. "Be stronger than it."

I shake my head. "I'm weak. I'm a weak, pathetic excuse for a human being."

Slowly, I stand up, wiping my face free of emotions like cleaning a blackboard in school.

"Don't say that," Cannon growls, standing up too.

With my mask firmly in place once more I say, "There was a reason I protected myself with booze, partying, and women. It was safe not having anything to care about, wasting my life away."

"Rush—" Cannon begins.

"It's time for me to realize that's all my life is, all it can be."

I turn on my heel, heading out of the room and for the door.

"Rush, stop," Fox pleads sternly from somewhere behind me.

"Don't do this," Cannon growls, his hand closing on my arm

as he flips me around to face him. "Don't throw everything away."

I stare back at him as I safely lock away the small bit of humanity I had slowly been gaining back these last few months.

"It's too late. I already have."

TWENTY-NINE

Kira

"I made the right decision," I tell myself, lying in bed.

It's been a week since I've seen Rush.

He hasn't texted or called me. I haven't reached out either.

"It was for the best ... for both of us."

I roll over, curling my hands under my head.

I wish I believed my words. If I could, then maybe I wouldn't feel sick all the time—the kind of sickness I know isn't caused by the baby.

Rush telling me he loves me is the scariest thing I've ever heard. I wasn't prepared for it, not at all. I couldn't lie and tell him I loved him back, I can't go down that path with him or anyone. I learned a long time ago the only person I can rely on is myself. To hand my heart over willingly to someone is asking for them to toss it to the ground and stomp all over it.

I endured nothing but heartache for years, never being loved by the family who should've loved me unconditionally—so why would I freely start down that path with someone?

I should've been honest with him, opened up and explained where I was coming from, but he stormed away too quickly. I couldn't do or say anything.

One minute he was there admitting he loved me and then ... then he was grabbing his shit and leaving.

It's further proof to me how people say one thing, but when the going gets tough they haul ass as far from you as they can.

If he really loved me he couldn't have possibly left, right? Or tried to abandon me at the train station?

I'm pregnant with his child and he was so mad at me he was willing to leave me there.

That's not love.

I roll back over onto my back, covering my face with the crook of my elbow.

I need to go to sleep. I have class tomorrow and real responsibilities that don't include obsessing over Rush and his stupid actions.

Sleep, however, has become a mockery—something I can feel fluttering at the edges of my consciousness but it never fully takes control because my guilty conscience keeps it at bay.

I hurt Rush and I feel sorry for it, I do. The last thing I wanted to do was hurt him, but I didn't give him what he wanted and now here we are.

Throwing the covers back I stuff my feet into a pair of fuzzy boots, yank on a sweatshirt, and head down to my car.

A few minutes later I park outside Mia's building.

It's a risk coming here, she might be going at it like rabbits with Hollis, but I need my best friend. I need a shoulder to cry on.

It's not late, barely after nine, so I doubt they've gone to bed. Otherwise I would've stayed home suffering alone in my misery.

I get out of my car, closing the door behind me and I climb the three steps to her building's door. Stepping inside I take a breath, pausing while I decide if I'm really in a good state of mind to be around people, but in the end, I realize I've been at home suffering in silence for too long.

I trudge up the steps and knock on her door.

I should've called or sent a text, before I showed up, but I wasn't thinking straight. I only wanted my best friend and common sense didn't matter.

The door opens and Hollis stands there in a pair of low hanging pajama pants and no shirt. His brown wavy hair flops over his forehead and he grins at me.

"Kira, to what do we owe this pleasure?"

I roll my eyes and push past him. "I need to see my best friend."

He chuckles and closes the door. "I figured that much. She's in the bath."

I wave a hand. "I've seen her naked before so I don't give a shit. I need to talk to her."

His grin widens further. "You have, huh? How naked are we talking? Like completely naked? Were there pillow fights involved? Fingering? I need details."

I roll my eyes again and I'm surprised they don't fall right out of my head.

"Only when we were changing clothes. Don't pitch a tent. Make yourself useful and go get snacks. We're going to need white cheddar popcorn, crackers with that gross looking squirt cheese, and double dunker ice cream—two gallons to be safe."

"That bad?" He raises a brow in surprise.

I sigh, biting my lip. Hollis is one of Rush's best friends and I don't know how much he knows or what I should reveal.

"How's Rush been?" I ask. It's an answer in and of itself.

He looks away, exhaling a heavy breath. Slowly bringing his gaze back to mine, he admits, "Not good."

I bite my lip, dropping my eyes to the old weathered floor. "That's what I figured."

"He told you he loves you."

I bring my eyes back up but I don't find any judgment or anger in his.

"He did."

"Rush has been through a lot," he explains slowly and softly. "A lot of shit he's never dealt with. Loving you isn't something he could plan for. It was unexpected. I think it was healing him in a lot of ways, but..."

"But?" I prompt.

"You rejected him." I open my mouth to argue or explain, I don't know, but he raises his hand to silence me. "Rush doesn't do well with rejection, especially when it comes to things he feels passionately about. He might not know it yet, but he's not going to truly be capable of loving you or anyone until he deals with his shit. He has to stop burying it like it doesn't exist. Nothing we do or say does any good. He's going to have to hit rock bottom before he decides to fix himself. I'm afraid he's almost reached that point." He runs his fingers through his hair and I notice the lines of worry around his eyes.

This hasn't been easy for me so I know it can't be easy for the guys to watch their friend crash and burn.

"He has things to work through," I agree. "Now, it's not just me I have to worry about." I place a hand over my bump. The tiny little life growing inside me is dependent on me to keep it safe and I'll do it, no matter the cost.

Hollis gives a sad smile. "Don't give up on him. Maybe you truly don't love him, and perhaps you never will, but he *is* a good guy and he'll be a great dad. He just ... needs to grow up." He shrugs as if the simple raise of his shoulders explains the situation.

"I can't wait forever," I whisper.

Hollis looks at me sadly. "I hope you don't have to." Hooking his thumb over his shoulder toward the bedroom he says, "You go crash Mia's bath and I'll run to the store and get your snacks."

"Thank you," I tell him.

"You're welcome," he replies with a small smile.

"No, I mean it. Thank you. Thank you for taking care of my best friend, for loving her like she deserves, and thank you for being a good friend to Rush."

He nods and follows me into the room. He grabs a shirt and puts it on, grabbing a jacket and then his keys off the dresser.

"I'll be back," he calls to Mia.

"Okay," she responds, having heard our entire conversation already. Her place is small, so it's not like you can have a conversation in secret.

He heads out and I push the bathroom door open.

I laugh when I find her practically hidden by all the bubbles.

"Enjoying your bath?" I ask her, sitting down on the closed toilet lid.

"Yeah, I was *trying* to relax before some crazy person showed up demanding to see me."

I smile and it's a real one. Already, with only a few words, she's managed to make me feel better. "When you need your bestie, you need them now. I'm sure you heard everything."

"Of course." She lifts her foot, turning the nozzle on the faucet to add more hot water.

A weary sigh gusts out of my lips.

"Did you lie to him?" she asks me, not holding back.

"I don't know," I answer honestly. "I'm ... confused. You know me, I've never had a serious relationship before, let alone a boyfriend. Things between Rush and I changed. I didn't want them to, it sorta happened." I stare at a tile on the wall, it's easier than looking at her. "Then I got pregnant, and here we are." I lift my hands and let them fall to my lap in defeat. "He said he loves me, but Mia," I sniffle, my eyes flooding with tears, "how can I believe him? My parents told me they loved me, but they didn't. Everything they did always proved the opposite. Their love was toxic. It smothered me and distorted my perception. How can I ever trust that someone's love is genuine? The kind of love you read about in books?"

Water sloshes as she reaches out and grabs my hand in her wet one. "You can't trust that, Kira. Love is a risk. When you give your heart to someone there's always the chance you'll get hurt. But being hurt is a fact of life, would you rather live with only ever experiencing the bad things or would you take the good things too, even if it meant possible hurt?" She looks at me with wide blue eyes, encouraging me to *think*, to *feel*. "I'm your best friend—if you knew ten years from now we'll get in a fight and never speak again, would you not want to be my friend now? You can't predict the future. What ifs exist to hold us back. Ask yourself different what ifs. What if you never take a risk?"

I wipe away a stray tear, sniffling.

"I know I have to put myself out there, but it's scary."

"So is crossing the street, Kira," she says sarcastically. "But you still do it."

"He's so mad at me," I whisper, my voice choked.

"Give him space. He's ... he's not doing well," she admits solemnly. "He's not what you need right now. Rush needs to fix himself, and you need to fix *you*. Then maybe the two of you could talk and work things out. But it's obvious you both need to work through your pasts, deal with things, before you try to pursue something more. You'll be nothing but toxic to *each other* unless y'all finally cope. What are you going to do? Huh? Are you going to focus on school, mope around, and let every shitty thing your parents ever did or said hold you back? When will it become enough for you? When will you reclaim your life?"

A sob escapes and I cover my face. Water splashes as Mia steps out of the bathtub. I feel a towel brush my arm and once she's wrapped tightly, she hugs me.

"I love you, Kira. Like a sister. You're my best friend. I want you to be happy. I'm tired of seeing you throw your life away because of what those horrible people did to you. Confront them if that's what you need to do. See a therapist. Just scream if that's what will make you feel better." She bends down and moves my hands away, taking my face between hers like a mother would a child. "This is *your* life," she reminds me. "It's yours to make something of. Until you let them go, they'll always be chaining you to the past."

I nod and hug her again.

She's right. I have to change. I have to let go. There's no sense in me holding on to those toxic people. I don't see them, I don't speak to them, but they're still constantly there, a heavy burden on my shoulders.

She shivers and stands up. "I'm going to put my pjs on before I freeze to death. You go pick out a movie or something to watch —and you're staying the night. No objections. Hollis can sleep on the couch."

I bust out laughing, which is comical since I'm still crying. "I'm sure he'll love that."

She grins and winks. "He does what I say."

I shake my head and laugh around my tears. "Got him wrapped around your finger, huh?"

"Obviously." She saunters out of the bathroom, making sure to flip her hair over her shoulder for good measure.

I roll off some toilet paper and use it to dry my eyes.

Dropping the paper into the trashcan I stand and assess my appearance in the mirror. My eyes are bloodshot with dark circles purpling the skin beneath them. My cheeks hollow. I look tired and not healthy at all, which is bad since I'm pregnant. I haven't been eating enough the last week and I've barely been sleeping. It's clearly taken its toll.

With a groan I turn away from the mirror.

Mia has already pulled on her pajama bottoms and top, and sits down, yanking on some knee-high socks with donuts on them.

"I'll go pick a movie now," I tell her.

She gives me a sad look. I know she wishes she could make this all better for me, but she's right. It's time for me to deal with my shit. The end of August will be here before I know it, and with it, this baby. It deserves a good, decent mother, one who isn't bogged down by the demons of her past. I want to be the parent my child deserves, the one I know in my heart I can be.

Sitting down on the black leather couch I curl my legs under me and pick up the remote. I find *The Wedding Planner* and select it. I've always loved that movie. It's probably surprising to some, knowing my personality, that I love chick flicks.

Maybe it's because I think I'll never have a simple, fun love like that, that attracts me to them.

Mia pads into the room and over to her kitchen area. "Want something to drink?"

"I'd say Coke, but I better have some water."

She laughs. "One water coming right up." She grabs two bottles and joins me. She holds one out and I take it, unscrewing the cap and taking a sip to dampen my parched throat.

Leaning over she grabs a blanket out of the wire basket beside her couch and tosses it to me before grabbing one for herself.

I cover up with the blanket decorated with dancing penguins. I draw it up to my chin, trying to disappear with a whisper of fabric, as the movie plays.

We're at the part where she's saved from the rogue dumpster when Hollis comes back.

"You're the best," I tell him, as he sets the grocery bags on the counter.

"Thanks, babe." Mia gives him a look that says he'll definitely be rewarded heavily for this at a later time.

I glance at her and mock gag. "Stop giving your boyfriend sex eyes while I'm sitting right here. It's gross."

She laughs. "He's hot. I can't help it."

"Later." He winks at her.

I throw the blanket off. "I'm gonna go now."

Mia grabs my arm and pulls me back down on the couch. "Nope, you're not going anywhere."

"I didn't buy all this shit for nothing," Hollis says, and tosses the bag of white cheddar popcorn at me.

I throw my hands up and manage to catch it. "Fine, I guess I can stay for the snacks." I sit back down and fix the blanket over my legs.

I open the popcorn bag and a small cloud of white cheese powder floats up.

Setting the bag between the two of us I grab a handful, while in the kitchen Hollis puts the ice cream away.

"Thank you," I say to both of them. "I didn't want to be alone tonight."

"You're always welcome here." Mia wraps her arm around me, hugging me from the side.

"Yeah, Kira. You're family," Hollis adds, looking up from where he's crouched over the bottom door freezer.

I start to tear up again, because coming from Hollis it means a lot. He could hate me for what I've done to Rush, but he doesn't, because he *gets* it.

Rush and I aren't ready to love each other. Not yet. Not until we can love ourselves first.

THIRTY

Rush

"What do you guys think of this for your logo?" Hayes asks, with the four of us huddled behind him in his back office at the studio, staring at a computer screen.

"Dude, that's fucking awesome," I blurt.

"Yeah, that's insane," Hollis pipes in.

"I like it," Cannon adds.

"I like the colors," is the only input Fox gives.

"I thought it went well with your band name," Hayes explains. "I'm pleased with it, but it's your band's logo. You four get the final say on this."

The geometric lion, with multi-colored hues is amazing, better than anything I'm sure the four of us would've come up with on our own.

Our band's name is scrawled across the bottom in a cobalt blue color with a hint of pink glowing behind it.

It's unique. I've never seen another fucking band logo like it.

"Should I tell the designer you're pleased with it?"

"Hells yeah," I say, clapping a hand on Hayes's shoulder. "Wrap it up, my man. Can we get this shit on shirts or something?"

On Hayes's other side Cannon glares at me.

I give him a look that says *what?*

He gives me a look back that says *you know what.*

I blink innocently, trying to look like the sweet little angel I'm not.

"Can I talk to you for a second?" he asks me.

Hayes looks between the two of us. "Everything okay?"

"Just fine," Cannon tells him with a fake smile. When his eyes fall on me once more, he looks like he wants to kill me.

"Go on," Hayes tells us, waving his fingers in dismissal.

Cannon makes sure I head out of the room in front of him. He closes the door behind us and then urges me further down the hall.

"What is it?" I snap at him.

He grabs my shirt in his hands and shoves me into the wall.

"What the fuck, man?" I look at him in shock. "What's your problem?"

"My *problem*," he spits with venom, "is the fact we're here to *work* and you're fucking plastered."

"I'm not," I defend vehemently, but my tone falls flat.

His eyes flash with anger. "I'm not stupid, Rush. I've seen you at all stages of drunkenness and I'm surprised you're not flat on your face."

"I'm *fine*," I snap, shoving him off of me.

He grabs me again, holding me against the wall with one strong hand. He's the fucking Hulk or some shit.

"Let. Me. Go." I bite out the words in a dangerous tone.

"No." He jerks me slightly. "What you're doing ... you're throwing *everything* away."

"Hollis fell in love with Mia and everything was fine. Hayes isn't going to lose his shit because I've had a few drinks."

His eyes turn lethal, his top lip curling. "You think I'm *mad* because of what this could do to our band? I'm *pissed*, because you're practically a brother to me and you're throwing your Goddamn life away. Do you have any fucking idea what it's like to watch someone you love completely give up on everything?"

I shake him off of me again, this time taking a few steps away from him. My jaw clenches and I glare at him. "I'm not your problem."

He lets out a breath and glances upwards, like he's waiting for something or someone to give him the answers to the world.

"You have to help yourself," he tells me, sounding completely and utterly defeated.

"I am. I'm fine ... I'm ... happy."

"Are you?" He stares at me, waiting for a response he won't get. "You're a fucking coward, Rush. Your parents died, it's sad, it'll always be sad—but you won't fucking deal with it. Kira rejects you, it sucks, but again you won't fucking deal with it."

"I AM DEALING WITH IT!" I shout so loud, I'm surprised the others don't come bursting out of the room down the hall.

Cannon shakes his head back and forth. "You're a boy pretending to be a man. Grow the fuck up, Rush."

He turns and heads back down the hall, opening and closing the door to the office.

I stand there for a few seconds longer, debating what to do.

In the end, I do what I do best.

I leave.

The glass dangles from my fingers as I sit sprawled in the black leather chair in the private room of the club. I don't even know what drink the bartender made for me. All I asked was for it to knock me out.

For eight years I've had ups and downs with my alcohol use. I've never, not once, believed I was an alcoholic. Now, I'm even beginning to question that. I feel certain I could stop if I wanted —but I don't want to. I like this feeling. I like the numbness. When I'm sober all I can think about is things I'd rather not.

When I'm in this state I'm free, floating on a cloud where nothing bad exists.

Music blares and my head throbs, but I don't care. With this much pain echoing through my skull I can't think of much else. Though, the ass shaking in front of me is nice to look at.

The girl lifts her dark hair up and gives me a flirtatious look over her shoulder. Her eyes are full of mischief.

I like mischief.

I drop my glass where it shatters on the ground. Nobody notices.

I stand and wrap my arms around the girl. She grinds her ass into my dick, rolling her hips to the beat of the song.

My hands slide down to her bare thighs, my fingers inching up her skirt and stopping there—for the moment at least.

Her laughter is a soft vibration against me.

She reaches one arm behind me, her fingers grazing my hair. Tilting her head back to look at me over her shoulder she says, "You can touch me."

I close my eyes, at war with myself.

I've never felt this feeling before.

Confliction.

I'm confused.

But the girl I love doesn't love me back, never will, so what's the point?

My hands move back to her hips and I spin her around until she's facing me. She's pretty, with dark hair, tan skin, full lips and brown eyes. They're not the warm brown of Kira's. Darker, more like black.

Kira.

NO!

I shove all thoughts of her out of my mind. Before I can talk myself out of it, or think twice, I kiss her.

She kisses me back with fervor, her tongue finding mine. She's a good kisser, but she doesn't taste right. Not bad, but just ... not what I was expecting.

We kiss wildly, with no beginning and no end. There's no control to it. It's a frantic clash of lips and teeth. Before I know it, we're stumbling down a hall.

My mind yells at me to stop, but I don't.

I just want to lose myself for a moment.

My back pushes into the restroom door and we stumble inside. Some guys cheer, but I pay them no mind, dragging her into a stall.

She tears my shirt over my head, her fingers raking over my abs. "You're so fucking hot," she purrs.

"Shut up." I kiss her again to silence her.

I don't want her to talk. It ruins the illusion.

I pick her up and her legs wrap around my waist. Her skin-tight, already too short dress slides higher up until her lacy black thong is exposed. I growl low in my throat at the sight of it and yank my lips from hers. She gasps as I pull down the top of her dress, exposing her pert bare breasts. They're large, naturally so —I can tell—and I bend my head taking a nipple into my mouth.

She throws her head back, and grips the hair at the base of my skull. "Yes," she cries. "Oh God, please."

"Don't talk," I plead with her. When she speaks it ruins the illusion. I swirl my tongue around her other nipple, my tongue leaving behind a trail of wetness.

"Put me down then."

I let her down, expecting her to slap me or leave, but instead she drops to her knees in the bathroom stall.

She makes quick work of the buckle on my belt and slides the zipper down on my jeans. She yanks them down, along with my boxer-briefs, and takes my length in her hand.

"Oh fuck," I blurt when she wraps her mouth around me. She's fucking skilled at giving head, but...

But.

BUT.

I shove her away and she falls back on her ass, her tits bouncing. "What the fuck?"

She looks at me with surprise in her dark eyes.

"Go," I growl. The one word is both a warning and a plea. I'm already putting myself away and redoing my pants. When she doesn't move I raise my voice. "Leave! Just fucking leave!"

She stands, teetering in her heels. She pauses, righting her dress and maybe waiting to see if I change my mind.

"Go," I say again, this time deadly calm.

"Asshole," she mutters under her breath, unlocking the stall and walking out.

"I'd fuck you, baby," some jerk says.

"Leave her alone," I tell the man I can't see as I lock the stall door back.

I drop to the floor, my ass colliding with the hard, dirty tile. I lean my back against the wall, drawing my knees up. Resting my elbows on my knees I bury face in my hands, yanking on my hair so hard a few strands pull free.

A scream tears out of my throat. It's filled with anguish, pain, self-loathing—too many fucking emotions.

"What have I done?" I sob, my chest shaking. My face is wet with tears, and I have no fucking idea when I started crying.

I want desperately to go back to twenty minutes prior—to before I ever stood up from the chair.

"What have I done?" I repeat. Thrashing my legs and tugging on my hair I scream those words over and over again.

I've completely lost my shit.

Cannon warned me one day I would reach rock bottom.

I didn't believe him—and if I had I would've never imagined it'd be like this.

Kira might not love me, but I love her. I fucking do. This is a betrayal to her.

I was ... I was going to fuck that woman.

I was going to fuck a woman that's not *her*.

I can barely catch my breath. I've never felt like this before, this mix of fear, pain, hatred.

My stomach rolls and in the blink of an eye I'm over the toilet and emptying every bit of alcohol from my body.

I'm not sick from the drinks. I'm sick from what I've done.

"I never meant for things to end up like this," I whisper to myself.

"Buddy, stop talking to yourself. It's weird," someone says from the next stall.

"Shut up," I mutter, as I resume my former position, wiping my mouth off with the back of my hand and letting out a groan.

I don't know what to fucking do. I can't change what I've done, or what I planned to do.

I've been living on borrowed time.

For eight fucking years I've been spiraling further and further down into this.

Things were better at first when I came to Virginia, but even that was borrowed time too, a small reprieve from the inevitable.

Cannon's known this was going to happen for a long while. I was too fucking blind to see it, and too stupid to believe it.

I always thought I could win at everything.

I believed I could beat my grief—that if I ignored it long enough it would go away.

Wrong.

Now, here I am, with the pain just as raw and fresh as it was the moment I was pulled away from the wreckage.

I hear my mom's voice in my head saying, "You can run, but you can't hide," in her playful sing-song voice as we played tag when I was a small boy.

Her words were true then, and they're true now.

Like a coward I've been running from my issues, drinking to dull the pain, fucking to fill the ache. I felt like I was safe as long as I kept my mind far enough away.

I've never been safe.

Now, I've really gone and fucked everything up.

When I look back at that naïve eighteen-year-old *boy* I was then, I'm nothing like him now. That version of me would be appalled at all the things I've done, but especially at what just transpired and how it taints the love I have for one special woman.

How could I do that to her? To myself? How do I make this right?

There is no simple answer, but it's time to admit defeat.

I pick myself off the floor and call for an Uber. I took one here so at least my truck won't be abandoned here like some mockery of Clifford the Big Red Dog.

An hour later the guy lets me out on the street. I stand there, staring at the building.

I'm far from sober yet—drinking practically non-stop for the last two weeks will do that to a person—but I know this is where I have to be as stupid as it probably is.

I wish when Kira had said she couldn't love me I could've

accepted it, or talked about it like a normal human being, but that's not me. Or who I was, since I never want to be that guy again.

I'm tired of always turning to shitty ass things when I'm angry, or scared. I'm tired of using them as a crutch, a security blanket. I'm tired of not recognizing who I am and being a man I should be ashamed of, but one I know my parents would be appalled to see I've become.

If I don't get my ass in line now ... I'll die.

Fear strikes my heart, but I know it's true.

With the band, with more success around the corner, and tours with God knows what substances around ... I'd die.

Live fast, die young.

I don't want that to be the legacy I leave behind to my unborn child. I want my kid to know me, to love me even if no one else in this world does, I want my kid to know I'll always be there.

I want to tell Kira my love is true, even if she doesn't love me, and I'm so fucking sorry for what I've done—what she's expected of me all along.

I'm exactly the man she feared I would be.

She'll never forgive me for this. I know it. But I won't keep this a secret.

A splatter of water hits my cheek and I tilt my head back, looking up at the dark cloudy night sky.

April showers bring May flowers, I think to myself.

I can't help but feel it's significant somehow.

Forcing my feet, one in front of the other, down the sidewalk and up the stairs I beat my hand forcefully against her door.

It's fucking late, nearly two in the morning, but if I don't do this now, I'll chicken out and I'll never tell her.

I keep banging my hand, hoping she hears it.

A minute later the door is pulled open roughly and I

stumble as she appears with a robe wrapped around her body, tied above her bump, and a baseball bat held ready in her hand.

"Rush?" she blurts. "What are you doing here? You're drunk," she states, taking in my bloodshot eyes and disheveled appearance.

It rains harder now, plastering my hair to my forehead.

"I had to see you," I tell her, pain ripping through my body.

"It's after two in the morning. This couldn't have waited?" She starts to close the door and I slam my hand out, barring her from shutting it.

"No," I say forcefully. "I needed to see you now."

"Go to the hotel and sober up." Her tone is final, but I don't listen.

"Kira!" I shout. "I'm trying to talk to you. I ... fuck." I look away from her. How do I tell her this? How do I possibly admit the sin I've committed? "I did something bad."

"If you killed someone, I can't be an accessory." She starts closing the door again.

"I fucked someone else!" I yell at the top of my lungs.

You shouldn't have just blurted it like that you fucking idiot.

Her face pales, her lips parting. "W-What did you say?" Her face crumples in pain, pain I know she wishes didn't show.

"It didn't get that far," I correct, "but it came close."

"How close?" She swallows thickly, her brown eyes brimming with tears.

"Too close," I confess. "But I stopped Kira, I stopped because I love you." I reach out, trying to hold her, but she jerks away.

"This is *exactly* why I said I could never love you," she seethes, pointing a shaky finger at me. "I *knew* something like this would happen. All those men growing up told my mom they loved her too, but guess what Rush, it was just *words!* None of them ever actually meant it. I knew it would be the same with you—and now what? You've come here to rub it in my face?"

I grab the top of the doorframe, leaning in close to her as rain courses down the sides of my face.

"I do love you," I plead with her to believe me. "I love you so damn much, Kira, but *you* said you could never love me. I shouldn't have done what I did tonight. I know that. I will regret this for the rest of my *life*," I speak passionately, needing her to understand.

She shakes her head. "Get help, Rush. Deal with your demons and stop making them my problem."

"Kira," I beg. "Please, believe me. I love you—I couldn't let this lie fester between us, I had to admit what I did tonight, what I was going to do." In the distance I swear I hear thunder rumble.

"You're a liar, a cheater, an alcoholic and God knows what else." Her eyes are fire burning amidst the rain. "Leave me alone. Let me raise our child on my own. Our son doesn't deserve to grow up with such a pathetic excuse for a father. I hope you get better, I do, but I don't want *anything* to do with you. Come near me again and you'll regret it. Try to fight me for rights to our son and I promise you'll *never* see him."

My breathing is ragged, and I'm stunned into silence for a moment.

"Son?" I blurt.

"I found out this week," she tells me. She looks me over, almost like she's trying to memorize what I look like. "Goodbye, Rush."

Before I can stop her, the door closes and locks.

"Kira!" I yell, pounding on the door. "Come back! This isn't over!" *It can't be.*

I pat my pockets, looking for her keys, but I don't have them on me and when my eyes drop to the doorknob I know it would do me no good anyway. She's changed the fucking doorknob.

"Kira," I yell, begging, pleading, praying for her to come

back. To understand I *know* I fucked up. I'm admitting it. I'm an asshole.

I drop my ass down onto the step of the wooden decking. I'm soaking wet, shivering, but I don't care. I deserve the physical suffering too.

This isn't how I meant for any of this to go. On some level I believed falling in love with her was the cure-all for my grief, that I could be responsible, and we would live in blissful happiness and raise our child together.

Be a family.

But my family is gone, and my chance at one in the future is gone now too.

I've thrown away everything *good* in my life, for a tryst in a bathroom stall, for a bottle of alcohol that's only dragged me deeper and deeper into something I can't crawl out of.

I'm staring at rock bottom, and I don't like it at all.

I could keep digging farther; see how far this hole goes, essentially digging my own grave. Or I could rise to the surface for the first time in years.

It won't be easy, child, but you can do it. You know why? Because you have a warrior's heart.

I press my fingers over the beating organ and I swear I can feel the ghost of my mother's fingers there too.

It was something she told me every time I wanted to give up.

She was always there with a hand to haul me back up.

This time, I have to do it on my own.

THIRTY-ONE

Kira

"Kira!"

I put my hands over my ears, sobbing. I can't hear his voice. I can't hear any more of what he has to say.

Showing up here to tell me he almost fucked another woman? What was he thinking? And why does it hurt so damn much?

"Kira!"

"Go away," I whisper brokenly, and I know there's no chance he even heard the two words.

I drop to my knees, wrapping my arms around myself as I cry.

You don't even love him. You don't love him, Kira. You don't love him.

I tell myself this over and over again, but each time I do it feels less and less true.

I can blame him all I want, but the fact is, we've both made a ginormous mess of things.

I gag at the image I conjure of him and some nameless woman when only weeks ago he was touching me on the hotel bed.

Jumping up, I run to the bathroom and yank my hair back just in time to throw up in the toilet.

My biggest fear has always been ending up like my mother. Attracted to men who hurt me, crying over losers who aren't worth my time.

I've become an exact replica of the woman I never wanted to be.

When I'm certain I'm done throwing up I sit with my back against the wall, bowing my head.

How did things get so screwed up? Where did I go wrong to end up like this?

I press a hand to my growing belly, at the little life I was so hesitant of in the beginning and now I cling on to as a source of hope.

My *son*.

I have to make things better for him, and that means cutting Rush out of my life. Maybe he can get his shit together, I want to believe that, but my life and our son's life is better off without him right now.

I rub a tear off my cheek, wondering what would've happened if I told him I loved him back in the hotel.

Would we still have ended up like this—or would we have lived blissfully ever after?

I want to believe we could've been happy, things could've been good, but I know in my heart it's not true.

We're both train wrecks waiting to happen—his just did, and

mine ... mine must be around the corner. Waiting to sneak up on me.

I pick myself up off the floor, dust myself off like I always have, and brush my teeth before getting back into bed.

I tell myself not to think about it, Rush isn't my concern, but my heart aches for him and anger still simmers at what he did—because at the end of the day, I might've told him I can never love him, but it was a lie.

I already do.

THIRTY-TWO

Rush

"I fucked up."

"Jesus Christ!" Cannon comes awake, his limbs flailing wildly as he finds me standing over him. "Why the fuck are you leering over me?"

"I fucked up," I repeat.

"What time is it?" he asks, squinting at the clock.

"Five."

"Great, then let me sleep for at least two more hours before I have to deal with you and your shit." He crooks his tattooed arm over his face

"Cannon, please, man," I beg. "I need you."

He sighs and drops his arm. Stifling a yawn, he sits up. "Go start some coffee. Something tells me I'm going to need *lots* of strong ass caffeine for this."

"Thank you," I tell him, and nearly wince when he gives me a pitying look.

He knows.

Of course he doesn't know exactly what I've done, but he knows it's bad or I wouldn't be coming to him.

After I finally plucked myself off Kira's stairs I walked around for a while. I was already soaking wet, so it didn't make much difference to me.

I stopped in front of a building downtown with paper cranes hanging from strings in the window. Emblazoned across the window was a sign—The Paper Crane Project, it deemed. There was a paper with information about what they did taped to the inside of the glass. I've probably passed by that building hundreds of times since we came here, it's not far from the studio, but I never stopped to pay attention.

I did tonight, and if it had been daytime I would've gone inside.

Reading what they do ... I felt a connection to their mission.

They write messages, positive ones, and then fold them into an origami paper crane. They leave them around town, in public places for people to find. The sheet of paper said their mission has spread across several states and they're hoping it catches on even more.

I want to be a part of something like that. Something *good.*

But I also have to help myself.

I brew Cannon's coffee and I'm pouring it into a cup as he comes out of his room, tugging a shirt over his head. I'm glad I had the forethought to change into dry clothes as soon as I got back here. Otherwise, I'd be a popsicle.

"Give me that," he demands, reaching for the coffee with a tattooed hand. He takes a sip and sighs. "That's good." Inclining his head toward the couch he says, "I take it this is the kind of conversation more easily swallowed when sitting."

"Yeah, probably," I sigh rubbing my hands together.

I feel completely sober now, but who knows what the fuck I'd score on a breathalyzer test. I'm probably lucky I didn't get arrested when I was walking around town so late, or early depending on your perspective, in the pouring down rain.

Cannon sits down and takes a large gulp of coffee before setting it on the table.

"What'd you do?" he asks, as I sit down in the chair across from him.

"Something horrible. Something unforgiveable." I scrub a hand over my tired face. I haven't slept in almost twenty-four hours.

"It must be bad if you look so dejected."

"After ... after I left the studio ... I mean, I was already fucked up. I took an Uber to D.C., walked around a while, that kind of shit, and then ... well, I went to a club." I rub my face. How I told this to Kira is beyond me, because she's the one I betrayed, who I hurt the most besides myself—but telling Cannon is like confessing to a parent that you took a joyride at fourteen in their car.

"Spit it out. I'm not awake enough for your babbling." He's peeved sounding, and frankly, I deserve it. I've been a jerk to him. To everyone. I'm a mess—a mess I couldn't see until I took things too far.

"I drank some more, and there were chicks there, hot ones. I started dancing with one and we kissed—"

He sits up, glaring at me with narrowed eyes. "Please tell me it was *only* a kiss." I give him a sheepish look. "Hold up, I need more coffee for this." He picks up the mug, holding up one finger signaling me to wait while he gulps down more of the dark liquid. "Continue," he says with a flourish, setting his mug down once more.

"Somehow, we ended up in the bathroom. There was more

kissing, then there were tits, and ... I just wanted to forget, Cannon." I plead with him to understand where I was coming from, to not hate me too. "After she started to suck me off, I stopped it. You have to believe me, it didn't go any farther than that. I felt like shit, I still do. I don't know if I'll ever feel okay again for what I've done."

He shakes his head at me, biting his tongue. "How could you? Do you not really love Kira, because I can't imagine loving a woman and then cheating on her?"

"I know." I bury my face in my hands. I can feel the sickness creeping back up my throat.

"You're an asshole," he tells me. "A real fucking idiot."

"I know," I breathe. "I'm a screw up, an asshole, an idiot. I'm an alcoholic, man," I choke, looking away from him. Admitting the words out loud was more difficult than I anticipated. Those words grate on my ears.

I'm an alcoholic.

But it's true, I am. Cannon's known all along, but I wanted to believe I still had some semblance of control over my life. I didn't.

The only control I have now is to accept I need help.

He stares at me, shocked I've finally accepted the truth.

"What are you going to do about it?" he asks me.

He's said all along *I'm* the one who has to decide I need help. It can't be forced on me.

"I'm going to join AA," I tell him matter-of-factly. "I don't know what else I'm going to do, but it's something. I saw this place in town, The Paper Crane Project. I thought I might start by going in there. I feel drawn to it for some reason." I shrug like none of this is a big deal, but it's *huge*.

It changes everything.

"Are you going to tell Hayes?" he challenges.

I inhale a shaky breath and exhale. "Yes. I can't keep this a secret."

"Good," he says. Leaning back, he assesses me. "What about Kira? Are you going to tell her about this ... romp?"

"I already did," I admit.

"Shit." He curses, running his fingers through the longer stands on top of his head. "I take it that went...?"

"Horribly," I finish for him. "I deserve for her to hate me." I look away, picturing her in my mind in the doorway of her place. Her look of utter devastation, anger, and the worst of all—the acceptance that this was what she expected of me all along, and why she could never love me.

I didn't prove her wrong. I proved her *right* and I'll never be able to forgive myself for that, for not being a better man.

"I guess this was the wakeup call you needed." He shrugs, and leans over to pick up his coffee cup.

"I hated I needed it to begin with," I grumble. "I hate myself for letting things get this bad."

He shrugs. "You've never dealt with shit. You ran from it. Now, it's caught up to you." He raises his glass in a cheers motion. "Make the best of it."

"How can I possibly make anything decent out of what I've done?"

"You can't take it back," he explains with a shrug. "But remember, actions always speak louder than words. Be the kind of man you know you can be."

"She'll never forgive me."

"So?" he counters. "You don't need to get better for *her*. You need to get better for *you*. The rest will fall into place."

"We're having a son, Cannon. A little boy." I feel tears filling my eyes and I dam them back. I don't know when I became so weepy, but I'm over it. "She told me I'll *never* see him."

He sighs. "Yeah, well she's pissed at you. Heat of the moment." He waves his hand in easy dismissal, like her words are no big deal. "Frankly, I don't blame her for telling you that. Go her."

"Go her? Are you on her side now?"

"I'm on the side where my best friend gets help and gets *better*. Now, you have the best motivation possible. Get better for you—then prove to her that you're not only deserving of being in your son's life, but hers too."

"She'll never take me back." I clasp my hands together and sigh.

"Maybe she won't," he reasons. "But you can still show her you're a decent man. Prove to her people *can* change. Go from there. I doubt it'll be easy, but you have to try. Stop sitting back and expecting everything to fall in your lap. It fucking won't, Rush. Get off your ass and work for it."

I reach out and clasp my hand to his.

"Brothers?" I ask.

He grins back at me. "Always." Letting go, he adds, "I'm proud of you, man. Now, don't make me take those words back. Prove to me, to Kira, to *yourself* that you're better than this."

"I will," I vow, feeling a blanket of acceptance fall over my shoulders.

I've accepted myself as I am now, who I've become, but I've also accepted who I can be.

It won't be easy, it won't be quick, but things *are* going to change.

THIRTY-THREE

Kira

Walking across campus, my backpack weighs me down. It's heavy with textbooks, and with my growing belly I feel lopsided.

I get looks on campus now, people staring at my pregnant stomach. I glare right back, because I don't have time for judgmental assholes. I covered my bases, but fate had other plans for me—a fate that seems to include a son.

It's weird to no longer call the baby an *it*. It's a he. A little boy.

A son I have the responsibility to raise right, not to be like my father or his. It's not going to be an easy task, but I'm ready to rise to the challenge. I owe it to him to give him the best shot at life.

My phone blares in my pocket and I curse, yanking my phone out.

I finally get the phone out of my pocket and answer. "Mia?"

"Why is it I see you loping across campus like the Hunchback of Notre Dame?"

"Where are you?" I spin around, looking for her.

"Answer the question."

"Um ... because I just got out of class," I explain in a *duh* tone.

"Today is your first session with Dr. Franklin. Get your ass over there."

"Shit," I curse. "I totally forgot."

"Well, unforget and get your ass in gear. Move, move, *move!*"

Suddenly she appears right behind me and I drop my phone.

"Don't scare me like that," I scold, slightly out of breath. "Scaring a pregnant lady should be a crime."

"Whatever." She bends down and hands me my phone. "I finally got you to agree to seeing a therapist and I'm not about to let you revoke on this promise. Now, *go*." She points to the parking lot.

"I'm going—you're the one who stopped me."

"But did you remember your appointment?"

I give her a sheepish look.

"That's what I thought." She flips her hair over her shoulder. "Now, leave. Skedaddle."

"Yes, ma'am."

I take off for my car and reach it in a few minutes. Placing my bag on the passenger side I quickly put the car in reverse and back out of the space.

Thankfully, Dr. Franklin's office isn't far from the campus.

I think I subconsciously forgot the appointment I reluctantly agreed to because it's fucking scary to sit down and talk to someone about my issues. They feel silly when I voice them out loud—childish somehow. But those issues are engrained deeply into me, because they hurt me.

Parking my car in the back lot, I enter the old building with peeling blue paint on the siding and find a kind looking older receptionist sitting behind a counter.

"Good afternoon, dear. You can sign in here." She points to a clipboard.

With a sigh I add my name and arrival time, before sitting down in one of the hard plastic seats.

I look around at the cornflower blue walls, and the painted pictures of historical buildings downtown.

Run, my subconscious tells me. The desire to flee is strong. Nothing good or useful can possibly come from this. What can this person help me realize that I haven't already?

My hands wrap around the armrest of the chair, knuckles turning white.

"Kira?"

My head jerks up at the sound of my name and I'm surprised to find a younger looking woman standing there. Her blonde hair is perfectly curled and I'm slightly envious of her red lip color. If I wasn't here to relive horrors, I'd have to ask her where I can get it.

Forcing my body out of the chair I stand and walk the six steps to her—yes, I count them.

"It's nice to meet you, Kira." She shakes my hand and I'm surprised by the warmth and softness of hers.

"You must be Dr. Franklin?" I ask, slightly shocked a woman this young could possibly be my therapist. She barely looks thirty.

She gives me a small laugh as she leads me down the hall and into a room where she closes the door.

"I am—but call me Della. I like my patients to think of me as a regular person. I'm just like you with my own problems. I don't want anyone to think I'm sitting there judging them or psychoanalyzing. In order for us to get to the root of your problem you have to learn to trust me—and I want to earn that trust. Please, have a seat." She gestures to a tan suede couch and sits down in a leather chair across, crossing her legs.

I look around the room, taking it all in. The wall across from the couch has built in bookcases full of books, anything from medical ones to children's. There's a little bit of everything, and for some reason that makes me feel a little more comfortable.

The walls in the room are painted a soft gray color with a hint of purple that's somehow soothing.

From the ceiling hangs a small chandelier that adds some elegance to the room. The old wood floors are covered with a fluffy white rug—the kind that makes you want to curl your toes into it.

It's such a vast difference from the front room that I'm slightly confused.

Sensing this, she says, "I just bought the building so I haven't decorated everything yet. I wanted to get this room fixed first. It's almost done."

"It's nice," I say, wiggling around on the couch.

Her appearance might've taken me by surprise, but that voice is still telling me to run far and run fast.

"So, Kira," she begins, smiling kindly. "Tell me something about yourself—anything, big or small."

"I like Coke and I feel like I need about ten right now."

She tosses her head back and laughs, her blonde hair swaying around her shoulders. Her blue eyes sparkle when she looks at me. "I actually have some Coke in the fridge if you'd like some."

"Please," I practically beg.

She stands and opens the door on a mini-fridge in the corner I hadn't even noticed.

She hands me a can of Coke and I give her a grateful smile before popping the can open. The liquid hisses and bubbles.

She waits for me to take a sip before she says, "Now tell me something else. I think you can do better, don't you?"

I sigh.

"Just something small, Kira."

At this moment, even something small feels like a huge admission.

"Um..." I bite my lip. "Well, I'm pregnant. Obviously. It was a huge surprise, definitely not planned, but..." I rub my stomach idly. "I wouldn't take it back."

Even in those moments where I lose myself to worry, I know I wouldn't change having this baby for anything.

She smiles. "Do you know the gender?"

"It's a boy," I say softly.

"A son." Her smile widens. "How amazing. I don't have any children yet."

"You don't?"

She shakes her head. "One day. How did you feel when you found out, since it wasn't planned?"

"Angry. Terrified," I admit to her. "I questioned whether I should even have him and if I did, if I should give him up for adoption."

"What changed your mind?" she inquires.

"I'm studying to be a nurse," I explain. "Seeing the babies at the hospital I knew then I couldn't ... I couldn't just get rid of this tiny little being—and I also knew in my heart I wouldn't survive my child going to someone else, and that I had to do whatever possible to give him as good of a life as I can."

"Thank you for sharing that with me, Kira. Is there anything else you'd like to share with me today? We have time."

I nibble on my bottom lip, my eyes dancing around the room and landing on nothing in particular.

Finally, I start speaking. "My best friend told me it was finally time I dealt with my past ... that's why I'm here."

"I want you to know, that there's not anyone on this planet that doesn't have a past. You're not alone in that."

I nod. "I've been carrying the baggage of it around for a long time. Growing up, even after my parents split up, any time my dad came around he was always roughing my mom up. It was nothing new, most of the guys she was with were the same way. But then my dad nearly beat her to death. He landed in jail and we moved here while I was in high school." I take a breath, noticing that I've been idly rubbing my fingers back and forth over the arm of the couch. "I thought she'd change after that, but even once we got here, she still sought out the same kind of men. The assholes and drunks. The druggies and abusers." I sigh heavily, because admitting all of this out loud is taking a lot out of me. I honestly can't believe I'm confessing all this so quickly to her, but if I don't open up then what's the point of being here? "I guess I'd hoped for once she might choose me, but like always, she couldn't stand the thought of being alone and I wasn't good enough."

She stares at me, seeming to assess what she wants to say. "Her choices aren't yours," she tells me in a soothing, calm voice. "There are people who get stuck in a cycle," she leans forward, closer to me, "and then they find it impossible to get out of. To someone on the outside looking in, it might seem like a simple choice to break this cycle but that's not always the case. For some people, what they have *is* love, because it's all they know. When you don't know any better it becomes easy to stay because it's what's expected. Something else might be better, but it's a foreign concept."

"Are you saying I've been too quick to judge?" I snap. "You don't know what it was like growing up with that—"

She holds up her hands to silence me. "But do you know what kind of background she grew up in?"

"No," I admit softly.

She sits back. "For you, seeing what you did, it made you go the opposite direction it seems from what you've said thus far. You're determined to never be that person. But for her, she might not have seen that choice as an option."

"I'm just like her, though," I blurt.

"What do you mean? Explain, please."

I sigh, and launch into the story of Rush and me. Of our hook ups and deals, of getting pregnant and pushing him away, of me starting to fall for him even though I told myself repeatedly I wasn't. I tell her about the New York trip and his confession, how I pushed him away even further this time, and what it ultimately led to.

"He sounds like a troubled young man," she murmurs when I'm done. "But he was never abusive to you?"

"Never, I swear," I add. "Trust me, I would've been done with him in a heartbeat if he was."

"Hmm," she hums.

"What?" I ask, almost plead. "What are you thinking?"

"I'm thinking maybe it's taken meeting each other, for you both to realize you can't continue living the way you are. You're here with me, making a step toward bettering yourself. I hope he's doing the same."

I look away from her. "I do too."

THIRTY-FOUR

Rush

My heart is a solid lump in my throat. I can feel myself choking on it.

Panic like I've never felt before threatens to smother me like a blanket dousing flames.

Speaking of flames, I feel like I'm on fire all over.

"I can't do this," I whisper into the cab of the SUV. "I can't, man." I shake my head rapidly back and forth.

Cannon reaches over from the driver's seat and claps a solid hand on my shoulder. "You *can*. You're strong enough for this—don't let fear make you think otherwise. You're going to go in there, sit down, introduce yourself, do whatever it is they have you do and you're going to be fine. After, you're going to feel better, and I'll be sitting here waiting for you. I have your back."

"I do too," Fox adds from the back, leaning up through the center console and making Cannon drop his hand.

"Why did we have to tell Fox what we were up to?" I grumble at Cannon.

"Because I'm your friend too," Fox reasons in a carefree tone. "I'm here for moral support."

I look in the backseat. "Or to read comics."

"Well, fuck, do you expect me to sit here twiddling my thumbs while you go to an AA meeting."

I wince—the words a verbal slap to the face.

I'm about to set foot in my first Alcoholics Anonymous meeting.

After telling Fox and Hollis I was going to start attending AA, I made all three guys swear not to say a word to Hayes until after I went to my first one.

Tonight, I sit down with other alcoholics, confess my sins, chant over a fire, say some spells or some shit. I have no fucking clue.

Then, tomorrow morning, I'll have to tell my boss, my fucking mentor and a man all four of us have looked up to for so damn long, that I'm an alcoholic.

"I'm an alcoholic," I whisper out loud.

"Uh..." Fox begins. "Thought we'd established that and that's why we're here?"

I slap him away like an annoying fly that won't stop buzzing.

"I'm still processing this shit. I don't need your peanut gallery bullshit."

"You know what would be great right now—peanut butter. Thanks for the reminder."

Turning around I watch him pull out a small round snack pack of peanut butter. He then proceeds to rip the foil back and dip a finger in the peanut butter.

"What?" he asks, blinking innocently like this is a normal occurrence.

Which it kind of is, with Fox you learn to expect weird and random.

I raise my hands. "I didn't say a thing."

I turn around and face the front.

"Go in, man. It's starting in five minutes," Cannon warns, his voice encouraging.

I sigh, looking at Cannon, then Fox.

Sobering, Fox says, "You're going to be fine, dude."

I press my lips together and exhale a gusty breath through my nose. Before I can talk myself out of it, I put my hand on the door handle and push it open.

"See you guys in an hour."

I close the SUV door and walk slowly into the building. I looked up the local AA online and found that they meet at a gym that's near our hotel.

Walking inside I'm surprised to find it's an MMA gym, and not the regular one I'd been expecting. Guess I should've paid more attention when I looked online, but the name was pretty standard.

ImBOLDen Gym.

I swallow in fear as I spot some people milling around.

The gym is closed at this hour of the evening, therefore, I know anyone I see is here for the AA meeting.

I walk forward and find a table with coffee and donuts. I grab a Styrofoam cup and fill it with the black coffee, dumping a heap of sugar in and dousing it with creamer. Stirring it, I take a sip to test it and wince.

"The coffee here is shitty, but the donuts aren't bad."

I look up to find a kind-eyed man who looks like he'd be my dad's age ... if my dad was alive. Wire-framed glasses sit on his nose, and his gray hair is cut short and receding, despite that he has a heavy gray beard of the same color.

"I'm Daniel," he says, holding out a hand. "I'm the head

around here—and *you* are a new face. I always try to introduce myself before we get started. I know the first time is scary. I still remember my first meeting like it was yesterday."

"You ... you're ...?"

He gives a small chuckle. "An alcoholic? Yes, I am. Sadly, we'll all always be one. Once it's in your system it's impossible to shake. It takes willpower to realize you'll never be okay with alcohol. A little voice likes to tell you after a while you can handle one drink, but it's lying. I'm speaking from experience. Ten years sober this time around."

"Ten years, huh? How long did you last before?"

He looks away, wincing slightly before he answers. "Only two." Looking back at me he adds, "The beginning is the most difficult part. This journey isn't easy. It's a constant battle, one we have to fight every day. It's a never-ending struggle inside ourselves. You have to wake up every morning and decide are you going to be an alcoholic or are you going to be the best version of yourself you know you can be."

I stare at him for a moment, mulling over his words. "I don't want to be this ... this person."

He claps me on the shoulder with a kind smile. "Good, then you're in the right place. Now, grab a donut and join us."

"I'm not very hungry."

"Just grab the donut, son," he tells me again, so I do.

I pick it up and carry it, along with my shitty coffee as I follow behind him.

My heart hasn't slowed since I arrived. With Fox and Cannon waiting outside I know if I ran out, they'd haul my sorry ass back in.

This is where I need to be.

Not for them.

Or Kira.

Or even my parents.

I need to be here for me. I *am* here for me.

"Grab an empty seat," Daniel tells me, indicating the chairs lined up in rows.

I pick one in the back, to myself, and Daniel chuckles—flashing me an amused smile. I don't think he's one bit surprised I've chosen to keep to myself.

I place the Styrofoam cup on the chair beside me, silently daring anyone to take that seat. Most of the ones in front of me are already filled and when I glance behind me, I don't see anyone else. I'm surprised by the variance of genders and ages in front of me. I expected it to be mostly males ranging in age from my age to maybe fifties.

I don't know why I assumed that, it was silly of me, I guess. Something like alcoholism can affect anyone.

I didn't grab a napkin with my donut, and since there's no point in wasting a good donut I take a bite and finish it in two more. I wipe my sticky hands on my jeans, which is gross, but I don't dare get up to get something out of fear that I might not come back to this spot. The last thing I need to do is give myself any excuse to not be here.

Daniel stands in front of the group, smiling warmly at everyone. He has the presence that somehow makes you feel at ease. I mean, look at me, I haven't run yet even if I thought about it.

"I'm so glad you all could make it out this evening. Chester, how was your daughter's recital?"

A man near the front who looks like he's in his thirties speaks. Yet again, I'm surprised because this man looks clean cut, like the suit and tie type. But he's here. Like me. Like all of these people.

"It was great," he answers, rubbing his palms on his jeans. "I think it's one of the first times my ex and I have been civil in a while. It was ... nice and she's supportive of me getting help. I'm hoping soon she'll feel comfortable to let me have the kids on my own."

"I'm so happy to hear that." Daniel's smile is wide and genuine. Clearing his throat, he says, "I suppose we should get started. We have a new face here and therefore I'm going to explain a bit about how I run things."

Even though Daniel doesn't point me out every head swivels in my direction anyway. I stick out like a sore thumb sitting by myself, but also these people *know* each other so even if I was sitting closer, they would still find me.

I lift my hand in an awkward wave, for once hating having all the attention in a room on me.

A light sweat begins to break out across my brow despite the fact it's fairly cool here.

Thankfully, Daniel clears his throat and they all face the front again like eager students in a classroom.

Daniel looks at me as he speaks. "This is a place of safety. For you, for all of us. It's a judgment free zone. We're all alcoholics for a reason, and we never look poorly on another for what that reason might be. Everyone is welcome to speak about their triumphs, their struggles and weaknesses, downfalls, any number of things. We often talk of other aspects of our lives and how they play into our personal struggles. But you're not required to speak. All that is required of you is to listen to others and be kind. Anger and fighting is not tolerated. While you're not *required* to speak and share your personal struggles, it is encouraged. There cannot be healing, nor progress, until you learn to share your burdens."

I nod as he finishes his speech. I'm not ready to speak today, and I'm thankful for that small reprieve. I can listen to the others, get to know them, and maybe learn to trust them all enough to share.

"One more thing," Daniel says, holding up a finger. "This is

Alcoholics Anonymous. The *anonymous* part being key there. Anything you share here cannot and will not be shared outside this room, and you aren't to share or speak about anyone else beyond these walls. Understood?"

I nod.

"Good, moving on," he continues. "Would anyone like to share first?"

A girl in the front row who looks like she's barely twenty-three, if that, raises her hand. Her hair is dyed a vibrant yellow blond color, with pink on the tips and her natural dark hair growing at the root. Taking in her clothes, she's dressed like a regular girl in jeans and a shirt with a band logo emblazoned across it. If I passed her on the street, I would never think she was an alcoholic—that she's like me.

I think I always believed someone *looked* like an alcoholic. It was part of how I've convinced myself for so long that I'm not one.

But there is no clearly defined label that marks an alcoholic.

"Come on up here, Holly." He waves a hand, motioning her to take his place in front of the group.

She clears her throat. "Hi, guys."

"Hi, Holly," the room echoes.

From off to the side I feel Daniel's probing eyes assessing me. I don't look at him. Holly's the one speaking so that's where my attention stays.

"I had a setback this weekend." She wrings her hands together and bites her bottom lip. "I didn't drink," she's quick to assure. "But I wanted to." She exhales heavily with the confession. "I went with my friends out to eat, and they ordered drinks. I know they didn't mean anything malicious by it, but it made me angry. I ... I wanted to order a drink to prove to myself, to them, that I could be fine with alcohol. So, I did. Order it, I mean." She tucks a piece of hair behind her ear, rocking back on the heels of her scuffed pair of Converse. "As soon as I ordered it, I knew what a bad idea it was. I left some money on the table, said goodbye to my friends, and left." She looks around the room, making eye contact with several people, myself included. "I'm almost a year sober. July tenth will be a year and I worked too damn hard to get to this full year, alcohol free, to lose it one night by trying to prove something I'll never be able to prove. I know one drink will never be enough for me. I'll always want more. I'm a better, healthier person now and I never want to be the girl I was before. I almost made that choice because of my own stupidity. Everything is a choice. To take the drink or not. We each have the power to decide. This time I made the right choice, but that doesn't mean I might not make the wrong one in the future."

Daniel begins to clap and the others join him. After a moment I clap too.

"Thank you for sharing that with us, Holly. Anyone else?" A man stands and Daniel motions him up as Holly sits down. "Tim, I'm so glad you're sharing with us today."

The man laughs. He's an older gentleman with a heavy gray beard and a baseball cap covering his head. He wears a plaid shirt and jeans, reminding me of a lumberjack—a scrawny one.

Clearing his throat, he begins, "My wife of forty years threatened to leave me if I didn't do something to help my sorry ass." The way the others nod I know these are details they already know and Tim has added them for my benefit. "Francis is a good woman. She's always put up with my shit, but I knew she was serious. I was goin' to lose her if I didn't give up the bottle. The sad thing is for a minute there I truly contemplated the choice—think about that, I considered giving up the woman I love, my soul mate, for a *drink*. What kind of bastard does that make me? But I'm four years sober now, my relationship with my wife is better than ever, our children respect me and ... I found out this past weekend I'm going to be a grandpa. Me? A grandpa." He shakes his head. "When my kids were growing up I was the worst of the worst. I was drunk all the time, even on the job—which is shit poor behavior when you're a construction worker." He gives a small laugh. "Maybe it's dumb of me but I can't help wonderin' if this grand-baby is my second chance. A small little do over of sorts. I can't go back and change how I was during my children's childhood but maybe I can sort of make up for it." He shrugs, giving another small laugh. "Ignore this old man's rambling. I know nuthin'."

Daniel steps up to him and shakes his hand. "You'll be an amazing grandpa, Tim. Congratulations."

"Thanks."

Tim sits back down and Daniel asks again who would like to speak.

Another person raises his hand. I'm surprised by how quickly and readily they are to share their triumphs and failures with one another. This might be Alcoholics Anonymous but it's obvious they've formed a camaraderie with one another, a family of sorts.

When the hour is up everyone disperses, some leaving immediately, some hugging, and others who just seem to linger, like myself.

Daniel plops down in the chair beside me. "What did you think?"

I search for the right words. "It was different than I expected."

"What did you expect?" He pushes his glasses further up his nose.

I grin. "Sitting in a circle, holding hands, singing *Kumbaya*."

Daniel laughs outright at me. "We only do that every other week. You caught us on an off week. Such a shame." He stands up, tugging his shirt down. Narrowing his eyes in a fatherly look of warning he says, "We better see you next week."

"You will," I promise.

"Good." He gives me an awkward thumbs up and laughs at himself. Shaking his head he asks, "Are you ever going to give me your name?"

I didn't even realize I hadn't.

"It's Rush."

He nods. "Good to meet you, Rush. See you next week." He points at me in warning before walking away to speak with someone else.

I let out a sigh I didn't know I was holding in and stand, heading for the exit.

I'm almost to the door when I hear a call of, "Hey, you! Hold up!"

I turn to find Holly standing in front of me.

She comes to a stop in front of me, her sneakers squeaking against the concrete floor.

"I just wanted to say hi and properly introduce myself. I'm Holly."

"Rush," I answer, shoving my hands in my pockets. I look over my shoulder, toward the exit.

She laughs. "You want to get out of here, I know. That's how I was the first few times." She smiles at me, her eyes a light and clear blue. "I wanted you to know this isn't always easy, but you've made a huge start by coming here."

I nod. "Yeah, uh, thanks," I mutter, because it feels rude to leave her hanging.

"Just remember you're not alone," she says, taking a step away. "We've all walked this path."

"Thank you," I say, and somehow I actually mean it.

Being here is fucking hard—it's the biggest admission I can

possibly make that something is wrong, that I'm not completely in control of my life.

She waves goodbye. "See you next week."

Somehow, she seems to know I'll be back.

Heading outside I climb in Cannon's waiting Land Rover. "How'd it go?" he asks, setting his phone down.

I exhale and shove my fingers through my hair. I didn't realize in there that my hands are shaking, but I can tell now. I look down at them, taking in the slight tremble that betrays my nerves.

"Not as bad as I thought," I finally reply.

"My man," Fox congratulates me, smacking me on the shoulder from the back.

Looking out the window I mutter, "I can't believe I let things get this bad."

I see Cannon's frown in the reflection of the glass. "All that matters is you see it now, and see how important it is to keep going."

I nod, thinking about Tim and the story he shared of hoping for redemption with his grandchild since he was too drunk when his kids were growing up to be a decent father.

I don't want my child, my *son*, to grow up without a decent father because I choose to drink over being there for him. I want to be the kind of man he looks up to and aspires to be. It won't be easy, getting better, but I can do it.

One day at a time.

Cannon's phone buzzes again and he picks it up, groaning. He proceeds to call someone and when they answer he bites out, "You can't come here." There's mumbling on the other end. "No," he growls. More mumbling, and he sighs. "Fine, but I'm not paying for your fucking plane ticket so you can come here and be a pain in my ass." The person says something else. "Yeah, yeah—I'll pick you up. I'm not that much of an asshole." He pinches the bridge of his nose. "You can stay in Hollis's old room. He lives with Mia now. Mhmm. Yep, just let me know."

He hangs up the phone.

"What the fuck was all that about?" I blurt and Fox leans forward between the two seats so he's more a part of the conversation.

Cannon sighs. "My sister needs a 'break' and wants to get away and 'spread her wings' or some shit."

"So?" I prompt, already knowing where this is going.

He lets out an irritated groan. "She's coming here. To Virginia. To live with us. She's going to be the end of me," he mutters.

The end of him? I don't think so.

With a smirk, I look back at Fox who has grown pale and is slowly slinking back against the seat.

Cannon has *no clue* how close Fox and Calista have been in the past.

I only know because I put two and two together and then Fox spilled the beans when I asked him about it.

Fox and Calista made a pact to lose their virginity together.

Those two have always had some strange bond—I think because Fox is the youngest of the four of us, and she was always tagging along, so they formed a sort of camaraderie since the three of us always picked on them.

But, if you ask me, Foxy boy has always had a thing for Cannon's little sister. I'm not sure what her feelings are.

Now, the poor guy is going to be living with the girl he likes, under the same roof as his best friend and her brother.

At least I won't be the only one with a permanent case of blue balls anymore.

THIRTY-FIVE

Kira

My feet ache from the hours I've spent on them working at The Sub Club. Work is necessary, though, so I power through. I really need to pick up a second job, but there's literally no free time in my schedule. I honestly don't know what I'm going to do. There's barely enough money now to cover rent, food, and necessities and now I'm going to have a baby with needs to care for—not to mention, I *really* need a nicer place in a better part of town, and there's always the chance my car could die.

To say I'm stressed is the understatement of the century.

I know I could always take Rush to court and get child support—but my stubborn ass wants to prove to him, to myself, to *everyone* that I can do this on my own. Plus, I frankly don't want to ever see him again—or have to deal with him.

Truth be told, I'm as angry at myself as I am him, because I know the only reason I feel hurt over what he did is because I do have feelings for him—deeper feelings than I'd care to admit.

I never wanted to get involved with a man for this very reason—I knew if things went beyond sex, it would get messy, and here we are.

"You okay?" Mia asks me, wrapping a sandwich.

"Just peachy," I snap back.

I instantly feel bad the moment the sarcastic words leave my lips. She's not the one I'm mad at. I'm not even sure I'm *mad.* Tired, and cranky? Yeah, definitely those.

"I'm sorry," I mumble, but she's already moved on to the register to check out the person she's waiting on and doesn't even hear me.

It's an hour until closing and the way I'm feeling even one more minute seems like too long.

The customer leaves, slinging the plastic bag containing their sandwich from their fingertips.

"I'm going to go wipe down tables," Mia tells me. "Why don't you ... go to the back and just find something to do."

"Yeah, okay," I agree, and take off my apron. I hang it on the hook and toss my plastic gloves in the trash.

In the back is our break room, stock area, and refrigerators housing supplies.

I pull out the chair in our break area and sit down, propping my feet up on one of the others.

I'm already a grouchy bitch and this baby isn't due until the end of August. True, it'll soon be May, but that's still a full three months before this boy makes his appearance.

I keep trying not to think about things—about how quickly time flies, because even though it feels like forever before he comes, it's truly not that long, and there are so many things he'll need before he arrives.

A car seat, stroller, crib, clothes, bottles, blankets, bibs, diapers—God, so many items and even though I have limited knowledge of screaming infants I know there has to be much more than that.

My eyes fill with tears and I sniffle. "I'm so screwed."

"Are you okay?" Mia asks as she sets down a box in the doorway.

She approaches me slowly, like she's encountered a wild animal or something. I suppose, lately, that's how I've acted.

I wipe my tears away. "No," I answer honestly. "I can't do this, Mia. I was crazy to think I could work, go to school, and take care of this baby."

She pulls out one of the other chairs and sits it in front of me before plopping down.

"There's no way I can provide any kind of decent life for him. I'm struggling enough on my own. I don't want my son to think I'm a failure."

She takes one of my hands, holding it in hers. "He would never think that."

"How can you possibly know that?"

"How could you possibly know he *would?*" Shaking her head, she continues, "I *know*, because he'll grow up seeing a mom who loves him unconditionally, who works hard to provide for him, in you he'll see quiet strength and he'll grow up to be the kind of man who respects women because *you'll* show him how important that is. You're the best thing for this little baby. I know it. I wish you could see it too." With her other hand she presses it to my growing stomach. "Besides, he'll also have me—the most kick ass aunt ever. You can do this, Kira. You're not alone, not like you think you are."

"This isn't how I imagined my life," I confess on a whisper, my voice cracking.

"Does anybody's life turn out like they imagine? I mean, I *never* wanted to get involved with a rock star. Now look at me."

She tosses her hands in the air. "He's the love of my life. I can't say it was love at first sight, but I know now he's it for me. That's the man I'm going to marry one day. When I was five, I wanted to marry a prince. There's no point in holding on to an ideal your life can never live up to." She pats my knee and sits back. "Let all that go. Live in the present and stop holding onto things that are only weighing you down. It's only when you let go that you can fly."

I laugh around my sniffles.

"Thank you." I let my feet drop from the other chair and lean forward to hug her. "I'm so lucky to have you."

Not many people are lucky enough to have a best friend that's practically like a sister. I don't know what I would do without Mia, without her family too.

When you're not good enough for your own flesh and blood, it's nice to know there are other people in the world who love and accept you for who you are. I don't have to pretend to be something I'm not.

This is my family now.

"We better get back to work. You know Chester can't handle the front on his own." She rolls her eyes, talking about the new guy who was hired about a month ago who is still fucking clueless.

I snort. "You're right. Yesterday he asked me if he was holding turkey—it was Canadian bacon."

She shakes her head in disbelief.

"That boy," she mutters.

I stand and stretch before following her out. Thanks to her, I feel a little lighter than I did before.

SITTING DOWN ON MY COUCH WITH MY PLATE OF DINNER, I LOOK AT the textbooks spread around me. I have a quiz coming up this week and I need to be prepared. I expect to get an A and nothing less.

Grabbing my notebook from the coffee table I balance it on my knee and take a bite of the chicken I made. It's not bad, but I'm not hungry—I just know I need to eat for me *and* the baby. I flip a page in the textbook on my right and jot down some notes in my notebook.

I start to yawn and I silently curse myself.

Pregnancy makes me not only incredibly tired, but sleepy too, and I have no time for sleep at the moment.

Finishing up my dinner I get comfortable—well as comfortable as I can—to finish studying for the evening.

When the words blur together on the page, and nothing I read makes sense I decide to call it a night. I close my textbooks and stack them on the coffee table along with my notebook.

I grab my phone from the table and then a bottle of water from the refrigerator.

My phone rings in my hand, startling me and I drop the bottle.

Shaking my head I reach down and grab it before answering the call.

"Hello?" I rest the phone in the crook between my ear and shoulder, with my head tilted to hold it in place as my feet pad across the floor, back to my room where my bed is calling my name.

"Kira?"

"Yes, that's me."

It's late, so I don't know why I'm getting a call right now—the only logical explanation is telemarketer.

I open my mouth to tell the person I'm not interested in what they're selling when they exhale a sigh of relief.

"I've been trying to get ahold of you, but every phone number I had for you was disconnected.

I plop my ass on the end of my bed, my brows furrow in confusion.

"Who *are* you?"

"Mitchell Williamson—I'm Quinton Marsh's lawyer."

My heartbeat pounds in my ears.

"W-What?" I stutter. "Why are you contacting me?" I practically yell into the phone.

"I'm terribly sorry for reaching you at such a late hour—but as time is limited, I—"

"Spit it out, Mitch," I snap.

"Your father ... he's sick. Cancer. He has only a week, two tops, left, and all he wants is to see you before he dies."

"Tell him I'll see him in hell."

I press end on the call.

THIRTY-SIX

Rush

I walk into the quiet studio the Monday after my first AA meeting.

Everything looks different somehow, and I find my eyes scanning every item, every picture like it might be the last time I ever see it.

I don't know what Hayes is going to say when I lay my sins out before him. He might decide I'm not good enough to stay a part of the band—that I'm too much baggage.

It doesn't matter if I've been there from the start, I won't let my actions weigh down my friends' hopes and dreams. I won't be the reason they don't reach the stars.

I asked them to come in a half hour later—to give me time to face Hayes alone.

Their support would be nice, sure, but I know I need to do this on my own.

I have to face my reality head on, and part of that includes telling my boss, and mentor, that I've hit rock bottom.

Following the sounds of movement, I find him in the studio, tweaking with things on the soundboard and muttering to himself.

I pause for a moment, unsure of the right way to announce myself.

Do I speak? Or knock? Or—Jesus fuck I'm out of my mind.

Running my fingers through my hair nervously, I clear my throat.

Hayes turns around and raises a brow in surprise. "You're here early."

He starts to turn back to the board, but I say, "I needed to talk to you."

"To me?" he asks, in disbelief and sits down in the swivel chair, facing me. "About what?"

His tone conveys how he seriously doubts I could have anything of importance to share with him.

I lick my lips looking around awkwardly.

"Sit down," he tells me.

I'm not one for taking commands, but this time I do. I need some sort of direction in this moment.

I sit down on the couch and he spins the chair to face me.

Behind him, the recording booth is lit up, our equipment waiting for us. I itch to get behind my drum set—to lose myself in the music and beat.

"Well?" Hayes prompts in a tone that says he's waiting.

Hayes is a decent guy, he really is, but he doesn't like to think his time is being wasted.

I wring my hands together, gathering myself. This hasn't been an easy thing to admit to myself, let alone someone like Hayes.

"I ... I attended my first AA meeting this weekend." I blurt out the words quickly, like ripping a Band-Aid off and sit up straight, squaring my shoulders. Hayes's face shows his surprise, so I continue before he can say anything. "My friends, and I'm sure you have too, have noticed how my drinking can get out of hand at times. I always believed I had it under control. I never thought I was an alcoholic. I could stop if I wanted, it's a lie I told myself and one I believed wholeheartedly. Until I did something unforgiveable."

His eyes narrow on me. "And what is this unforgiveable thing you did?"

"I hurt the woman I love in a way I can't change or take back. I'm afraid I've done irreparable damage to any chance I might have had of having a life with her."

"With Kira?" he clarifies.

I nod solemnly. "She said she could never love me, but I think she lied—"

"Why would she lie?" He butts in.

"Because she's scared, I guess. Isn't that why most people lie? Because it's easier to live in fear than to step out on a limb?"

He shrugs. "You're right. What exactly did you do that you think you can't take back?"

I wince. This is the last conversation in the entire world I want to be having with Joshua Hayes of all people.

"Something unforgivable."

He rolls his eyes. "I need more details than that if I'm going to give you advice."

I jolt back in shock. "You want to give me advice?"

He shrugs, raising his hands. "You said you love her—is that true?"

"Yes," I answer without a moment of hesitation.

"Then level with me and be honest, then we'll go from there."

I wince. "It's bad."

He sighs heavily, rolling his eyes. "I've done things in my past I regret and wish I could take back. Life isn't rainbows and sunshine, son. It's constantly falling down and picking yourself back up—learning from your mistakes. Now tell me before you irritate me too much and I decide not to help you."

Taking a breath, I tell him all of it—about how I've been falling for her for a while, but was terrified to admit it to myself. About the trip to New York and how I finally confessed my feelings and what she said. As much as it makes me ill to talk about what I did at the club, I do. I tell him all of it. I tell him about my guilt, and about my parents' deaths—how I've been spiraling out of control ever since. It feels good to get all of this off my chest, and even to tell it to a father sort of figure. I mean, he *is* a father, but he's not mine and our relationship has always been a purely working one.

He leans back in the chair, rubbing his jaw.

"Fuck," he blurts, and for some reason it surprises me to hear the word leave his lips. "That's quite the mess you've dug for yourself."

"I know." I hang my head in shame.

I've never been ashamed of my actions before. I've always owned every decision I've made, even when I knew they were bad. This is the first time I've ever experienced true regret for something I've done and it makes me feel physically ill.

"I already think you're on the path to redemption."

"You do?" I raise my head.

"You went to AA—that's a big step, now keep going, keep proving to her *and* yourself that you can do this. Prove your worth by getting sober. She's angry, so give her time and space to calm down. While you're giving her that space, keep working on yourself—not just with not drinking, but with other things. Deal with the death of your parents, because you never have. Go back home if you have to. Lay to rest everything you've been holding on to. Through it all, don't forget your love for her, and think of your child. You're going to be a father now."

"It's a boy," I whisper.

"Really?" He smiles. "I didn't know yet."

I nod. "I'm going to have a son." I exhale the breath I was holding. "I still can't wrap my head around it. Me, a father."

He chuckles. "You better get used to it. It's a label that belongs to you now and you can't take it back."

"I want to be a good father," I confess to him. "I want to be a man worthy of my son looking up to. I want to be the kind of man Kira deserves to have."

"It's as simple as this—decide what kind of man you think that is, and prove that you're it."

"I can do that."

He gives me an encouraging smile, but even as I say the words I wonder, *but what if I can't?*

THIRTY-SEVEN

Kira

"You have to go see him," Mia admonishes me, yanking out the chair across from me at Starbucks.

I pick at my croissant, glaring at my drink that's very much *not* coffee, since I'm trying to cut out caffeine.

"I wish I would've never told you about that call," I grumble as she plops down.

"I'm your best friend—you tell me everything."

"Exactly. I'm beginning to see what a bad idea that is."

She sighs. "I know he wasn't a good man, Kira. I'm not saying you need to go see him, and forgive him, and pretend the past didn't happen. You don't owe him anything, but you owe it to yourself."

"How?" I look at her in disbelief.

When we decided to meet at Starbucks for lunch during our break on campus, I had to tell her about the phone call I got last night from my father's lawyer. Now, I regret that decision immensely.

She huffs out a breath like I'm too dense to get what she's saying—which is true, since I see no logical reason for me to go out of state to see the father I haven't had anything to do with for years. I've already laid him to rest. In my mind, I packed him up in a box and buried all my memories of him in the backyard.

He might not be dead yet, in the real sense, but in my mind, he's been dead for years.

"Don't you think you deserve to have a proper goodbye—to tell him anything that's been weighing on your mind?" She looks at me with those piercing blue eyes of hers, and raises her iced coffee to her lips.

"What's the point?" I shrug indifferently. "There's no chance of closure, unless you're proposing I speak to my mother as well." I raise a brow in challenge.

Her lips turn down in thought and she gestures with her hand. "It might not be such a bad idea."

I glare at her. "If this drink hadn't cost nearly five dollars, I would throw it at you."

Her eyes sparkle with amusement. "Go ahead, I'm the one who bought it after all, so it's not like you'd be out of the money."

I roll my eyes. "You know I'd never actually throw my drink at you."

"Yeah, I know." She grins, fluffing her glossy red hair. Sobering she adds, "I'll go with you. We can at least drive to the prison and if you decide you don't want to go, no harm no foul."

I roll my eyes. "I can save you the nine hour trip—I don't want to go."

She sighs in exasperation, like she's a mother dealing with an unruly child.

"I'm so proud of you for seeing the therapist—truly, I am.

But I don't think you'll ever move on until you confront your demons head on."

"And by demons you mean my parents?" I stir the ice in my drink, for something to do because looking at her is becoming a bit too much. The sincerity and true concern in her eyes bothers me. She wants what's best for me, and for some reason she thinks this is it.

"Yep." She nods.

"If I go—" She perks up at my words. "*If*, and that's a big if, it won't be to forgive him for what he did. He doesn't deserve my forgiveness. She doesn't either for that matter."

"I think it would be a great opportunity for you to get everything off your chest before it's too late."

I swallow thickly. "It's not him I'm the most angry at," I confess. "Yes, he was mean, and he did bad things, and I am still mad at him—but I wasn't around him as much as I was my mom. She's the one I lived with, the one who raised me, and the one who continually chose assholes over her own daughter. It wasn't like she was trapped in a bad relationship—she chose these guys time and time again. She didn't care how they treated her, or leered at me Every bad thing that ever happened to her, she always told me it was my fault."

Mia looks at me sympathetically. "Then go see your dad, tell him what you need to, and then say your peace with her. Be done with it. Be done with harboring these ill feelings, and move on, because you can tell me all you want that you have but we both know you haven't. It still haunts you."

I shake my head. "How did this go from me saying absolutely no to seeing my dad, to suddenly you talking me into seeing both of them?"

She shrugs, fighting a grin. "I'm talented like that." Sobering, she reaches across the laminate tabletop and grips my hand. "I love you, Kira—like a sister. I want to see you thrive, not hold yourself back from every single good thing in your life because you're scared of committing to it."

"You're talking about Rush," I snap. "He's an alcoholic, Mia. He ... he basically cheated on me."

She frowns. "I know," she says sympathetically. "But isn't everyone worthy of a chance of redemption?"

"Even my parents?" I retort.

"Even them," she whispers softly. "Whether they do anything to warrant that redemption is up to *them*, not you. Don't you think if Rush proves he's on the right track, that he gets better for *himself*, and deals with his shit—he's worthy of being forgiven?"

"Possibly," I mutter.

She grins and counters, "Don't you think if you move on from your past, and learn it's okay to love—that not all love ends in heartbreak—you're deserving of his forgiveness too?"

"*His* forgiveness?" I blurt.

She tilts her head, appraising me. "You broke his heart."

I wince.

"Your parents broke your heart—surely you of all people know how much damage and pain heartbreak can cause."

The lump in my throat grows harder.

"Rush has been through a lot," she continues. "He's *lost* a lot. Tragedy changes people, and sometimes it sends them spinning out of control, down a path they never intended to go. When the time comes, listen to him." I open my mouth to argue, but she holds up a hand to silence me. "I'm not saying you have to forgive him, fall in love, and ride off into the sunset. All I'm asking is for you to listen to him and truly hear what he has to say. Then, once you do, you go from there."

"It sounds like you're on Team Rush," I grumble. I'm not angry, I understand where she's coming from.

Rush and I do owe it to ourselves, and our son, to one day sit down and be honest with each other. About our pasts, our fears, our feelings—about everything.

She laughs lightly. "I'm on team-Kira's-happy. That's all I want for you—for you to be happy."

Happy. It's such an ambiguous word. I'm happy in moments, sure, but is anyone ever truly happy all the time? Is such a thing possible?

"Do you really think I can be happy?"

She stares at me for a moment, emotion swimming in her eyes.

"I think everyone has the opportunity to be happy, as long as you let go of the burdens weighing you down."

"What if those burdens are too heavy?" I counter softly, wiping condensation off my clear plastic cup.

She contemplates for a moment and then says quietly, almost hesitantly, "Then I guess they drown you."

It's a funny choice of words considering that's how I feel almost all the time. Like I'm drowning in my emotions, in the baggage I carry with what's been said and done to me.

I have the power to sever those ties, to cut away the bonds and swim to the surface, but can I?

THIRTY-EIGHT

Rush

I grin as I work on laying down drumbeats for a new song we're working on. Drumming has always been easy for me, just like basketball was, but now that I'm one week sober suddenly it's clearer, the beat pouring from my veins.

One week seems like so little time, but I haven't gone this long without a single drink in ... fuck if I know.

My head bobs along and I *feel* it. I feel my passion again—the spark I've been missing for years. I've been going through the motions for so long that it began to feel real and not like I was faking it.

It's sad to realize I've been lying to myself for so long I've deluded myself into believing a false reality.

Hayes's voice enters the recording booth. "That's great, Rush. Take a break."

I hop up from the stool, tucking the drumsticks into my

pocket.

As I exit the booth, Mia enters the studio with coffee.

"Ah, yes. I love you." I smack a kiss against her cheek and grab the one I know is mine.

"Don't mack on my girlfriend," Hollis growls.

"That's my daughter," Hayes warns.

I roll my eyes. "Please, I don't have a death wish."

I sit down on the couch, with my coffee, between Fox and Cannon.

Mia passes out the rest and then Hollis tugs her down onto his lap in the chair.

Hayes's face tightens, but he shakes his head and it clears. I'm sure it's tough for the man, seeing his daughter fall head over heels for Hollis, but my man Hollis is just as crazy about her. I thought he'd join me in bachelorhood forever—now look at us, him in love with the girl he never knew to hope for, and me ... well, I'm tied up in knots about a girl who can never love me.

Hayes claps his hands together. "We need to talk about things."

"That doesn't sound good," I mutter, which earns me some glares.

Clearing his throat, Hayes leans back in his swivel chair. One of these days I'm convinced he's going to lean back too far and fall right out of it. Not gonna lie, I'll laugh.

"The album is coming together great, but I think we should look at a later launch. I'm leaning toward November. That way, we have time to market more and I can find you guys the best manager and PR team—people who are truly going to take care of you."

"Makes sense," Cannon mutters.

Our rise to success is ass backwards.

We started out playing only for ourselves in Cannon's basement. Then, as teens we moved on to performing some around our small town. Just small events, like park activities and school functions. Then we moved to L.A. and played some clubs, got a decent following with our singles, and started playing festivals. It was hardly glamorous and a lot of times we went hungry because we needed the money for gas to get to our next venue. When Hayes discovered us, it felt like a miracle. We'd had interest in the past from a few managers, and even a few studios who almost signed us, but it never went anywhere. Typically, you'd get a manager first and they'd get you signed to a company.

But Hayes was just beginning this venture into producing with his very own studio, and he wanted us to be his first project. You don't just say no when one of the world's biggest rock stars and a badass guitar player believes in you.

So, we signed, but it's left us without some of the necessary things we need.

"I'm looking into people, and Willow Creek's manager is interested in you guys as well, and I, of course, trust her. But I want to entertain others, and let you guys pick who you feel you'd work best with. For the time being there are some local fairs coming up this summer. Willow Creek is booked to play—and I have you guys booked to open for us. These are usually small town affairs, not to toot my own horn," he grins widely, "but Willow Creek brings in a huge amount of people. Fans come from all over and even if they can't get onto the grounds, they park where they can hear the show. Once the album is wrapped, you guys will go back to L.A. and the real work will begin."

"When ... when do you think we'll go back to L.A.?" I ask, hesitant because all my thoughts go straight to Kira and the baby. I don't want to be away from them. She can hate me for what I've done, I don't blame her, but that doesn't stop me from wanting to be near her and my son.

"Probably sometime in September." My face shadows with worry, my heart thumping. "Is that a problem?" Hayes asks me, not rudely but curiously.

"The baby is due at the end of August," I say quietly. I can feel Mia staring a hole into the side of my face. She hasn't said much to me, and I'm sure she knows from Kira what I did.

"Ah." Hayes nods. "Well, you're not required to go back to L.A. at least not right away. But you will have to go back eventually. L.A. is a necessary evil in the music industry."

The thought of going back there, to a city where corruption and temptation is on every block scares the shit out of me. I've only been sober *one* week. My second AA meeting is in two days. How can I possibly get in good enough shape to be okay in a city like that? More so, how am I going to be able to prove myself worthy to Kira before I leave? I've already accepted she might never forgive me. It's a fate I've accepted, but it doesn't mean I won't try to defy it.

I know Kira and I are made of the same stuff. We're meant to be, even if she can't see it.

"That's all I have to say for now." He claps his hands together. "Now let's get back to work."

Walking out of the studio with Cannon and Fox on my heels I turn to them. "You guys head back to the hotel. There's somewhere I want to go."

Cannon narrows his shrewd green eyes. "You better not be going to a fucking bar."

I roll my eyes. "Such little faith in me, Rhodes. No, I'm not going to a bar."

"We'll come with you," Fox pipes up.

I shake my head. "This is something I want to do on my own."

Cannon sighs and looks at his watch. "Be back at the hotel in two fucking hours. If you're not I will find your ass and you'll regret it."

I exhale a heavy, world-weary breath. "Okay, father, I'll be home then. Don't worry. It gives you wrinkles."

Fox chortles at my comment.

Cannon watches me, his look daring me to fuck up.

"See y'all in *two* hours," I emphasize, and finally part from them.

I hear the two of them muttering behind me, but I refuse to turn around.

I know they have every right to be worried, but I'm not up to no good.

For once.

Strolling down the street and a block or so over, I find myself standing outside The Paper Crane Project once more. I shove my hands deep into the pockets of my jeans, staring at my reflection in the glass.

My blond hair is disheveled, and my cotton blue t-shirt is wrinkled from sitting for so much of today. My eyes don't look nearly as hollow as they did, but they're still lost. Sad. I'm not sure I'll ever stop being sad over what I've lost.

Knowing I look like a weirdo standing outside the front of the place, I force my feet in front of me, one step at a time, and open the door.

Inside, I'm surprised to find more of the strings of cranes hanging from the ceiling. There are so many it looks like a fucking unicorn was murdered and rainbow exploded everywhere.

With so many colors my eyes don't seem to know where to look first. Thankfully, the walls are white, and so are the tables

—though, those are lined with colored paper, just waiting to be turned into cranes.

"Hello?" I call out.

"Just a minute," a male voice answers.

Crossing my arms over my chest, because I feel awkward as fuck being here, I wait.

A man appears, carrying a baby. A fussy little boy who wiggles insanely in his arms, squawking and reaching for something over his father's shoulders with his chubby hands.

"Can I help you?" the man asks.

"Um ... shit ... yeah. I ... uh ... read about what you guys do. Thought I might like to help."

"Oh, thank God!" Another voice cries from the back and a tiny woman with dark hair barrels around the corner. "We're in desperate need of more volunteers. This thing has exploded and I'm overwhelmed." When the baby sees her, he reaches wildly for her and she takes him. "I'm Blaire," she introduces herself to me. "This is my husband, Ryder, and this little one is Wyatt." She bounces the baby in her arms and he blows bubbles in his spit. "People will be arriving soon, but we need to make at least one thousand today. A few of my volunteers live in Harrisonburg and they're trying to get this going there, but we've found the more cranes we have left around towns the quicker it catches on."

"Um ... so what do I do?" I ask hesitantly. "I'm Rush, by the way."

Handing the baby back to her husband she says, "Here, I'll show you. It's easy."

She motions for me to follow her to one of the tables. I sit down and she hands me a bright green piece of paper.

"The gist is—write something positive and fold it up into a paper crane." I look at her like a deer in headlights and she laughs. "I'll show you how to make them, don't worry."

"So ... what do I write? You have a nice ass?"

She snorts. "That might brighten someone's day, but we prefer to keep it G rated, or at least PG, please."

I think for a moment and scrawl across the piece of paper; *it gets better.*

"Good," she tells me. She picks up a purple piece of paper, writes something down, and holds it up. "Now for the folding."

I follow her steps and when I'm done, I glare at the offending *thing* I've created.

"Mine looks like a fucking turkey."

She laughs heartily. "It's not bad for your first one."

She continues to work with me and by my tenth I can actually make a decent looking crane.

"What brought you in here?" she asks curiously. "Truly. I find most people don't wander in here by accident."

I clear my throat and look into her kind eyes. "Let's just say, I've lost some things, and ... because of that I've done things I'm ashamed of. I'm trying to atone for my mistakes, and it seems like making the world a happier, kinder place is a good point to start."

She smiles kindly at me, crossing her fingers together. She looks to be the same age as me, maybe a few years older, but not much.

"Do you know why this whole thing started?" She motions to our surroundings and I shake my head. "My fiancé died," she continues, sadness creeping into her eyes. "He died, and I was lost. I didn't know what to do with myself."

"That sounds like me," I admit.

"After I lost him, I spiraled into depression. When I found out I was pregnant with his child, it felt like I had something of him I could still hold onto, but at the same time my grief was so strong I worried I couldn't be the kind of mother I always wanted to be. Anyway, Ben always left me these sweet notes, which he folded into paper cranes. He'd hide them in random places for me to stumble across. I kept finding them after he died, and it became something I held on tightly to. Those words became the only buoy I had holding me up while I was adrift at sea. I ended up joining a group for grief, which is how I met Ryder. He had lost his wife," she explains. "The Paper Crane Project was born from that grief—from wanting to bring something good into the world when I was afraid only bad was left."

"Wow," I breathe.

"Sorry to dump all that on you," she gives a small laugh, folding another piece of paper, "but I felt like it was important for you to understand this place. What it means and what it stands for. We still host grief meetings once a month."

My head shoots up. "You do?"

"Yes—have you lost someone?"

I nod reluctantly. "Yeah," I reply. There's no point in denying it.

"You should come. Our next one is in two weeks. We'd love to have you."

"I might drop by," I answer. Truly, I might, but by not committing I won't feel obligated. "I think I might like to come here a lot," I reply.

She smiles, and there's no sadness or pain in her eyes. It's been eight years since I lost my parents and I've yet been able to shake that look from mine. "We'd be happy to have you. Stop by any time." She stands and taps her hand against the table. "I'll leave you to it. If you need any help feel free to ask anyone or holler for me."

"Thanks."

I glance at the time and I decide I have about an hour before I better head to the hotel or fear Cannon's wrath. Normally, I wouldn't care about defying him—fuck, I'd do it for fun—but I know his worry comes from a good place, and the last thing I want to do is piss off the friend I'm depending on the most.

Cannon's always been the rock of our group. This impenetrable force that nothing can shake. We need him far more than he does us, and while we might joke about how he's such a dad, I don't know what we'd do without him keeping us in line.

I start writing my notes and making the cranes. Mine are far from the perfect ones hanging from the ceiling, but I feel like for a novice they don't look too bad.

Never give up on what you believe in. I write on one note.

On another I scrawl, *Life's short. Do something epic.*

There's something therapeutic about writing the notes, in putting good vibes out into the world. There's far too much negative, not only inside ourselves but in the world around us. In some small way this helps balance it out.

Checking the time, I silently curse and finish folding my yellow crane.

I leave my pile on the table and go in search of Blaire. Other volunteers sit at tables, but pay me no mind. It's nice not to be stared at. I feel like that's all anybody who knows me is doing lately. Staring and wondering if I'm going to screw up.

I find Blaire in the back and clear my throat. "Excuse me?"

She turns around and smiles. "You heading out?"

I nod. "I'll be back another day. Where do you want me to put the ones I made?"

She waves a hand. "Leave them on the table. We gather them up at the end of the day."

"All right, well, bye."

You're an awkward fuck when you're sober, I tell myself.

She laughs lightly. "We'll see you soon. Don't be a stranger."

Leaving the building I feel a little lighter than I did before.

I walk the streets back to the hotel in a few minutes and head up to our suite. Inside I find Cannon making tacos.

It's like a pang to my chest, seeing those fucking tacos. All because of Kira.

"You're back," Cannon states. "I'm impressed." He uses a spatula to push something around the pan.

"'Atta boy," Fox says from the couch, looking at one of his comics with those weird plastic blue and red 3D glasses.

"Dinner will be ready in a few," Cannon announces, lining up hard shell tacos.

"You mean, you're not going to tell me I'm not allowed to eat your dinner?" I mock gasp at him and he rolls his eyes.

"Fucker," he mutters. "If you don't act like a dick, you're welcome to a taco."

"They're not my fave, but for you I'll have one," I joke.

"I should punch you in the face," he grumbles, turning his back to pull out some ingredients from the refrigerator.

Originally I thought it was dumb as fuck to basically have a full size kitchen in a hotel suite, but now I see the benefits.

"But you won't," I quip. "You love me too much. I'm like a rainbow on a rainy day."

He turns around and narrows his eyes on me. "No, you're the rain."

"True," I agree. "Without me, there'd be an endless drought. Look at me bringing good things to the world."

"Stop sassing me and help."

"Yes, Mother," I salute him, and join him in assembling the tacos.

A few minutes later the three of us sit down to eat together. Soon, it'll be four of us when Callie arrives this weekend.

I have no fucking idea how that's going to work out, but right now it's the least of my concerns.

Getting sober is number one, dealing with my shit is two, and proving to Kira I'm the kind of man she can rely on for herself and our son is third—it would be number one, but I know if I don't accomplish the first two, the third will invariably come crumbling down.

THIRTY-NINE

Kira

"Don't you think we should've taken a more inconspicuous car?" I glance over at Mia, her hair whipping around her shoulders from the open car windows as we speed south down the interstate, heading for North Carolina. "A bright red Audi sports car seems like a target at a prison."

She slides her sunglasses up her nose. "The prisoners won't be seeing my car. You usually take a shuttle from parking to the actual prison."

I stare at her like I don't know her—because I'm honestly questioning that fact at the moment.

"How could you possibly know that?"

She shrugs and gives me a sheepish look before her eyes return to the road. "Criminal Minds, duh."

"You weirdo," I snort.

Mia is one of those beautifully gorgeous girls who is actually a total dork. I'm pretty sure if her TV broke and the only channel she could watch was National Geographic, she'd die happy.

I look out the window, at the passing trees, and the green that has suddenly blossomed as spring hits us in full force. It'll be May soon, and I wish I could slow down time. I feel like the closer it gets to August the faster it goes, and I'm scared.

I'm scared of the unknown, of what's to come, of how I can possibly handle motherhood on my own.

My mom might've practically raised me, but she's not the kind of parent anyone should look to for how to do things.

Sometimes I envy Mia. Not for her dad's fame, or growing up with money, but for having two parents who love each other whole-heartedly and who would do anything for their children.

The sad thing is, I've learned in life there are more people like me than Mia.

"This is fun, don't you think?" she asks, picking up her stainless steel travel cup and taking a sip of water. I, on the other hand, have a large size Coke from the Sheetz we stopped at to get gas an hour ago. It was a bad idea, since I already have to pee.

"How is this fun?" I counter. "We're trapped in a car headed to a *prison* to see my estranged father. Nothing about that rings *fun* to me."

She rolls her eyes and replaces her cup of water in the holder in the middle. "I mean, *this*." She waves her fingers between us, eyes steadily on the road. "It's like ... a road trip or something. A *girls'* trip, before the penis inside you arrives and has to tag along everywhere," she jokes.

"Bleh, when you say *penis inside me* it sounds way too sexual."

"Well, I mean, there is a penis growing inside you. You're having a boy."

"God, Mother Nature is weird," I mutter. "I can't believe I have to see my father, for the first time in years, knocked up. I wanted to be everything my parents weren't. I wanted to go to school, get a degree, have a decent job and be successful. Now, I'm just like them."

There's an exit coming up and she changes lanes, getting off and pulling onto the side of the road. I'm silently grateful, because I *do* have to pee—but I also know I'm about to get a scolding. She unbuckles her seatbelt and twists around in her seat to face me.

"You are *nothing* like them. Having a baby, in no way, shape, or form makes you like them. You're still going to school, you're still going to get a decent job, you're still going to be successful, you'll just also wear the title of mom while you do it. There is no shame in becoming a mother, Kira. Motherhood is the hardest damn thing in the world. Some people throw it away like it means nothing while others struggle to get pregnant. Life's not fair, it's true, but there's nothing in the rulebook that says because you had an unplanned pregnancy it lumps you into the likes of your parents. The only thing that could ever make you like them is if you *act* like them—and I don't see it happening, do you?"

"You always know what to say." I brush a tear away.

I never used to cry, ever. Crying doesn't solve anything and it makes your eyes burn, but ever since I got pregnant I'm a weepy mess.

She reaches over and hugs me—well, as best she can within the small confines of her car. It might be sporty and cute, but it's about as small as one of those tiny clown cars you see at the circus, and with our bags stuffed in the back it's even more claustrophobic than normal.

"I love you, Kira." Pulling away, she holds my shoulders forcing me to look at her. "You're my sister. Not by blood, but by choice—and remember, we all have a choice. They made theirs, now you make yours."

She sits back and tugs on her seatbelt. "Um," I start, placing a hand on her arm, "I need to pee before we get back on the road."

She laughs, shaking her head. "With as many pee breaks as you've already had, we'll be lucky to make it there in a week."

"Ha, ha," I intone sarcastically. "Make fun of the pregnant woman who has no bladder control."

"You're not even that pregnant," she remarks.

I narrow my eyes as she pulls back onto the road from the shoulder and heads down the street to a McDonald's. "Tell that to me again when you get pregnant."

She snort-laughs. "Yeah, that's not happening for a good long while."

"That's what I thought, too," I sigh, touching my stomach. I should start feeling the baby move soon, which both excites me and freaks me out.

She gives me a sympathetic look.

"Have you thought about any names?"

I bust out laughing. "Are you crazy? I'm so tired and stressed I can barely function, let alone think about naming a human being."

"You'll have to come up with something eventually." She turns into the fast food parking lot and finds a spot near the door to park the car.

"Nameless Marsh has a nice ring to it," I quip, undoing my belt.

Her brows raise in surprise. "Not Nameless Daniels?"

I narrow my eyes. "What has Rush done to deserve the baby getting his last name?" I counter defensively.

She shrugs nonchalantly. "He might've fucked up, but he's a decent guy at heart and I know he feels guilty." Tapping her chin she adds, "I know, you could make a new last name out of both of yours." She thinks for a moment and shoots a finger into the air. "I've got the perfect one ... wait for it."

"I have to pee," I warn her, "so unless you want me to pee on your leather seats, you'll spit it out."

"You're no fun," she grumbles. "But if you combine your last names you get Danish."

"I'm not giving my kid Danish for a last name. Nice try."

I hop out of the car and she scurries after me.

"I might as well pee while we're stopped," she explains, when I look back at her.

I speed walk inside to the bathroom and thankfully one stall is open.

A sigh of relief escapes my lips at the pleasantness of emptying my bladder. I swear the thing is the size of a pea already.

Finishing, I flush the toilet and yank up my leggings—my poor ass can't afford maternity jeans. Opening the stall, I wash my hands and dry them.

"Kira?" Mia says from behind one of the stall doors.

"Yes?" I hedge, worried she's going to start in again on Rush.

"I want to get a frappe while we're here. You want anything?"

"No, I'm good," I answer. "I'll meet you at the car."

I head outside, feeling the heat of the sun pierce my skin. The farther south we go, the warmer it's gotten. I hope it means heat is headed our way.

I hop up on the back end of the sports car, swinging my legs while I wait for her. A few minutes later she comes out, sipping on a caramel frappe with a brown bag emblazoned with the large golden M on the front.

"I swore I thought I heard your stomach grumbling so I got you a Big Mac and fries. You're welcome."

I laugh. "We have snacks in the car."

"I also got me one," she continues. "You cannot stop at McDonald's and not get food. It's blasphemy."

I roll my eyes, but smile. "Thanks, Mia." Hopping down I take the bag from her when she holds it out and we climb in the car.

We sit there and eat, staring at the fence in front of us. The brown paint on it is peeling, and I idly wonder why anyone would paint wood brown. Seems like such a waste of time.

"What do you think you're going to say to him?"

"To who?" I blurt, thinking of Rush.

She stares at me. Blinking once. Twice. "To your dad," she answers.

"Oh, him," I mutter. "No idea. Whatever comes to me in the moment, I guess."

"Who did you think I was talking about?" She probes, one brow raised shrewdly.

"Um ... no one," I mutter.

"Mhmm." She purses her lips. "You thought I meant Rush."

"No, I didn't," I defend. "I don't even think about him."

She smirks. "You're so full of shit I'm shocked this whole town doesn't already reek of it."

I playfully push her shoulder. "Give me a break."

"I can't," she says seriously. "Because you love him and he loves you, and I just want to see you two happy."

Picking up a fry I rip it into pieces. "I accepted a long time ago my life isn't meant to be happy."

"Don't say that," she pleads, our food lying forgotten in our laps.

"It's the truth," I sigh heavily, wishing I could exhale my burdens as easily as I do my breath. Instead, they stay bottled inside, forever trapped in a prison of my own making. "Some people are meant to soar, while others stay behind with their feet planted firmly at the roots. That's me, Mia. There's no escaping this life."

"There is a way," she reasons. "There's always a way. You're just too stubborn and you're afraid of having your heart broken."

"I *have* had my heart broken," I snap at her. "I've had it punched, slammed, stepped on, thrown—you name it, it's happened. Whatever is left of it ... I have to protect at all costs."

"Life's nothing without a little risk."

"Then I guess I'll only ever have nothing."

IT'S DARK WHEN WE ARRIVE AT OUR HOTEL. I DON'T EVEN KNOW what town we're in. Mia might've gotten me to agree to this shit show, but I made her call the lawyer back and take care of all the details. I wasn't interested in being here and I didn't want to know any more than I had to or put in any effort.

I wanted my father to feel as insignificant as he and my mom always made me feel.

I drop my bag on the bed nearest the wall. "I'm going to shower," I mutter to Mia, who's already calling Hollis to let him know we got in okay.

Selfishly, and despite myself, I wonder if Rush knows where I am and what I'm doing.

It shouldn't matter to me if he knows, or if he cares, but dammit it does. I keep trying to convince myself I hate him and want nothing to do with him, yet half of my thoughts are occupied by him. I wish I could cleanse him from my brain with bleach, but since that won't work, here I am.

I close the door to the bathroom behind me, and pee, before I get out of my clothes to shower.

It's a pretty nice hotel Mia booked—nothing extravagant but

way better than the thirty dollar a night room I could've afforded.

The warm water cascades down my body, soothing my aching muscles, but doing little to make me feel better overall.

It'll take a miracle for that to happen.

I've always been so strong, I've had to be. I couldn't let things tear me down and make me a shell of who I am, but lately I feel like a weak and pathetic version of myself. As if layer by layer I'm finally being exposed for who I truly am, which is a frightened girl begging to be loved and accepted.

Those two things seem like such simple, easy things to expect, but they're not. Not for me, not for anyone really.

Stepping out of the shower I dry off my body with the towel and fluff it against my hair to help it dry faster.

Wrapping the white towel around my body I step into the room and rifle through my bag for my pajamas.

"My turn," Mia chimes, hopping off her bed and heading for the bathroom.

I tug on the pair of gray cotton shorts and a white tank top that hugs my bump. I dig out my hairbrush and stand in front of the mirror near the door, smoothing the dark strands. They hang limply over my shoulder like a discarded dishrag. My brown eyes look sad, haunted. I hate to admit it now, but the only time I've seen them light and almost happy was during the months I spent with Rush. I didn't even notice it then, how happy he was making me. I think it happened so slowly, so gradually, I became immune to the symptoms—of happiness, caring, I guess even love.

Turning to the side, I cup my hands around my growing belly.

A piece of Rush and me, created from our pain, but also from the good parts of ourselves too.

Maybe that's our issue—maybe the tiny bit of good we had

left went to our son and that's why things are so fucked up now and we're both in the position of facing the pain of our pasts head on.

But if that's true, I'm glad our child got those good pieces. I don't want him to be like us, hanging onto a past that's only sinking us like a ship.

The bathroom door opens and I jump, my hands flying from my stomach and my hairbrush flinging across the room.

Mia looks at me in shock, her lips slowly curling into a smile at having caught me admiring my bump.

"I didn't mean to scare you," she says, picking up my brush and putting it in my bag. "But I'm kind of glad I did."

"Oh, shut up." I playfully push her shoulder and pass her to climb in bed. I'm exhausted, but I doubt I'll sleep knowing what I face tomorrow.

She laughs and changes into her pajamas before burrowing into the other bed. She turns the TV on and flicks through the channels, stopping on Discovery Channel.

"Why am I not surprised?" I mutter.

"This is good," she defends. "You'll see."

I roll over, and close my eyes, choosing to ignore her and to my vast surprise, I fall right to sleep.

Cracking my eyes open I find it's pitch black in the room, not a hint of light leaking in through the curtains. I spare a glance at Mia in the other bed and have to stifle a laugh. She's passed out with her hands clasped under her head, with a light snore emanating from her open mouth.

Picking up my phone from the side table it immediately lights up and I squint at the time.

It's a few minutes before five. I know there's no chance I'll fall back asleep—I was lucky enough to sleep the first time—not with only hours to go until we have to be at the prison to meet my father and his lawyer.

I fiddle with my phone, and for some God forsaken reason, decide it'll be a dandy idea to look at my old texts from Rush.

One reads: **You in that tight ass red dress = instant boner. You enjoy torturing me, don't you?**

Another: **Every time I see you at work all I can think about is bending you over the counter and showing you what I can do with my foot-long.**

I giggle at that one, but my heart aches—for pushing him away, for being a liar, for ... well, *everything*.

But shit happens for a reason, and I guess we both need to walk these paths we're on.

I read a few more of his messages and finally toss my phone onto the bed away from me before I decide to do something stupid, like text him, or call him.

Despite the early hour, I know—I *know*—he'd answer right away.

That only makes me feel worse instead of better.

Rolling onto my side to face the wall, I clutch the other pillow against my body, hugging it like it's a person.

"I've made a mess of things," I whisper out loud, the words bouncing off the walls of the barren hotel room.

"You know what you do with messes, you clean them up."

I flop over and find Mia blinking sleepily at me.

"I didn't mean to wake you up," I tell her, feeling bad I've disturbed her rest.

She shrugs. "I couldn't sleep much anyway. I was worried."

"About what?"

She sits up, her vibrant hair looking like a swath of bees have attacked it and made a hive inside the strands. "You, stupid. I'm worried about you. I might've convinced you to come here, but that doesn't mean I don't understand how difficult this is for you. The last thing I want is for you to be hurt, but I know you have to do this. It's time to clip the bonds holding you down."

"I know," I breathe, staring across the small space at her. "You were right to make me come here. Even if nothing good comes of it, I think I would've spent the rest of my life asking what if I had come. Now, I have the chance to know."

She runs her fingers through her hair, trying to make sense of the mess. "Should we go get breakfast? I know it's early, but I'm already hungry and surely something is open."

I nod in agreement. I don't feel hungry, my nerves are too tightly wound, but I'd much rather be anywhere than stuck in this room.

"Cool." She stands and heads for her bag, pulling out her clothes.

An hour later the two of us are dressed, with hair fixed, make up on and walking out the door in search of food. I don't know what it is about looking nice that instantly makes me feel like a badass ready to take on the world.

I am Kira. Hear me roar.

We slide inside onto the buttery leather seats of her car and she pulls out her phone, searching for places to grab breakfast.

"There's a Waffle House nearby, is that cool?"

"Nothing wrong with that," I reply.

She snickers. "We'll have to take a picture and send it to Hollis. Waffle House is his favorite place in the world—do you know he found an article on the internet that says they have a food truck that caters weddings now? He told me that was his one request at our wedding."

I snort. "Aren't there like ten Waffle House's where we live? Why do we need to send him a picture? Also, what did you say to that?"

"We have to send him a picture just to fuck with him, duh.

He thinks that's our thing, so he'll be jealous—and if he's jealous that means hot, fuck-me-until-I-can't-walk sex when I get home. And I told him not to give me any wedding requests until he puts a ring on it." I open my mouth to speak but she finishes with, "To which I added, I didn't want a ring any time soon."

"Good for you, girl. And I guess if it means you get bang-me-against-the-wall-and-pull-my-hair sex then I'll pose for your silly picture."

She laughs and puts the address into her navigation system.

"Speaking of Hollis, how did you finagle bringing me to a *prison* without him or your dad demanding they have to tag along?"

"Well, Hollis has to work, and I didn't tell my dad. All I said was I had to work extra shifts at The Sub Club so I couldn't help at the studio for a few days. No biggie, he'll never know."

I stare at her wide-eyed as she exits the hotel parking lot. "Who are you and what have you done with my goody-two-shoes best friend? The Mia I know would never lie to her father."

"That's before he tried meddling in my love life so much ," she mumbles.

"He is extremely overprotective of his kids." And me too if I'm being honest. Hayes always wants what's best for the people he cares about. He just has a tendency to go overboard.

She flicks her blinker on with far more aggression than is necessary. "He still doesn't need to be so ... so *him*. I'm twenty-three years old and it's exhausting dealing with him. I love him, you know I do, but sometimes I want to shake him."

"Just wait until you have kids," I warn her. "Then he'll really go off the deep end."

She snorts. "Yeah, Hollis won't have a dick left when that happens."

She zips her tiny car into the parking lot and parks in front of the yellow and black themed building. No matter where you go, these places all look the same.

Unbuckling my seatbelt I say, "I hope you're paying for Awful House."

She gasps. "Waffle House is delicious. You take that back."

I laugh, opening the car door. "You're so easy to rile up. It's too much fun."

She gets out of the car and it locks with a pleasant honking sound. I didn't know a honk could be pleasant, but apparently on sports cars it's a requirement or maybe you can pay extra for such extravagances, I wouldn't know.

Opening the door, we're greeted with a chorus of, "Welcome to Waffle House."

I pick a booth hidden in the corner and Mia slides in across from me.

"Mornin' y'all," a plump waitress greets us in a cheery tone —far too cheery for this early in the morning if you ask me. "What can I get ya to drink?"

"Coke," I reply, while Mia glares at me.

"A water for me," she says, and the waitress heads off to fill those bubbly looking clear plastic cups.

"You're going to rot your teeth with all the Coke you're drinking."

I flash her my middle finger and she giggles.

"Don't take my Coke from me. It's all I have left in this world," I joke.

She shakes her head. "You're nuts."

I cross my arms and lay them on top of the table. "Tell me something I don't know."

"Here you ladies go." The waitress sets our cups down and pulls two straws out of her apron, dropping them on the table between the drinks. "Y'all ready to order?"

Mia looks at me and I nod.

"All right, what can I getcha?" The waitress poises her pen against the paper, waiting for us to speak.

"I'll have the cheese omelet," Mia orders. "Hashbrowns with onions, please."

"Egg sandwich for me—with cheese and bacon. Make the bacon crispy—dark, black, and crumbling like my soul."

The waitress gives me a distressed look.

"Ignore her," Mia tells the woman. "She's stressed, and she says weird things when she's that way."

"I'll put this order in for y'all." She flashes Mia a smile and glances at me nervously.

"Stop scaring people," Mia scolds me. "It's rude."

"You know what else is rude—jiggly bacon. Bacon. Should. Not. Jiggle."

She stifles a laugh, shaking her head. "You're impossible."

"Again, tell me something I don't know." I look out the window of the Waffle House. There's a Holiday Inn next door, and across the street a Hardee's. "Why didn't we go there for breakfast?" I accuse. "Hardees trumps Waffle House any day. Everyone knows that."

She waves a dismissive hand. "I can't taunt Hollis with Hardees," she scoffs. "Which reminds me." She picks up her phone and twists in her seat trying to get a shot of the two of us in the restaurant, while also making it obvious it's a Waffle House. "This isn't working," she groans. "Here, hold this." She shoves a menu at me to hold up. "Better," she declares and takes her precious pictures.

She finishes and grins to herself as she types out a message to him.

"I hope this works in your favor," I sing-song. I rest my elbows on the table, interlacing my fingers where I rest my chin. "It could backfire."

"Not likely."

I laugh, smiling at her. "Look at my little Mia—all grown up and gaga over hot, fast, dirty sex. I never thought the day would come."

"You could've never predicted I'd meet Hollis Wilder," she quips.

"No, but I knew the minute I saw him that first time him and Rush stopped by The Sub Club that you two were going to fuck. Did I realize you'd fall in love with each other? Nope—but the sexual tension was too hot to handle."

"What about you and Rush?" she asks, arching a brow seriously. "Did you know then you guys would fall into bed together."

"God, no," I snort. "I mean, he's hot—but I wasn't interested at all at first. He was too cocky and sure of himself. I like men to have a *little* humility."

"Sure, sure," she dismisses my words. "You two still happened."

I stick out my tongue at her. "Only because I saw his cock bouncing in those gym shorts he was wearing. A cock that large and delicious looking swathed in clothes was not something I was about to pass up. Now, look at me." I lean back and point at my belly. "I knew he was trouble from the first time I saw him, and that's exactly what he's done for me. Given me a big heaping spoonful of trouble."

"Oh, please," she scoffs. "When that baby comes out you're going to fall so in love you won't know who you are anymore."

"I didn't say I wouldn't," I counter with a smile, touching my belly. "But it's still trouble. This boy is half of Rush and half of me, which means he's bound to be crazy and bouncing off the walls. I'm going to have my work cut out for me."

"Here you ladies go," the waitress puts our plates down. "One omelet, and one egg sandwich with super crispy bacon."

"Thank you," we both say.

"Can I get y'all anything else right now?"

"Nope, we're good," I tell her.

She walks away and Mia grabs the ketchup bottle, giving it a good shake before she squirts some ketchup on her hashbrowns. "I can't stand when I forget to shake it and it's all liquidy. It makes me gag," she says, and does just that, apparently from the thought alone. "Ketchup should not look like bloody water. I see enough of that at period time."

I snort. "A major plus side of pregnancy—no periods."

"Yeah, well no babies for me yet. Sorry." She frowns mockingly. Sobering, she says, "I always thought we'd have kids at the same time. Now we're not."

"There's always next time," I joke.

"Do you think you'll have more kids?"

I bite my lip, thinking seriously about her question. "I never imagined I'd have *any* kids. Well, I guess it depended on certain things."

"What kind of things?" She spears a bite of her omelet.

I pick up my sandwich and take a bite before I answer her. "I wouldn't want to be one of those women who has a bunch of kids and ends up on welfare and yelling at her children all the time. That's just ... not the life I want for myself. So, yeah, I guess it would depend on if..." My cheeks bloom with red like a flower opening its petals to the sun.

"If...?" she probes, raising one brow.

I feel my breath come faster, each inhale short with not enough oxygen, while my pulse rapidly picks up speed.

"I didn't believe in love—didn't want it, and had no use for it, but yes, somehow, somewhere, some way I fell in love with Rush. I didn't want to admit it to myself, let alone him or anyone else. But I ... I love him, despite all this," I toss my hands in the air, "I still do. But I'm also enough of a realist to know love doesn't get you everything or anywhere in life. Love can sometimes be the greatest burden of all, dragging you down into the deepest pit of despair, and I won't let him drown me."

"What if he's your air?" she counters, and I'm not surprised. Mia might not have wanted to fall for Hollis, but that doesn't mean she still doesn't believe in true love and the prince saving the princess.

Only, in this story, I'm the witch and Rush is the demon.

"What if he's not?"

MIA AND I HOP ON THE SHUTTLE TO TAKE US OVER TO THE PRISON —just like she thought we would from all her Criminal Minds watching.

Looking around at the few others on the bus I feel extremely out of place. I don't know why, they're average looking, normal people, but somehow I feel like ... I guess like I'm better than them, than *this*. But the fact of the matter is, you don't choose your family and anyone on the street could be in this same position.

"This is fun, right?" Mia asks, rubbing her hands together excitedly.

I shoot her a look. "Fun?" I blurt. "How is this *fun?*"

She gets a sheepish look and sinks toward the window. "I've never been to a prison," she whispers under her breath. "I've only seen them on TV."

The woman behind us snorts. "Oh, honey, this is nothing like on TV."

"What's it like?" I ask her, twisting around in my seat.

"Well, you'll get patted down to make sure you're not hiding anything, they'll even make sure your bump is real." She nods toward my stomach. "There are metal detectors, ID checks. It's serious business."

"Okay, so maybe *fun* wasn't the right word." Mia looks sheepishly between the woman and me.

"Ya think?" I retort.

I don't mean to mock her, but I'm nervous, and when I'm nervous I'm more rude than normal.

Not only am I about to walk into a prison, which is panic inducing as it is, but I'm about to see my father for the first time in years. Hell, I barely saw him before that. He only popped in and out of my life when he wanted something from my mom—usually sex, money, or drugs.

The only fond memory I have of him is one year at Christmas he gave me a Barbie doll. She wore a red dress with gingerbread men on it and had green earrings. She was one of my most precious possessions for the longest time. I thought it was proof my father loved me. But then I grew up and learned material items don't equal love, and he'd probably stolen it anyway.

The bus comes to a stop and the doors open with a squeak and pop of air.

If I thought my heart was beating fast before, it's tenfold now. I can't control the out of sync rhythm and I worry it's not okay for the baby.

"Come on," Mia says, coaxing me off the bus when I don't move.

I blink and look around, realizing everyone is already off the bus and the driver is waiting impatiently for us.

I stand up and force my feet in front of me down the aisle and to the steps. When my feet touch ground I feel sea sick, which is ironic since my feet are rooted firmly to the earth.

Mia hops out behind me, and the doors screech closed behind us. The bus pulls away, leaving behind a puff of exhaust smoke and the lingering stench of fuel.

Ahead of us, the prison looms like a dark gray bleak fortress

—which I guess is exactly what it is. It looks like something out of a futuristic movie, where the world has ended and it's left looking gray and bleak with no hope at all.

Mia and I follow the others and begin the procedures to get in.

They do in fact check my belly—I kind of thought the lady made that one up, but apparently women have been known to put on a fake belly and try to smuggle stuff in. The lengths people will go to makes me question humanity at times.

I expect to end up sitting at one of those phone booth type things to speak to my father—but apparently since he's going to die and all, they're allowing us contact, as if I *want* that.

An officer leads us to a room and closes the door behind him. There's a mirror and Mia taps me on the shoulder and points at it. "I wonder if we're being watched."

I don't answer her because I'm too busy looking at the man seated at the table, behind him in the corner is a man in a nice suit speaking on the phone who must be his lawyer.

I've seen people, thanks to my studies, close to death because of cancer—and it's obvious this is the case with my dad, so at least that wasn't a ploy to get me out here.

He's dying, and from the looks of it, any day now.

His skin is sagging, like even it has lost strength and the will to live and now only flops loosely over his body like an oversized blanket. His eyes are sallow, and sunken into his skull. I can't remember the exact shade of hazel his eyes were—whether they were more brown or green—but now they're a muddy dirty color, and clouded like mud has been smeared across. His once auburn colored hair is gone, but a few tiny little tufts stick out from his skull haloed by the light filtering in through the window. His lips are almost non-existent, as if they've shriveled up like raisins.

He's a stranger to me, and not because of how he looks.

He's my father, but only because I happened to come from his sperm. He's none of the things that truly makes someone a father.

The man in the corner hangs up his phone and I feel Mia's hand reach down and take mine, squeezing it. She doesn't let go and I'm silently thankful for the small amount of strength that seeps into me from her.

The lawyer comes around the table to stand in front of me. "Mitchell Williamson," he sticks his hand out and I reluctantly take it with my right one. "Your father's lawyer. And I guess he needs no introduction. Who is this?" He indicates Mia—how he knew I was Quinton's daughter is beyond me.

"This is my best friend. She's here so I don't have to be alone," I reply with a bite to my tone.

I don't give her name and she doesn't offer it. It's better if neither of them know who she actually is. People act differently if they manage to put two and two together and figure out who her father is.

"Sit down, please," Mitchell indicates the two plastic chairs across from my father, and he takes the one beside him.

My dad has yet to say a word. I don't know what he's waiting for, since apparently I'm here at his request. You'd think he'd be a bit more forthcoming.

Mia and I sit down. She flashes me an encouraging look.

I steel my shoulders, raising my chin slightly—not haughtily but defiantly. I won't cower to this man. I won't be made to feel less than I am, because I'm worth more.

He looks me over with those sick tired eyes of his.

Normally, I would begrudge such scrutiny from *anyone*, but today I'll tolerate it because after this he'll never see me again. He might as well get his fill.

"Kira," he whispers, his voice as weak as he looks.

Before he says more, I look him over more fully and decide

he reminds me a snail without its shell, pale, slimy, and gross looking.

"Quinton," I finally reply.

No way in hell am I driving this conversation. He wanted me here, so he'll have to do the talking or he won't get anything out of me. Perhaps, not even then.

"You look ... grown up."

"That's what happens when years pass and you don't see someone because you're locked away in prison for nearly beating their mother to death."

The words pour hatefully out of me and I'm shocked by them. Each word seems to pierce him like a bullet. I didn't know I'd been harboring this inside me, but the venom in my words is raw and real, not something that can be faked.

"I would tell you I'm sorry for that, but I know you wouldn't believe me." His voice is so soft, like a thousand tiny butterflies fluttering their wings.

"You're right," I state. "I wouldn't." My tone isn't nasty, not this time, just honest. I'm not here to lie and make him feel good about himself. I'm not a fucking cheerleader. He's a prisoner, I'm his daughter, and that's it.

"I can't believe how old you are now," he continues, like my blunt statement doesn't mean anything at all. I guess it doesn't.

"People get old," I mutter.

He chuckles and it turns to a cough. "That they do."

"Look, Quinton." I cross my arms and lean closer to him over the metal table. "I'm not here for niceties. In fact, I don't really know why I came at all. But the fact of the matter is, I am. Let's get on with the real purpose now shall we? I don't like my time wasted and well," I quirk my head, "it doesn't look like you have much time left at all."

I see anger simmer in his eyes and I smirk to myself, because while he might be a shell of what he used to be, he's still the same underneath that saggy paper-thin skin.

"Is it so unbelievable to think my dying wish would be to see my daughter?" The question ends with a hacking cough.

"Yes," I sigh sadly. "Yes, it is. I never mattered to you or mom. I was an object. Something to place on a shelf and pull out when I became useful. I was nothing then, so why would I be something now?"

"I'm sorry," he whispers. "For what it's worth, I am. I'm sorry I was such an angry fuck. I'm sorry I was a liar, a cheater, a druggie, an abuser. I'm just sorry I *was*."

"Sorry doesn't change the past, but good news Quinton, it's just that. The *past*. We all have to move on with our lives eventually."

For some reason my words strike a chord within myself as I realize I've been holding on to this hatred for him, for my mom, for everything and it hasn't mattered. Holding onto this hatred hasn't been healthy for *me*—and it hasn't affected them at all. They're untouched by it, while I've continued to suffer.

A weight lifts off my shoulders with the epiphany and I feel good, better than I have for years, because I'm no longer weighed down by their burdens or mine.

I choose my path. They don't forge it for me. From this moment forward I'm my own person. I exist separately from them and their sins. I don't have to be like them. I don't have to punish myself.

I am me, and they are them.

My future is what I make it.

I stand up suddenly, the backs of my knees shoving the chair back where it scrapes roughly across the floor—the noise loud and obnoxious, not at all pleasant.

"Mitchell," I nod my head at the lawyer, "Quinton. This has been ... enlightening. I'll be going now."

"B-But," my dad stutters as Mia follows me to the exit. "That's it?" he asks, his tone angry and stronger sounding than before.

I turn around and look over my shoulder at him with Mia hovering in my peripheral.

"That's it," I respond. "I don't owe you anything, and you owe me nothing—even if you did, I don't want it. From this moment forward I'm my own person and I won't let myself rule my life by other people's sins. Not anymore."

Straightening my shoulders, I march out the door with Mia on my heels.

"That was bad ass," she says.

"Thank you," I reply, smiling.

It's a real, genuine, happy smile—not one I've forced.

I choose my destiny, I choose my path, I *choose*.

I finally understand why Mia felt I needed to come here. She was right all along. It wasn't my dad I needed to see, it was *me*. I needed to see that I'm not him, or my mom. I'm my own person and this is *my* life to live.

So, it's time I actually started living it.

FORTY

Rush

"I'm sitting up front," Fox calls, sprinting around me and heading for Cannon's Land Rover.

"Nuh-uh. No you don't."

I take off after him and since I'm taller, I pass him easily, snagging the coveted shotgun spot.

"Stop acting like children," Cannon scolds, coming up behind us and unlocking the car.

As he heads for the driver's side Fox hisses at me, "You know why I have to sit up front you prick."

I grin back. "I know why, and that's *exactly* why you're sitting in the back. No way am I missing out on the opportunity to watch you squirm."

"I fucking hate you," he grumbles, yanking open the back door forcefully and climbing inside.

When I'm seated in front of him, he gives the seat a rough kick.

"Hey!" Cannon snaps, twisting around to glare at Fox. "Are you fucking five? Don't kick my fucking car seats or you can pay to have this baby detailed."

"Whatever," Fox grumbles, glaring out the window at the hotel's garage.

Shaking his head, Cannon starts the car.

"You could stay behind, you know," I sing-song to Fox.

"Fat chance," he mutters.

I grin to myself. The idiot might not want to sit in the back stuck beside Calista, but he *does* want to see her when she gets here.

Beside me, Cannon is completely oblivious to Fox's turmoil. Personally, I don't think he's as unaware of the whole Fox and Calista thing as he seems. Do I think he knows about the whole virginity sex pact? I doubt it. But Cannon's perceptive and he has to know Fox and his sister have a thing for each other. Maybe it doesn't bother him, out of all of us, Fox is the most tame next to Cannon.

"Why did you two want to come anyway?" Cannon asks, pulling out of the garage.

I snort. "Callie is like our little sister, too," I jab at Fox, fighting a grin. "We want to see her."

"Yeah, but she's going to be living with us so it's not like you wouldn't see her."

"We just want to roll out the welcoming mat, C-Man. It's what friends do."

"Mhmm," he hums doubtfully. "Here, put something on and shut up." He hands me the AUX cord, which is a very, *very* dangerous thing to do.

I smile gleefully.

"Oh for fuck's sake, he's got that weird look on his face. What have you done, Cannon?" Fox complains in the back. "Never give Rush the fucking AUX cord."

"Too late now," Cannon mumbles, heading toward the interstate. "Don't make me regret this," he warns me.

"Never." I grin widely and crazily, like the Joker.

Moments later *He's A Pirate* by the amazingly talented Hans Zimmer begins to play.

"Oh no," Fox says, and I glance behind to see him throw his head back. "He's going to do the dance."

Calling it a dance is a bit of a stretch, but there a ton of hand gestures and flailing involved.

"For the love of God," Cannon mutters. "I don't think they predicted you when they wrote the laws that constitute distracted driving."

"That's because nothing in the world can prepare you for pirate Rush."

He shakes his head. "Drunk pirate Rush is a nut case, but the sober one is just as insane."

"I can't help it that I was a pirate in another life," I retort, still dancing to the orchestra song.

When the song ends Fox pleads from the back, "For the love of God, pick a normal song."

I scroll through my playlist and switch to *What Does The Fox Say?*

"Nope, no, *no*," he shakes his head rapidly back and forth, "this is not what I meant."

"I have the AUX cord and I'm in charge. Deal with it, motherfucker," I cackle merrily.

Cannon grins back and even Fox cracks a reluctant smile.

This is the first time in months I've felt so light.

By the time we pull up to arrivals at the airport, I've played every annoying song I can think of to irritate the shit out of them.

"Do you see her?" Cannon asks, squinting at arrivals.

"She's right there," Fox murmurs softly. When I turn around, I find him staring out the window with a look of longing—coveting something he feels he has no right to.

Cannon looks where he's pointing and spots Calista.

She stands by her suitcase, with large black sunglasses on. Her dark hair curls down past her breasts. Short and curvy, guys nearby can't help but check her out. She's hot, even I'll admit it—but unlike Fox, I never had the balls to go after her, besides, she's far too much like a little sister to me and that'd be gross.

Cannon puts the Land Rover in park and hops out to greet her, wrapping her in a massive hug.

Those two might argue non-stop and send each other idiotic pictures, but they're closer than any other siblings I know. It's kind of comical seeing Callie be swallowed by Cannon's massive tattooed arms. She all but disappears.

Fox sighs forlornly behind me.

"You can say hi to her," I tell him. "It's not like you're going to kiss her in front of him or strip her naked. Hellos are okay."

"You wouldn't get it," he mutters.

I suppose I wouldn't. I've fucked around, but I've never pined for someone I can't have. Unless you count Kira, but I don't. I could've had her, if I hadn't fucked things up. If I'd been patient, and waited, she would've realized how right we are.

Instead, I went off the deep end and nearly fucked another woman—someone I felt nothing for, just to what? Be an asshole? Prove to myself I don't need Kira?

It doesn't matter what my intentions might've been, they were shitty and ill-guided. Every day I feel sick over it, but I know I can't change it. All I can do is move forward and better myself, so I never do anything as stupid ever again.

Cannon heads back to the car, wheeling Callie's suitcase

behind him. He opens the trunk and puts it in, then takes the duffel off her shoulder and puts it beside the suitcase.

"Hey, guys." Callie waves through the open trunk.

I raise my hand, my neck aching from sitting turned around so long.

"Hi, Cal," Fox says, his voice higher than normal and forced sounding.

She looks back at him, but I can't get a read on her—if she's as lovesick as good ole Foxy boy.

Cannon closes the trunk and then they're walking around the side of the vehicle. She opens the passenger door, sliding in beside Fox.

I can tell he would love nothing more than to look out the window, away from her, but it would become suspicious if he avoided her completely.

"How have you been?" he asks, as she places her purse between her feet and reaches for the seatbelt.

"I'm good—just needed to get away for a while. Debra was smothering me. I need to spread my wings a bit, maybe suck some peen while I'm at it."

Cannon bumps the horn by accident at the word *peen* as he gets inside the car.

"Calista," he grumbles. "Don't make me shove you on a plane back home myself."

"I'm only kidding. Basically, the Tinder dick pic pile was growing thin. I thought if I came here, I might get some good shots to replenish my stash so I can keep bugging you," she tells her brother.

Fox's face grows red, but nobody but me seems to notice.

Cannon mutters something under his breath as he pulls away from the terminal. "Remember, I kindly agreed to let you come here. Don't shove it in my face."

She snorts. "Kindly? You didn't agree kindly, big bro."

"I did speak with Mom on your behalf," he reminds her, glancing briefly in the rearview mirror at her.

"And I thanked you for convincing Debra I would be fine. I'm twenty—not twelve. She needs to stop suffocating me."

"Don't call Mom by her first name, that's rude."

"You always were such a goody-two shoes." She leans forward and playfully ruffles his perfectly coifed hair. "But you still have your rebel ways, so stop giving me grief." She grins and pokes his tattooed arm. "*Mom* almost shit a brick when you came home with the first one."

"Why is it I feel like by letting you come here I've basically allowed myself to be taunted for an undetermined amount of time?"

"Uh ... because that's exactly what you did," she says in a duh tone.

Cannon makes eye contact with each of us guys. "Pray for me, fellas. I'm going to need it."

"WHERE ARE YOU GOING?" CALISTA ASKS ME, FROM WHERE SHE lays on the couch, a fashion magazine glued to her hand.

"None of your business, that's where I'm going."

She rolls her eyes. "I was just curious, that's all. You don't have to be a dick about it."

"I'm a dick about everything," I counter. "I'll be back later."

I doubt Cannon's told her about me joining AA and I'm not planning to inform her either. The less people who know, the better. Not that I think Callie would go blabbing her mouth all over social media ... no, that's exactly what I think.

Speaking of social media, I've barely been looking at mine. I wonder if my fans have even noticed. I used to be on it practically twenty-four-seven before we came here and started focusing on the album. Then Kira happened and took up even more of my time, because I wanted to be with her.

I guess that should've been my first tip-off things were different with her. She's the first female since my parents have died that I willingly wanted to spend time with and actually *wanted* to have sex with. Don't get me wrong, I enjoyed all the sex I had prior to her, but that's all it was about. The sex. The release. The *who* didn't matter.

When I finally reach the street outside the hotel I pause for a moment, inhaling a breath of the fresh spring air.

Two seconds later a sneeze explodes from me.

"Fucking pollen," I mutter, and get a dirty look from a passing little old lady on the street.

Shaking my head, I let my feet carry me to the MMA training gym where the meeting is held. I arrive earlier than I did the first time, and only a few people linger around.

I pick a donut covered in chocolate icing and sprinkles, devouring it in two bites. I ignore the coffee this time, having learned better than to attempt to drink it.

Strolling over to where the chairs are set up, I pick a seat closer to the front this time, but more in the middle, because there's no fucking way I'm sitting smack dab in the front row. I might enjoy being the center of attention when it comes to most things, but this isn't one of them.

Somebody drops into the seat beside me, and I'm not surprised when I turn and find Daniel seated beside me. He smiles widely, pleased, his eyes warm.

"Welcome back, Rush."

"Did you think I wouldn't come?" I question, wanting his honest answer.

Looking at me through his thin wire framed glasses he says, "Most people think the first time you come to a meeting is the hardest, but they're wrong. It's each time after, because each meeting is a step closer to leaving the alcoholic behind. But like any addict your mind rebels, urging you to go back to what you know, because up ahead ... the journey is unclear. But you're here, and that's good."

"I'm here," I echo.

"I'm proud of you." He squeezes my shoulder and stands, going to speak to someone else.

Those four simple words hurt more than he can possibly know, but they also mean a lot, a whole lot, because I haven't heard them since I was eighteen-years-old in the back of a car moments away from my life changing forever.

Daniel is practically a stranger to me, but I sense kinship within him, and maybe it's a common bond all alcoholics share. After all, I'm only beginning to accept the fact I am one. I've spent years denying it. To myself. To my friends. To everyone.

As the meeting starts, I listen carefully to everyone who chooses to share. I know I need to get up there and open up, but this is only my second meeting and I'm not there yet. I need more time to sort through my thoughts, to figure out how I truly feel.

When the meeting ends a few people speak to me. I'm the new guy and I guess they're curious. I give as little information as I can, because so far, I don't think anyone knows I'm in The Wild, and here recording with my band. The last thing I need is word getting out and spreading to the media that I'm in AA. I know it's supposed to be anonymous, but money talks and there are a lot of people who would willingly sell you out for a few thousand bucks.

I toss up my hand in a goodbye wave at Daniel before I head out on the street. The sun is beginning to set, but I'm not ready to go back to the hotel yet.

I look left and right, then start walking, letting my feet guide me wherever they want to go.

Twenty minutes later I find myself standing on the street, looking up at Kira's second-story apartment and the stairs leading up to the door. I didn't mean to come here, but I guess my subconscious led me here. I know from Hollis she's gone with Mia this weekend out of town—a girl's trip, he said. She needed to clear her head, because of me, I guess.

I hate that I'm such an asshole, that I hurt her so much she had to get away.

If I could drop to my knees and say I'm sorry a thousand times and I knew she'd forgive me, I would.

But I know that's not enough.

I have to work on myself before we can ever work together—and even then, she might not give me another chance. She might truly not love me, but I don't believe it, not anymore.

Being sober brings a new clarity to things, and looking back to that night in the hotel ... I scared her. My *words* scared her.

Her parents, the two people in the world who should've loved her unconditionally and moved mountains for her, didn't. That love was used against her, tossed in her face until love was no longer pure to her and represented something disgusting, something to be *used* and exploited. I would never do that to her, not even drunk off my ass, but she couldn't know that—couldn't let herself believe it either.

I inhale a shaky breath and exhale it slowly.

"Forgive me, Kira," I whisper into the growing dark. "Forgive me and let me love you until my dying breath."

She's not there to hear, to listen, but it's not meant for her ears yet anyway.

It's a promise, a vow to myself that I *will* get her back.

Not today, not tomorrow, but one day—because we're a flame, one that will never burn out.

FORTY-ONE

Kira

"You think you're good?" Mia asks, setting my bag down in my apartment. She insisted on carrying it up, because to quote her *you're pregnant, sit back and let people do shit for you.*

"I'll be fine." I mean it too. "Thank you."

I'm thanking her for so much more than carrying my bag up. For convincing me to go to North Carolina, for taking me, for being there for me through all these years, and all the ups and downs. She might be my only friend, but when you have a friend as good as her you don't need any more.

"I love you, girl," she says, and hugs me tight. "I'm so proud of you."

"For what?" I ask, holding her at arm's length and looking at her. I can't think of anything I've done to be proud of.

"For facing things head on. For being the bad ass you are."

"I'm nothing remarkable." I shake my head and let her go, taking a step back.

"That's where you're wrong. You're strong, and resilient. You're so much more than you give yourself credit for. You handled everything this weekend with dignity when you could've ranted and raged. You're admirable, Kira—and I do, admire you that is. I'm lucky to call you my best friend."

"Stop!" I scold her, fanning my face. "I'm pregnant and emotional. You can't say things like that. I cry over the dumbest things these days."

She laughs and pulls me into another hug. "I love you, Kiki."

I bust out laughing. "You haven't called me that since high school."

She shrugs. "I thought it was time to bring out the old nicknames."

I roll my eyes playfully, grinning widely. "All right, get out of here then, *Mimi*. Go see your man and have that hot sex you've been talking about."

She gives a little shimmy. "I'm gonna get sexed up tonight. Bye, girl." She blows a kiss my way and then she's gone, the door clicking closed behind her.

I lock it and then collapse on my couch, exhausted—mentally and physically.

My eyes are heavy and I know I could fall asleep right here if I let myself, but this couch is not the best thing for me or my back.

I give myself a total of three minutes before I get up and carry my bag down the hall to my room.

Dumping it in the corner of the bedroom I take a shower before changing into my pajamas and getting into bed. Turning the TV on, I hope something mindless will help me fall asleep. Tomorrow it's back to school and my endlessly busy schedule. Summer can't get here fast enough.

I keep eyeing my phone on the nightstand, and I feel stupid and ridiculous, because I'm hoping Rush will text me. I don't even know why he's on my mind or why I'm hoping for it. I still don't know if I think we're what's best for each other, but I miss him. I didn't feel so alone when he was around. He didn't even have to be in the same room as me, but knowing he was a text or phone call away brought a comfort I didn't know I had until it was gone.

Picking up my phone I open his contact.

Me: I miss you.

I type out the words, staring at them, but I don't press send—because while I might miss him, he *hurt* me, and I know from Mia he joined AA. I don't want him to think I forgive him and that means he doesn't have to keep working on himself.

For now, as much as it hurts, I know we're both better apart.

He needs to grow on his own, and so do I. Seeing my father might've been a big step, but there's still more baggage I need to let go of. One moment of clarity doesn't erase years of mental and emotional abuse.

I backspace the words and close my eyes, tossing my phone so I don't see where it lands—that way, I can't be tempted to pick it up and do something stupid.

Eventually, I fall asleep with the feel of phantom arms around me.

Parking my car outside the post office I dig through my bag and procure my key to my box. I rarely check it, because I don't get anything important, just junk—all my bills are either taken care of directly with my landlord or online. It's been probably two months since I checked it, which is longer than I normally go.

The bell tied around the handle jingles as I enter. The post office is long and narrow, lined with rows and rows of boxes for all the apartments around here. I locate mine and open it, pulling out the stack of fliers and advertisements someone has wrapped a rubber band around. A piece of yellow paper flutters to the ground and I bend down to pick it up. I squint at it, finding that it tells me I have a package too large to fit in the box.

I march up to the empty counter and slap it down.

"I didn't order anything—so I think this was put in my box by mistake."

The man picks up the slip of paper and looks at it. "Kira Marsh, right?"

"Um ... yeah," I answer reluctantly.

"It's the right one then."

He gets up then and heads into the back returning with several Amazon boxes.

"There you go." He shoves them at me and air whooshes out of my lungs as I struggle to carry them out and to my car. I end up having to make several trips since the boxes are heavy.

I still think they were sent by mistake, but my name *is* on the label.

Once they're loaded it's a short drive to my apartment and I have to make *five* more trips to and from my apartment to get the boxes and my other stuff inside.

Finally, I lock the door behind me and pause to catch my breath. My pregnant ass is not equipped to walk up and down the stairs that many times in a row.

Once I don't sound like I'm wheezing on my last breath I grab a knife and begin opening the boxes.

Each one contains baking supplies—cake pans, cupcake pans, a glass display, a sheet for piping out macarons, icing bags and tips, basically anything and everything I could possibly need to bake whatever I want. Opening the last box, my jaw goes slack at the sight of the bright red Kitchen Aid mixer. I've dreamed of having one for years but I never believed I could afford one. Now one's been handed to me and I know there's only one person who could've possibly done this.

Despite my better judgment I pick up my phone.

When he answers I blurt, "You shouldn't have done this. You didn't need to buy me all of this stuff. Rush, I can't accept this."

"I wondered when you'd get it." I can hear his smile on the other end.

"I don't deserve this." I press a hand to my head, trying to ignore how my heart picks up speed at the sound of his voice.

"I wanted you to have it."

"How long ago did you send it? Surely after everything you'd rather me return this so you can get your money back."

"I bought it all the minute this beautiful brown-eyed girl spoke of her passion for baking and her dream of opening a shop one day. I know you'd make an amazing nurse, Kira, but you shouldn't give up on your dreams."

"Most of us have to be practical," I reason, exhaling a breath. "We can't all be rock stars."

He sighs, but it's not a disgruntled sigh—more one born of defeat and maybe despair. "I had to give up on my dream once, not by choice, but by force of circumstances. If it's something that can be avoided, it should. At least now, you can bake when you have time. Even if you never open that shop like you dreamed, you'll still be baking. Did you get the card?"

"No, I didn't see the card, but I haven't gone through the mail portion yet. And what did you mean? What dream did you have to give up on?"

I hear a door close in the background and some rustling. "I wanted to play basketball. I got a full ride scholarship to Duke University on the same day I was in the car accident that took away my ability to play. It's the day I lost not only my dream, but my parents."

"Rush," I gasp, my voice breaking along with my heart.

"There are no excuses for what I've done and who I've been, but maybe you can understand just a little bit more."

"I still don't feel right accepting this," I say, before I blurt out something I can't take back.

"It's a gift," he says softly, almost sadly. "It's not given with the expectation of getting anything return. I want you to have it."

"Well, thank you," I reply. I know I should hang up the phone, but I don't want to. I want to linger in this moment a little longer.

"It's good to hear your voice," he says. "H-How's the baby?" he asks hesitantly.

"He's doing good. I should feel him moving soon."

Clearing his throat, he says, "I better go, Kira. It was good to hear from you."

Strangers, it's what we're acting like—and it doesn't feel good. I don't like this one bit, but everything is fucked up and I don't know how we can ever repair it. We are both on our way to fixing ourselves, so maybe there's hope. I'll hold onto that—to hope, because without hope there's nothing left in this world.

"Bye," I whisper.

He lingers on the phone a few seconds longer and then he exhales a breath and the line goes dead.

I feel warm all over from the sound of his voice and now in its absence I can feel a chill starting to seep into my limbs.

Grabbing the stack of mail I rifle through it and find the card he sent.

Tearing it open, I slide it out of the envelope, nearly giving myself a paper cut in the process.

I read the front and out the side five-hundred dollars falls into my hand with a note attached:

For ingredients.

Inside the card in his scrawl he's added:

We might make new dreams, but it doesn't mean we should give up on our old ones. Dreams are fuel to making the impossible become possible. I'll thoroughly enjoy eating whatever you bake—and eating other things if you let me. –Rush

I grab my phone and send him a text.

Kira: You shouldn't give up on your old dreams either. Even if you couldn't play basketball in college and go pro if that's what you dreamed of, you can still get on a court and make the best of it. Maybe it'll fill a blank space.

A moment later the message shows it has been read, but he doesn't reply. Regardless, I hope my words will impact him in some way.

FORTY-TWO

Rush

"I come bearing cupcakes," Mia sing-songs as she dances into the studio in the afternoon. We've been at it for hours, and since I'm no longer drinking, I suddenly understand why Cannon's always lighting up a cigarette. I need something to take the edge off and I guess a cupcake will have to do. "And before you ask," she adds, setting a cupcake carrier down on the chair, one I'm familiar with since I added it to my Amazon shopping cart months ago when I ordered supplies for Kira, "no, I didn't make these. Kira did. Apparently, there's a Martha Stewart in her that I didn't know existed."

A pleased smirk lifts my lips and I hide it behind my hand. I'm happy, because I knew something about Kira that Mia didn't. It's something Kira could've shared with her years ago, but like so many things, kept it to herself. It's one small piece of herself she gave willingly to me and only me.

"They're chocolate with chocolate icing and chocolate chips sprinkled on top, because apparently Kira is having a chocolate craving or something. Honestly, I think we're all lucky they're not Coke flavored and we should count our blessings," she rambles, passing them out.

I give her a small smile when I take mine. Staring at the blue cupcake wrapper with white dots, I wish selfishly I could've watched her bake them.

Does she sing when she bakes? Does she dance? I wonder if she wore the apron I sent?

I force the thoughts from my mind as I peel back the wrapper, exposing the chocolate cake part. It looks moist and delicious. Even the icing is applied expertly. The care and love she put into creating these is obvious.

When she gets to Hollis she gives him a saucy grin and I suppress the urge to roll my eyes. Not only are they grossly in love, but for the first time in my life I'm jealous of it. I've always looked down on lovey-dovey couples, finding their devotion annoying and overdone, but I'd give anything to have Kira smile at me, to touch her freely.

More importantly, I wish we could exist in a world where our demons could be easily defeated and being together was easy.

Even if she does forgive me at some point, there will be nothing easy about our life. I'll always be an alcoholic and her past will always exist. But hopefully we could keep each other from being pulled under by the tide.

I take a bite of the cupcake and it tastes fucking *good*, even better than it looks, which is saying a lot.

"Tell her thanks for the cupcakes," I say to Mia, raising my half-eaten cupcake.

"I will." She gives me a sympathetic smile and it makes me want to cringe. I don't need her sympathy or anyone else's. I made my bed, now I have to lie in it.

Speaking to Kira on the phone almost a week ago was nice—hearing her voice made me pathetically happy. I could send her a text myself and thank her for the cupcakes, but I don't want to push myself on her. I want her to know she has as much choice in this as I do. If she doesn't want to give us a shot, I'll be okay with it. Will I be happy about it? Hell, no. But I won't be an asshole about it either, because I understand she doesn't owe it to me to give us a shot.

I want her to know she can come to me when *she's* ready and I won't crowd her.

This whole trying to be a better person, and doing the right thing, is fucking hard.

I finish the cupcake and toss the wrapper in the trashcan. I take a swig of Mountain Dew—my new vice of choice, I guess—as Hayes directs us to get back to work.

We'll be flying out to L.A. soon for a short trip to meet with a couple of managers and PR people to see if we can find a fit. I don't want to fucking go, and I'm hoping I can talk my way out of it. The last thing I need right now is to step back into that city. It's the kind of place that demands a price to be paid. I've been paying it for years and didn't know it, with my drinking, with women, with my pure and uncontrolled self-destruction.

It's weird looking back, at all the times I believed I was in control, that my choices were mine, and I realize now that the alcohol had taken hold and numbed me to it, all while making me believe I was fine.

A couple hours later we're heading out of the studio. Fox turns for the hotel and Hollis is still inside with Mia while she straightens things up—hell, they're probably fucking instead. I'm slightly jealous at the thought, but there's only one woman I want, and she doesn't want me right now. Probably, not ever.

But I also know it's better if I don't have sex right now, either. Like alcohol, I was using it to fill a void in my heart. One I was trying to cover with dirt, but it kept sifting away. None of the things I've been doing were helping me. They were only making things worse instead of better.

Cannon leans against the exterior of the building and lights up his cigarette. A girl passing by on the street eyes him up and down. She pauses, nibbling on her bottom lip and my brows knit as I watch her.

"Can I help you?" Cannon asks in a polite tone. "Are you lost? I'm not from here and I'm shit at directions." He blows the smoke from his mouth away from her. Even still, she inhales it likes it's the most pleasant aroma she's encountered.

"I'd love to call you Daddy," she blurts. "Oh my God, did I say that out loud?" I stifle my snort and give her a nod that yes, in fact, she did confess she wants to call my best friend *Daddy*.

I can imagine her cries of passion now.

Yes, Daddy. Harder, Daddy. Oooh, right there, Daddy.

I've never gotten the appeal of calling a man *daddy* in bed. It just sounds ... disturbing to me, but to each their own. The ironic part is, he acts like such a dad, but I know that was not where her brain was going.

In fact, I'd say she was more likely imagining the length of his rod and how fun it would be to take for a ride.

Cannon looks like a deer caught in headlights. "Um..." He begins, not sure how to respond.

The girl, her pale skin entirely flushed now, says, "I'll just be going now. Pretend this never happened."

She takes off down the street as fast as her legs will carry her.

Cannon shakes his head. "I always get the crazies, man."

I chortle. "Remind me to tell Hayes we need to make Daddy Cannon shirts for sale."

He pushes me. "Don't you fucking dare." He tosses his cigarette down on the ground, grinding the toe of his boot into it.

"I better get going," I tell him.

"Where?" he asks, but for once his eyes don't narrow in suspicion.

"I ... I'm attending a grief counseling meeting," I admit. There's no point in me being ashamed of the truth. I've been spending a lot of time with Blaire and Ryder at The Paper Crane Project, getting to know them and listening to their story. Somehow, through their heartbreak they found the power to continue on, to even fall in love with each other. Already they've helped me to understand I'll never forget my parents and the ache will never truly go away, but it does get better once I accept that it can.

"Really?" Cannon raises a brow.

"Yeah." I nod, exhaling a sigh.

"I'm proud of you, man. Truly, I am. You've made a lot of progress the last few weeks, and if you stay on this path, I know you'll get even better. You're like a brother to me. I've only ever wanted what's best for you. Seeing you throw your life away hasn't been easy."

"I'm sorry," I say, and I mean it too. "I'm sorry you, Fox, and Hollis had to watch me spiral out of control. I'm sorry I couldn't see what was going on. I was blind to everything I was doing and becoming. I'm sorry you've had to shoulder so much because of my sorry ass."

He claps me on the shoulder. "That's what friends are for, and anyone who doesn't think so isn't a real friend. You always do whatever you can, in any way, for the people you love."

"Thanks, man. I better go." I hook a thumb over my shoulder.

"See you later," he calls as I head off.

Ten or so minutes later I open the door to The Paper Crane project. The tables are pushed out of the way, to each side of the room, with the chairs arranged in a circle in the center of the now empty space.

I'd be lying if I didn't say my heart races with fear.

I feel incredibly vulnerable looking at those chairs, some already filled, knowing I'm about to face the loss of my parents head on. Somehow, this is worse than attending AA and I don't know what that says about me.

"Glad you could come," Ryder says, and I jolt away in surprise since I didn't realize he was practically beside me.

He gives a small chuckle, watching me from behind his thick-framed black glasses. His dark hair is slicked back and his smile is kind. He knows how hard it is for me to come here, and what exactly it means.

Acceptance.

The final step to grief.

Accepting that they're gone and not coming back.

Accepting that it's okay to hurt some days, but not all of the time.

Accepting that I can move on with my life and it doesn't mean forgetting or loving them any less.

"We have drinks, coffee, snacks, whatever." He indicates a table. "Help yourself if you want anything. We'll be starting in a few."

I nod my thanks as he moves off. I spot Blaire speaking to someone and when she sees me, she waves with a smile.

I grab a bottle of water, not because I'm thirsty, but because I know I'll feel better with something in my hands instead of nothing.

Heading over to the chairs I take a seat and brace myself for what's to come.

A couple more people trickle in, but all total, including Ryder and Blaire, there are only eight people.

Ryder speaks, but I barely hear what he's saying. It's like

there's thunder rumbling in my ears and I can't hear anything else over it.

One by one everyone in the circle speaks. Some losses fresher than others. There's even one person attending who is facing the imminent death of her father.

Each story pierces me like an arrow shot into my body, because while we might all be grieving different things, we are all still *grieving*, and there's a bond born of that kind of grief.

Finally, everyone has spoken but me.

I know I don't have to speak, it's a choice, but all these people were brave enough to share their story so I might as well too. I *can* do it. I know I can. I'm stronger than I give myself credit for—that's something else I've come to learn the last few weeks, the strength I thought I had was nothing but a farce, something I manufactured to once again trick myself into thinking I was okay.

Clearing my throat I say, "Eight years ago I was involved in a car accident that killed my parents and injured me. The other driver was killed on impact. All the paramedics and doctors told me I was lucky." I laugh at the word, shaking my head. "I didn't feel lucky. My parents were gone, my dreams of the future..." I sigh, thinking of the text message Kira sent me after we spoke on the phone. "I felt like I had nothing worth living for and that I was the unluckiest person on the planet. For years, I've been masking my pain with alcohol and sex," I admit softly, ashamed. "It's only recently I've come to understand I can't keep throwing my life away like that. I have people to live for, ones I care about, and a girl I've fallen for but am completely undeserving of." I shake my head back and forth, leaning forward with my hands clasped. "I've made so many shitty mistakes since I lost my parents. The pile is endless and sometimes I don't think I can see my way past them, but then I hear my mom's voice telling me there's always a way, and even though it hurts hearing her voice, it feels good too. For the first time in a long time I don't feel angry every waking moment. Most of the time it wasn't even an all-consuming anger, just something that hovered at the peripheral of my mind, waiting for something to set me off. It fucking hurts knowing they're gone," I confess quietly. "I hate knowing I'll never see them again, not in this life anyway, and maybe not even the next. I wish I didn't miss them so much, but then ... if I didn't miss them, wouldn't I forget them?"

Across from me, Ryder clears his throat. "It's okay to miss them. You'll *always* miss them. I can see the progress you've already made since I first met you and you did that all on your own, Rush. You're stronger than you give yourself credit for. We all still have our weak moments from time to time, important dates like birthdays, anniversaries, the day they died, whatever it might be. But when those days come, accept the hurt, don't fight it, don't try to numb it or pretend it doesn't exist. Instead, *own* it. Let that pain give you power, a reminder. You're a fighter and nothing, not even this loss, can beat you."

I hear his words echo through my skull. "Thank you," I murmur. "I just hope I can atone for my behavior. I want to be the man they were proud of."

"You already are," he replies with a kind smile.

I give a small smile in return, but I don't feel that way, not yet.

"The loneliness has sucked," I admit. "I have my friends, and we're close, practically like family, but it hasn't been the same. They've never lost someone, so they don't *get* it. They try to, I'll give them credit there, but there's only so much sympathy someone can have when they haven't been through it."

An older woman to my right speaks up. "You should get a pet."

"What?" I look at her stupidly.

"That's what I did when I lost my husband. The house was

too quiet, too empty without him. I ended up adopting a dog. Now, it feels like there's life again."

I mull over her words. I doubt the hotel allows pets, but I've *always* been a rule breaker. Even when my parents were alive. They encouraged it actually, claiming the most successful people in the world would've never gotten where they were if they weren't willing to break the rules.

"Maybe I will," I murmur.

She smiles at me and adds, "It really does help."

"That's all the time we have today. We'll meet again next month. If anyone would like to stay behind and make cranes, you're welcome to."

A couple people trickle out, but the rest, myself included, stay behind to help them put the room back in order.

"How are you feeling?" Blaire asks, the two of us carrying one of the tables back to where it goes.

"A little better," I admit, and she smiles. "It's nice being around people who've been through it, you know. Loss isn't easy."

"It's not," she agrees. "Don't get me wrong, I love my husband, and I'm blessed with our children, but I still think about Ben all the time. Especially here." We set the table down and she points to the cranes. "He's everywhere, and while that makes me sad sometimes, it also makes me happy, because while he might be gone, he still exists. In my heart, in my memories. People don't disappear because they're gone."

"There's something I've been thinking about doing, but I'm not ready yet."

"And what's that?" she asks, as we walk over to the chairs to carry some over to the table.

Picking two up, one in each hand, I say, "I have to go back home, to the house. It's time for me to clean it up and sell it. I inherited everything when they died, but I didn't want it. I couldn't even set foot in the house again after they died. I stayed with my friend's family. But I have to face it."

"You do," she agrees, placing a hand over mine.

She pulls her hand away and grabs a chair. I set my two chairs at a table to her one.

"You'll know when you're ready," she adds, flipping her dark hair over her shoulder to get it out of her way. "If you're thinking about it, that says a lot."

"I'd like to do it before my birthday. I don't really know why I came up with that," I shrug at my words, "but that's my goal."

"It's important to implement goals," she agrees, nodding her head. "It makes you work harder instead of wallowing in self-pity."

"I'm happy I found this place."

She smiles back at me, her eyes crinkling at the corners. "I am too. That's what I've always wanted this place to be. A safe haven."

Once everything is back in order I head out.

The days are getting longer, and while normally that makes me happy, this time I'm not—because I'm reminded of all those nights I spent out with Kira, and now I'm afraid I might never get them back.

Thinking about that woman's advice I head the few blocks over the hotel's garage and get my truck. It doesn't take me long to find the address for the nearest animal shelter on my phone.

We had a dog when I was little, but when it ran away and we never saw it again, my mom was too devastated to get another and I was too little to really feel heartbroken about it.

I'm not planning on getting a dog, or any sort of pet—but I figure it can't hurt to check out the shelter and spread a little love.

It's across town, but I don't mind the drive. With the

windows rolled down and the breeze rolling in I feel my head clear bit by bit.

Arriving at the shelter I drive up to the newer building and park my truck. Grabbing my baseball cap from the passenger seat I slip it on backwards and hop out.

Inside there are two women sitting behind the desk, one probably in her fifties and the other in her thirties. I give them my most charming, trademark smile. It's getting late and they're probably near closing time, but I've learned with that smile I can get pretty much anything I want.

"I'm here to take a look around, spend some time with the pooches."

"Y-Yeah," the younger woman stutters. "Through that door. Don't take any of them out on your own, but if you want to interact with one just ask us, or Anna is in the back cleaning cages, and she can help you."

"Thanks." I give them another smile, and I have my hand on the door, pushing it open when the other, older woman, whispers, "He can spend time with my pussy anytime he wants."

I glance over my shoulder and wink. She blushes at being caught but I don't mind. I personally think women should be more free to express their sexual desires, even if that means telling a random guy on the street you want to call them Daddy.

A sign points me toward the dogs, so I head that way first. Cats aren't really my thing.

I come across a golden retriever first, bending to give it lots of love—well as much as I can—through the cage. The sign on the cage says it's a male named Cupid and he's two years old. Looking down the line of cages it makes me sad all these animals are stuck here without a home and someone to love them.

I move to the next one, giving the lovable pit-bull next to Cupid some attention. The piece of paper says her name is

Francesca. Her long pink tongue swipes between the links of the cage and kisses me. I chuckle at the wet streak she leaves behind.

I make sure to pay attention to each and every dog, and then I head over to the cat section, knowing I'll feel like a selfish bastard if I don't say hi to them too.

The first cage houses three kittens ranging in colors from gray with black, to solid white, and the last tuxedo colored. They play, rolling around together, and I can't help but laugh at their playfulness.

There are loads more cats than dogs and it takes me a while to get to them all. Finally, I reach the last cage and I'm surprised they haven't kicked me out yet—but maybe they forgot I was in here. Doubtful, though. More than likely those women are somewhere ogling my ass. Can't say I blame them. I have a great ass.

Looking into the final cage I almost think it's empty at first, but a nametag dangles proclaiming this small cubicle the home of Patch, an older male cat. I peek into the cage and nearly jolt back when a glowing green eye looks back at me.

A low meow leaves the cat's throat, and he gets up, stretching his limbs.

His fur is shades of brown and black with gray thrown in for good measure.

Once he's in front of me I understand why he's named Patch. He's missing his right eye, a scar running from the corner of his eye over the top of his pink nose, and half of his left ear has been ripped off.

I stick my finger up for him to sniff, which he does, and then begins to rub against the cage.

"He never does that for anyone," a small female voice says behind me.

I turn around and as my eyes connect with the girl's, her skin turns the shade of a tomato.

"I know you." My lips lift up in a grin.

"Oh, God," she blurts. "Can we pretend that never happened?"

"Um ... no, not possible. You told my friend you wanted to call him Daddy. That's not something anyone forgets easily."

Squaring her shoulders, she lifts her narrow chin. "In my defense, I've never said anything like that in my life—but your friend is stupid hot, and I couldn't help myself."

"It was the neck tats wasn't it?" I joke.

If possible, she gets even redder. "Perhaps," she hedges. "Anyway," she shakes her head rapidly back and forth like her brain is an Etch-A-Sketch and she wants to rid the memories from her mind, "do you want me to get Patch out for you?"

"Oh, no," I say, stepping away from the cage. The cat looks a little sad as I distance myself from him. "I need to go."

She bites her lip and says, "He doesn't get a lot of love, and he's old so no one wants to adopt him, maybe you could stay a few more minutes and play with him? It might do him some good."

I can't very well argue with that. "Yeah, sure. What's your name?" I ask.

"Anna," she answers. "And please, for the love of God, don't tell your hot friend you ran into me. I can't handle any more humiliation. It's basically my full-time job to make a fool of myself."

"He might like you." I shrug. "He's fond of pussies—the cat kind," I blurt, realizing she's not in on the inside joke between Cannon and his sister. "Though, he likes the other kind too."

She snorts. "Yeah, I haven't been too lucky in love, so I think I'll pass."

"Whatever you say."

She reaches up then and unlocks Patch's cage. He shies away from her, and she looks at me. "You want to grab him? I think he likes you better."

When I step up to the cage sure enough Patch creeps closer to me. I grab him and pull him into my arms. As I pet his head he purrs and Anna grins from ear to ear.

"It's nice to see him happy. I've been volunteering here since high school and he's been here for years."

"Years, huh?" I look down at the patchwork of a cat, and suddenly I know I'll be damned if he spends one more night behind those bars.

"Yeah," she exhales sadly. "People don't want old cats who look like they've been chewed up and spit back out. I would've taken him home with me a long time ago, but my place is small and I already have three cats in my apartment, not to mention the three strays that won't leave me alone."

I wave a hand at her Crazy Cat Lady shirt. "It all makes sense now."

She gives a small shrug, her lips tugging up in a smile. "I've learned to embrace it. I'm the crazy cat lady at twenty-three. Life could be worse."

"Yeah, you could be calling random men on the street Daddy," I snort.

"Oh my God," she blushes again. "Stop bringing it up."

I snicker. "It's too funny. I can't help myself." Patch burrows his scarred face into the crook of my elbow. "I'm going to take him home with me," I blurt before I can change my mind.

"Really?" She raises one dark brow in surprise. "Are you sure?"

"I am. He doesn't deserve to live like this."

And neither do I. Patch didn't ask for his cage, but I made mine.

I swear she gets tears in her eyes. She reaches out, scratching him on his head. "Everyone deserves love."

I know she's speaking about the cat, not me or anything else, but I still find myself saying, "Even assholes like me?"

She gives a small laugh. "I don't know you, but in the few minutes I've spent with you I wouldn't label you as such. Even when I acted like a total weirdo over your friend you weren't a jerk to me. But assholes deserve love too, maybe more than anyone else."

"Why is that?" I ask, and she looks up at me with wide dark eyes outlined by a purple pair of glasses. The purple matches the color streaking her short black hair.

"Because, love is the only thing capable of redeeming even the darkest of souls."

I mull her words over as I fill out the adoption papers for Patch. Then I'm given a few small toys and a sample size of food to get me through tonight and the morning until I can swing by the pet store and get him the shit he needs. The two ladies who were sitting in the front are thrilled Patch is going to a good home—a home I lie about and give Mia's address for, because I know there's no way in hell they'll let me take him if they know I'm currently living in a hotel. But Patch is mine and I'll be damned if I leave him behind.

Patch falls asleep in my lap on the drive to the hotel and since it's not cold out, meaning I have no coat to hide him in, I have to stuff him into my gym bag—leaving an opening so he can breathe but not escape.

When I get on the elevator a man steps inside, dressed in business attire and speaking on his phone.

Patch let's out a meow and the man looks over at me.

"Stomach," I explain. "I haven't had dinner."

He nods and gets off a few floors beneath me.

Reaching my floor, I swipe my key in the door and as soon as it clicks closed behind me I crouch down and let Patch out.

Calista screams. "Is that a cat?" She rises off the couch, a fashion magazine falling from her hands to the floor.

Cannon looks over his shoulder from the chair. "The fuck," he mutters.

I walk over to him. "Don't worry, man. I got you something too."

Patch is hot on my heels as I stop in front of Cannon and pull the piece of paper out of my pocket. "If you ever want to be called Daddy, call her." I slap the piece of paper against his solid chest and he grabs it.

"What the fuck?" He blinks at the numbers scrawled across the paper.

"I convinced Anna to give me her number, so I could give it to you. She's embarrassed about the whole *Daddy* thing, but she's a cool chick. Give her a shot." I shrug and sit down. Patch hops up onto my lap and curls up.

"Who the fuck is Anna?" he asks.

"The chick from earlier today, the one in the cat clothes," I explain. "The one who said she wanted to call you Daddy."

His mouth opens in a surprised O shape.

"Whoa, whoa, whoa, what did I miss?" Calista asks, fully invested in this conversation now.

"Not important," Cannon mutters, but I notice he tucks the piece of paper in his pocket and doesn't crumple it up. "You can't keep that cat," he tells me. "We'll get in trouble."

"Patch is staying," I say like a defiant child. No fucking way am I sending him back to that shelter. "We've bonded," I defend. "Besides, we keep Fox around and he's a woodland creature."

Calista stifles a laugh and Cannon rolls his eyes. "If we get caught, it's on you." He points a finger in warning at me. "I'm going to bed. It's too late for me to deal with this shit."

"Night, Dad," I call after him and he gives me the finger over his shoulder.

"He's kind of ugly," Calista muses.

"Cannon? I know—he got beat with the ugly stick. You lucked out."

She laughs. "Not him, though that is true." She flips her dark hair over her shoulder. "I meant the cat."

"Patch has character," I defend vehemently. "He's lived a battered life and he's come out better for it."

But have I? Am I a better man? Can I be a better one?

"Whatever you say." She stands and heads for Hollis's old room, leaving me alone with Patch.

I scratch him on the back of the head and exhale a weighted sigh. "It's just you and me now, man."

My heart pangs in my chest, because what if that's the truth? What if it's only ever me, this battered cat, and my friends? What if Kira never wants to work things out? What if I never get to see my son?

I push those thoughts from my head, I refuse to let that be my reality.

I haven't fought for my life, for myself, in years.

But I'm fighting now, and I'll fight for Kira and my child too.

I'll fight until the very end.

FORTY-THREE

Kira

I stick the macaron shell on top of the other, smooshing the delicious filling in between. I lick a little off my fingers, the sweetness zinging on my tongue.

My phone begins to ring and I curse, wiping my hands on the apron—a solid red color with black dots making it remind me of a ladybug.

The number flashes across the phone, the city listed beneath it, and I almost don't answer. But I do anyway, because I know I can't ignore things forever.

"Hello?" I answer, tucking my cell between my shoulder and ear so I can continue to assemble my macarons.

"Hello, Kira? It's Mitchell Williamson—Quinton Marsh's lawyer."

I roll my eyes. "I know who you are Mitchell," I intone dully.

"I wanted to inform you your father passed away last night."

"I figured," I sigh. "It was inevitable, so I don't really see the need for this chat." I forget about the macarons and rest my hip against the counter. "If that's all you have to tell me—"

"No, no," he rushes quickly before I can hang up. "There's the matter of his will and burial."

I roll my eyes and tug on my hair slightly. The bite of pain in my scalp serves to remind me I truly am having this conversation.

"Mitchell, I honestly don't care about any of that." It's probably rude of me to call him by his first name and not *Mr. Williamson*, but I don't give a shit.

"Everything is arranged for the burial here in North Carolina—you don't have to worry about that. I thought you might want to attend—"

"*Nice try*," I draw out the words. "Then what is this about?"

He exhales on the other end of the line and I decide I better go sit down on the couch, because I have the feeling this is going to turn into a lengthy conversation.

"All your father's assets have been left to you. You're the last living family."

I snort. "The man was a drunk, abusive, asshole who could barely hold down a job. What kind of assets could he possibly have?"

"Well," Mitchell clears his throat and I can hear the sound of papers shuffling, "when his parents died he inherited everything, a house, a small bit of land, and some money. Since he was in prison, he couldn't do anything with it, so it all goes to you now."

"How much are we talking about?" I ask with a sigh. Yeah, I could use the money but the last thing I want is to accept anything that in any way is a part of my father.

"If you sell the land..." He muses, and there's more shuffling. "North of a million."

My phone drops to the ground with a clatter. I bend over and quickly pick it back up, pressing it to my ear.

"What did you say? Repeat it slowly," I beg, sure I've heard him wrong.

"Including the value of the house, land, the money and investments left behind, it's worth over a million dollars."

Seconds, that's all it takes for me to go from a broke ass bitch to having wealth I could've never imagined.

Even though the idea of not having to worry about money sounds amazing, it feels wrong to accept it. I hated my father, I didn't know my grandparents, and in my mind that in no way adds up to me being deserving of this.

But it's not just *me* I have to think about anymore. My son's future is far more precious and important than my pride and dignity.

"What do you need from me?" I ask, and Mitchell begins listing off what I'll have to do.

When I hang up the phone, I toss it on the coffee table and lean back against the cushions of the couch.

"Is this real life?" I murmur aloud.

That's when I feel it, the small little fluttering in my stomach as the baby moves, and I begin to cry, because this is very much real and for the first time in perhaps my entire life, I have hope.

FORTY-FOUR

Rush

"I swear I blinked and it's July," I mutter, banging my drumsticks against my knees.

"You're telling me," Cannon replies, grabbing a bottle of water and tipping it down his throat.

We're minutes away from going on stage to open for Willow Creek at the county fair.

Fox slings his electric guitar over his shoulder and flicks his dark hair out of his eyes. It might seem like a normal gesture, but when he does it, I notice he uses it as an opportunity to check out Calista in the corner sitting and talking to Mia. He barely speaks to her and avoids being around her at all costs. One day soon I'm going to have to have a talk with him, man to man, that he needs to grow a pair and tell her how he feels.

Looking around at the people gathered in the tent—the four of us, Mia and Calista, Hayes and the rest of Willow Creek, plus some of the board members for the fair and people on Willow Creek's team—I can't help noting the visible and very prominent, at least to me, absence of Kira.

I haven't seen her since the day I showed up confessing my greatest sin of all—betraying the love I had for her, and whatever fragile trust that had been built between us.

I've been sober two months and it's getting harder to stay away. I miss her. I want to see her and make things right, but I know words will mean nothing to her, and she deserves proof I'm better and I'm changed. So I keep going to AA and hanging out at The Paper Crane Project, and when I'm not at those places I'm either in the studio drumming my heart out, pounding my pain and heartache into my kit, or I'm at the hotel hanging with Patch. I've grown even more attached to the cat. If I could take him everywhere with me, I would. He might be old and lived a rough life, but he's living the life of a king now.

A guy pokes his head into the tent. "You guys are on in one minute."

"It's show time, boys." I grin and clasp my drumsticks in one hand. "You all warmed up?" I ask Hollis.

He grins back. "You betcha."

"Ready?" This time I address Fox.

"Fuck, yes."

"You?"

Cannon straps his bass across his front and stretches his fingers. "Hell yeah."

It's been too long since we've been up on stage playing a crowd. I've missed it like crazy. We had a small gig at Griffin's, a local coffee shop, but it hardly counts. This too might be a small venue, but it's not shabby and at this point I'll take anything. I love the feeling of being on stage. The adrenaline. The cheering. The music pumping around us like a tangible force.

It's the closest we'll ever come to real magic in this world.

"Ten!" Someone calls out.

I stretch my wrists and then fist bump each of my friends before we're jogging on stage to cheers. Most of them might be here for Willow Creek, but after our set, they'll never forget us.

Hollis grabs the mic and speaks into it. "How you doin' Clarke County? You ready for a show you'll never forget?"

Cheers echo back as Fox and Cannon get into position, hooking their instruments to the speakers.

Hollis looks over his shoulder at the three of us and I raise my drumsticks.

He counts down on his fingers.

Three.

Two.

One.

Magic.

MY BOOTS THUD AGAINST THE STAIRS AS THE FOUR OF US EXIT THE stage after the end of our set. I'm soaked in sweat, and I'm fucking glad I wrapped a bandana around my forehead, keeping my hair at bay while I played.

We crash into the tent, all of us grappling for a water.

"You were amazing," Mia cries, wrapping her arms around Hollis's neck.

"They weren't too shabby," Mathias mutters, always the cynic.

His icy blonde haired wife smacks him in the chest. "Shut up, they were good. Don't be rude."

"Yeah, ignore Mathias. He lives with a stick up his ass. It's very uncomfortable," Emma, who is Maddox's wife, pipes in.

They weren't here earlier so they arrived after we went on. We've never met their wives before, except for Hayes's—Arden

—but they're equally recognizable from all the tabloids they're always pictured on.

"I don't have a stick up my ass," Mathias defends. "I'm a fucking realist."

His wife, Remy, rolls her eyes. "If you were a *fucking realist* you would've never started a band in the first place, so give me a break, you oaf."

Their ease and camaraderie as a group makes my chest pang, because once again my thoughts are zeroed in on Kira. I want that with her. I want to laugh, and poke fun at each other. I want to be a family.

The thought hits me like a ton of bricks.

It seems like something I should've already realized, loving her and all, but for some reason I haven't truly grasped how much I want her to not only be my family, but to make our own together.

Across the way, Mia's eyes connect with mine, despite the fact Hollis is holding her against his side. Her eyes are sad, like she knows exactly what I'm thinking about.

I dip my chin in a nod to her, a gesture that I know, and I'm going to get her back. I'm going to prove myself worthy. One day at a time.

FORTY-FIVE

Kira

I sign my name on the line, feeling both excited and scared. It's a strange combination, but not an entirely unpleasant one.

The salesman holds out his hand to shake mine. "I'll go get the keys for you."

"Thank you so much," I say, smiling.

Thanks to my inheritance, I can say goodbye to my clunker and buy a reliable car to cart this baby around in. It's still scary putting so much money into a car, but I want my child to be safe.

Unfortunately, I'm going to be stuck in my lease on the apartment until it ends. My slimy bastard of a landlord somehow learned of my inheritance and wants to charge me an arm and a leg to get out of my lease. I'm not sure that's even legal, but I'll lose even more money trying to fight him. So, I'll be there until my lease is up in November and then it's good riddance to that shit hole too.

Ten minutes later I'm sliding behind the wheel of my shiny red Toyota RAV-4.

I rub my hands over the black leather steering wheel, inhaling the scent of brand new car.

I had planned to get something used, with low mileage and in good condition, but ultimately decided I might as well indulge while I can since I plan on keeping this car for a very long time.

With a wave at the salesman I pull out of the lot. Mia invited me to come with her today to the Clarke County fair to see The Wild and Willow Creek perform, but I declined—insisting I *had* to get a car today, because frankly, and stupidly, I'm scared to see Rush.

It's pathetic, I can't avoid him forever—but I need more time.

I know the more time I let go between us the more likely it is he'll start sleeping around if he hasn't already, or worse, move on—but I'm learning while I have to be open with my feelings, and willing to speak about them, I also still have to protect myself.

I've been going to therapy twice a month and it's helping a lot.

I'm understanding I can't change people and I can only change how I react to them. She's helping me learn that not everyone's promises are empty, or their love conditional. There are good people out there, like Mia, and her family.

I shouldn't be so quick to judge. I make mistakes, we all do, and I'm learning to evaluate and decide what kind of mistakes are unforgivable.

Now that it's summer I don't have to worry about school, and I've been enjoying every moment by learning everything I can about becoming a mother, and baking. I didn't feel comfortable at first, accepting the gift of baking supplies from Rush, even after we talked, but I realized he was truly doing it because he wanted to, not because he expected anything in return.

Instead of heading back to my crap hole apartment, I go to Target, strolling down all the baby aisles. I've bought a few things, mostly stuff I've ordered from Amazon, but there's so much more I need to get and have—but Mia made me swear not to buy a whole bunch of stuff before my baby shower which is only days away. With the baby due a little over a month from now, it's crunch time.

I pick up a box of baby blankets, a set of four in a soft muted blue, nearly green, color, white and gray. Touching my fingers to the soft fabric, tears well in my eyes, because through most of this pregnancy I've been scared to death, and now ... now I feel excited, and picturing my sweet baby boy wrapped in a blanket, held in my arms, makes me emotional. I can't help wondering what parts of him will be me and what parts will be Rush. Regardless, he'll be perfect.

Moving down the aisle I pick up a pack of small white socks. It's crazy to me that he'll be so tiny. I've been around babies before so it's not like I'm unfamiliar with the concept of their size, but somehow it's different realizing this baby is mine.

I still haven't picked a name, and I think it's because any time I start to think about it I feel sick. In my heart I know Rush should be a part of such an important decision.

I hang the socks back on the rack and browse through the different bottles and binky's wondering how anyone ever decides what to get. There are far too many choices.

When I start to get overwhelmed, I decide it's best to leave—after all, according to Mia I won't need to even think about buying most of this stuff for myself.

Getting behind the wheel of my brand new car, I cradle my now large stomach.

So much has changed since I got pregnant. I fell for Rush

even though I didn't know it, I pushed him away and lost him because of it, but most importantly because of that mistake I've learned so much about my past and bit by bit, I've started to move on from the wrongs that have been wrought against me.

Everything is a ripple effect—this baby the biggest one of all, but I have a gut feeling that once the waves settle, my landscape will be entirely different—better, because when you learn to love yourself it lights up your world.

FORTY-SIX

Rush

"What the fuck are you doing?" Cannon asks from the doorway of my room.

"What does it look like I'm doing?" I retort, tearing off a piece of tape and applying it to the package.

"Wrapping a fucking car seat, that's what it looks like."

"Ding, ding, ding. Mr. Rhodes you are correct. You win the award for He Who Asks Dumb Questions."

I'm being a dick, but my friends are going to the baby shower for *my* kid while I'm not invited. I'd be lying if I didn't say the snub stings, but since I'm giving Kira space, I'm not forcing the issue.

Even though I won't be there, I researched my ass off to get everything my kid will need and what will be safest. I don't want Kira having to worry about this stuff on her own.

"You should just come." Cannon sits down on the floor beside me, tearing a piece of tape and handing it to me.

"I wasn't invited," I grumble under my breath.

I'm being sulky, but it *hurts*. It's like a kick to the stomach to feel like people think my kid is better off without me in the picture.

Several months ago this would have sent me running for a bottle of alcohol, while saying I was fine, but not now.

Instead, when they leave, I'll be heading to my AA meeting.

"Don't tell her these are from me," I beg him, waving my hand at the crudely wrapped packages already stacked by the door to my room.

He raises a brow. "Why the hell not?"

Adhering one last piece of tape to the car seat box I answer him. "I don't want her to think it's charity, or guilt, or whatever the fuck else she might assume if it comes from me. This is me wanting to provide for my child, so he has the best I can give him, and even if we never work things out and I don't get to be around him much, I'll still feel better knowing he's taken care of."

"You're going to work it out," he declares adamantly.

I shrug indifferently, like it's no big deal and isn't weighing heavily on my mind every minute of every day.

I can see now how I leaned on alcohol like a crutch, thinking it made me feel better, gave me some sort of freedom from the pain when really it was only masking it.

It made me do stupid shit, like thinking hooking up with that chick in the club was a good idea.

I don't think I'll ever be able to clear that mistake from my conscience.

Fox pokes his head in the door. Cannon and I both look up at his intrusion.

"We better get going," he announces. "Are you coming?" His gaze swings to me.

I shake my head. "I have AA," I answer him, because it sounds better than saying I wasn't invited.

His brows furrow. "Can't you skip one?"

"Fox," Cannon warns, standing up. "It's important he goes to his meetings."

Honestly, even if an invitation had been extended to me, Cannon probably would've made me turn it down and go to AA anyway. I can picture him now, dragging me inside the building and plunking me in a chair, telling me in his stern voice to get my shit together.

"I'll help you guys load this stuff up," I mutter, standing and grabbing one of the larger boxes that contains a stroller.

It takes us several trips to get everything loaded and before the trunk closes on Cannon's SUV, I stand back and take it all in.

"I might've gone overboard," I admit, seeing the large vehicle stuffed full.

"Ya think?" Calista blurts.

I send her a scathing look. She doesn't even know Kira, but she gets to go.

"Y'all better get going," I tell them, taking a step away.

Kira's baby shower is being held at Hayes's house, which is about an hour away. Mia organized the whole thing, and I'm sure it's going to be far more than Kira would ever want, but I can't blame Mia, because it's not like I held myself back with getting gifts.

Fox gets in the back while Calista heads for the front passenger seat.

Cannon watches me with his eerie light green eyes, twisting an unlit cigarette between his fingers.

"You're doing good, man. Don't screw it up."

"Don't worry about me. I'm not going to go off the deep end. I have too much to lose."

He stares at me, thinking silently, and finally says, "Don't get too comfortable. Don't think because you've been without alcohol you're magically cured with time. You're going to struggle all the time and there will be moments when the temptation to reach for a bottle threatens to overwhelm you. When that happens, don't be afraid to ask. We're here for you. We're family."

"Thank you," I say, and I mean it.

I'm not naïve enough to think it won't always be a struggle to stay away from alcohol, but with so much on the line ... I don't want to lose more than I already have. Hearing other people talk about their stories, the resounding ripple effect of their alcoholism on their significant others, friends, and family is a constant reminder to keep my shit straight.

"I'll see you later."

He pushes the button to close the trunk and lights up his cigarette, still watching me.

"Be careful," he warns.

Be careful to stay away from alcohol.

Be careful of your decisions.

Be careful with your heart.

I tip my head at him and get behind the wheel of my truck and drive away.

It's not exactly necessary for me to drive to my AA meeting, but I figure the last place I need to be when I leave the meeting is an empty hotel suite. If I have my truck, I can at least drive around and it'll keep me from getting into trouble.

I arrive early and pour myself a cup of coffee—because I took it upon myself to make sure better coffee was provided. No one should have to sit through these meetings without a hot coffee.

"Good to see you." Daniel claps a hand on my shoulder and I turn to him with a smile.

"You see me every week," I remind him and he chuckles.

"Yes, and it's still good to see you. I'm proud of your commitment."

I dump a pile of creamer into the coffee and swirl the cup a bit to combine the creamer with the coffee.

"When you commit to something, you give it your all."

He nods. "I like that saying."

"It's what my dad always used to tell me," I exhale a sigh. "I don't want to fail at something as important as this," I confess to Daniel. "I want to make the change and never go back to who I was."

Every day I feel more confident and sure of the path I'm on. I feel better, too. At the time I had no idea the way the alcohol was clouding my mind and all my decisions. It's like I'm finally clearing a film from my eyes and seeing things as they truly are and not as the alcohol wanted me to believe.

"You're well on your way there."

He smiles before heading over to speak with Holly who has walked in.

I make my way to my seat, my heart beating an out-of-control rhythm inside my chest. It's nothing like the steady beat of my drums. Today, I want to get up and talk about my story, about the addiction to alcohol that somehow happened without me even realizing it. I became dependent on a substance instead of myself and I was completely oblivious to the hold it had on me.

I feel jittery and I haven't even taken a sip of coffee yet. Its warmth seeps through the Styrofoam and the liquid sloshes around, threatening to spill over as my knee bounces up and down restlessly.

For some reason, speaking up at the grief group wasn't

nearly as nerve wracking. I think it's because I don't feel ashamed of being sad over my parents' deaths, but I do feel ashamed of being an alcoholic. There's such a negative connotation with alcoholism, but for a lot of people it's a coping mechanism, like for me.

I look around at the quickly filling room and lift the coffee to my lips. It burns my tongue, but I barely even feel it. My mind is elsewhere and not even pain can refocus me.

Much quicker than I'd like, everyone is seated and Daniel is speaking. Some meetings are different than others, where we all sit facing each other and speak about our thoughts and feelings, our dependence and the struggle, and others, like the first meeting I attended, he sets it up like this—an encouragement for people to stand on their own and speak what they need to. I think it's done in an effort for people to prove to themselves they're strong enough to face their demons.

Today, I'll finally be facing mine.

I listen carefully to everyone who stands up and speaks, with each passing second knowing I'm going to have to soon be up there.

"We have time for one more," Daniel announces, and I swear his eyes linger on me.

Before I can change my mind, or allow someone else to take my place so I can make an excuse to myself that I didn't have a chance, I stand up and say, "Me."

My voice is quiet. Probably quieter than it ever has been.

Heads turn my way and I wish I could fucking disappear.

But I think of the person I want to be.

Of Kira.

Our son.

And so I move my feet, one in front of the other, as Daniel motions me to the front.

I've gotten to know these people, to hear their stories, but I am still fearful standing in front of them. They're the least likely people to judge me, but as harshly as I judge myself I can't help thinking everyone else is doing the same.

Clearing my throat, I scrub my hand over the stubble on my jaw.

"Uh ... hi, guys," I begin awkwardly. "I've never been up here before and it's ... scary as fuck."

They laugh a bit at that.

"I've been coming here since April now, listening to your stories, getting to know you and it's helped me to realize I had placed such a stigma on what makes an alcoholic. It might be a label, but it doesn't fit one type, most labels don't." I rock back on my heels, feeling awkward as hell. I thought I might feel better after I got up here, but that's not the case.

"Being sober has been a strange experience, an enlightening one. I think I felt like because the majority of the time I only had a beer or two, I didn't have a problem. But I did, because even when I didn't drink much—I craved it. I needed it to get through things. Without it, I felt like I'd fail or I couldn't let loose." I pause, gathering myself. I've shared in AA about my parents and how it led to my drinking, so that's nothing new but I haven't truly explained how deeply their deaths scarred me. "When I lost my parents, it felt like I had nothing left to live for. I wanted nothing more than to join them. I thought about killing myself often, and when I drank ... I felt light, free from those thoughts. When I was drunk, I became a whole new person, one who was wild and unchained. I partied hard and fucked harder, all while the alcohol burned its way through my system. It became my fuel, the thing controlling my body instead of ... *me*."

The words begin to pour out of me suddenly.

"I let other things control my life, because if I did ... I'd have to face reality, that they were gone and not coming back, that my chance at playing basketball in college and going pro was wiped away, that my entire life plan was suddenly ripped away. I should've seen a therapist like everyone suggested, but I was stubborn, certain I could heal on my own, but I didn't. The more time that has passed the harder it has become to change the man I turned into. But then..." Kira's face enters my mind, her dark hair, round brown eyes, full lips, and that dimple in her chin she dislikes so much. "I fell in love when I swore I never would. But I guess you don't necessarily choose to fall in love, do you?" I muse, looking away and fighting a smile. "It just happens —in the blink of an eye, the span of a heartbeat. Everything changes."

I run my fingers through my hair, it's a nervous gesture, but thankfully I don't feel the nerves anymore. With each word and sentence that leaves my mouth I get a little lighter.

"Neither of us was looking for love, but I think she loves me too. Or ... *loved*. I hurt her, and I hurt myself, with a disastrous decision. But I think if everything I've gone through with her hadn't happened, I wouldn't be here right now, standing in front of you all." My lips twitch with a memory. "My mom used to tell me everything happens for a reason and one day I would understand the meaning. I still haven't figured out why they had to die, but I do know why things had to happen the way they did with Kira. We were both two incredibly broken people trying to make a whole, but when your broken pieces can't even fix you, you can hardly mend someone else. I think we had to fall apart to have any chance of falling back together." I clear my throat, my palms suddenly sweaty. "You see, I cheated on her. Kind of, I guess, but the way I grew up—what I did is considered cheating. Kira and I weren't together, but my heart belonged to her. It has from the moment I met her, even though I didn't know it then. Even when she broke my heart, those pieces were still hers, and what I did..." I shake my head. "I'll never stop regretting it. I told her I loved her and when she said she couldn't love me, my reaction was to get drunk for days on end and finally nearly fuck another woman. I can't be that person anymore, not just because I want her forgiveness, but because I can't stomach being the kind of man who treats the woman he loves like she's nothing. I hate this feeling."

I take another moment to think about what I want to say. I know the meeting is beginning to run long, but no one says anything. They all sit there, letting me speak and get this off my chest.

"I guess all I have to left to say is, I know this journey is only beginning, and I know it won't be easy—but I'm putting everything I have into staying sober. I want to be proud of who I am, and I want my parents to look down on me with pride."

"Well said." Daniel claps his hands and the others join in.

I smile—a wide, full, happy smile not weighted down by grief or fear.

"You've come a long way in a few short months," Daniel tells me, shaking my hand.

"And I hope to go a lot further."

"You will."

FORTY-SEVEN

Kira

It's Sunday morning, the day after my baby shower, and I can't wrap my head around all the stuff gifted to this baby.

I wipe away a tear, knowing how much these people care about me and the baby, when for the longest time I convinced myself I was unlovable.

The pile from Rush is the largest and includes some of the most needed things—like a crib, stroller, car seat, and so much more. The guys said Rush wanted them to claim the gifts and he didn't want any credit, but they thought I should know.

I told them he could've come, but Cannon said Rush thought he wasn't invited.

Silly, silly man. I don't think anyone felt it was necessary to extend a formal invitation since he's the father, but I guess considering the circumstances I can see why he'd assume otherwise.

It's still early, the sun has only been up for around thirty minutes, but I text him anyway.

Me: Are you up?

I sit down on my couch with a bowl of cereal, waiting for his reply.

I'm on my second bite of cereal when the chime sounds.

Rush: Yup. I'm at the gym.

Me: Think you could come over after? I could use some help.

Rush: Yeah, of course.

I tuck my phone between the couch cushions where I can't look at it. I haven't laid eyes on him since that fateful night where he showed up drunk, confessing what he'd done.

I've missed him, but it'll be strange seeing him again.

Finishing my cereal, I wash the bowl out in the sink, change out of my pajamas into clothes, and start to unbox some of the items I'll need help putting together.

I read some of the directions in the hope I could possibly get started on some of these things, but there's not a chance. It all sounds like it's written in a foreign language.

My phone dings with a text message and I dig it out of the couch.

Rush: I'm outside.

Inhaling a breath to calm myself, I smooth my hands down the front of my t-shirt dress. I'm *not* a dress kind of girl at all, but it's one of the most comfortable things I can wear these days.

I open the door, propping my hip against it and look down to see Rush coming up the stairs.

He stops a few stairs below me, so we're eye level.

"Hi," he says in that husky, too-sexy-for-his-own-good, voice of his.

"Hi," I say back.

"I brought this for you." He extends his arm with a Dairy

Queen milkshake grasped in his hand. "If you don't want it, it's fine. It's a chocolate malt, though."

I take it from him and offer a small, awkward smile. "This is great, thank you." Clearing my throat, I blurt, "I'm sorry you thought you weren't invited to the baby shower. I didn't think it was necessary to send a formal invitation, and for that I'm sorry. I should have anyway. I just ... pregnancy brain, I guess."

"It's okay," he murmurs, but I can still see the hurt in his eyes despite it. "I needed to go to AA anyway. It's important I don't miss a meeting."

"O-Oh, of course. Thank you, though, for everything you sent the baby."

He curses and shakes his head. "Those dickheads," he grumbles, but he's smiling anyway. "I told them not to tell you it was from me."

I reach out and grab his hand. "I'm glad they did."

He looks down where my hand touches his.

When he looks up, I say, "I'm learning human contact isn't such a bad thing."

He gives a small chuckle. "Not going to catch cooties anymore?"

I press my lips together, my eyes flickering away. "I don't need to worry about cooties when I already caught feelings."

Holding the door open wider I motion him inside.

He doesn't remark on my confession, which I'm thankful for.

"If you're going to buy the baby all these big things the least you can do is put them together," I joke easily. "I have no chance of doing this on my own, but I'm an excellent helper."

He cracks a grin and I can't help but be taken aback by how different he looks. I was afraid to really look at him before, but now as I study him I see how much healthier and happier he looks. His skin has more color, even his blond hair seems brighter, and his eyes don't have light purplish gray circles beneath them anymore. They're all things I didn't really notice, but now they seem glaringly obvious.

"I'm sure you are." His voice is deep, his blue eyes steady.

I've never had the urge to wrap my arms around someone and hug them and never let go, but suddenly it overwhelms me.

"You look good," I tell him. The words seem inadequate, but I mean them.

"I'm doing good," he replies, his eyes glancing around my small apartment as if he's seeing it for the first time. It's no different than the last time he was here, only cluttered with boxes from the baby shower and with more kitchen supplies.

I take a tentative step toward him.

"Can I ... can I hug you?" My voice shakes as I ask the question, but I can't resist my desire to wrap my arms around him a second longer and then be enveloped by those same arms.

His eyes darken, his lips down turning, and I fear he's going to tell me no.

If he does I'm not sure how I'll feel.

"Any time, beautiful."

He opens his arms and I wrap mine around his muscular torso. My belly doesn't allow me to get all that close to him, but I hug him like I've never hugged anyone else before. He tightens his arms around me, burying his face into my hair and inhaling the scent of my shampoo.

"I'm so sorry, Kira," he murmurs softly in a regret-filled voice. "I'll never stop being sorry for what I've done."

"I'm sorry too." Tears leak out of my eyes, but I don't move to brush them away because I'm not ready to let go of him yet. I'm afraid if I do, he'll disappear and this all will have been a dream.

He cups my face, tilting it up so I'm looking at him. I feel so small looking up at him like this. Somehow, in the time we've been apart I forgot how larger than life he is. He towers over me. I'm pretty sure he could shield my entire body with his.

"I've missed you, so much," he tells me, his voice soft. "Just being around you. Seeing you smile and ... exist."

Exist.

That one word tells me so much about his own feelings. When you truly love someone, it's enough to just be around them.

I reach up, touching my fingers to his smooth, freshly shaved jaw. "I forgive you, Rush. This time apart, therapy, just dealing with all my past shit has helped me move on and see things differently. Not only with you, but ... all of it. And I want you to know I forgive you. Even if this never goes anywhere further with us, I want you to know that. And ... I hope you can forgive me too. For being closed off, for lying when you said you loved me." Tears spill down my cheeks. "I lied because the truth was scary and overwhelming. I lied to protect myself, but all I did was hurt both of us."

"There's nothing for me to forgive." He wipes my tears away with his big thumbs. He presses his forehead to mine. "We've been two fucked up people, but I think we're finally getting our shit straight."

I crack a smile. "I think so, too."

He takes a step away. "I don't want to rush things with us."

"Slow and steady wins the race?" I joke, cracking smile. I swipe a tissue out of a box and dry my cheeks.

"Something like that."

I hate the space between us now, but I know he's right.

I've been working on myself, and he's been working on himself, but now it's time for us to be sure we work together. Sometimes two people might love each other, but they're better off apart—I hope that isn't the case with us.

"What can I help you with?" he asks, getting right to business.

I stir the whipped cream into the malt shake. "I have everything laid out in piles already, with the directions."

He takes a glance at all the piles that take up so much space I had to scoot my couch out of the way the best I could.

"You don't want to open the crib?" he asks in a confused tone, his brows furrowing.

I shake my head. "He'll sleep with me or in a bassinet to start. I figure it'll be easier when I move if it's still in the box."

"You're moving?" He doesn't sound surprised, but it's not like I've made it a secret I don't want to keep living in this dump with a baby.

"Eventually. My lease is up in November, and the baby won't be in a crib by then. I ... uh ... my dad passed away and I came into some money through him and that's how I'm affording it." I don't know why I feel the need to explain, I just do.

Rush moves over to the pile of parts for the stroller. "I'm sorry about your dad."

"Don't be. He was an asshole," I sigh.

He looks over at me with those deep blue ocean eyes of his that leave me breathless. "Then I guess I'm sorry for what should've been."

He bends down and picks up a part, looking it over before addressing the directions. Glancing over his shoulder at me he says, "Sit down. Please. There's a lot we need to talk about. I ... I want to tell you everything. I think we've both kept a lot of secrets from each other, because we were trying to protect ourselves. I realize now I was never protecting myself. I only brought myself more pain and I hurt those around me because of it."

I tuck a piece of hair behind my ear and sit down on the

floor beside him, curling my legs under me. Placing the shake beside me, I face him.

"We're a lot alike," I state, letting out a breath I'd been holding and didn't even realize.

"We are," he agrees.

He grows quiet, reading the directions and looking at the parts.

Once he starts putting it together, he speaks again. "Nine years ago now, I was involved in a car accident," he begins softly, his voice barely above a whisper. His eyes flicker to mine, like he's hesitant to make eye contact, but knows he needs to. "A driver hit our car, and my parents were killed instantly. I sustained some injuries, none of them life threatening, but it killed my chance at playing basketball."

He screws some pieces together and doesn't speak for a minute or two.

"My parents and I were close. I'm an only child, and I only had them. They were older when they had me and didn't have any family themselves. Losing them ... it was like losing a vital part of what made me who I am. I didn't want to live without them, and I spiraled down a dark hole. I started doing things I had never done before. I drank an insane amount, I partied, even tried some drugs at one point but discovered that was too far even for me, and I fucked. My friends tried to be there for me, but I didn't want to listen to reason. Once we headed for L.A., I fit right into that lifestyle. It was exactly what I craved. Hollis had always been a partier, so he was right there with me, Fox isn't much of a drinker but he likes the scene, and Cannon ... well, Cannon thinks he has to take care of all of us."

The stroller starts coming together and he focuses on it while I sit there sipping the chocolate malt. I smile around the straw, because I don't know of any guy who would take care of me the way Rush has. Even when we weren't anything but fuck buddies, he wanted to do things for me, much to my chagrin.

I stay quiet, giving him time to sort through things, because it's obvious he has more to say and I want him to have the chance to say what he needs to.

"I don't feel angry like I used to," he murmurs, pausing to look at me. "All day, every day I used to be angry—that they were gone, that the asshole hit us that day."

"I don't feel angry anymore either," I admit. "Mostly just sad at times, for what could've been, what *should've* been." I place my hand on my round stomach. "At least with him I have the chance to make it right—to be a good mom."

His lips lift in a small closed-mouth smile. "You'll be the best mom."

"I've been going to therapy," I confess, tucking a piece of hair behind my ear. "It's helped me to see things clearly where my parents are concerned and ... I'm letting it all go. My life is mine, and I shouldn't live holding onto something that's done nothing but drag me down. I won't be drowned by someone else's mistakes anymore."

"You shouldn't," he agrees, adding the wheels to the stroller.

"It's progress I should've made a long time ago," I admit, clearing my throat. I lean my back against the couch, spreading my legs.

"Yeah," he sighs. "Same here." He looks at me with sad eyes. "Do you think we would've ever bothered to fix ourselves if we'd never met each other?"

I nibble on my lip, picking a piece of lint off my dress. "I'd like to think so, but I don't know. We never will know for sure."

"You gave me something to fight for." He stares into my eyes. I can't help but see so much in their depths. I *feel* it too. An infinite amount of thoughts and emotions can be conveyed in one simple glance. "And I have to thank you, because in fighting for you, I finally fought for myself."

"I'm happy for you, Rush." I mean it wholeheartedly. On one hand we're the same two people we've always been, on the other we're not. Healing changes you, it makes you better, but it can also make you a stranger, and in a way that's what we feel like now.

The baby starts to kick and I let out a laugh.

"What is it?" he asks, his head flying up at the sound of my laughter.

I scoot over to him and grab his hand, another one of the stroller wheels falling to the ground, and press it to my stomach.

"Do you feel that?"

The baby kicks again.

His lips part and his eyes widen in surprise, lifting to meet mine.

"That's him?"

"Mhmm," I hum. "He likes to kick all the time—but mostly at night. I think he's giving me a heads up that I'm never sleeping again."

He grins crookedly. "That's amazing." He places both hands against my stomach, gazing down with a look of wonder. "Such a miracle," he murmurs softly. Raising his head to look at me he asks, "Does he have a name?"

I shake my head. "It's scary naming a baby. Whatever we pick ... it's his name forever."

"We?" He grins, his eyes lightening.

I smile back with a shrug. "We'll see. You better come up with something good. I have veto power if it sucks."

He sobers, moving his hand over my stomach as he follows our son's kicks. "I'll come up with the best name ever. You just wait and see." Dropping his hands, he sits back and meets my eyes. "I would like to be there—in the delivery room, if you're okay with it."

I press my lips together, thinking. I had planned for only Mia to be with me.

"Can I think about it?" I ask him. "I'll let you know."

His shoulder sag in defeat, but he nods anyway. "That's fine."

Silence descends upon us as he finishes putting together the stroller and moves on to the car seat, making sure it fits in the base and everything is connected. When the last of my chocolate malt is gone, I help him, he orders me not to but it's pointless—I do what I want.

There's something almost therapeutic about working together.

"We're like a team," I blurt, and he glances at me with a questioning gaze. "We ... we work well together," I explain awkwardly.

He smiles back. It's a soft, hesitant smile—not at all like the cocky one I grew used to. "Yeah, we do."

Being around him like this fills me with warmth and gives me hope for what could be. I've missed him, sure, but I don't want to invite him back into my life fully until I feel confident we're both on the right track.

It would crush me to give us a chance and Rush start drinking again. I need someone I can rely on, a steady rock to cling to, a shield against the darkness and storms.

I haven't decided yet if he's the rock or the storm.

But I know what I hope for.

It takes several hours for the two of us to finish putting everything together, but I enjoy the time spent with him, especially as we loosen up and begin to laugh and joke. It's different between us than it was before, but I can still feel the attraction and chemistry thrumming between us and I'm grateful it hasn't gone away with all the other changes.

I walk Rush to the door and the urge to get on my tiptoes and kiss him is strong, but I know we're not ready for that. If we have any chance of making this work it means taking things slow and I'm happy he's on the same page. I might have forgiven him, but it doesn't mean we need to rush things, and after the way I hurt him he needs time as well to see if things between us are salvageable.

"You should come to my appointment on Friday," I tell him suddenly. "The baby looks like an actual human being now. He's huge. He's measuring really long, I think he's going to be tall like you."

Rush's face warms and his genuine smile nearly knocks me off my feet. "I'd love that. I'll pick you up."

"You don't have to—"

"Please?"

I don't think Rush has ever said please to me over anything and somehow, I find I can't deny the request.

"Okay." I nod slowly. "My appointment is at eleven in the morning so pick me up at ten-thirty."

"I'll be here," he promises.

"Thank you for helping today with all of this stuff." I motion inside my apartment. "You really didn't have to buy all of it."

"I wanted to. I'll see you Friday, I guess."

"Friday," I echo. It's Sunday now, which makes Friday feel like a lifetime away, but the point of taking things slow is to not spend every waking moment together now that we've made contact again.

He nods and jogs down the steps, hopping in his truck a moment later.

He looks up at me through the truck's window with hope in his eyes and it nearly knocks me to my knees.

I lift my hand in a wave, and he mimics it then gives two sharp honks on this truck's horn before pulling away.

Stepping inside, I close and lock the door before leaning against it.

Slowly, I raise my hand to my chest and feel the pattering of my heart beating against my palm. Color floods my cheeks and I let out a squeal.

I, Kira Marsh, have a full-blown crush on Rush Daniels.

I guess there's a first time for everything.

FORTY-EIGHT

Rush

I pull my truck up outside Kira's apartment and shoot her text to let her know I'm here. A moment later she comes down wearing a loose dress like she had on the other day, a pair of red Converse, with her dark hair pulled back into a ponytail. Her face is free of makeup and she looks ... happy.

I think she's the most beautiful thing I've ever seen.

She opens the passenger door and glares at me and I have to suppress a laugh, because I've fucking missed her pissed off looks.

"How do you expect my heavily pregnant ass to haul myself into this massive beast of a truck?" She sticks her hands on her hips, staring me down.

"I can help you."

I hop out of the truck before she can retort and meet her at the passenger side.

"My equilibrium is way off thanks to this thing." She points to her stomach.

"I think it's perfect."

Her eyes sparkle at that. "Stop trying to woo me with sweet words and help me in here, or else we'll be taking my car."

I give her my hand and she takes it. With my other at her waist I help her climb into the truck.

"This truck is not baby friendly," she scolds me. "You need a minivan."

I snort. "I'm *never* driving a minivan, Kira. Don't even start."

"Good luck trying to put a car seat in the back. I'm just saying." She raises her hands innocently, smiling at me. I don't know a time when we've ever been like this, joking and lighthearted.

"It's a good thing I'm six-foot-six then. I'll be fine."

"Whatever you say." She gives a small shrug. "We better get going."

"Right," I agree, closing her door.

Luckily, the hospital where her doctor is happens to be a ten-minute drive tops, so we should still be early.

Once I've pulled into traffic, I clear my throat. "I thought maybe we could get lunch after your appointment ... if you want."

I've never sounded this idiotic in my entire life. My voice even squeaks like a prepubescent boy. I've always been unapologetically confident, even before the accident, but Kira has me feeling all kinds of vulnerable.

"That'd be nice."

"Your choice," I tell her.

"Cheeseburgers," she sighs dreamily.

I shake my head. "Have you craved them the whole time?"

"Yes," she admits. "Those and Coke. I've probably gained

twenty pounds because of those two things alone. I hope these cravings go away as soon as he's out, I miss my tacos."

"I miss your taco." I grin at her, waggling my brows.

Her only response is an exhaled sigh of disbelief.

I turn into the hospital and loop around, searching for the right parking lot section.

"It's that one." She points it out and then it becomes a game to find a parking space.

Eventually we find one and hurry inside before she ends up late to her appointment. So much for being early.

We step onto the elevator and it's the just the two of us, standing side by side. My arm brushes hers and I lower my head to study her.

"Why are you looking at me like that?" she whispers, tilting her chin up as she raises her eyes to meet mine.

"Because I want to memorize every detail of you."

Her lips part, but anything she's about to say gets cut off as the doors open and we step off the elevator. We walk side by side into her doctor's office and I sit down while she signs in.

I can't help thinking of all the appointments she's come to without me. It stings, but I also know we've needed this time apart to grow as individuals.

She plops into the chair beside me, holding her purse on her lap protectively like a paranoid ninety-year-old named Barbara.

"I hate doctors offices," she mutters under her breath. "They all look so depressing."

I chuckle. "And you'd think one like this would be a little happier."

"I guess they don't want us to feel too comfortable," she reasons, wiggling in her chair.

"Kira?" A nurse calls out and the two of us stand.

We're led back and down a hallway where the nurse takes Kira's weight and blood pressure before putting us in a room.

Kira hops up on the table and I sit in the chair beside her.

She wraps her arms around her belly and tilts her head in my direction. "I'm a whale."

I roll my eyes. "No, you're not. You're beautiful."

I'm not lying, either. She's more gorgeous than she's ever been, and I can't quite understand the pride I feel knowing she's round with my child.

Her cheeks redden. "Thank you, but I don't feel that way. I'm tired all the time, my feet hurt, and I burp like a redneck competing in a burping contest."

"Your body is growing a human, you're bound to have side effects," I reason, clasping my hands together. I lean forward slightly in the chair. My nerves are far worse today than the first time I came with her.

"It's hard sometimes, not feeling like me." Her eyes sadden and she nibbles on her bottom lip nervously. "I didn't want this baby to start with," she admits, which is nothing new to me. "But now ... I can't wait to hold him and see him. I already love him so much and I didn't know it was possible to feel something so powerful for a person you haven't even met."

"He's your child—*our* child—it's a love that transcends everything."

"You love him too already, don't you? I've heard sometimes the dad doesn't connect with the baby until it's here. It's different for the mother since you're growing it. And since you haven't been able to be around..." She trails off.

"I do," I admit. "That doesn't mean I'm not scared or worried, but I do love him. He's a piece of you and me, and that's ... well, it's a real kind of magic that exists in the world, isn't it?"

She grins at me. "When did you become so philosophical?"

"I've always been this way. The alcohol made me a loon." I wink at her.

I'm definitely much more serious not drinking. Don't get me

wrong, I still laugh, joke, and have the amazing talent of turning practically anything into a dirty conversation, but I'm subdued. I don't have this unchained wildness constantly needing to be released to keep me sane—and I'm not sure if I can blame that entirely on the alcohol. Not coping with the loss of my parents led to a lot of built up thoughts and emotions and they needed to get out in some way.

"How are you feeling?" she asks softly, hesitantly like she's afraid to voice it. "Is ... is it weird to be sober?"

"In a way, yes—mostly because I truly believed I was sober the majority of the time. I thought there was nothing wrong with liking to let go and drink until I lost all control. Now, I see what a disaster I've made of things because I refused to accept I'm an alcoholic. I feel better without it, but that doesn't mean there isn't a part of my brain telling me I'm fine and I can have a beer if I want. It's lying to me, and I have to ignore that voice so I don't lose myself again. It's been difficult doing this once, I can't imagine doing this again, but a lot of people do," I exhale a sigh. "I want to be strong enough to never pick up a bottle again, but I'm not naïve enough to think it won't be difficult—especially with what I do. When we go on tour ... alcohol will be everywhere, in easy reach, and I'll have to fight that voice even harder."

She reaches out, touching her fingers to my cheek and I place my hand over hers.

"You can do it. I believe in you."

I take her hand, pressing a kiss to her fingertips before letting go.

"Thank you." I mean it wholeheartedly. Her faith in me gives me all the more reason to fight for my sobriety.

The door opens and the doctor comes in.

I barely hear all the things she says to Kira, even though I try to pay attention, because all I can think about is seeing our baby.

When I met Kira nearly a year ago now, I never could've fucking imagined we'd be here, in a doctor's office getting ready to see our baby.

I couldn't have imagined *any* of this journey.

It's been a long, difficult road to only be a few months—it feels more like years, instead—but I wouldn't change a thing. Even if Kira and I don't get back together, I'm still glad we've both faced our demons. Otherwise, they would've kept haunting us and our lives would never reach their full potential since we'd always be clinging to a past long gone.

"You two ready to see your baby?" Dr. Wren inquires, looking between the two of us with a kind smile.

Kira looks over at me with a smile, extending her hand. "We are," she answers.

I wrap my hand around hers, still surprised at the ease in which she touches me now, when she was so afraid of any kind of contact unless it was sex.

Dr. Wren turns the screen so the two us can see it easier and squirts some gel on Kira's stomach before pressing the wand against her.

A moment later our baby appears on the screen.

Somehow, it's even more amazing than the first time.

"He's a wild one," the doctor jokes. "I hope you two are ready to never sleep again." She gives a small laugh, moving the wand around. "Look," she points, "he's sucking his thumb."

I lean practically completely over Kira's body, gazing in awe at the squirming baby inside her belly.

"It's incredible," I murmur.

My gaze leaves the screen and I look down at Kira. The urge to kiss her is strong, but for once I restrain myself. I can't do what I want, when I want, anymore. I have to think before I act.

"He's amazing." Kira smiles up at me. "I hope you're thinking of a really good name."

I chuckle. "It has to be epic so you can't use your veto power."

I know it's a big fucking deal, her giving me the chance to name our child, and I don't want to blow it. I don't know yet if she wants him to have her last name or mine. I'm selfishly hoping for mine, but I won't push the issue, not with her giving me this opportunity.

"Make it count," she says, her brown eyes soft and shining with the promise of so much more.

"I will," I vow, and I know we're both talking about so much more than his name.

I SIT DOWN ACROSS FROM KIRA, DROPPING THE GREASY PAPER BAG between us.

"God, I love Five Guys," she moans, diving for the bag and quickly pulling out her fries and cheeseburger.

"I bet you do."

She pauses unfolding the foil from her burger and glares at me like she wishes she could incinerate me. "I'm so glad to see your delightful, dirty sense of humor is still intact."

I pull a fry out of the bag and pop it in my mouth. "So are other parts of me."

She rolls her eyes dramatically and lets out another low moan with her first bite of burger. An older couple a few tables away look over.

"She's pregnant," I defend.

"Who cares what they think," she retorts, going in for a second monstrous bite.

I can't help but grin at her, because I fucking love the way she refuses to be anything but herself.

I finally take a bite of my own burger and it's damn good.

"I have something to ask you," I begin, my voice soft and hesitant, because frankly I'm scared of her answer.

"This sounds dangerous." She raises a brow and wipes her hands on a napkin, listening carefully.

"I need to go back home, to Tennessee—to finally clean out my parents' house and put it up for sale."

"Okay," she replies, dragging out the word. "What does this have to do with me?"

"I want you to go with me."

I hate admitting this weakness out loud, but pretending to be strong is just as weak.

"Me? Why?" she blurts.

I answer honestly. "Because you get it."

Our situations might be totally different, but she understands what it's like to struggle and let go of the things holding you back. I know my friends would pack up and go with me but ... this is going to be a big fucking deal for me and I don't need too many voices and conflicting talks about things. I need one steady and solid presence at my side and that's her.

"I don't know," she hedges, breaking a fry in half. She lifts her dark eyes to mine. "I don't want to push things too far, too fast with us."

"Please?" I'm resorting to begging now. "As friends, nothing more. I promise I won't try anything."

She sighs, but a smile slowly lifts her lips. "Why is it I can't say no to you? I really hope our son doesn't inherit that trait from you or I'm screwed."

"You'll go then?" I dare to hope.

She nods resolutely. "But don't make me regret this, Daniels." She points a finger at me in warning with her adorably cute mad face.

"Never," I vow.

FORTY-NINE

Kira

"Are you sure this is a good idea?" Mia asks, sitting on the end of my bed as I pack my bag.

"No," I answer honestly. "But I can't believe you're not gung-ho for this. I know you're secretly Team Rush."

She puffs out a breath of air, blowing her hair out of her face. "I like Rush, I want to see him redeem himself and you two ride off into the sunset—I'm a romantic now, sue me. But you're also my *best* friend, and I want you to be happy and not rush into anything you're not ready for."

"I'm not planning on sexing him up, if that's what you think." I push down on the clothes inside so I can zip it easier.

"That's not what I thought. I don't want to see you hurt, that's all."

"I'll be fine," I tell her, blowing hair out of my eyes with a breath. "Besides, I think this will be good for Rush and me. It'll give us time away, the two of us, to talk about things and see where we want to go with this whole thing."

"Do you know where you want things to go?" she hedges, knowing she's treading on thin ice.

I shove my zipped knock-off Vera Bradley looking bag out of my way and park my ass on the bed beside her.

"I don't know," I answer honesty, exhaling a sigh. "For the first time I'm hoping for more, but I'm not counting on it. I'll be okay either way."

"Are you sure?"

"Yeah," I answer with a nod. "Because I am enough."

She smiles, her blue eyes shining with the threat of tears. "I'm so proud of you. You've come so far."

"Don't go getting all sappy on me now," I warn her, feeling tears forming in my eyes.

"Oh, shut up," she scolds, practically tackling me into a hug so we both fall back on my bed. "I love you."

"Love you, too." I'll never understand what I did to deserve a friend like Mia, but I'll never stop being thankful for her.

Letting me go, we both sit up and she points a finger at me like a bossy mother reprimanding her child. "If you get uncomfortable, or things go south, whatever—you call me and I'll be there to get you as fast as I can. I don't care what kind of traffic laws I have to break."

"It'll only be a few days—a week tops."

"Still, Rush is newly sober and this is going to be a big test for him, going to his childhood home. Hollis says he hasn't been inside since his parents died. It's bound to be in terrible shape. Watch out for rats," she warns me.

"I doubt there are rats." I roll my eyes at her dramatics.

"You never know." She shrugs in a whatcha-gonna-do-about-it gesture.

There's a knock on the door and I look at her. "He's here."

"I don't know why I feel like you're leaving me and I'm never going to see you again," she sniffles, wiping at the corner of her eye.

I smile and grab her hand. "Things are changing, and with that comes a feeling of loss—but you're not losing me, Mia. Just like I haven't lost you to Hollis. This is just ... the next phase of life."

"You're right," she agrees with an exhale, still looking sad.

There's another knock on the door.

"I better let him in before he barges his way in here." I stick out my tongue and roll my eyes dramatically, even though Rush would never do that.

Mia grabs my bag and carries it as she stays behind me.

I swing the door open to reveal Rush standing on the opposite side. He's so large he fills up the entire doorway and he has to duck when he walks inside.

"We better hit the road," he says, sliding his sunglasses off and sticking them on his shirt. "Traffic is going to start getting heavy."

"Unless we left at three in the morning—it's going to be heavy no matter what."

He chuckles. "You're right. This your bag?" He points at the bag Mia holds.

There's an awkwardness in the air between the two of us and I know it's because neither of us really knows how to proceed. Are we just friends? More? What is this weird in-between state and how do we deal with it?

"Yeah, that's it."

He holds out his hand to take it from Mia and she glares at him. "I might be rooting for you, but if you hurt her, I will not hesitate to punch you in the nuts."

He chuckles, his eyes flickering over to me. "Noted."

She finally hands him the bag and I turn to her. "I have to go. Stop acting like a crazy over-protective mom."

"I can't help it."

"You're being silly."

She hugs me goodbye and follows us outside as I lock up my place.

With one more hug on the street, she finally gets in her car and drives away.

"What's wrong with her?" Rush asks, standing beside his truck with my bag slung over his shoulder one-handed. "She's not pregnant too, is she? Because she's acting super fucking emotional."

I snort. "Absolutely not. I think ... a lot of changes have happened for her and me in a short amount of time. It makes you ... nostalgic, I guess—desperate to hold on to what was, but we all have to move forward eventually."

"Makes sense." He opens the back passenger door on the truck and places my bag on the seat beside his duffel. "Do I need to boost you in?" he jokes, shutting the door and opening the front one for me.

"If you'd get a footboard, I wouldn't need a boost," I scold him.

"Where's the fun in that?" He grins boyishly at me—so light and playful. His blond hair flops over his forehead, draping into his eyes and he pushes the strands out of the way. "Up you go." He motions for me to get in, holding out his hand.

With a dramatic sigh, I take his hand and let him help me into the truck.

He starts to close the door but I hold my hand out, stopping him. "I have to go pee." He looks at me in disbelief. "I'm *pregnant*," I remind him. "I pee a lot. It's not my fault this baby likes to use my bladder as his personal trampoline."

With a sigh, he helps me back out and I waddle up the stairs and into my apartment to empty my bladder before we finally get on the road.

Because I'm evil, I commandeer the AUX cord. As soon as the opening notes begin Rush shakes his head.

"No, nope, turn that shit off."

I sing dramatically to Celine Dion's *My Heart Will Go On* from the Titanic soundtrack.

"You're the worst," he tells me, shaking his head, but there's no hiding his smile. "Absolutely awful."

His complaining only encourages me to sing louder and add in lots of flailing and hand gestures.

When the song ends, he breathes a sigh of relief, but it's short lived when I put a remix of it on instead.

"This is my punishment for all the times I've tortured the guys in the car," he gripes.

"Payback's a bitch," I say, even though I have no idea what he's talking about.

After the remix is done, I put one of my regular listened to playlists on, because I don't have the energy to keep messing with him even if it's fun.

I stick my phone in one of the empty cup holders and wiggle around, trying to get comfortable, which is pretty impossible these days.

"Are you nervous? To go back home?"

He exhales a heavy breath, flicking the blinker on to change lanes. "Fucking terrified," he finally replies. "But I'll never be ready for this. It's something I just have to do."

Noticing the way his fingers tighten around the steering wheel, I can't help wishing I hadn't asked, but we're hours away from him having to face this reality ... and if it becomes too much, I'm afraid of what he might do and how helpless I'll be to stop him.

Only an hour into our trip I have to stop for a potty break.

"Are you regretting asking me to come?" I ask, exiting the bathroom to find Rush standing across the way with his back against the wall, one leg propped against it, and his arms crossed over his muscular chest.

"Not at all." He grins, slipping away from the wall to fall into step beside me. "In fact, I was thinking about how happy I am I asked you along."

"Is that so?" I say in a sarcastic tone.

He slips in front of me, walking backward. "Oh, yeah. Who would complain about a hot chick for their road trip companion?"

"I'm sure most males would *love* a very pregnant, moody, has to pee all the time, woman tagging along. Sounds like the dream."

"You're my dream."

I push his shoulder and brush past him. "If you start with all that sappy Disney rated crap, *I'll* punch you in the nuts and Mia won't have to."

He laughs fully, and it makes butterflies flutter in my stomach.

He slings his arm over my shoulders and steers me outside the double glass doors of the gas station to his truck.

"No sappy shit, noted. Just us."

HOURS LATER RUSH SHAKES ME AWAKE.

"Wh-What's happening? Where are we? Are we here?" I blurt out each question in a short and clipped voice, my blurry eyes swing in every direction as I take in our surroundings. "Why are we at a Holiday Inn?"

"We're stopping for the night," he explains. "We have about four more hours to go before we get there." He stifles a yawn. "I didn't get much sleep last night, and we've already lost a lot of time stopping, so I figured we'd take a break."

"Are you making fun of my non-stop need to pee?"

He grins, holding up his thumb and index finger a slight width apart. "Only slightly."

Sobering I ask, "Did you need more time?"

He looks away from me, out the windshield and the muscle in his jaw ticks. "Maybe," he admits. "I don't know what I'm going to do seeing that house again, going inside it ... packing away their stuff. It's like I'm packing *them* away as if they never even existed."

"They existed, Rush, and they'll always exist. Right here." I reach across the console and touch my fingers to his chest where his heart thumps steadily.

"You're right," he breathes, hesitantly reaching across to place his palm against my stomach. "They'll exist in him, too. I'll make sure he always knows his grandparents."

"I wish I could've met them," I confess on a whisper. "They sound like good people."

"The best," he sighs, the weary kind full of regrets. "They would've taken you under their wing and my mom would've doted on you. They would've wanted you to know what real parents are supposed to be like."

I smile at his words. "One day, you're going to have to tell me more about them."

"I will," he vows.

After a long pause, the two of us grab our bags and head inside. He gets one room with two beds, which surprises me since I expected him to ask for one. I'm actually kind of sad we won't be sharing a bed, but I don't tell him, because again I have to remind myself how important it is for us to take things slow.

Rush slides the keycard into the door and swings it open.

Immediately to our right is the bathroom and then we walk a

little further to find two queen beds, a TV stand with a TV, and a small desk.

Rush tosses his bag onto one of the beds.

"You want to shower?"

I shake my head. "I showered this morning."

"Me too," he replies.

Awkwardness falls between us, heavy and pulsating like a living being.

I clear my throat. "I guess we should go to bed then—get up early."

"Y-Yeah," he stutters, and it makes me happy to see his composure slip. Since I met him, he's always been so together, never letting his emotions glimpse through, but now there's a vulnerability to him. It's a reminder to me of how human we all are, even if we try to pretend we're not.

He closes the curtains and I yank my pajamas out of my bag.

"Turn around," I command him when he comes back over.

"Why?" He grins boyishly, a challenge in his eyes. "I've seen you naked numerous times and in many positions."

"But never with a basketball attached to my stomach. *Turn around*," I hiss, shooing him with my hands.

He sighs dramatically, like I'm such a pain in his ass, but finally, thankfully, turns around to face the opposite way.

I make sure he stays looking away as I change out of my clothes and into a maternity tank top and a pair of cotton shorts.

"I'm done," I announce, and he turns around.

"Fuck," he groans hoarsely. "Your tits have gotten so big."

"They're enormous," I sulk forlornly, because they *hurt* at this size. "It's miserable and this baby isn't due for another month so it's only going to get worse."

"I'm sorry I missed your birthday," he blurts suddenly.

"How do you know? I never even told you when it is."

"Mia," he answers.

I sigh, lifting my bag off the bed and dropping it on the floor. "I should've known." Facing him with my hands on my hips, I say, "We've needed this time apart. There's no need to apologize."

"Still," he shrugs, not quite meeting my gaze, "I wish I could've been there."

"It wasn't exciting," I promise him. "Mia took me to get some kind of pregnancy massage—which was amazing by the way—and to get our nails done. Then we went back to her place and gorged ourselves on Double Dunker ice cream."

"I hope I can celebrate next year with you," he confesses vulnerably.

"I hope so too."

I hope for a lot of things I refused to even dare think of a few months ago, one of the main things being working things out with Rush. I never believed we were right for each other, that we could possibly raise a child and be a couple, but now I see how wrong I was. If there's anyone in this world who is made for me, it's Rush.

But it doesn't mean it'll be easy.

Any kind of love is work. None of it is smooth sailing, and I credit my therapist with showing me that.

"All right, your turn to look away." He spins his finger in the air, encouraging me to give him my back.

"You have to be kidding," I retort. "You're not pregnant."

"If I don't get to look, neither do you."

I roll my eyes. "And society says it's women who are dramatic," I grumble, as I turn around.

I hear him chuckle and barely a minute passes before he tells me I can look.

"You had me turn around so you could strip down to your fucking boxer-briefs," I scoff. "You really are a drama queen." I brush past him and turn back the bed I'll be sleeping in. "I'm going to sleep, so I don't have to deal with you."

"Don't be mad." He mock pouts at me, jutting out his delectable bottom lip. He looks too fucking delicious for his own good standing there all muscular and ripped, his tattoos on full display barely concealing the visible veins in his arms, with his boxer-briefs hugging every inch of him—and I do mean *every* inch. He grins, and his tongue slides out to moisten his lips. "Like what you see, Kira?"

I turn my head. "Not at all."

He laughs huskily and flips the covers back roughly on his bed. "Keep telling yourself that."

I cross my arms and roll over, away from him. "I will, because it's true."

He doesn't say anything more, but I can feel the cockiness radiating off of him even as I fall asleep.

FIFTY

Rush

My truck rolls to a stop outside the perfectly normal and average suburban home.

Brick front, siding on the sides and back, red front door, dark gray shutters.

The lawn is perfectly manicured, not a weed in sight. There's a twelve-year-old Nissan Altima in the driveway—my mom's. In an alternate reality, I can pretend Dad ran to the store and he's going to be right back, but in the real world the home is cold and empty. There hasn't been life here for a long time.

"This is it?" Kira asks in surprise, pointing out the window.

"Yes," I say, switching the truck into park.

"Does someone live here?"

"It's empty," I answer with a sigh, slipping my baseball cap off to scratch my head before putting it on backwards.

"Empty?" She looks at me in surprise. "But ... it's in such good shape—it's been taken care of. I—"

"I pay people to clean it twice a month, and lawn maintenance. Anything that needs to be kept up ... I make sure it's taken care of. I might not have wanted to be here, but that doesn't mean I was going to let it fall into disrepair. It's still my home," I sigh, draping an arm over the steering wheel and looking out Kira's window at the house.

She reaches over, placing her small hand on my knee and giving it a squeeze. "We'll go in when you're ready."

I place my hand over hers, soaking in the comfort of having her here—to not have to do this alone.

I wish I could jump inside her mind, see what she thinks when she looks at the house from a stranger's eyes, but I can't. I can only see it from my eyes—the memories of learning to play basketball with my dad in the driveway at the hoop he put up for me. Running through the yard with my friends and the neighborhood kids, playing tag or jumping through sprinklers. Barbeque parties thrown by my mom who loved having people gather at our house.

I have so many good fucking memories, but I've let the pain of one day overshadow them all.

Lifting my hand off of hers I take the key from the ignition and exhale a breath.

"I'm ready." Her brown eyes meet mine, questioning. "I am," I vow.

Climbing out of the truck I grab our bags and help her out. I feel like I'm being stared at from every house around, but I know it's my own paranoia and guilt plaguing me, because I shouldn't have stayed away for so long.

She stays by my side as we walk up the asphalt driveway to the side door.

My breath passes through my lips in a low whistle at the

sight of the flowered curtains hanging over the window in the door. They're faded now, nothing like the bright hue I remember from before.

I set our bags by the door and pick up the frog holding a yellow umbrella from the ground, pulling out the hideaway key tucked within.

Even though I know they're dead and gone some part of me keeps expecting the door to swing open and my mother to pull me enthusiastically into her arms. I would give anything for one more chance to tell them I love them, how much I appreciate everything they ever did for me.

They made me a good man, and I'll never stop being fucking sorry I lost sight of who I really am.

I slide the key into the knob and swing the door open.

The smell hits me first.

Lemony with disinfectant and not at all like the cookies and brownies my mom was constantly making for local charities.

This isn't home, not anymore. It's a shell, a fragment left behind. It's simply a house without a heart now.

I pick up my bag from the ground—Kira's still slung over my shoulder—and push the door open further so she can easily step inside.

Reaching for the familiar switch on the right, I flip it up and the laundry room floods with light. White cabinets line the top of the left wall with the washer and dryer below with a small counter area and sink. The walls are a bright canary yellow. I remember my dad and I thinking my mom was nuts when she made us paint it this atrocious shade, but looking back now, I'm thankful for that day spent with my dad. At the time it seemed like such a chore. Now, it's something to be cherished.

"It's cheery," Kira says, looking around.

"Kitchen's through there." I point straight ahead and she

moves forward. I flick on another light and the kitchen comes to life.

The cabinets are a blue color my mom referred to as *cornflower* and the counters are a laminate designed to look like marble.

Everything is exactly the fucking same, and I don't know why I expected it to be any different. Even her damn black and white polka dot chicken sits in the corner with cooking utensils sticking out of it. An embroidered dishrag that says *The Daniels' Home* is tucked into the arm of the oven. I set both of our bags on the floor and spin around, finding the calendar on the wall—dreading what I'm sure I'll no doubt find, but instead it's gone and in its place is a new calendar for this year. I'm sure it's something the cleaner put up, maybe trying to bring some life to the place, but with the hummingbird in the picture it looks like something my mom would've picked out.

Kira doesn't say a word as I take everything in. I'm thankful she lets me absorb this on my own with no interference. It's crazy to think it's been nearly ten whole years since I came home, set foot in my own house.

I move to the next room and Kira follows silently behind me like a shadow.

The sectional still takes up much of the space in the family room, the purple stain in the curved part from a glass of wine my mom knocked over is still there. The wall of family photos shines without a hint of dust on them.

I take in my mom's sandy brown hair and brown eyes so similar to Kira's. I never noticed that before. Perhaps I wouldn't allow myself to see it.

My dad stands beside her, with his arm wrapped around her waist smiling at the camera. His dark hair is speckled with white, while his beard is almost completely white. On my mom's other side is me, standing taller than the both of them. Blond hair spiked up and bleached on the ends—why I thought that looked good is beyond me—holding a basketball trophy from my junior year. When we took that photo we had no idea nearly a year later they'd be gone.

"They look kind," Kira speaks softly.

"They were," I whisper. "The kindest. The best. They didn't deserve to die."

I swallow past the lump in my throat, feeling tears well in my eyes.

Kira's small warm hand presses against my back, rubbing slow circles.

"I'm here, Rush. If you need to scream, then fucking scream. If you need to get angry, get angry. If you need to cry, then cry. Let it out. You owe it to yourself. Emotions demand to be felt and when you smother them that's when they turn and suffocate *you* instead."

I turn and wrap my arms around her, bending so I can bury my face in her neck. I don't cry at first, I just need to feel her, but then the tears do come.

I've kept too much shit bottled up for too long and it comes out painfully. I didn't know crying could physically hurt, but this does. I feel the emotions and raw wounds tearing open over and over again, but as I let it out, I can feel them being cleansed.

It feels like we stand there for fucking ever, but eventually I manage to let her go. I don't feel like a wuss for letting all of it out, instead I feel stronger than I have in a long time.

"Are you ready to move on?"

I know she's asking if I'm ready to go to another room, but I feel like I'm ready to move on in a bigger way.

"Yeah." I take a step away from her and instantly I miss her warmth. A year ago I never could've imagined I'd be standing in this house again, but here I am. We've both changed so much and power comes from embracing your demons, accepting them, and finally being set free.

Forcing my feet one in front of the other, I explore the rest of the downstairs—a bathroom, my dad's office, and the game room. The game room used to be one of my favorites. My dad was obsessed with arcade games and one whole wall is lined with them. In the center is a pool table and there's a dartboard on one of the walls.

Upstairs are two guest bedrooms, my old room, theirs, and two more bathrooms.

Their room is at the end of the hall with the door shut, mine is on the right.

My heart thrums in my ears and I can't hear anything.

But then Kira slips her hand into mine and holds onto my arm with her other, leaning into my body.

"We can do this together," she promises me. "One step at a time. As long as you focus on one step the distance doesn't seem so terrible."

I grin at her. "Did your therapist tell you that?" I joke.

She shrugs. "She's actually a smart lady."

With a shake of my head I take one step, then another, and another until I'm standing in front of my bedroom door.

I swing it open, taking in the small space.

The walls are the same grayish blue color my mom insisted was perfect for a teenage boy. My bed is tucked against the wall, with my small desk at the end and blue swivel computer chair. Above my desk is shelving, lined with trophies and medals. On the other side of the room is my closet and dresser. The window beside my bed looks out on the street below and my red truck looks like a fucking beacon it's so bright.

Something clangs and I turn to find Kira giving me an apologetic look, a picture frame clasped in her hand and since I know where she got it from, it's safe to assume she knocked it against one of my trophies.

She looks down at the picture and then back at me. "You were already taller than all the boys." She gives me a small smile. "How old were you here?"

I take one step and peer at the picture, even though I already know. I just want any excuse to be closer to her.

The grainy picture shows me standing in the back of the group shot. My hair is cut haphazardly and way too short, because my mom got the wild idea she could cut my hair. My smiling face showcases a mouthful of braces, but my eyes ... they're happy, not haunted by the ghosts of one fucking night that changed everything.

"I was thirteen. It was my eighth grade year."

"What happened to your hair?"

I snort. "My mother, that's what happened."

"She cut your hair?" she surmises.

"Yep. It was unfortunate and the ladies were not a fan."

"Already a charmer at thirteen?" She rolls her eyes. "Why am I not surprised?" She lifts onto her tiptoes to replace the photo on the shelf but I grab it from her so she doesn't strain herself.

"I can't help it if I've always had a way with the ladies," I joke, looking down at her once the picture is back where it belongs.

She makes a noise in her throat.

I reach out, brushing a stray hair off her forehead before I touch my finger to her chin, raising her head.

"There's only one woman I want attention from now."

"Is that so?" Her voice drops, taking on a husky edge.

I nod. The urge to kiss her is fucking strong, but I hold myself back.

I've always taken what I wanted, when I wanted it, and this whole waiting thing is new for me—but I remind myself it'll all be worth it in the end.

I hope, at least.

The air between us grows taut and thick with desire, but neither of us acts on it.

I take two steps away from her and the bubble evaporates as if it never existed to begin with.

"Do you want to ... should we?" She points outside the room, and I know what she's trying to say.

"Not yet. I can't..." I pause, shaking my head. "I can't yet."

She nods. "I understand."

"Pick the guestroom you want," I tell her. "I had the cleaners get new sheets and bedding for those rooms so we could use them. I'll grab our bags and bring them up."

She nods and heads down the hall, while I jog down the steps to grab our shit from the kitchen.

It's weird how this house was once so full of life, buzzing like a beehive, and now it's empty—like some relic left behind from a lost world.

It's going to be fucking hard going through all this shit to throw away, donate, or keep.

I carry our bags up and find her in the green room as I call it. My mom liked color, and every room in the house is a different shade. Growing up I thought it looked like a fucking rainbow threw up in here, it still does, but now I see how her personality is sprinkled in every room.

Kira stands looking out the window that overlooks the backyard. There's a covered pool, a gazebo, and a grill. The lawn guys have done a good job of keeping leaves swept away and the flowers in bloom. I've made sure to always pay the staff keeping this place up a decent wage with holiday bonuses. I wanted them to know I appreciated all the hard work they put into taking care of my childhood home. I couldn't come here, but I couldn't let it fall into disrepair either.

She hasn't noticed me yet, and she cradles her growing

stomach lovingly, a wistful smile on her face. I didn't think it was possible, but she's even more beautiful now than when I first met her.

I set the bags down softly and lean against the door watching her.

It's selfish of me to lust after her like I do, but when you've touched heaven, you want as much as you can get. It's more than anyone as corrupt and fucked up as me deserves. She's messed up in her own ways too, but I think that's what makes her more beautiful to me. Broken things have character, a story to tell, whereas a shiny new polished vase is better kept up on a high shelf never to be touched or felt.

At the end of the day, all I want is for her to be happy. That's how I know my love is true. Even if her happiness doesn't bring her into my arms, I'll never begrudge it, because seeing her light up with joy is more than I deserve after everything I've done.

I push my body away from the door and clear my throat before she can turn around and find me staring at her. Her heads twists in my direction, her lips lifting in a small smile. The brown of her eyes is lighter than it used to be, no longer weighed down by fear and anger.

"I brought your bag," I tell her unnecessarily. I'm a pathetic fuck.

Her smile grows. "I see that."

I shove my hands in my pockets. "I thought we could relax for the day and start going through things tomorrow." I don't say it out loud, but I need time to process actually being here again after so long before I start getting rid of things. I know it's going to fucking hurt, but it has to be done. I can't keep all this shit forever and this house ... it deserves to have a family living in it again.

"Okay." She nods, her hand still rests on her stomach. I don't think she even realizes the way she holds her belly. Protectively. Motherly. "I think I'm going to shower."

"You know where it is." I run my fingers awkwardly through my hair. I've never been like this before, nervous and like a prepubescent schoolboy crushing on a teacher. "I'm going to run out and get some groceries—is there anything you want?"

Her smile is nearly blinding and it hits me like a punch to my gut.

"Double Dunker ice cream if they have it."

"I'll drive to five stores if I have to."

"And Coke," she adds.

I laugh, rubbing my jaw. "I was already planning to get that. I don't have a death wish."

She grabs a pillow off the bed and tosses it at me. "You asshole," she laughs, "take that back."

"What?" I defend, easily deflecting the pillow where it thumps against the wall and falls to the floor. "You drink the stuff non-stop lately."

She crosses the room and lays her palms flat against my chest, trying to move me. "Get out of here already."

My feet go nowhere and I bust out laughing. "It's cute you think you can push me." I grab her hands, tucking them into mine, and duck my head to whisper seductively in her ear, "I'm not going anywhere, Kira."

She shudders against me, not in fear but lust, and I can see her nipples pucker against the cotton of her dress. Sadly, I know it's my cue to back off before we do something stupid.

"You get that shower, explore, whatever the fuck you want," I say lightly. "You're the queen of this castle." I spread my arms wide.

With that, I jog down the stairs and out the side door, getting out of there before we fall into bed or I admit she's also the queen of my heart.

FIFTY-ONE

Kira

Rush raps his knuckles against the open bedroom door and I look up from the trashy gossip magazine I bought at the last gas station we stopped at.

"I want to take you somewhere," he announces.

I glance at the clock on the nightstand. It's after seven already. We've spent most of the day apart, except for lunch, because I wanted to give him his space. I stayed close enough that I'd know if he was about to get into trouble or spiral out of control. There's no way I'd completely abandon him.

I close the magazine, leaning against the fluffy pillows. My back is killing me, but I've reached the stage in pregnancy where I'm a miserable lump anyway.

"Where?" I hesitate to ask, studying him closely and finding his blue eyes to be calm and clear like a smooth pond and not the raging ocean I'm used to.

He takes a step into the room. "I was thinking," he curls his fingers around the footboard of the bed, "I wouldn't tell you." He gives me a rakish grin, reminding me of some rogue pirate desperate to covet my heart like a treasure chest.

"Aren't we past secrets?" I raise a brow at him in challenge.

He drops his head, shaking it slightly. "You have me there—we're going to pick up fast-food and then I'm taking you to one of my favorite places in this crappy town. Technically it's in the next town, but who cares about the details." He winks.

"Well, since you're saying food is involved, I can't say no. This baby says he's hungry."

Rush chuckles. "He gets that from me."

I slide off the bed with a groan, pressing my hand to my aching back.

"Are you in pain?" he asks, his eyes wide with worry.

I point to my stomach. "I'm carrying a bowling ball with me everywhere, it's natural for my back to hurt. My feet also ache, and I pee all the time." I slip my feet into my flip-flops and grimace. "Which reminds me, I better pee before we go."

"I'll wait for you downstairs." He tosses his thumb over his shoulder.

"Meet you there," I promise, and head for the hall bathroom to empty my bladder.

I barely sit down on the toilet when my bladder empties itself. It's probably been thirty minutes—less even—since I last peed, but it feels like I'm emptying an entire gallon of water.

I finish and wash my hands, then meet Rush downstairs in the kitchen.

Following him out through the laundry room, he helps me into his massive truck.

"I wish I never had to look at this truck again," I grumble as he places a 'helpful' hand on my ass.

He laughs. "Why is that?"

"It's mocking me."

He closes my door and walks around the front. After he's in and buckled he inquires, "It's mocking you? How?"

"It's mocking me, by forcing me to need help to get in and out. I could barely manage before, and now my equilibrium is all off thanks to this chunk." I rub my stomach fondly.

I don't know how I went from being so scared and terrified of being a mother, to loving this tiny human I've never met so completely.

He shakes his head sadly as he backs out of the driveway. "Don't hate the truck. She's a beauty."

He caresses the steering wheel like you would a lover before shifting the gear into drive.

"Do you have anything planned for your birthday?" I ask him, making small talk.

His head whips toward me and he grins. "You remembered my birthday."

I roll my eyes. "It's not like it was hard to."

"But you wanted to remember it, didn't you?"

I don't answer him, and I guess that's all the answer he needs anyway, because he faces the road once more sporting a proud smirk.

A few minutes later he rolls into the drive-thru of a burger joint—bless him.

He doesn't even ask me what I want on mine, he already knows, as he places our order—adding a chocolate and strawberry milkshake on at the end.

"Stop trying to fatten me up," I grumble playfully.

"First off," he holds up one finger, "you would've killed me if I hadn't ordered one—don't even try to deny it. Secondly, these are the best fucking milkshakes *ever*. You can quote me on that. Thirdly," he sticks up a third finger, with a grin, "well, I don't really have a third—but I'll just say, I'll be telling you I told you so in no time."

I roll my eyes dramatically. "Keep telling yourself that."

It's a lie. I know I'll love it. I can't resist a milkshake.

He pays for the food and drives forward to the next window. He hands the carrier filled with our drinks and shakes to me and then takes the food bag, placing it in his lap.

As he drives through the town, I study every detail I can, as if by getting to know the town, I can know Rush better.

We end up on an open road, with farmland on each side.

"Man, there are a lot of cows. Just like back home." I can't help but laugh.

He gives a small chuckle and stuffs his hand inside the bag, pulling out a French fry. "That's what happens when there are farms every-fucking-where. Cows, cows, and more fucking cows."

Eventually he turns onto a gravel road and the setting sun nearly blinds me. I yank down the sun visor for some relief.

I spot some cars up ahead, but I can't figure out what anyone is doing. There's a small hut built by the road and Rush slows down, coming to a stop.

He rolls down his window and leans out.

"How much?"

"Five bucks," the teenager replies.

Rush pulls out a ten and hands it to him. "Keep the change."

He drives forward and backs his truck in near the others.

"Out you go," he tells me and I glare at him. "Right," he grins, "you need my help."

"You're eating this up," I grumble.

"Yes, yes I am," he chortles. The jerk. "Just wait here," he orders.

I raise one brow, because where the hell else am I going to go?

He hops out of the truck and heads around the back, putting the tailgate down. I turn my head around, looking out the back window, and my jaw drops because the back is filled with pillows and blankets on top of what I think must be an air mattress.

Beyond him, I squint and make out a ... screen.

When he opens my door I smile at him. "You brought me to a drive-in."

He grins, his hair pushed back messily like he can't get it out of his eyes quickly enough. He looks boyish and at ease, so much younger.

"I did."

My heart fills with something I don't quite understand. Hope, longing, and something else.

He takes the drink carrier from me and offers me his other hand. I slip my hand into his and watch the way his closes over mine.

I've never wanted to give my heart or myself to anyone. It always felt like too big of a risk. But somehow, piece by piece I've been handing them to Rush long before I realized I was.

We've both made mistakes, been hurt by each other and our pasts, but I still know my heart chooses him. *I* choose him. The words stay locked in my throat as my feet touch the ground and he lets go to close the truck door. I know I'll let them out soon, I have to or I'll go crazy, but now isn't the time.

He places his hand low on my waist and guides me to the back of the truck.

"This seems kind of cheesy now," he admits with a small shrug and an adorably sheepish smile, "but I used to love coming here as a kid, and I thought you might like it too."

I place my hand on his arm and tilt my head back to look up into his eyes.

"This is perfect, Rush. This is the sweetest thing anyone has ever done for me."

His smile nearly blinds me and makes my chest pang.

He sets the drinks down on the tailgate and grabs my waist. "Up you go."

"Rush, no!" I cry, but he's already lifting me onto the back of the truck as if I weigh nothing.

"Even pregnant, I bench press more than you weigh." He levels me with *the look*—you know, the one where someone is clearly telling you without words you're crazy.

"Whatever," I grumble, and scurry awkwardly toward the back of the truck where the mountain of pillows is.

Rush hops into the back of the truck in one lithe movement that's too fucking sexy to be legal. I almost want to ask him to take his shirt off and do it again, but he'd get way too much pleasure from my request, so I bite my tongue. Literally.

It takes a few minutes for us to get settled with our food and drinks.

"What movie is playing?" I ask.

"No fucking idea," he answers, and shoves some fries into his mouth.

"They could be playing a chick flick," I warn, unwrapping the burger. "Or Titanic."

He shrugs. "Tonight, it doesn't matter."

"Why is that?" I pause my movements and tilt my head toward him.

"Because," his eyes meet mine, the blue swirling with an endless pool of shades, "all I care about is being with you."

I duck my head before he can read too much from my eyes.

"You're killing me," I confess on a barely there whisper, the words slipping out unbidden between my lips.

He brushes my hair away from my face and lifts my chin with the backs of his fingers so I'm forced to stop avoiding him.

"Not as much as you're killing me."

It seems illogical that out of all the millions of people in this world, the two of us would find each other. We're so much alike, but so different at the same time. With him I feel complete. I've found a part of me I've been missing and didn't even know I needed. Now that I've found him, I never want to let go.

I scoot closer to him and his eyes widen a fraction of a second before I press my lips to his.

He's stiff at first, caught off guard, but it takes only a moment for his lips to become a soft pillow beneath mine. His fingers delve into my hair and he kisses me back with such passion and fervor I wonder how I've ever lived my life without this feeling.

Without *him*.

I give, he takes, he gives, I take. We know this dance well and it's been too long since we've stepped on the dance floor.

My fingers tangle into the cotton of his shirt, begging and aching to pull him closer.

He grabs me by the waist and pulls me onto his lap. My burger tumbles onto the blankets, but I don't care.

Suddenly, I'm only hungry for him, and I'm positive if I don't get my fill I'll die.

He kisses me desperately, like a man on death row begging to hold on for just a minute longer.

Our time apart has been necessary, I know.

I needed to heal and to accept my role in the way things played out. I needed to grow up and stop holding on to things that were only weighing me down. You can't soar if your wings are clipped.

Rush, too, needed time apart to come to grips with his reality. I think if I'd told him I loved him too that night in New York City, he would've continued on his merry way—drinking and never dealing with his parents' deaths. He's been forced to overcome those obstacles in a way he never would have if we'd tried being together from that moment on.

I know in my heart, all the way down to my soul, if that day would've gone differently, we would've never made it as a couple. We still might not, nothing is a guarantee in this world. But before, we were standing on a shaky ground crumbling beneath our feet, now we have a solid foundation to build upon.

Time is fleeting. It ebbs and flows. Moments end only to never return.

Our moment could've ended in that hotel room in a city that means nothing to us.

But something tells me it's only starting now.

His lips break from mine and he holds my cheeks in both of his massive hands.

I can see every small freckle dashed across his nose. Every fleck of gold and green sprinkled in his blue eyes. Every eyelash. Even a small scar on his forehead normally hidden by his hair.

It's only when you let your guard fall away that you can truly see one another for who you are. We're more naked to each other in this moment than we've ever been, and we're fully clothed.

"Hi," he whispers, staring back at me.

I don't shy away. For the first time in perhaps my entire life, I don't feel like I have anything to hide. "Hi."

"You kissed me."

"I did." I curl my fingers into the hair at the nape of his neck.

"*You* kissed *me*," he repeats with a grin.

"I did," I reply once more with a smile.

His smile fading slightly, he sighs. "I didn't want to push you for too much too soon."

"You didn't push me," I remind him, moving my hands to lay them flat against his chest. "I kissed you, remember? I got tired of waiting for you to make the first move," I laugh, and it feels good to let such a carefree sound tear out of my throat.

"So, what does this mean?" he asks, gliding his fingers gently through my hair.

"It means..." I begin slowly, moving my lips to his jaw and placing a kiss there. "I'm finally..." Another kiss to his neck. "Ready to..." I place a kiss on the opposite side of his neck. "Say..." I kiss his jaw, again mirroring where I kissed him on his right side. I bring my lips leisurely up to his ear and whisper, "I love you."

His breath catches slightly and I know I've surprised him. I smile against his skin and his arms tighten around me. He buries his head into my neck and his stubble scratches me, but I don't care.

He pulls back, but only enough to meet my eyes. His are filled with happiness, relief, and...

"I love you too, Kira. You came out of nowhere, like a falling star—no, like a whole fucking meteor shower, and you lit up my world. Nothing is right now without you."

"I know what you mean."

Behind me, the movie begins to play but I don't turn to look. It's the last thing on my mind.

In this moment, all that matters is him.

Us.

"You want to give this whole thing called life a try with me?" he asks jokingly.

"Yeah, yeah I do."

He hugs me again, and I never want him to let me go. I could stay in his arms forever and I'd be happy. I'm not an expert in love, far from it, but I think that's how you know you've found the one—when they're the only one you can ever imagine holding you, spending time together, simply *existing* with.

He finally sets me off his lap.

"All I want to do is fucking kiss you, but we better eat. Can't have little man getting hangry." He rubs my stomach.

"No, we can't have that," I agree. My eyes fall to my burger lying on the blanket, where several flies are attacking it. My lips curl in disgust. "At least I have fries."

Rush holds out his wrapped hamburger. "Have mine."

I shake my head. "I'm not eating your food."

"Kira," he says in a low voice of warning that makes my center clench. My God, it's been too long since I've had sex and I want nothing more than to rip off his clothes and make *him* my meal.

"Can we split?" I acquiesce.

He shrugs. "Fine, we'll split it."

I pull the fries out of the bag while he tears the burger in half.

He hands me my half and I take a bite. "Oh, this is good," I moan.

He gives a husky laugh. "You haven't even gotten to the milkshake. Brace yourself."

I wiggle my back against the pillows and sit side by side with Rush, my right leg touching his left.

Darkness has almost completely erased all the color from the sky.

I don't even care what movie is playing, because I'm so focused on Rush. He keeps stealing looks at me and it makes me feel warm and fuzzy. This giddiness is new for me, strange but exciting.

Sitting here with him in the back of his truck, among the pile of blankets and food, I realize this is pretty much a date. The first *real* date I've ever been on.

The irony isn't lost on me that I'm experiencing my first date weeks before our baby is due, but I've never believed in doing things according to society's standards—why start now?

Rush finishes his half of the burger and wipes his hands on a napkin.

"You're not watching the movie," he tells me. "You're staring at me. I can *feel* you looking at me."

"I don't care about the movie."

"What do you care about, Kira?" He tilts his chin down toward me, and even in the dark I can't escape the way his eyes feel on me. I never knew you could be electrified by a look before, but you can.

Rush proves the impossible is possible time and again.

"You," I whisper.

My stomach flutters to life with excitement and nervous energy as he cups my chin gently and presses a tender, barely-there, kiss to my more than willing lips. I'd love nothing more than for him to kiss me deeper, to steal my breath, but there's something infinitely more romantic about this. It's a reminder we have all the time in the world.

Sitting back, he passes me my milkshake and grabs his. He scoots lower, turning on his side and propping himself on his elbow so he faces me.

I wrap my lips around the straw and moan. "Holy shit, that *is* good."

He grins wickedly, his eyes sparkling with barely contained laughter. "I told you so."

I smack his shoulder playfully. "Don't mock me."

"I did warn you I'd be saying I told you so." He lifts his cup in salute.

"Yeah, rub it in," I grumble good-naturedly. "You know," I begin after taking another lengthy sip of my milkshake, "there's so much we don't know about each other yet."

"Only because you never wanted to get *that* personal." He winks at me and sets his milkshake aside where it teeters precariously on top of the blankets.

I duck my head. "It was easier that way. If I didn't know you, I couldn't get attached. Then, it wouldn't hurt when things ended."

"It would've still hurt," he sighs, rolling onto his back and pushing his hair out of his eyes.

"I realize that now," I admit. Rubbing my lips together, I think about something I can tell him. "When I was little, I spent an entire year thinking someone lived in my closet, so I wouldn't go near it. It was a vacuum cleaner."

A boisterous laugh rumbles out of his chest. "That's pretty fucking funny."

"What about you?" I ask. "Tell me something. Anything."

I've never been this desperate to know anything about anyone, but suddenly I want to know everything I can about him.

"I wouldn't ride a bike without training wheels until I was eight. I thought I was going to crash without them."

"And did you?"

"Within the first five minutes of them finally coming off I rode into a ditch and broke my arm."

I laugh. "Did you ever ride a bike again?"

"Of course," he scoffs, "I had something to prove. But my cast was a real hit with the ladies." His playful smile lifts my heart. I never imagined things could be like this with a man—easy, comforting, like being with my best friend. "How do you really feel about your dad dying?" he asks, and I grimace.

I pick at a loose thread in the blanket and my dark hair falls forward, hiding my face. "Relieved, and that makes me sad, because it shouldn't be that way. You shouldn't be so afraid and angered by people that you're thankful you know you'll never see them again. It's been years since I saw him anyway, thanks to his jail sentence, but like with my mom it was the constant fear of one day I could see him again."

"What about your mom? Have you seen her?"

I shake my head. "No. Confronting her is pointless. She'll never see the things she's done wrong, how she's hurt me with her actions. My therapist has helped me realize I'm different from her. Just because I'm her daughter doesn't mean I'm *her*. I'm who I choose to be."

He brushes my hair behind my ear, purposely skimming his fingers over my cheek. "I like who you are."

"You *are* a cheese-ball tonight."

"But I'm *your* cheese-ball, and that's what's really important here." He winks and leans over to kiss my cheek. I feel my face fill with warmth.

"I've missed you," I admit. It took me a long time to realize the constant ache in my chest was a Rush sized hole gaping in my heart.

He curls his fingers against my neck and gently pulls me forward until our foreheads touch. "I've missed you every hour, every minute, every fucking *second* since I stood in the pouring rain and confessed my sin to you. But I needed this and you needed it too. We needed to be stripped down to our rawest, barest, forms of ourselves in order to start clean. We had to accept our demons in order to move on. We could've never done that together." He swallows thickly. "In any universe, I'll always choose you and no matter what, I'll do what it takes to call you mine. This is what I—what *we*—had to do to have this chance here and now. It barely feels like any sort of sacrifice when I know we have forever. You might not be so sure yet," he adds when he sees the doubt on my face, "but I'll know for the both of us—and when we're old and gray, watching our grandchildren terrorize the cat, I'll be saying I told you so just like I did tonight. You'll tell me not to mock you and then together we'll remember this moment."

"We have a cat in the future?" I bust out laughing.

"Babe," he playfully pinches my side, "we have a cat *now*, and you bet your ass we'll have more. I've learned I'm quite the cat person."

Slowly, I ask, "We have a cat *now*? Where exactly is this cat?"

"Uncle Cannon is babysitting him this week," he explains. "His name is Patch. He's missing an eye and part of an ear, but he's fucking cute, I promise."

"You have a cat?" I'm stunned and can't wrap my head around this development.

"Yep," he nods, a smile spreading over his lips, "I have a cat."

"Wow," I suppress a laugh. "I wasn't expecting that. I can't believe the hotel is letting you have a cat."

He winces. "The hotel doesn't know, so *shush*."

"My lips are sealed," I promise, miming zipping my lips and throwing away the key. "I won't tattle on you."

"That's my girl." He kisses me, and it's strange, but exhilarating how he freely touches me and how I let him. Even when we were only sleeping with each other I wouldn't let him touch me like this.

Now, he's mine and I'm his, and that fact doesn't scare me one bit.

They say people can't change, but we're proof those naysayers are wrong. Anyone can change if they want to and we wanted to. Not only did any chance of us being together depend on it, but so did our lives.

FIFTY-TWO

Rush

I lie in the bed of the second guestroom, feeling too cold, even though, if anything, it's too hot. I miss the feel of Kira against me, in my arms, and it physically hurts knowing she's only one room away. When we got back home, she asked me to share her bed but I stupidly turned her down—trying to be a gentleman and take things slow like I promised myself I'd do.

She looked as disappointed as I feel.

I doubt I'm going to get any sleep tonight, but I can't feel too bad about that fact knowing Kira and I are together now. Calling her my girlfriend feels weird, but I guess that's what she is. She feels like so much more than that. Girlfriend sounds so fleeting and insignificant, when she's permanent—tattooed on my heart the way my arms and chest are inked.

The door to my room eases open and I sit up.

"You're awake," she whispers, tiptoeing into the room.

"Couldn't sleep," I confess.

"Me either. My back hurts and ... well, I missed you." She looks unsure admitting it. I know it's hard for her to accept someone as an equal, her partner, since she's so used to taking care of herself, but I'm fucking honored she's trying.

"Get in." I flip the covers back and she climbs into the bed. "Let me rub your back."

"You don't have to," she says, lying on her side to face me.

"Roll over," I command.

She stares at me for three whole seconds before she rolls over.

I begin kneading her back and she lets out a moan. "That feels so good. You have no idea."

"If you're hurting, I want to make you feel better."

"Have you thought of a name yet?" she asks me.

I chuckle. "Stop fishing—I'm not giving you any sort of hint."

"You suck."

I can't see her, but I instinctively know her bottom lip is pouted.

Fuck, I want to roll her over and kiss her until we're both breathless and she's writhing beneath me, begging for more.

"It's a good name," I promise. "I think you'll like it."

"What about a middle name?"

I grimace even though she can't see. "A middle name? He doesn't need a fucking middle name. I don't have one."

"You don't have a middle name?" She blurts out. "Why?"

"My parents said I rushed into their lives unexpectedly and Rush was the only name I needed, anything else would've diminished the meaning and power of my first name and that's how I feel about the name I've picked."

"I still have veto power," she reminds me with a soft laugh.

I give her a small, playful pinch before I resume rubbing her back. "You won't be using it."

"That sure of your choice, Mr. Daniels?" she jokes.

"Fucking positive," I vow.

I've thought long and hard about this name. A kid's name is a huge deal as it is, but her entrusting me solely with the choice made it an even bigger fucking deal than normal. I wanted it to be a powerful name and a name that means something to the both of us. I think I've nailed it, but she's not going to know it until he comes screaming into the world—otherwise I know she'll overthink it, but in the moment, she'll get it and understand the perfection of it.

"Ugh, right there," she moans when I hit a sensitive spot. I press my thumb a little harder into her back, rubbing in circles.

I lean over, chuckling under my breath in her ear. "You sound like you do when my cock is inside you."

"You're the one who dropped me off at my room like a gentleman," she reminds me.

"I'm an idiot."

"Yes, you are." I can feel her smile.

I press a kiss to her shoulder. "I love you."

She lifts her head slightly so she can see me. Even in the dark room the warmth of her brown eyes hits me. She's a different woman from the one I first met. That version of her was closed off with a tangible coldness emanating from her body. Now, she's softer, even her features are less pinched, and she looks happy—not pissed at the world.

She curls an arm around, touching her fingers to my stubbled chin. "I love you, too. It's weird to say, but it's true. I've never been in love before and I thought it would feel different."

"Like what?" I find myself desperate to know.

"Trapped. Confined. Imprisoned. It's the complete opposite of that. With you I feel freer than I ever felt on my own."

I kiss the side of her forehead and with a gentle nudge command her to roll back over, so I can continue rubbing her back.

"Does it feel any better?" I ask her.

"Loads," she breathes in relief, "don't stop. This is the best my back has felt in weeks."

I scoot close to her, spooning my body around her. This is the most intimate I've ever been with a woman and our clothes aren't even off. In high school, I had a few girlfriends, but our hookups basically consisted of us in the backseat of my car. After my parents died I went the route of meaningless one-night stands. I've never laid with any woman like this—no expectations, only the comforting feel of our bodies twined together and knowing we have all the time in the world. I'm still desperate for her, don't get me wrong, but there's something remarkably special about feeling content.

For the first time in years, I don't feel the need to run away. To be in constant motion. I'm happy to simply exist.

Kira's breaths even out and I raise up, peeking over her shoulder and smile when I see she's dozed off to sleep. I keep rubbing her back for a few more minutes before I too drift away.

Packing away years and years' worth of shit—trying to decide what to keep, donate, and trash—is a fucking exhausting process. Not only is it tedious, but it's emotionally difficult.

The first thing Kira and I did after having breakfast was go around with different colored tape and mark every piece of furniture in a color corresponding to what needs to be done with it. Once that was finished, it was time for lunch.

Now, we're getting into the nitty-gritty shit—going through

drawers and having to look at each individual item or pieces of paper contained inside.

It makes me want to pull my hair out from sheer boredom, but it's also emotionally taxing. This is my mom and dad's stuff. It's their life, their house, their possessions and it's being reduced to nothing.

"Are you sure you want to sell the house?" Kira asks me, rifling through a stack of documents. "It's your childhood home."

"I'm sure. It's the people that make a place home, not the structure—and with my mom and dad gone ... it's just a place now."

She nods, but she still looks unsure. *I'm* sure of my decision, and I know she'll respect it. I'll keep some things from here, some of their favorite items, but beyond that ... I'm okay. I used to think I'd never reach the point of being okay, but here I am.

Kira and I spend the rest of the day clearing things out. By the end, there are nearly ten bags full of trash and a shit ton of boxes to donate.

After dinner we're both so tired we climb into bed together, where I rub her back again, and we both fall soundly asleep.

The next several days repeat in the same pattern—except I start driving boxes to the local thrift stores and charities, as well as disposing of the trash.

It's the fifth day we've been here when we reach my parents' room. We cleaned my room out yesterday, and other than some naughty magazines and a couple of old condom wrappers, there thankfully wasn't too much for me to be embarrassed by. I kept a few of my trophies, but it was mostly the photos I wanted. Basically, photos are all I've pulled to keep thus far, except for a blanket that was my mom's favorite she always said my grandma had knit for her. I never met any of my grandparents, even though I wish I had. My parents were older when they had me and both sets had already passed away.

"Are you ready?" Kira asks me. Her voice is hesitant, and I know she won't push me to do this if I'm not ready. "We can do this another day. We're here two more days."

"No." I shake my head adamantly. "I have to do this."

The facts is, whether I do it now or two days from now, I'll have to do it.

Why put off the inevitable? It's not like I'm saving myself any pain—if anything, by delaying it I could make it worse.

As a family it's not like we spent much time in their bedroom, but it's the fact that this was *their* place. Their private space away from everything. I feel like it holds secrets and I'm not sure I'm ready to unearth them.

Kira reaches out and grips the knob in her hand, twisting it. The door opens with a grating creek and the darkened bedroom comes into view.

I reach instinctively for the switch on the wall and the light attached to the ceiling fan floods the room with a harsh yellow hue.

The walls are the same muted purple I remember. The bedding is the same too, gray *gingham* my mom kept correcting me on when I insisted it was plaid. The landscape painted canvases hanging on the walls are all the same. The trunk at the end of the bed is the same.

It's all the same, like every other room in the house. Untouched. A relic from a time long since passed.

Kira's hand slides into mine and our fingers clasp each other automatically. I'm holding onto her for dear life, like she's a buoy and I'm adrift at sea.

I take a step into the room and the plush carpet molds to my feet. I remember when they splurged and bought this obnoxiously fluffy beige colored carpet. My mom was ridiculously excited over it and my dad ... well, he was fucking happy because she was.

We haven't marked the furniture in this room yet, not like we did with everything else in the house on that first day. I had to keep this room closed up, sheltered away, until this moment. Until I was ready.

The absence of life hits me as powerfully here as it did when I first stepped into the house.

When a house has sat empty for a long time you can feel it. It's as if the walls breathe and speak to you, telling you how lonely they are without a family to reside inside. This home is begging to have life breathed into it.

My life is elsewhere now, and this place deserves to be a home again, to have joy and laughter echo between the walls.

"You're awfully quiet," Kira remarks, squeezing my hand.

"That tends to happen when one thinks about something," I joke.

She rolls her eyes at me and I'm tempted to spank her for it. "Stop sounding all formal. It's weird."

"I can't help it," I admit with a sheepish shrug. "It helps me cope."

She looks up at me with those big brown eyes of hers and quirks her head. "Like if you view the world through another lens it might not hurt you?" Her question is soft, but her tone says so much—that she's been in this same place and knows how it feels.

"Exactly," I whisper, releasing her hand.

I explore the room while she parks her pert ass on the trunk.

The room is spotlessly clean, but it's not like I banned the cleaners from this room, only myself, until now.

Kira sits quietly, watching my movements and not saying a word. Having her here brings me comfort, but I'm eternally thankful she doesn't try to press me to talk. If this situation were reversed, like me, she would need the quiet.

Placing my hands on my hips after ten minutes of inspecting, I announce, "It's time to get to work."

I grab boxes, tape, and markers from the hall. We divide the room between us and begin clearing out drawers. At this point Kira knows the types of things I want to keep for myself, what's trash, and what can be donated, so we work in silence. Occasionally she hums a little bit. I don't think she even realizes she's doing it, but it makes me smile. I love seeing her exist naturally and I don't think I'll ever get tired of it.

I clear out the closet, adding any decent clothes and shoes to the donate box, and stuffing anything that's ratty or falling apart into a trash bag. After about two hours the room begins to look empty. Even the bedding set is gone, taking up an entire box to itself.

I start on the dresser, while Kira sits down to go through the trunk.

After a few minutes she cries out, "Oh my God, look at you."

I turn and she holds up a picture gleefully and I wince. It's a picture of me as a baby completely naked in the bathtub. Apparently, it's a requirement in order to be a parent to have at least one naked baby picture hidden away somewhere.

Kira flips through the stack of photos she holds. "Aw, you look like a little cherub."

She pinches a picture between two fingers and flips it around for me to see. I sit on my mom's lap, a toddler of no more than two I'd say, with blond curls, big blue eyes and rosy cheeks.

"I look like a fat monster," I respond dryly.

"No, you don't," she scolds, sounding truly offended. "We should make a photo album out of all these."

"You'll probably run into some in there," I tell her, turning back to the dresser and tossing a pair of grass stained shorts my dad wore for mowing the lawn into the trash bag. "That's where my mom kept those. She called it her important-shit-catch-all-trunk.

She laughs at that. "Your mom sounds great."

I sigh, thinking of how things could've been.

But I have to stop myself, because if they would've lived chances are my life would look nothing like this. I would've never set out with the guys to make a go of our band. I would've never met Kira and ... and our baby wouldn't exist.

I'm not saying I'm glad my parents are gone, because otherwise I wouldn't have met Kira or be going places with the band, but it's interesting to think about how vastly different things would be.

I can hear Kira rifling through things behind me. She's having way too much fun looking at pictures and mementos from my childhood, while I'm over here actually trying to get rid of shit.

"Aw, look at this."

With a sigh I turn to look and she holds up a drawing. There are three stick figures labeled Mom, Dad, Me, written in my terrible elementary school handwriting—not that it's much better now—and if it weren't for the labels there would be no way to tell who is who. I've been lucky to be talented at several things—drawing is not one of them.

"Trash that," I tell her.

She gasps and clutches the yellowed piece of paper to her chest. "Never."

I exhale a small chuckle. "At least if our son sucks at drawing, I can pull that out and tell him he's not alone."

"I think it's adorable," she defends passionately, as if it's her own masterpiece. I won't be surprised if she doesn't try to put it on her refrigerator when we get back to her place.

She sets it aside and starts shuffling through more things.

She pulls out a large photo album overstuffed with pages with random pieces of scraps sticking out of the pages.

A piece of thick stock paper comes fluttering out of the album as she lowers it to her lap and drifts to the floor a few feet from her.

"Oh," she says, stretching to reach for it. Her fingertips brush it and she picks it up, flipping it over to view the front. Her face pales and her pink lips part. "Oh," she repeats in a different, more tragic tone.

"What is it?" I ask as her eyes scan the document.

Her eyes flick up at me, meeting mine over the top.

"Nothing," she says, but there's doubt in her tone.

I get up from my crouched position and cross the few feet to sit down beside her, stretching my legs out.

"Let me see." I hold out my hand and she places the paper in my open palm like she's offering me a loaded gun.

My eyes fall to the paper and the words at the top flash at me like the flickering lights on a Ferris wheel.

Adoption.

The word sticks out, it's all I can see for a moment until my eyes start hungrily reading the rest of the document. I devour it and read it again, not believing my eyes.

"Rush," Kira says softly, her fingers curl around my shoulder and she leans into me. I feel her breasts brush against me, but for once my body doesn't respond.

I feel like I'm frozen and on fire, all at the same time.

Six months ago, if someone had handed me this document I would've torn it up in anger, found the nearest bar, gotten shit-faced, and then done something reckless and stupid.

Now ... I take several deep breaths, trying to ease the pain seizing my body. Surprisingly I'm not angry like I would've been before. This piece of paper doesn't change a thing. My parents were and will always be my parents. This in no way erases their significance. They raised me, cared for me, loved me—that's the definition of a parent, not blood.

"Are you okay?" Kira hesitates softly behind me.

"I'm ... surprised," I reply honestly. "But I feel okay. This changes nothing," I voice my thoughts aloud. "They're my parents. That's all that matters."

She brushes her fingers through my hair and down my cheek to my jaw. "It's okay to be mad or hurt. Don't hold it inside."

"I'm not," I promise, and it's not a lie. I brush a tear away. "Things make more sense now," I admit on a shaky exhale. "I never really looked like them, but I always figured I looked like some other relative I'd never met. Never once did it cross my mind I was adopted, not even when my mom told me I was conceived in her heart. I just thought it was her hippy talk." My lips tip up into a crooked smile and Kira cracks one in return. "Don't feel sorry for me," I beg her. "I won the lottery with my parents. They chose me and ... we were a family."

I press my forehead to hers, cupping her jaw. She tugs her plump bottom lip between her lip. "And now we are." She places her hand on my chest and I feel the warmth of her hand seep through the cotton and burn my skin. "We chose each other too."

"We did," I agree, and place my other hand on her stomach. "And we made him with the best and most beautiful parts of ourselves before we even knew they existed."

A tear leaks out of her eye and I brush it away with my thumb.

"We're going to be okay," I vow. "One way or the other, everything always works out. Maybe not in the way you expect, but it does."

She sits back and I release her as she wipes away more tears on the back of her hands.

"I've been so hung up on my parents, wondering why they couldn't love their own flesh and blood, but this … the way your parents loved you. Blood means nothing. It's the choice to love, it's opening your heart up and giving it freely—that's true love. My heart is yours Rush Daniels, I'm trusting you not to break it."

She places her hand in mine.

We've held hands plenty of times, especially since the night in the back of my truck this week, but I understand what she's telling me without words.

Her fear is gone and she's mine completely. There are no barriers, no prisons of our own making.

This is us—Rush and Kira, a flame burning brightly and nothing, not our pain, not our sins, not even time can separate us. Some things are meant to be, they go together without an explanation, that's us. We're a truth that can't be denied.

Closing the distance between us I seal my lips over hers. I kiss her gently, savoring the taste of her.

The official adoption certificate flutters to the ground somewhere.

Inconsequential.

Unimportant.

All that paper tells me is my parents *chose* me.

Chose to love me.

Chose to cherish me.

Chose to give me the best fucking life they could—it's about time I started living it like I should, and that starts here and now with the woman I love.

"Rush," she breathes my name like a prayer, pressing her fingers under my shirt and against my heated skin. "I need you," she begs. The ache in her voice sends a shiver down my spine. All I want is to worship her, to show her how much I love her.

I kiss my way down the column of her throat and she arches her neck, pushing her breasts into my chest.

"More." Her fingers tug on the back of my head.

I force her dress down and tug at her bra, freeing her breast from one of the cups. I do the same with the other, weighing them in the palms of my hands. They're bigger, fuller, and more sensitive from the way she moans.

I lower my mouth, capturing one pert pink nipple in my mouth.

She lets out a gasp, her back arching.

My erection strains against my jeans, but I ignore it for the moment. I want to reacquaint myself with her body. It feels like it's been years since I've fucked her, not months.

But I know deep down what we're about to do isn't fucking.

I'm about to make love to the woman of my dreams, my future, the mother of my child.

My *everything*.

She's something I never knew to hope for, my savior.

She might not realize it, but she saved me.

I remove her dress and she writhes against me, rubbing her center against my jean-clad leg. She's aching and desperate, but I can't rush this. I won't. I've waited too long to have her like this.

With no rules, no lies, no sins.

Just us.

We're Rush and Kira, a phenomenon that doesn't make sense, but exists nonetheless.

I explore her body like I've never seen it before.

Every curve, every freckle, is something I want to memorize.

When I finally sink inside her I know one sound truth.

She's the destination I've been driving toward for nine years and I'm finally home.

FIFTY-THREE

Kira

Lying with my head on Rush's chest, our fingers intertwined, and our legs tangled, I'm absolutely positive I've never been happier or more at peace than I am in this moment.

What just happened between us on the floor ... it was nothing I've ever experienced before. It was eye-opening, inspiring, the things epic love songs are written about.

Rush nuzzles his face against my neck and his stubble scratches my neck.

"I love you," I murmur, pressing as much of myself as I can into him.

Now that I've admitted my feelings, I can't stop telling him I love him. I've always avoided this kind of connection, the thought of willingly handing my heart to someone was too scary, but now I see how powerful it can be to trust someone so completely.

"Love you, too." He brushes his lips against the top of my head.

"Are you sure you're okay?" I hesitate to ask.

Finding the official adoption document was a shock to me and I can't imagine how he feels.

He gives a soft laugh. "I'm okay, I promise. I know I've used sex in the past to cope, but this wasn't that," he promises, making slow circles with his thumb against my hand he holds. "They loved me," he adds softly, "that's all that matters to me. Do I wish they would've told me? Yes, but it doesn't change anything. I'm still their son, and I'm beginning to understand people have their reasons for everything."

"I'm proud of you," I whisper, drawing random designs on his chest with the index finger of my free hand.

He tips my chin up with a gentle nudge of his fingers. "Be proud of yourself."

Snuggling closer to him, I confess, "I never want to move."

His body shakes with laughter. "You won't be saying that when you get hungry."

I smack him lightly. "Stop teasing me. I'm growing your child."

"True, true," he acquiesces, kissing the top of my head. He lays his palm against my stomach, his large fingers splayed out. "I can't wait to see him."

"Me either," I admit. "I want to know what he looks like and hold him. I feel him all the time, but I want him in my arms."

"Not much longer," he sighs, twisting his fingers through my hair.

"I'm excited, but so, *so* scared," I confess on a breath. "There are so many things that can go wrong."

"And there are so many others that can go right," he reasons. "I'll be with you every step of the way. No matter what happens."

"Will you let me scream as loud as I need to?"

"I'll scream with you."

"Will you let me squeeze your hand as hard as I need to?"

"I'll squeeze back, so you know I'm with you and you're not doing it alone."

"Will you love me no matter what I say in the moment?"

He gives a small laugh. "I'll love you always, no matter what. It's an easy promise to make." He untangles his fingers from mine and sits up. "Get dressed, I want to show you something."

"If you want to show me your cock we don't have to get dressed for that," I joke, giving him a coy smile.

He gives my ass a light smack. "I see what you're trying to do and it won't work. This is important." His blue eyes sparkle with humor despite his words.

"Fine," I grumble good-naturedly, because from his tone I can tell whatever he wants to show me *is* important.

I dress as quickly as I can in my nearly nine-months pregnant state—which is to say I dress at the rate of a turtle, and Rush gets so impatient after tugging on his own clothes he helps me snap my bra into place and pulls my jersey dress over my head and down my body. At least I put my own underwear on, that's a win, right?

Rush leads me downstairs and swipes his keys from the kitchen counter.

I decide not to bother asking him where we're going. He's not going to tell me, so why waste my breath on it.

He opens the passenger side and helps me in. I give him a grateful smile. As time ticks away and I near the end of my pregnancy my entire body aches and I'm tired for no reason, but can't sleep. I know it's my body's way of preparing me for a screaming newborn, but it doesn't mean I have to like it. Come on, Mother Nature—let me have a few more weeks of decent sleep and rest?

The wind lifts the leaves of the nearby trees and I swear it's Mother Nature mocking me with a laugh.

Rush hops in and backs out of the driveway quickly.

Barely three minutes pass until he turns into a lot.

Squinting I spy...

"A basketball court," I breathe.

"A basketball court," he echoes with a reminiscent sigh. "*The* basketball court to be exact."

He hops out of the truck and grabs something from the back before helping me out. He keeps whatever he brought hidden behind his back, but I think it's pretty obvious what it is.

Sure enough, with a grin he shows me the ancient basketball. Seriously, the thing looks like it's falling apart.

"Can you shoot, Marsh?"

I roll my eyes. "I can hit you in the head with it, does that count?"

"Ooh," he hisses. "Aggressive. Me likey." He waggles his eyebrows up and down. I struggle to suppress my laughter.

"Come on, wife."

"Wife?" I stop dead in my tracks.

He exhales a breath and stops too. "Calling you my girlfriend seems weird, you're more than that. Calling you the love of my life would get exhausting. Fiancée makes no sense since I haven't proposed—"

"And wife does?" I argue, fighting a smile.

"Well, yeah," he shrugs, looking unsure of himself, "right now you're the wife of my heart, and one day, when *you're* ready I'm going to get down on one knee and ask you to marry me. Then you'll be tied to me forever." He gives a playful wink as we step onto the court.

"You're getting cheesy in your old age." I swipe the basketball from him. "Slow, too, apparently."

"I'll be twenty-seven in a week and that's *not* old," he argues, chasing after me.

He grabs me around the waist and I giggle as he captures the ball easily from me.

I love this freeness, the lightness I feel with him. Everything is so easy. I don't feel the torment and questioning I did several months ago. I'm not afraid. I only want to live, and I know the best way for me to do that is with Rush by my side.

He's my partner in crime.

"I don't hear you opposing the idea, so I take this to mean you're open to the possibility?" He bounces the basketball in-between his legs, being a total show off.

"Maybe one day," I admit, with a soft exhale. I'm not opposed to the idea of marrying Rush, not anymore anyway. What does still scare me is the idea of such a commitment. But if there's anyone in the entire world I would willingly tie myself to, it's him.

He grins and tosses the ball into the net. It swoops in easily, the net swishing.

He jogs after the ball and walks back over to me bouncing it.

"This was my favorite spot growing up." He pauses, canting his head to the side and embracing the feel of the wind on his face. "My dad and I spent a lot of time here. At the time I didn't understand what those moments would mean to me. When someone's gone ... it's not the things they gave us that we remember, it's the memories we made together."

"You're going to be an amazing father," I tell him, and my heart pangs as I remember the hurtful words I slurred at him the night he showed up drunk at my place.

"Leave me alone. Let me raise our child on my own. Our son doesn't deserve to grow up with such a pathetic excuse for a father. I

hope you get better, I do, but I don't want anything to do with you. Come near me again and you'll regret it. Try to fight me for rights to our son and I promise you'll never see him."

I was hurt and I lashed out. He was hurt and made stupid choices.

Through it all, it's led us here to this moment.

"You think so?" he asks, shielding his eyes with his hand so he doesn't have to squint from the sun.

"Yeah."

His smile is infectious. "You'll be a fucking amazing mom, Kira. We're going to raise our boy right." He holds out the basketball for me. "Take your shot, Kira."

I wrap my hands around the ball and step toward the basket. He stands behind me, hands on my hips. He ducks his head and rests his chin on my shoulder.

"Don't overthink it. Aim where your heart guides you and it'll go in every time."

I tilt my head, looking at him as best as I can.

"You," I whisper. "It guides me to you every time."

Without looking, I shoot the ball toward the hoop, but neither of us watches to see if it goes in.

It doesn't matter, because as he wraps me in his arms and steals my breath with a kiss, I know I've already scored the game winning point.

FIFTY-FOUR

Rush

I look around at the mostly empty house. Most of the furniture has been picked up by whoever bought it from Craigslist or is being donated. The pictures are gone from the walls, but the memories are forever.

"There's one stop I have to make before we start home," I tell Kira as she walks up beside me.

She leans against me and I instantly feel more at peace. She's like a balm, soothing my soul.

"Wherever you need to go."

We support each other and I didn't understand how valuable it is to have someone in your life who does that until now.

After one more moment to soak everything in we head out and I give her a boost into the truck. The back has three boxes of stuff I decided to keep and the rest is gone.

It's not easy giving it all up, a part of me would be content to hold on to it forever, but I know that's just fucking stupid. I have to let it go and move on. As long as the house sits here, full of their stuff, a piece of me will always be trapped.

I'm free now.

I start the truck and back out, driving away. I glance back in the rearview mirror, getting one last look at the house I called home practically my whole life.

It doesn't hurt as badly as I expected seeing it grow smaller and smaller behind us. I think it's because I know my future is planted firmly at my side, her fingers curled into mine.

It doesn't take long to get where I want to go and I park the truck against the curb.

"Do you want me to sit here?" Kira asks, eyeing the cemetery.

I shake my head. "Come with me. Please." I tack on the last word softly, a whispered plea to not have to face this alone.

She nods once and I hop out to give her a hand.

I've only been here once, on the day they were buried, but I still remember exactly where their graves are. I think I could find it with my eyes closed. It's one of those things you can't seem to forget, no matter how much you wish you could.

I stop in front of their headstones.

"It feels like I'm standing on them," I mutter to Kira.

She squeezes my hand. "You're not, but we can move."

"No." I shake my head. "This is fine." I work my mouth back and forth, trying not to fucking cry. I feel like I've cried more in the last few months than my entire life, but I guess that's what happens when you finally deal with shit. "I shouldn't have waited so long to come here." I don't know whether the whispered words are for my parents or Kira.

She squeezes my hand. "You're here now. That's all that matters."

I exhale the breath I was holding.

I've never noticed how eerily quiet a cemetery is—but it isn't like I've spent a lot of time in one.

I can hear every rustle of the leaves, chirping birds, a lawn mower a couple of streets over, and even dogs barking.

In the middle of chaos exists this place.

Swallowing past the lump, I say out loud, "I'm sorry. I'm sorry for abandoning everything you both instilled in me. I'm sorry for turning my back on you and everything. I'm sorry for not being the man I should've been. I'm sorry for letting my grief dictate everything in my life. I'm sorry for everything. Sorry seems hardly near good enough when you both are here, but even though you left me behind I'm glad you went together. I can't imagine one of you ever living without the other. Now that I'm experiencing the same kind of love, I can say I don't know how I would live without this girl." I tilt my head down to look at Kira. Her dark hair stirs against her shoulders from the breeze and her eyes are warm in the early morning sunlight. To her I say, "Thank you for giving me a reason to find my way back."

"You had a reason all along," she speaks softly. "It existed inside you, but you couldn't see it."

"Until you," I add, and she smiles.

God, I fucking love this woman. I never believed I'd feel anything this powerful in my entire life, but I do. I'm a lucky bastard. I don't deserve her, but I'm going to spend the rest of my days trying to prove I do.

Kira stands on her tiptoes and kisses me. Backing away she slips something in my hand.

"I found this in the trunk in the house, and I ... you should read it."

She takes more steps away and my brows furrow. "Where are you going?"

"I'll wait by the truck," is all she tells me.

I look down at the piece of paper folded into a tiny square in my hand. Looking over my shoulder and finding Kira to be a tiny speck in the distance I unfold the paper carefully.

I nearly choke on my own saliva when I see my mom's handwriting.

Bracing myself, I begin to read.

My dear, sweet, brilliant Rush,

It's your fifth birthday and I watched you blow out your candles on your dinosaur cake with a smile on your face. You ran around the yard laughing with your friends, having the time of your life. I've just tucked you into bed and you placed your tiny precious hand against my cheek and said, "I love you, Ma."

For years I believed I would never have a child. All I ever wanted from the time I was a little girl was to be a mom.

Years of infertility took a toll on our marriage and we'd given up hope when you came along.

You were unexpected, but our greatest dream realized.

All the years of hoping, praying, dreaming of a miracle were finally worth it.

We'd finally decided to adopt, and were lucky it didn't take us long to get you when we believed it would be years.

Your parents were young, teenagers, just kids themselves and they knew they couldn't raise a child. They selflessly gave you up and entrusted you to us.

It's been the greatest gift I've ever been given.

I love you so much. You're my little boy. Even if you didn't come from my womb, you came from my heart, and it's the same difference in my book.

It terrifies me to think about telling you you're adopted. I don't want you to look at us differently and I'm afraid it might crush me if you want to find your birth parents, even though I can understand.

I can't tell you enough how much I love you, how much we both love you. You complete our world.

You're a beautiful soul, my boy, and while you might be small, I know you're going to do amazing things. Your spirit is that of a fighter and I know you're going to take on the world and make it yours.

One day, I don't know when, we'll tell you the truth and I can only hope you'll understand. For now, I have to write my thoughts here and tuck them away, because for a little bit longer I want you to be completely ours.

I love you, Rush. With all my heart.

Always,

Mama

A tear falls onto the letter and I quickly blot it with my shirt, careful to let the liquid soak into the cotton and not smear the writing. I fold the letter up and tuck it into my jeans.

"I love you too, Ma. And you too, Pops."

My dad hated when I called him Pops, but I can't help doing it for old time's sake.

I don't know what might've happened if they'd told me when I was younger, but like now, I don't think it would've made any difference to me.

They raised me. *They* loved me. *They* tucked me into bed every night.

They were there every step of the way and the best fucking parents imaginable. I can only hope I can be half as good for my son, but I'll try my hardest to be the best possible.

Finding out they adopted me truly changes nothing for me. I have no desire to find my birth parents. They're less than strangers to me. I don't hate them for giving me up, I think it's damn admirable, but I don't feel like I'm missing a connection.

My parents showed me all the love in the world, and now I have my own family in my friends, in Kira, in our son.

Bending down, I kiss my fingers and touch them to each headstone.

"I'm sorry I'm not around much, but you guys are always with me. Always."

I touch those same fingers to my heart and stand up. Tilting my head toward the sun I inhale a breath and then take the first step into my future.

FIFTY-FIVE

Kira

"Wow, you weren't lying about the cat," I remark, entering Rush's hotel suite. As soon as he opens the main door a cat comes rushing from God knows where and meows at his feet, weaving between his legs.

"Patch, come on, I've got to close the door before someone sees you."

"I cannot believe you snuck a cat into a hotel." I shake my head, stifling laughter.

"The things we do for love." He presses a hand dramatically to his heart and sways. Setting his bag down he picks up the cat and scratches under his chin.

I wasn't ready for him to take me home, and I kind of wanted to see if he actually had a cat, so we ended up here. It's early afternoon since we spent last night in a hotel.

We shared a bed this time.

"Kira," Fox says in surprise, setting a magazine or something down on the coffee table.

I notice Cannon's sister draped in the chair by the couch, her dark hair piled in a messy bun, with a cup of coffee or possibly tea clasped in her hands. She's in her pajamas, clearly comfy and at home. I met her briefly at my baby shower and she seems nice and I was amused the entire time by how she pokes fun at all the guys.

Cannon comes from his room, I assume, and looks at Rush and me, a slow half-smile curving his lips. "'Bout time," he mutters, and his tattooed hands reach for the refrigerator door, pulling out a bottle of water.

Calista stands up and walks over. "Since these assholes are fucking rude, welcome home. Things went well I take it?"

Cannon closes the refrigerator door and crosses his arms over his chest. "Language, Callie."

"He thinks I'm twelve," she says to me with a conspiratorial wink. "I've seen a penis, you know," she hollers at Cannon, like he's not standing a few feet away.

He slaps his hands over his ears. "Shut up."

"Boys." She shrugs with a roll of her eyes. "So predictable."

Over her shoulder Fox is hiding his face behind a pillow and I'm not sure whether he's trying to hide his laughter or disappear.

Cannon lowers his hands. "Am I good now?"

"Cock, balls, penis, shaft—"

"Fuck, I'm leaving." Cannon hauls ass back to his room.

I bury my head against Rush's side, laughing.

"So, I'm glad to see Rush can say goodbye to his pining emo stage. You've forgiven him I assume, or you wouldn't be here?" she probes persistently.

I stifle a snort. "Um ... yeah, I have. I'm ... his ..." I look up at Rush and finish with, "person."

He rolls his eyes. "She's more than my person, she's my heart."

"Oh my God, I think that's the sweetest thing I've ever heard." She looks up at Rush with serious, but kind eyes. "I'm happy for you. You're like a brother, and you deserve this."

"Thank you," he says, and bends to kiss her cheek.

"Are you guys hanging out here for a while?" she asks, sashaying back to the chair and flopping into it. "We can put a movie on or something."

"I'd like that," I admit. Tilting my head back to fully see Rush I ask, "Do you think Mia and Hollis would come over?"

"I think they would."

In less than an hour Mia and Hollis arrive, bringing pizza, drinks, and cupcakes with them.

"This is not good for my ass," Calista says, picking up a slice of ooey-gooey pizza. "But I'm thoroughly going to enjoy eating it."

Fox clears his throat and his eyes shift to her every few seconds.

I give Rush a questioning look and he nods back in silent answer.

Those two have so boned and it's pretty obvious Cannon is oblivious.

Calista picked the movie and as *The Princess Diaries* starts the guys all groan, but I know they secretly don't care as much as they protest.

Looking around at my friends—*no,* my *family*—I don't think I've ever been happier.

I finally found my place in this world and as Rush wraps his arm around me, I know I'm not going anywhere. Acceptance and love ... it's a beautifully underrated thing.

FIFTY-SIX

Rush

"I have to get to the studio," I tell Kira, stuffing the last bite of toast in my mouth. "I'm going to be late."

I sit up and grab my wallet, depositing some bills on the table.

"Wait." She grabs my wrist to halt me from sliding out of the booth at our favorite breakfast spot. I never thought I'd be sitting here with her again, but I'm fucking glad for it. "It's your birthday, can't you be a few minutes late?" Her brown eyes are wide and begging. I'm a fucking sucker, because I give in.

"Fine," I agree. "We can grab coffee and then I'll head over."

She smiles widely. "Thank you."

She slides out from the booth and I do the same, placing a hand on the small of her back as I guide her outside. Griffin's is a short walk from the diner and we stand in the long line to order our coffee.

"I'm sorry I didn't get you anything for your birthday." She frowns, a wrinkle furrowing the skin between her eyes.

I smooth it out with my thumb. "You gave me *you*. That's all I need. Besides, it makes us even."

She twines our arms together and leans her head against me. I don't think she has any idea what her affection does for my heart. All those months she avoided willingly touching me, unless we were having sex, have all led to this—an openness between us.

I tilt my head down, kissing the top of her head as we move forward in line. Her hair smells like peaches, or something else equally as sweet. I think it's my new favorite scent, and I don't have a fucking care to give if that makes me sound like a pussy.

It's our turn to order and Kira gets some kind of caffeine-free iced coffee. I get an iced coffee too, but one with lots of flavoring.

When we head out with our coffees clasped in our hands she laughs and points to my drink. "I still can't get over your girly drinks."

I roll my eyes. "It tastes fucking better this way. Why am I going to drink black coffee just to seem more manly? That's the stupidest shit I've ever heard of."

She gives a small laugh, wrapping her lips around her straw. I stifle a groan, because I woke up in her bed this morning to those same lips wrapped around my cock.

"Are you headed to work?" I ask her. "Or back home?"

Her job's not far from here, since I'm already late I could walk her there before heading to the studio.

She shakes her head. "Not until later. I'll go with you to the studio. I need to pick up something from Mia."

I raise a brow as we pause, waiting to cross the street. "What could that be?"

She slaps my arm lightly—the sting of a mosquito. "Get your head out of the gutter."

I laugh as we cross the street and head to our right in the direction of the studio.

I don't know what I'm going to do heading back to L.A. in a matter of weeks. All I know is I want Kira to come with me. I can't imagine being parted from her or the baby. She can transfer and go to school there if she wants or—

"What are you thinking about?" she asks, interrupting my thoughts.

"You," I admit. "The future."

"What about it?" The straw of her coffee rests against her lips as she waits for my reply.

"We have a lot to talk about," I reply with a shrug.

"Yeah, we do—but it's your birthday. You're twenty-seven today. Let's celebrate and save the serious stuff for another day."

"As long as we *will* talk about it." I narrow my gaze on her as we stop in front of the studio.

"Of course," she scoffs.

I open the door to the studio, and before I say *what the fuck* because it's dark as hell inside, the lights shoot on in a blinding manner and my friends, Hayes, his wife Arden, Mia, and the other members of Willow Creek and their wives jump up yelling, "Surprise!"

"Surprise." Kira stands on her tiptoes, kissing my cheek and clasping our hands together.

She drags me into the studio, the door closing behind us, and I stare around in shock at everyone gathered. It's unexpected and I stupidly find my throat closing up.

There's a cake on a table in the corner, a couple of presents too, but I don't care about those things.

It's these people here in front of me that I find to be the greatest gift of all. I feel my once empty heart, that's recently begun beating again for Kira, swell with happiness and love.

I'm not alone in this world. I have these people. This family

I've made for myself—even if Mathias Wade sulks in the corner looking like he'd rather be anywhere else, everyone knows he's a secret softy or else he wouldn't be here.

I swallow past the lump in my throat as I think about all the bad shit I've done, but how far I've come.

Anyone deserves redemption if they choose to walk the path back into the light.

My path brought me here, back to my friends, to Hayes and his band mates, but most importantly back to my girl.

"Happy birthday, man." Hollis claps me on the shoulder and pulls me into a hug.

Cannon grabs me next and says in a whisper, "I'm so fucking proud of you."

His words make my chest expand. They mean more than he knows. Cannon has always been there for me, and he's also been the only one to tell me like it is, even when I didn't want to hear it.

I move from person to person before finally Hayes pulls me into a corner.

"I just wanted to say you've come a long way since you guys came here. You're a whole different person and I can see in your eyes you're happier. I know things haven't been easy for you, and there are bound to be details I don't know, but I want you to hear it from me that I'm here for you. I know I'm not your father, and you don't need a replacement, but if you ever need someone like that to talk to ... you have me."

Fuck, these people are trying to turn me into wreck. Maybe it's all the time without alcohol, or maybe it's embracing things, but I've never been more in touch with my emotions than I am now. Feeling this strongly makes things both easier and more difficult.

After my talk with Hayes I end up back with Kira, wrapping my arms around her and letting my fingers graze her belly.

"Are you surprised?" she asks, tilting her head back to look up at me.

"Fucking astonished," I reply. I lower my head and kiss the side of hers.

Soon they're singing happy birthday to me, and Emma—Maddox's wife—begins cutting the cake after I blow out all twenty-seven candles.

Sitting by Kira on one of the couches, her feet in my lap, with a forkful of cake halfway to her mouth, I say, "This is one of the best birthdays I've ever had."

Her brown eyes sparkle with happiness. "Good—and we have the rest of our lives to top it."

FIFTY-SEVEN

Kira

"Are you staying here for senior year?" Mia asks me, sipping her iced latte in the busy Starbucks a few blocks from campus where classes are starting in two weeks.

"I mean ... I'm signed up," I hedge nervously. "Aren't you?"

She shrugs, exhaling a sigh. "I told Hollis from the beginning school was important to me and I wanted to finish, so yeah, I'll be here when they go back to L.A. Long distance is going to suck, but we'll make it work."

I stifle a laugh, because once upon a time Mia believed long distance *never* worked. When you find the love of your life, though, all kinds of opinions change.

She sets her plastic cup down and wraps her hands around it absorbing some of the condensation in the process. "I thought you might be heading back to L.A. with Rush and were too scared to tell me."

I shake my head. "No ... well, I don't know exactly. We're figuring it out."

The last week Rush and I have had numerous conversations about life in L.A. versus here. My life has always been here, but his future is in L.A. I hate these kinds of serious talks and how they disrupt the recent bliss we've had, but I know it's not something that can be avoided.

"You guys are having a baby together," she reasons. "It's only natural you'd live together."

"He wants me to come with him," I admit. "But I'm scared."

Admitting it out loud feels like a weakness. I've always plowed through life like obstacles didn't matter. I didn't allow fear to be a part of my vocabulary, but here we are.

"You could go to school there." She dances her fingers through the air like it's oh so easy. "Finish your degree. You wouldn't be missing out on anything. You might even be able to finish online, and then you could stay home with the baby."

"You sound like you want me to go." I raise the cup of purple colored lemonade to my lips.

"I don't *want* you to go, but I'm being practical here, Kira. You guys love each other, right? You're having a baby—naturally you should try to be together."

I worry my bottom lip between my teeth. I know she's right, it's the same conclusion I came to early on, but it doesn't mean I'm ready to accept it.

The idea of living in L.A. is daunting. I've never been, but I can't imagine it being my kind of scene and more than anything I worry about Rush being thrust back into that kind of lifestyle and environment so soon after getting sober. What if it ruins us?

"I need more time to think about it," I tell her. "He's not leaving until September."

"Does it really make sense for you to start classes?"

I don't reply because we both know the answer.

She sits back in her chair with a little smirk that tells me she knows she's right.

"Maybe I won't go back," I hedge. "I could take a semester off to be with the baby."

"That would probably be smart," she agrees. "He shouldn't be separated from his mom so young."

"You make us sound like wild animals."

"Humans *are* wild animals. We're barely civilized. Don't you watch the news? People hate people for the most ridiculous things these days. It's nuts."

"But I'll be alone if I go to L.A."

She shakes her head. "No, you'll have Rush. Hollis, Cannon, and Fox will be there too—and Calista I assume. She's pretty cool and I'm sure she'd love to help with the baby."

I shift uncomfortably in the chair. My back has been hurting more than usual for the last two days.

"The baby's not even here yet," I evade, this whole line of conversation making me entirely uncomfortable.

She sighs exasperatedly. "You're going to pop any time."

"He's not due until the end of the month. He could come later," I reason.

She narrows her eyes. "Whatever you say."

I take another sip of my drink, wincing at a piercing pain in my back.

"See!" She yells at me, pointing an accusing finger. "You're having a contraction."

"No, I'm not," I defend, breathing deeply to ease the pain radiating in my lower back. "I'm practically nine months pregnant, I can't sleep, every surface hurts my back, and my body has had it. *That's* what's wrong."

Not to mention my aching and heavy breasts, swollen ankles, and the fact I spend the majority of my time urinating.

And they call pregnancy beautiful.

At the thought of pee suddenly my bladder reminds me it's time to go.

"I have to use the bathroom," I tell her, standing up suddenly.

I feel wetness between my legs, but that's unfortunately normal. I've peed myself several times—okay, more than several times—since getting pregnant. But that's what happens when a giant baby tries to use your bladder as a trampoline.

I waddle to the back of the shop and lock the bathroom door behind me and yank my panties down hurriedly before holding up my dress as I sit down.

As I start to pee I look down, noticing redness on my thighs. It's not much, but it's definitely blood. I lean over, peeking into the lining of my underwear and find more blood there.

"Oh my God," I blurt, quickly grabbing a wad of toilet paper to wipe myself clean.

There's not much blood on the paper, which I take it to be a good sign, but the fact that there's any blood at all means I need to get to the hospital as soon as possible.

I wash my hands and rush out to Mia. "We have to go to the hospital."

"What?" Her eyes widen in surprise and I know I've completely caught her off guard even though she was the one only moments ago arguing she thought I was having contractions.

"Hospital. Now." I bite out the words. "I'm bleeding," I add, the fear leaking into my voice.

"Oh my God." She hops up, grabbing her drink, bag, and digging for her keys all in the span of a few seconds.

I grab my purse and follow her to her car. By the time I'm inside and buckled I have my phone in my hand and I'm dialing Rush.

He doesn't answer and I curse. He might be in the booth recording something.

I call Hayes instead and he answers immediately.

"Kira?" he asks in his worried dad voice. "Is everything okay?"

Sure enough, in the background I can hear drums.

"I need to talk to Rush. It's an emergency."

Barely thirty seconds pass until Rush is on the phone. "Kira, what is it? Are you okay?" His voice is even more concerned than Hayes's.

"It's the baby," I say breathless. "I went to the bathroom and there was some blood—not a lot, but enough. Mia is taking me to the hospital." Another pain pierces through my back and I wince.

"Maybe it's your bloody show," he responds, and I can hear shuffling in the background. "If it is ... fuck, he's coming. Oh, fuck. Jesus Christ. It's happening. It's happening, people! The baby is coming!"

"Bloody show?" I repeat. "How do you even know about that?" The fact Rush knows it means a sign of labor does something to my heart.

He stops freaking out long enough to respond, "I read the baby books. Guys, I've got to go," he says to them. "Where the fuck are my keys?"

Hearing him freak out would be amusing any other time. "Just get to the hospital," I beg, my bottom lip starting to wobble with the threat of tears. *"I need you."* The three words leave my throat in a broken plea.

"Fuck, Kira. I'll be there as soon as I can."

"We're all coming." I hear Hayes say in the background.

"I love you, Kira," Rush says, still sounding half out of his mind.

"I love you, too." I hang up the phone and lean back in the seat. We're not too far from the hospital, thank God.

"Do you think your back pain is contractions?" she asks me, her eyes darting to my side as she white knuckles the steering wheel.

"Fuck if I know," I blurt. "It's not like I've done this before. I don't even have my bag, it's at my apartment." I curse under my breath. "This isn't how this was supposed to happen."

"Calm down," she says as soothingly as she can. "Once Rush is with you, I can go get it."

I know the bag should be the least of my worries, and honestly it is, but in this kind of moment it's a nice distraction to think about something so miniscule and not nearly as life changing as the prospect of having a baby.

Mia parks in front of the main entrance to the hospital, urging me to stay in the car.

Naturally, I don't listen.

I waddle inside with her and she grabs a wheel chair, commanding me to sit down. She speaks with the people at information who call upstairs for a nurse to come get me.

"I'm going to park the car and I'll be right up," Mia promises. Grasping my hand she says, "I love you, you're like a sister to me, and I know you're absolutely going to kick ass at this."

I send her a grateful smile before she runs outside to her idling car. She didn't even take the keys out of the ignition. Honestly, in the few minutes we've been here it's a miracle someone hasn't driven off with it.

I'm freaked out by this entire situation and everything I've ever learned about childbirth seems to have decided to flee my mind. I guess nothing can ever truly prepare you for being the patient.

Mia's only been gone three minutes, five tops, when a nurse steps off the elevator. She smiles kindly at me.

"Hi, I'm Amelia. I'm going to take you up to the maternity ward to get checked out. How far apart are your contractions?"

"I'm not sure," I admit, feeling like an idiot for not timing whatever it is I'm feeling. "I'm feeling pain in my back, but I'm not sure if it's contractions. I went to the bathroom and there was blood, so that's why I'm here."

She nods her head in understanding and wheels me to the elevators.

We reach the maternity floor and she takes me into a room. "Can you get into a gown on your own?" she questions.

"I'll be fine," I promise.

"Once you're changed, we'll check everything out and see what's going on. Who's your doctor?"

I tell her and she leaves the room, closing the door with a soft click behind her.

With shaky hands I change into the atrocious gown. Nerves are getting to me, because if the baby is coming today that's *huge*, but if something's wrong ... it terrifies me.

I've gotten myself settled on the bed when the nurse reenters with Mia.

"She says she's with you," the nurse, Amelia, says.

"She is."

Mia sits down on the plastic looking couch by the window. Rush should be here any minute. The studio isn't as far as the Starbucks we were at.

Sure enough, I hear a commotion outside the room and seconds later a frazzled looking Rush bursts into the room. His blond hair is spiked in every direction from repeated tugging of his fingers and his blue eyes are frantic.

"Kira," he breathes my name like a prayer and rushes to my side.

"I take it this is the daddy-to-be?" Amelia asks with a slightly amused smile.

"He is. Where are the other guys?" I voice my question to Rush.

"Waiting room," he replies.

"I'll let them know what's going on once we have answers," Mia says from her corner.

"Thank you." Rush sends her a grateful smile. "Thank you for getting her here."

"She's my best friend. There's nothing to thank."

What feels like an hour later, I'm hooked up to monitors and my lady bits have been thoroughly checked out.

"You're definitely in labor," Amelia announces. "You're already four centimeters dilated. Looks like you guys are having a baby today."

Rush grasps my hand and leans his body over the bed into me. "We're having a baby."

Me, being my sarcastic self, retorts with, "I kind of knew that already."

He chuckles as Amelia heads for the door. "I'll call your doctor," she announces. "Let her know how things are going."

Once she's gone Mia stands. "I'll let the others know the baby is actually coming."

"Mia," I voice her name and she hesitates halfway across the room. "Thank you." So much is laced into those two small words. "Please, come back. I want you here with me—if you're okay with it."

"I'll be back," she vows before slipping from the room.

When it's only the two of us, Rush presses his forehead to mine. "You're going to kick ass at this, Kira. I love you so fucking much."

I tilt my head up and press my lips eagerly to his. Grasping his hand I say, "*We've* got this. We're a team. In this together."

"Till the end."

"Till the end," I echo.

FIFTY-EIGHT

Rush

Watching Kira power through contractions gives me a new and deeper respect for women. They're powerful creatures who can do far more than men ever could.

Her contractions start coming more forcefully, lasting longer, and I can see her wearing out as the hours pass.

Her brow dampens with sweat, her dark hair slicked back.

"It hurts," she whimpers to me, squeezing my hand as another contraction hits.

"Should I tell the nurse you're ready for an epidural," Mia asks, at her other side.

"Yes," Kira cries, her nose scrunching from pain. "Please."

Mia lets go of her hand and dashes out of the room to retrieve a nurse.

When Mia returns she tells us the nurse is putting in the order.

Kira whimpers in pain, her lips quaking. I've never felt so fucking helpless in my entire life. I wish more than anything I could take away her pain. I would do it in a heartbeat.

Finally the man comes to give her the epidural and I sit holding her hands as she leans forward.

"I'm scared," she whispers to me, squeezing my hands.

"Look at me," I command.

Her eyes raise a small amount to peer into mine.

"You're strong, and fucking resilient, you've got this."

"I've got this," she echoes, letting out a breath as the needle goes into her spine. Once she settles against the pillows she gives my hand a light squeeze. "I don't know what I'd do without you."

I know the words are a huge admission from her. Bigger, perhaps, than *I love you*, because she's admitting she's come to depend on me.

Sitting down in a chair beside her bed, never dropping her hand, I admit with a laugh, "Even though the baby books said this could take hours, even days, I still thought it would be really quick for some reason."

She lets out a snort. "If only."

"Feeling better?" Kenzie, the nurse on call for the night hours, asks popping in and rubbing disinfectant onto her hands.

"Much," Kira admits with a small smile.

She checks Kira out and then leaves like she's done thus far.

Waiting, that's all we're doing now. Waiting for our son to decide to join us in the world. The sun begins to set outside the window, bathing the sky in vibrant oranges and deep purples.

"Are you okay here with Mia for a few minutes? I want to talk to the guys."

"Yeah. I'll be fine."

On the opposite side of the bed Mia smiles. "I'll take care of her, I promise."

Exhaling a breath, I stand up and head for the door.

Looking over my shoulder at Kira in the hospital bed, her belly large and round with our child, I've never been more enamored. I don't know what I did to deserve this girl, but I'll never stop thanking the universe for it.

Her eyes meet mine, and in them I see more love than I deserve, but I take it anyway, because I know no one will love her back the way I do.

I close the door softly behind me and find my friends in the waiting room. Hayes is still there too, but now Arden has joined him, and even Calista has shown up.

"You guys should go home," I tell them. "It's going to be a while yet until he makes his appearance. There's no point in hanging around."

Cannon stands up. "We're not going anywhere, man. We're here for you, and we'll still be here when your son comes into the world."

"You don't have to—"

"We want to," Hollis adds, standing up too.

Fox joins them. "We're your best friends. You can't get rid of us that easily, even if you are an asshole most of the time."

I shake my head. "Come here, you fucking losers." An older couple in the corner glares at me for my use of language, but I don't care.

I open my arms and my friends and I share a group hug. I've felt closed off from them for a while now, my own doing, but now I feel like we're back to where we always were. I'm fucking lucky to have them in my life.

Stepping back I clear my throat. "I'll keep you guys updated."

They nod their appreciation and I head back down the hall to join Kira in her room.

Another hour passes and when she's checked again Kenzie gives an apologetic smile. "You're progressing very slowly, and the baby's heart rate is beginning to drop. We're going to watch things for a little while longer, but if his heart rate drops any more we're going to have to do an emergency c-section. I don't want to scare you, c-sections are normal and nothing to worry about, but I know it's not ideal or what you had planned, so I want you to know that's where things are looking like it's headed so you can prepare yourself."

Kira bursts into tears and I don't know what to fucking do. It's a helpless feeling watching the woman you love try to bring your child into the world and you can tell it's wearing on her. Then, something like this happens and throws an even bigger wrench into things.

"Kira..." I begin, but it's pointless, because I know she can't hear me over her sobs.

"I'm sorry," she blubbers. "I know we have to do what's best for him, but I wasn't expecting this. I-I'm s-sorry." Her whole body begins to shake with her sobs.

I wipe her tears away with my thumbs, wishing I could just as easily make this whole thing better for her.

I hate feeling helpless and out of control, but when it comes to having a baby, I'm not sure there's any other feeling.

Mia brushes Kira's hair from her damp forehead. "No matter what happens you're going to rock this."

I wipe away another tear from Kira's cheek. "Whatever's best for the baby, we have to do." She turns to me with pleading eyes, seeking my approval.

"That's right," I agree. "And you might not have to."

I'm trying to be optimistic for her and myself. It fucking terrifies me to think about them cutting her open to get the baby out.

It isn't long before the doctor enters the room with a forlorn expression.

"I'm afraid his heart rate is still dropping," Dr. Wren tells her. "We're going to get you prepped and into the operating room as quickly as we can." She pats Kira's leg covered by a blanket. "I don't want you to be scared or worried, so if you have any questions let me know."

Kira swallows thickly. "Is he going to be okay?"

"He's going to be fine. We just can't leave him in there any longer, okay?"

Kira nods. "Do what you have to do, Doc." She sounds resigned, but her eyes hold a flare because in every fiber of her being she's a fighter.

Things start to move quickly with a flurry of activity as people move in and out of the room. Mia says her goodbyes and goes to join the others in the waiting room. A nurse hands me scrubs to put on and I yank them on over my clothes.

Kenzie adjusts a hair net onto Kira's head and smiles at me. "It's almost show time, Daddy. You wait here and we'll take her back to the operating room to get prepped. I'll come back and get you. It won't be long."

"Okay." My voice croaks on the word. I grab Kira's hand and bend down to press a soft kiss to her lips. "I love you. I'll be back by your side, where I belong, in no time."

"I know." Her lips curve into a smile. "We're going to have a baby."

I chuckle, kissing her knuckles. "Yes, we are."

"All right, I've got to take her away now," Kenzie says, and I step back.

I watch Kira being wheeled away and feel like a huge chunk of my heart has been yanked out. I hate being separated from her in this moment, even if I know it's only for a few minutes time.

I pace the mostly empty hospital room as I wait. I feel close to ripping my hair out waiting for Kenzie to return, as promised, to take me to the operating room.

I don't like the thought of Kira being alone in a clinical operating room while they prep her, but I know she's strong and is probably handling this whole thing better than I am. She's stronger than I'll ever be.

Before I wear a hole in the floor I sit my ass down on the plastic looking couch. I cover my face in my hands and exhale a breath.

I've known for months we're having a baby, that one day he'd be here, but I wasn't prepared for how I would feel when the day came. I'm scared shitless knowing this new life is going to depend on me. I want to be a good dad, the kind of man who raises my son to be respectful and care for others. I want to teach him things and spend time with him the way my father did with me. I know I can do it, but it's still fucking scary to think about. A child is the biggest commitment you can make. Fuck those people who say it's only until your kid is eighteen—this is for *life*.

"We're ready for you," Kenzie says softly, interrupting my thoughts.

I say a small prayer and exhale a heavy breath before I slowly stand on my feet.

I follow Kenzie through the halls and down the elevator to the operating room.

Seeing Kira strapped to a table, a blue paper screen blocking her view, knocks my breath out of me. I love her and seeing her helpless like this feels like a hand has reached into my chest and squeezed my heart.

I sit down beside her on a stool and she turns her head toward me. Her brown eyes are swimming with barely contained tears and it chokes me up. I wish I could erase all this for her, that she didn't have to go through this, but I can't. All I can do is be her rock, her foundation.

I brush my fingers over her cheek. "We're going to meet our son."

She nods and sniffles. "This isn't what I wanted."

"I know." I swallow past the lump in my throat. "God, I know, Kira. I'm so fucking sorry."

"But I want him to be okay. He has to be okay." She nods her head rapidly, her teeth chattering.

"I know you do, baby." I keep rubbing her cheek, refusing to not touch her.

"What if he's not okay? What if they're not telling us something?" Her voice becomes hysteric.

"Shh," I hush her. "This baby is made of both of us, and since we're both tough as shit he's going to be doubly tough."

A small laugh bubbles out of her throat and then she grimaces as they do something to her.

I'm not even paying attention to what they're doing or saying. Kira is my sole focus. I want to keep her distracted, centered, because right now she doesn't need to think about them cutting her open to get to our baby.

"It's been almost a year since I first saw you," I murmur and her eyes drift back to me. "I had no clue when I saw you what you'd come to mean to me. You've changed my life, Kira. I'll never stop being grateful to you for showing me the light again."

"I thought you were a hot asshole the first time I saw you." Her eyes twinkle with something other than tears. "I didn't want anything to do with you."

"And then," I lower my mouth to her ear, "you got an eyeful of my cock and couldn't resist."

Her lips twitch with laughter. "What can I say? It was highly impressive through those gym shorts."

"And even better in person, am I right?"

She doesn't answer me as her face screws up. I hear the doctor say she's going to feel a lot of pressure.

"Stay with me," I tell her. "Focus on my voice. I'm with you, always."

Another minute passes and then...

A cry.

More like a wail as our son says, "Hello, I'm here. I'm real."

The doctor lifts our son up and over the divider so we can see him.

Even covered in blood and God knows what else, he's still the most amazing thing I've ever laid my eyes on.

"Fuck, he's beautiful, Kira." I lean over to kiss her forehead.

"Go with him," she pleads with me, tears spilling out of her eyes, as they carry him away.

"But—"

"I'm fine," she says with surprising strength. "Go with him. That's what I want."

With one last press of my lips to her skin, I pull away and go to be by our son's side.

He wails as a nurse wipes him clean and gets his measurements.

He looks so fucking small to me. How am I not going to break him? He's barely the size of a football.

After he's cleaned and swaddled with a hat hiding his tuft of dark hair the nurse holds him out to me.

I stare at her blankly, my arms hanging at my sides. "Uh ... what do you want me to do?"

I've never held a fucking baby before and I don't want to drop him. That would not score me any dad points.

She gives a small laugh. "Just hold your arms like I have mine and be sure to support his head. That's all."

"But ... he's so *small.*"

"Babies are small." Her grin tells me she's amused by my reluctance.

Taking a deep breath, I hold my arms like she has hers and she slips him into my hold.

I've never understood the term *takes my breath away*, but in this moment my child has rendered my lungs of the ability to breathe.

Rocking him in my arms I carry him over to Kira and sit down on the stool at her side once more.

She tilts her head, peering at his small wrinkled face.

"He kind of looks like a pug." She stifles a laugh. "But a very cute pug."

"He's perfect." I rub my index finger against his soft cheek.

"He's so little," she remarks.

"Just over six pounds," Kenzie responds, coming to Kira's other side. "How are you feeling?"

"Uncomfortable, but it's tolerable."

Kenzie gives a small smile. "You'll be in recovery soon and you can do skin on skin with him."

As Kenzie walks away to tend to something, Kira lifts her eyes to mine. "Are you going to share this brilliant name with me now? I don't want to keep calling him Baby."

I chuckle as our son tries to open his eyes. "I've never seen anything more perfect."

I tilt him in my arms so Kira can see him better.

"He has a butt-chin," she remarks. "I knew it. But he is pretty perfect."

I kiss his forehead, and I can't believe how soft his skin is. "As for his name..."

"Yes?" she pleads and I grin.

I've held out this long and now I'm worried she won't love the name as much as I do—won't see the utter perfection of it.

"His name is Phoenix," I murmur, looking from our son to her.

"Phoenix?" she repeats, crinkling her nose in contemplation.

Before she has the chance to open her mouth and voice her veto I explain my choice as I gaze down at my son, ironically wiggling his nose like his mother.

"Yes, Phoenix, because he's our redemption. From our ashes came him. He's our rebirth."

When I turn my eyes to Kira, I find hers shimmering with tears.

"It's perfect," she breathes. "Just like him."

In the chaos and despair of our lives, this tiny soul was created, and in him I see more than our redemption.

I see our future, and it's fucking bright.

FIFTY-NINE

Kira

Finally back in a regular room, and nearing one in the morning, a new nurse hands me my son and presses him against my bare breast. Like a hungry little fiend, he searches for my nipple and latches on. His tiny fist rests against my chest and his dark lashes fan his cheeks.

Rush hovers over the both of us, a physical protective shield.

"He's a natural," the nurse says with a smile. "I'm going to leave you two alone, but don't hesitate to push your call button."

"Thank you." My voice trembles with emotion. I've never felt so happy, sad, confused, and hopeful all at once.

While I was in recovery Rush let everyone know the baby was here, and I was doing well, before sending them on their way with instructions to come back tomorrow to meet him. I wish Mia could've been with me in the operating room, but only one person could be with me. Naturally, I chose Rush.

Now, I'm so thankful to have this moment just the two of us ... *three*—there are three of us now.

Phoenix is only in his diaper, but I grab a swaddle from the bed and drape it over us. I don't want him getting cold. As promised, Mia went and got my bag for me and dropped it off.

"You should sit down." I peer up at Rush as he leans over us, his large hand hovering over Phoenix's head.

"I don't want to," he murmurs in awe.

Ever since Phoenix came screaming into the world, Rush has barely taken his eyes off of him.

"I can't believe he's barely over six pounds," I remark, rubbing my finger over his downy hair. His dark curls seem to be the only thing he got from me, because even though he's only a few hours old there's no mistaking who his father is. He's Rush's brunette clone. There's always the chance his eyes could turn brown later on, but something tells me they're going to be the same deep ocean blue as his father's. "I thought he was going to be huge," I admit with a small laugh when Phoenix gives a small hiccup but immediately goes back to suckling.

"He's a few weeks early, if he'd kept cooking he would've been a lot bigger."

"That's true," I agree. "God," I breathe out, feeling tears fill my eyes once more, "I can't believe he's actually here. I can't believe I have him and you. It's more than I ever allowed myself to dream of. I love you, Rush." The words leave me in a torrent, filled with more feeling than I knew I possessed.

"I fucking love you." Rush kisses the side of my head as tears fall down my cheeks. "Thank you."

"For what?" I look up at him, confusion marring my brow. His tousled blond hair tumbles into his eyes and he sweeps it back with his fingers.

"For loving me despite my faults."

Reaching with my arm that's not cradling Phoenix I touch

my hand to his. "I love you *for* them, because it makes you human."

Phoenix finishes nursing and since I'm sore from surgery, Rush changes his diaper. One of the nurses showed him how and he's a pro at it already. I shouldn't be surprised. I think Rush strives to succeed in all things.

He puts the baby in one of the sleepers I had packed in my bag and swaddles him—sloppily, he hasn't mastered that one yet —before rocking him to sleep in his arms. He gently lays Phoenix in the bassinet as I struggle to keep my eyes open.

"Go to sleep, Kira." He kisses my cheek before kicking off his shoes and hooking his thumbs in the back of his t-shirt to take it off.

"I just want to keep staring at him."

He grins, stretching out on the uncomfortable looking couch in his jeans. "He'll still be there when you wake up."

"You sure?" I crack a smile.

"Positive."

Even though I don't want to, there's no fighting it and sleep claims me.

PHOENIX WAKES US UP SEVERAL TIMES IN THE NIGHT TO NURSE AND have his diaper changed. He doesn't even cry much when he grows hungry, he just stirs and makes these little noises.

Now, the sun is entirely up and I munch on a chicken biscuit Rush snagged for me from the Chick-fil-A in the hospital. While I eat, Rush sits in a chair doing skin-to-skin with Phoenix, who sleeps peacefully on his father's tattooed chest. Rush rubs the baby's back humming softly.

I didn't think it was possible for me to love him more, but here we are.

"Why are you smiling at me like that?" He doesn't even lift his eyes away from Phoenix, he simply knows.

"Because you're hot."

His chest rumbles with laughter. "Keep talking like that and we'll have another one of these soon." Phoenix emits the tiniest yawn and I swear my ovaries weep.

"I'd be okay with that." The words pass through my lips in a quiet whisper.

His head snaps up and a grin tugs at his mouth. "That so?"

I never wanted kids, *ever*, but things change. "Yes. At least one more."

"I want a whole brood. This is what life's about."

Hearing Rush say that warms my heart, because I know after losing his parents he never wanted a family either. Somehow the two of us found each other and within ourselves found the power to forgive and embrace a future we thought didn't belong to us.

"Knock, knock," Mia's voice sounds by the doorway.

I turn my head and a smile breaks across my face when I see her, Hollis, Fox, Cannon, and Calista hovering outside.

"Come in you guys." I wave them inside, stifling a grimace. A c-section is no joke. My body feels like it's been split open and I've been turned inside out.

They pour inside and I notice some of them carry gifts for the baby. Calista even holds an IT'S A BOY balloon.

Mia peers over Rush's shoulder at the baby's face. "Oh my God, he's precious," she coos, touching his nose. "Does he have a name?"

She looks from Rush to me, begging for an answer.

I give Rush a nod for him to tell them. "Meet Phoenix Daniels."

"Aww, it's a perfect name," Mia cries, clapping her hands together.

"He's pretty cute, I guess," Calista adds, crinkling her nose.

"It's fucking weird seeing you hold a baby," Hollis blurts.

"But he looks like he's a fucking natural at it," Cannon adds in.

Fox tilts his head to the side, appraising the baby. "I can't believe you have a kid."

I smile to myself as I look at the three friends crowding around Rush. Those boys grew up together, have been through so much over the years and always there for each other, and now ... here's this new life joining the bunch.

I guess it's like they say, the circle of life.

"You're next," I tell Mia. "He needs a friend."

She blanches and takes two steps away from the baby like she could get pregnant just from being near him. "Nope, no way. Not happening."

Hollis grins at her, his curls flopping into his eyes. "What? You don't want little mini-Hollis's running around? I think they'd be cute."

"They might be cute, but your sperm is not fertilizing one of my eggs any time soon."

Hollis busts out laughing. "One day, then."

She smiles back at him. "One day." She nods her head in agreement.

"Y'all are weird," Calista snorts. "Let me hold the baby. That's what we're here for, right?"

For the next hour Phoenix is passed to each of our friends before he finally demands a boob to be fed on. It's pretty hilarious when he tries to latch onto Cannon who immediately shoves him into my arms and says, "Take this."

This, not him. It's hilarious seeing the normally most-together member of the band lose his shit over a baby.

They leave and it's only Rush and I with the baby once more.

Our family.

He curls his large body into the bed with me as much as he can and the two of us stare at the beautiful innocent life we created. I lean my head against his shoulder and close my eyes for a moment, relishing in all the gifts I've been given.

You can choose to focus on the bad, all the wrongs that have been done to you, or you can rise up from the ashes like a phoenix and choose a rebirth instead.

"I love you, Phoenix," I murmur, and lower my head to kiss his tiny wrinkled forehead.

Thank you for saving me. For saving us.

"You know you have to put the truck in *drive*, right?" I question Rush as he sits at the hospital entrance refusing to drive away.

I sit in the back beside Phoenix in his carrier. He sucks on his green binky and his eyes flutter behind closed lids in a beautiful and peaceful dream world.

"Yeah, I know—but fuck, I've never driven with a baby in the car before. This is scary."

I laugh. "We'll be fine. My place isn't too far."

"Yeah, but—"

"Rush, we can't stay parked outside the hospital all day."

He exhales a breath. "You're right."

"I know I'm right." I grin at him in the rearview mirror and he slowly, blessedly, pulls away.

Rush looks back at us every few seconds, driving at a snail's pace.

"We'll be lucky to be at my apartment by next week," I remark casually and he huffs a breath.

"I'm driving precious cargo here."

When cars start honking, he realizes he can't drive at his slow pace and starts going the speed limit.

He parks the truck on the street when we arrive and helps me out. I wince, holding my stomach.

"You okay?" he asks, holding my arms to steady me.

"Yeah, just sore." I give him a smile, showing him I *am* okay. Childbirth is hard and my body has been through hell. Not only did I labor for hours, but I had to get cut open too. Thankfully, the band the hospital gave me to wrap around my abdomen has helped a lot.

Rush reaches inside the car and lifts the car seat from the base.

I notice my car is parked back in its normal spot. I don't know who brought it back here from Starbucks but something tells me it was Hollis and Mia.

Rush and I take the steps up to my apartment slowly and I give him the keys to unlock the door.

Inside, he carefully extracts Phoenix from his seat without waking him up and hands him to me.

My apartment is stuffed to the brim with baby items and it's a reminder of how small this place is and how desperately I need to move.

I rock back and forth with Phoenix in my arms. I don't even know why I do it. It feels natural, though.

Rush stands with his hands on his hips, his head lowered.

"Rush," I hesitate. "Is something wrong?"

He lifts his impossibly blue eyes to meet mine and I see worry and fear in them. My heart braces for what he might say, what I *fear* he's going to say.

My mind yells at me that he's backing away, that he's about to tell me he can't do this, but my heart tells my head to shut up and stop being a liar. I *know* Rush. I know his heart, his soul, his very essence and I see how much he loves Phoenix. Whatever is bothering him has nothing to do with what my mind wants to think it is.

He swallows thickly and pulls something from his pocket, dropping to one knee.

My heart skips a beat, and my eyes widen with fear as he opens the small black jewelers' box in his hand.

"Kira Elizabeth Marsh, I fucking love you. You're my person and I never want to be separated from you ever again. I want you by my side always, not because I want to keep you caged, but because I can't imagine my life without you in it. You set me free, and I think maybe I've set you free too. I fucking hope so, at least." He pauses, swallowing thickly. I swear I can see his pulse racing in his throat. "This is a promise for a future together, a life, a happy ending. I want you to move to L.A. with me, to live with me. I want us to be a family completely. You can go to school there if you want to get your nursing degree, or fuck—open a bake shop if that's what you want. Whatever it is, I'll support you one-hundred percent. You've got my back, and I've got yours." He inhales a breath and lets it out slowly. "Say yes, Kira. Say yes to our future, to a home, to a life, and to a promise that one day when you're ready I'm going to get down on one knee and put a fucking ring on your finger."

My eyes overflow with tears and they wet my cheeks as I gaze at the key in the jewelry box. Phoenix stirs in my arms, like he knows I'm an emotional wreck, but I've never in my life been this happy.

I've always been tossed aside, forgotten, a burden—something in the way, as easy to get rid of as a piece of trash.

But I've found my worth, and I've found my love.

"Yes," I croak and Rush's grin lights up his entire face.

He stands quickly and grabs my face, pressing a bruising,

passionate kiss to my lips. Phoenix lets out a cry in my arms, not liking being caged between the two of us.

Rush grabs the house key from the jewelry box and places it in my palm, curling my fingers around it.

"To our future."

"Our future," I echo.

EPILOGUE

Rush

One month later

I pull into the driveway of the Spanish style bungalow on the outskirts of L.A. We came here straight from the plane and Phoenix sleeps peacefully in his car seat in the back of the car. I don't know how we got so lucky, but he's truly the best baby.

"What do you think?" I ask Kira hesitantly, nervous for her reaction.

I bought the house sight unseen just from the pictures online and then hired an interior decorator to make sure it was furnished and ready to go when we got here. It was pricey, but my parents' house sold quickly and for a decent buck, so it made the perfect down payment.

She looks at me in awe. "It's perfect, Rush. More beautiful than I imagined."

She hasn't seen pictures or anything. She told me she wanted to be completely surprised and that she trusted me.

We've come a long fucking way.

"Should we go inside?" I suggest with a raised brow.

"Yes," she cries, squeezing my arm. "I'm dying to see more."

She scurries out of the car and goes to get Phoenix, but I grab his car seat before she can. That thing is fucking heavy and awkward and she doesn't need to carry it no matter how stubborn she is. I also grab Patch's carrier—I hope he likes L.A. At least he'll have more freedom here than in a hotel room.

We walk up the brick pathway to the front door. It's rounded on top with a little window in the middle.

"Got your key?" I ask her.

She grins and pulls it from her pocket. From it, a keychain dangles with a picture of the two of us on one side and one of Phoenix on the other.

She slips it into the lock and pushes the door open.

Inside, the home is open with wood floors, wooden beams, and a creamy off-white paint. The furniture is all neutrals and dark woods. I felt like that was more us. There are some baby items already set up in the living room, which boasts a sectional couch in front of a fireplace with a big flat screen TV.

I needed a big fucking TV, what can I say.

I set the carrier and car seat down, unzipping the carrier to let Patch run free through the house, before I gently extract Phoenix from his car seat. He fusses a bit, but the minute he nuzzles my neck he calms right down.

In the past I thought I'd hate being a parent, but I love it. I was meant to be a dad, and Kira was meant to be a mom. It's sad to think if we'd never met this might never have happened for us.

"I want to show you his room." I reach for her hand and she fits her slender hand into my massive one.

I worked the hardest with the interior designer on his room. I wanted it to be perfect for him and Kira, something special and more than she could've ever dreamed of having.

I lead her up the stairs and down the hall, swinging open his bedroom door. Light streams in from the backyard where a tire swing sways lazily in the wind.

The walls are a soft gray I think the interior designer called dove gray or some shit. The wall with the crib has a gray, black, and white wallpaper she insisted would look *chic*. I didn't care as long as the end result was fit for my future rocker. Or basketball player. Or scientist. Or whatever the hell he wants to be when he grows up.

Kira walks over the crib, running her fingers over the black frame of the modern crib. She spins in a circle looking around at the changing table, rug, giant stuffed black dragon in the corner and all the other items, like the play mat and bouncer.

"You worked really hard on this didn't you?"

I shrug. "The designer and her team did all the work."

"But this is *you*. It's us. It's perfect." Tears fill her eyes. "What did I do to deserve you?" She closes the distance between us and rises on her tiptoes to kiss me.

I wrap one arm around her waist, keeping a careful hold on Phoenix with the other.

"You love it? You love the house?"

"I love *you*." She pokes my chest. "All this," she waves her hands to encompass the room, "it's just a bonus. You're all I need now. You and Phoenix."

"I feel the same." She smiles and I swear I've never seen her happier. This last month of us adjusting to being parents has been ridiculously blissful. I'd tell someone to pinch me, but if this is a dream I never want to wake up.

I know my battle with alcoholism will never end, it's always going to be a fight, but the thought of losing them trumps my need to turn to a bottle of alcohol.

Kira curls into my body and leans her head against my chest peering at Phoenix.

I rub my thumb against her arm, never wanting to let go of the loves of my life.

And I don't have to.

They're my forever, and forever starts now.

If you loved Blaire, Ryder, and The Paper Crane Project pick up
Bring Me Back today.

Note From The Author

I could have put the typical blurb here.
Boy meets girl.
They fall in love.
Live happily ever after.
The end.
But this isn't *that* story.

ACKNOWLEDGEMENTS

This book has been a whirlwind to write from the moment I sat down and started it. Rush and Kira took me on a journey I wasn't expecting at all. It might sound crazy but I'm beyond proud of these two characters and how much they grew through this book. I love when a book I'm writing surprises me, and this one definitely did.

To you, dear reader, thank you for reading and supporting my books and me. Because of you I get to live my dream, and that's the best gift ever.

See you in the next one.

ALSO BY MICALEA SMELTZER

The Wildflower Duet

The Confidence of Wildflowers

The Resurrection of Wildflowers

-

The Boys Series

Bad Boys Break Hearts

Nice Guys Don't Win

Real Players Never Lose

Good Guys Don't Lie

Broken Boys Can't Love

The Wild Series

Wild

Rising

Trace + Olivia Series

Finding Olivia

Chasing Olivia

Tempting Rowan

Saving Tatum

Willow Creek Series

Last To Know

Never Too Late

In Your Heart

Take A Chance

Willow Creek Box Set

Always Too Late Short Story

Willow Creek Bonus Content

Home For Christmas

Light in the Dark Series

Rae of Sunshine

When Stars Collide

Dark Hearts

When Constellations Form

Broken Hearts

Standalones

Beauty in the Ashes

Bring Me Back

The Other Side of Tomorrow

Desperately Seeking Roommate

Desperately Seeking Landlord

Whatever Happens

Sweet Dandelion

Say When

The Road That Leads To Us

The Game Plan